HARD ROCK HEAT

HARD ROCK HEAT

FAME AND FLAMES™ BOOK 1

ELIZA LOCKHART

FLORID
Romance

To those who write from the heart, whether that's poetry, messages to loved ones, or the fantasy another might enjoy.

Published by Florid Romance
an imprint of LMBPN Publishing
2375 E. Tropicana Avenue, Suite 8-305
Las Vegas, Nevada 89119 USA

Version 1.00, February 2024
eBook ISBN: 979-8-88878-331-3
Print ISBN: 979-8-88878-839-4

THE ROCK HARD HEAT TEAM

Thanks to the JIT Readers

Veronica Stephan-Miller
Jan Hunnicutt

Editor
SkyFyre Editing Team

CHAPTER ONE

Juno

The insides of my stomach churned as I sat waiting. Today was the big day. My first TV interview, and I'd been asked to wait in some side room alone. Not that I had any idea what to expect, but every time I'd imagined how it would go, it hadn't been me waiting alone in a room for thirty minutes while the interview time ticked closer.

I'd imagined being unable to find the correct section of the studio and wandering lost in the building for hours or turning up in my pajamas. The sorts of nightmares everyone had. But I'd also dreamed of it going well and pushing my career to a whole new level.

Although I'd been up since six to get ready and travel to London for the interview, I felt wired, my hands shaky and my pulse fast. Once more, I checked my hair and makeup still looked okay.

I'd tried to do my deep brown hair in an elegant French plait but was so unused to bothering with it that I wasn't sure I'd done a very good job. Similar with the makeup, although I'd heard they were likely to redo it anyway.

I ignored most of my facial features, a sort of self-defense mechanism. My nose was a little too wide, my eyebrows too bushy, and my forehead too tall. Instead, I tried to focus on my eyes, the intense blue one of my best features. I also loved my ears, the shape of them almost elven and quirky in their lack of earlobes. My face wasn't the most attractive, but it could definitely be worse.

Sighing, I put my little compact mirror away and sat back. My stomach was still in knots, and my hands were beginning to sweat.

Not good.

I subtly wiped them on my skirt and hoped it wouldn't show.

To try and give myself something to focus on, I pulled out the sheet of questions I was going to be asked again and looked through them. There were the ones I'd expected about my work, the current book I was there to promote, and how I juggled everything.

There was also one about my separation. It had come as a shock to a lot of people. Almost fifteen happy years of marriage, including those of the recent pandemic, suddenly ended. I'd planned my answer to that one very carefully. I had to make sure people believed my reasoning.

Almost instinctively, I reached down to the bruises on my right-hand side and smoothed my clothes over them. They still hurt, but the pain was finally fading. I'd taken painkillers to take the edge off, but it was important that no one noticed them.

I was thinking about my answer to the final question, what I was planning on doing next, when the door finally opened.

My mouth fell open as I recognized one of the most attractive men on the planet being shown into the room by another of the studio assistants. He gave me a brief smile, the gesture lighting up his tanned cheeks and showing the chiseled jaw in the best frame.

He glanced at the woman showing him in before moving over

to a seat on the opposite side of the room, and I couldn't help but follow him with my gaze.

I finally shut my mouth, hoping the click it made wasn't too audible.

"Someone should be with you to take you to hair and makeup in just a few minutes," the woman said to Jack Starling, billionaire rock star and actor, before she noticed me.

She seemed to do a double-take as if she didn't expect anyone else to be in the room.

"Oh, are you waiting here for Dominic?" she asked.

"I don't think so," I replied. "A lady called Faith asked me to wait here for my interview."

"Interview?" The woman frowned and pulled the folder she'd been clutching against her chest far enough away to look at it. She seemed to scan down some sort of list.

"I think you might be in the wrong place. This is the section of the studio for Keith O'Sullivan's talk show."

"Great. That's the show I'm on today," I said as I exhaled, feeling my body relax with relief.

"Me too. They must be doing a double interview," Jack said as he leaned forward and once again offered me that dazzling grin. His words were like honey, a blend of American deep South accent and something more mystical and almost Caribbean.

"No, no," the woman said, suddenly appearing flustered. "It's just Jack today. What's your name, miss?"

"Juno. Juno Fernsby. The author and narrator."

"Audiobook narration?" Jack Starling asked as the woman continued to look through pieces of paper she held, dropping one.

Both of us got up and tried to pick it up for her. Jack beat me to it by just a fraction, our hands brushing together. I straightened, feeling my cheeks grow hotter as he handed it back.

"I'm sorry, I don't have you down at all. There must have been some sort of mix-up. Your interview must be another day. Do you think you could come back another day?"

I frowned and held up the paper I'd been clutching, my question sheet with a clearly printed date at the top.

"It is the ninth of July, right?" I asked.

"Of course. All day," Jack replied for the woman, although she nodded as well.

"Then I'm meant to be here today," I added, feeling my stomach knot even more.

Of all of the things I'd imagined going wrong, having the studio forget I was coming hadn't been one of them. This couldn't be happening.

Not only had it cost me several hundred pounds to get here and stay the night at a hotel nearby, but the time it had taken and the preparation I'd put in was massive. My new agent had assured me this would do wonders for my career. It was supposed to be something hugely exciting, not a train wreck.

"I'm really sorry. I don't understand how there's been such a mix-up, but you can't be interviewed today. Mr. O'Sullivan doesn't do double interviews."

"But I've had this interview planned for months. I was told he doesn't get many openings..." I trailed off, aware I was rambling.

I felt mortified, my cheeks beginning to heat. Not only was I not going to get my interview, but I was being given the brushoff in front of my favorite actor.

I looked between them, not sure what else to say or do, but the assistant appeared entirely sure of herself. No interview for me.

"Why don't you go check," Jack said. "There's a chance we're both meant to be here, and this lady has no doubt come a long way for this. I'm sure something can be worked out to accommodate both of us and waste no one's time."

The woman gulped, but his calm suggestion had far more

weight than my pleading denial had achieved. Eventually, she nodded.

"If you could both wait here, I'll be back as soon as I can."

She turned on her heels and strode out, pulling the door shut behind her with a bang.

I backed up a little, not sure what to do now, and very aware I was alone in a room with Jack Starling, the most attractive man in the world. He didn't move, his gaze on me, and I felt my cheeks flush again, so I looked away, taking in the jeans he wore and the brown boots beneath them. He had a quirky dress style, as did most of the rockers he spent time with.

"I'm sure the whole thing will be sorted out soon," he said. "Have you come a long way?"

"From Bath," I replied, instantly grateful for his ability to make conversation. I'd heard he was shy, but my normal, confident exterior was taking a while to catch up to the situation.

"Beautiful city. I love it there in the summer."

"It's stunning when the sun shines," I said, immediately hating the small talk, but what else did I say to this man? My mind went blank, and my heart hammered in my chest, the pain down my side suddenly a thousand times worse.

This was a bad day.

CHAPTER TWO

"Are you in London just for the interview or for other reasons, too?" I asked, the words tumbling out of my mouth in a rush.

"Other reasons. We're recording a couple of songs here. Didn't know if I'd have time for interviews, but they begged me to come on only a few days ago. I figured, why not?"

"Right," I replied and looked up.

Our eyes met, and I was pretty sure we were thinking the same thing. I'd been ditched from the schedule because they'd managed to persuade him to come instead. And they didn't have the courtesy to tell me.

"I wouldn't have agreed to do it if I'd known they were going to cut someone else from the show," he said quietly a moment later.

"It's not your fault. I'll probably have to go home and come back another day. It's not that big a deal," I replied, embarrassed again. "It's not as if I can force them to interview me anyway."

I sighed and pulled out my cell phone to quickly message my agent and let them know what was happening. He was going to be more than a little angry. Keith O'Sullivan was a friend of his and had shafted him.

After tapping away for a moment, I realized Jack was still staring at me, now sitting back, his strong arms folded across his T-shirted chest. On his hands were multiple rings and tattoos, and my eyes were drawn to them.

I gulped as I wondered if the silence was awkward again.

"So, tell me more about what you do. What sorts of stories do you like?" he asked, not hiding his interest in me or trying to make me feel more comfortable.

While part of me found it intimidating, the rest of me began to feel a little braver. Talking about my interests was something I could do.

"Fantasy," I replied. "Urban fantasy and epic fantasy mostly, but I've dabbled in most sub-genres."

"Like elves and stuff?"

I nodded, "Like Tolkien, and then those races put into the modern day, like dragons in LA."

"Sounds like a lot of fun. Does it pay well?"

"It pays the bills, and each new series seems to do a little better than the last. I'm not making millions, but I'm at the point where I'm having TV interviews now. This was supposed to be my first," I said as I sighed.

Before either of us could say anything more, the assistant returned.

"Look, I know you think you're supposed to be here today, and we've clearly told you that," the woman said, ignoring Jack and looking straight at me. "But I'm afraid Mr. O'Sullivan is adamant. He's interviewing Mr. Starling today."

"No," Jack said as he got to his feet again. "Tell O'Sullivan that he can interview us both or neither of us. Let's not waste anyone's time unnecessarily."

"But we don't have any questions prepared for Miss Fernsby."

"It's Mrs. Fernsby, actually. My husband and I might be separated and getting a divorce, but I'm still married for now, and you must have questions prepared because you sent them to me," I replied, holding out the sheet of paper I still clutched and feeling a lot braver knowing I had such a powerful ally.

The woman gaped at us for a moment before she took the questions and added them to the stack she carried on top of her folder.

"Right. I'll go inform Mr. O'Sullivan, but he isn't going to like it, and we'll struggle to get you both through makeup in time."

"You'd best get someone to come to us and begin while you're on your way, then," Jack added. "Or tell us where to go, and *I'll* make sure we're both ready on time."

She seemed to hesitate again but nodded and gave him directions. It was clear he understood them, a good indicator he'd been here before.

"Come on," he said to me as soon as she'd left. "Let's make this an interview to remember."

I smiled, feeling a rush of warmth as gratitude swept over me. He'd handed me a lifeline and my dignity all at the same time.

I let him lead me through doors and down corridors with a confidence I marveled at, and then we were in a larger room with several chairs in front of mirrors. There were three women standing at one end of the room. They looked our way, pausing in the middle of looking over makeup samples.

"We need to both be ready for O'Sullivan's show," Jack said by way of introduction. Immediately, two of the women came forward and headed toward the chairs.

I did the same, almost copying his actions as he sat in one.

For a moment, there was silence as the women pulled out makeup and brushes. The woman closest to me smiled as she looked me over.

"Do you mind if I take all this off and start again?" she asked.

"Go for it," I replied and heard Jack chuckle.

"This is her first interview. Make sure she looks stunning," he said.

"Yes, boss," she replied, flicking him a grin and pulling out some wipes. Within only a few minutes, she'd removed all the makeup I wore and revealed my naked face.

It felt a little strange to be surrounded by people I didn't know and letting them decide details about what I wore and how I looked, but every time the makeup artist had a decision to make, she asked Jack what he thought and which shade of lipstick, eye shadow, or style to choose instead of me.

Not sure what else to do, I let them pick it all and continued to sit and be made glamorous.

We were almost finished and trying to determine if I needed to emphasize my eyes a little more when the flustered assistant came in.

"O'Sullivan has agreed to interview you both on one condition."

"What's that?" Jack shot back as his artist finished him and declared him good to go on stage.

"He wants to change the questions slightly. The research team found some areas of your lives and work that relate and cross and would like to ask you about them in relation to each other to make it feel more like a joint interview."

"Sounds wonderful," Jack replied. "I'm sure we can be accommodating and answer on the fly if needed."

Again, he'd answered for me, but I could do no more than open my mouth to try and ask what area of our lives appeared to be related before the assistant was gone again.

I had to close it again as my artist added a slight detail near one eye and then leaned back to get a better look. Jack came over, standing behind my chair and staring at me in the mirror.

"Perfect," he declared. "The writer transformed."

The artist moved so I could get up, and then Jack took my hand and led me somewhere else entirely.

"Thank you," I called over my shoulder, Jack already at the door on the other side of the room from where we entered and going through it.

It felt strange to have my hand in his, but his grip was a strange combination of light and firm. I would've had to tug hard to remove my fingers from his.

We were soon in a much more comfortable-looking room, a large sofa along one wall with a few chairs on either side. On a small table were drinks and snacks, no doubt laid out for him.

He took me to the sofa and sat, giving me little choice but to follow. While I tried to get comfortable and have my mind catch up to what was happening, he grabbed a couple of bottles of water, unscrewed the lids, and poured them into two nearby glasses.

"To your first interview," he said as he held mine up to me and gave me that lopsided, amused grin again.

I took it, hoping my hands wouldn't shake too badly. Not only was I about to be interviewed, but right now, I was sitting beside one of the most gorgeous men on the planet, and I had his complete attention.

When I woke up this morning, I'd been sure the day would go its own way and nothing like I imagined it might, but this was a whole new level of unexpected. And I wasn't sure how to handle it.

CHAPTER THREE

Leaning back, one arm over the back of the sofa and his body turned toward me, the rock king and phenomenal actor looked at me.

"So, when is the new album going to come out?" I asked, not wanting to be the kind of person who only remembered to talk about themselves.

"Oh, sometime early next year," he replied as he waved his hand. "But they'll no doubt ask me about that in a moment."

I frowned slightly. What could I get him to talk about if he didn't want to answer questions they might ask in the interview? As I caught him looking at me again, a slightly amused expression crossed his face, and a twinkle lit up his eyes. I lifted an eyebrow, an unspoken request for an explanation.

"You're very expressive subconsciously, aren't you? No secrets, no pretense, just this little, shy author who has some steel on the inside when she needs it."

"That's direct of you," I replied. "You think you know me already?"

"No, not at all. To truly get to know someone takes a lifetime."

I nodded, surprised by the words but not the wisdom in them.

I just couldn't make out this man and what his angle was. On the one hand, he appeared mysterious, but on the other, confident and kind. A juxtaposition of self-assurance and a sort of shyness of his own. It kept throwing me off.

We weren't on the sofa sipping water together and trying to find interesting topics of conversation for long before someone wearing all black and hooked up to a radio came in.

"We're going to do Miss Fernsby first and then you, Mr. Starling. We'll just get you both pinned with a mic."

I lifted an eyebrow, but no one explained what they meant by doing me first. Did that mean I was going to be interviewed first? Just introduced first, or something else?

The newcomer came forward and attached a small clip-on mic to my blouse and then did similar to Jack, putting his on the edge of his collar.

"We'll be turning these on as you walk out, so feel free to talk to each other while you wait," the technician said, giving us both a brief smile before he retreated again.

I looked down at the small mic, noticing it was no bigger than an apple seed. How could something so tiny pick up my words? I had no idea, but I looked up to find Jack grinning at me again.

"First time with one of these kinds of mics, too?"

I nodded, feeling my cheeks flush.

"It's really obvious, isn't it?"

"A little, but not in a bad way. It's…" He trailed off, making me wonder what he would have said.

"So, do you have any tips for making a good impression out there?" I asked a moment later.

"Ugh, sure, I guess. I could give you some advice, although I wouldn't say I'm an expert."

"Compared to me, you're practically God, so…" As the words came out and I realized I'd just called him a god, I could have hit myself. Way to play it cool.

He let out a little chuckle but seemed to almost blush as well.

We both took a moment to calm, the pause somehow less awkward than talking would have been.

"Well, try to relax, obviously. Women seem to be expected to sit properly, but you can also go for a more casual, laid-back look if you wish. Tilt your body toward Keith a little, even if I'm on the other side of you. And don't take yourself too seriously. If you can say something funny, do it because the laughter will help everyone relax and warm to you—even you."

I listened, trying to take it all in as he gently gave me all this info. He spoke slowly enough for me to follow, but my nerves made it hard for me to process all of it.

"I think you'll be great, though," he added and smiled.

I found myself returning the gesture, probably looking calmer than I was but still clutching my glass in one hand.

We didn't get much longer before the technician came back.

"Miss Fernsby, can you come with me, please? We're almost ready for you to go on."

Instantly, I got to my feet, going toward him. As I did, Jack reached out and took the glass from me, reminding me it wouldn't make a good prop.

"Thank you," I said, meaning more than just this latest rescue.

"I'll see you in a few minutes. Knock 'em dead."

"If I do that, there will be no one left to interview you," I replied, but I smiled as he chuckled.

"Just rough 'em up a little, then."

"Deal." I grinned and finally followed the technician, who had begun tapping his feet.

The black-clad man led me down yet another corridor and passed other people waiting in the wings, some with props and others monitoring elements of the broadcast. Out here, I could hear Keith O'Sullivan talking to his audience. It was a live audience, but the show wouldn't go out until later in the day. It gave them time to edit out anything absolutely awful, but the idea was that the whole thing was shown as it happened.

I tried to focus on my breathing and taking deep breaths, my hands clasped behind my back so no one could see how much they shook, but the nerves mounted so badly that I began to have full-body shakes.

The technician noticed almost instantly.

"That's it. Keep taking deep breaths, and why don't you tell me what your favorite color is?" he said.

"My favorite color? Do you need to know?"

"No, but it gives you something else to focus on," he replied, grinning.

"Oh… Purple, then. That deep purple they have on chocolate bars."

"That's a gorgeous color. Do you like the chocolate, too?"

I nodded as if it was just a passing fancy, but the truth was I loved it. It was the first thing I'd ever eaten. My grandma had broken a tiny piece off a bar and fed it to me on the end of her finger as a baby. I'd only been about four or five months old, and my mother had been horrified. Not that I remembered it, but it was a story I'd been told many times by both women.

"There. Whatever you just thought about, it helped," he said as I realized I'd drifted off into my thoughts. "Now, he's about to introduce you. You just need to walk past me and through the gap to your left. Then you'll see him standing in front of a chair and a sofa to your left again. All you have to do is wave at the audience and greet Keith before sitting down."

"You say 'all,'" I replied. "But women have fallen on their faces doing far less."

"You'll be fine. All those women were wearing heels far too big for them and hadn't practiced. You've got gorgeous little boots on. Not going to fall at all."

I exhaled again and nodded, grateful for the pep talk from a stranger. In truth, I was only wearing the low-heeled boots because of my bruises and aches. It hurt too much to walk in anything else.

There were no more opportunities to think about anything else or even truly be nervous. Keith called my name as the technician moved to the side and ushered me past.

I appeared out of the gap and into the bright lights of the studio about half a second after he finished speaking. For a moment, I was almost too confused to know where to go, my arm waving automatically. Within seconds, my senses caught up, processing the audience clapping and Keith looking toward me.

Walking to him, I let him pull me into a brief top hug, and then I moved to the sofa.

I slipped onto the end closest to him more from a desire to be seated sooner than any other reason, curling one leg up and under myself without really thinking. It was how I sat when I was getting ready to write, and there was a chance my foot would go dead before I could move, but I'd done it now and didn't dare shift.

"Thank you for coming," Keith said, his words sounding sincere even if they now weren't.

"Thank you for having me," I said, hearing my words come out and, with them, most of my nerves.

I was doing this interview now, and I couldn't run away.

CHAPTER FOUR

"So, you're an author, and you've got quite an impressive backlist. Is that right?"

"I think others will have to decide if it's impressive, but I think I've got something like eighty or so stories out there now in various forms."

There were gasps from the audience, and Keith nodded, adjusting his suit as he did. It was dark gray and fit his slightly short frame well.

"That seems like an impressive amount to me. Am I right?" he asked, looking at the audience.

Cheers came back, making me smile with gratitude and feel even more relaxed.

"And your latest one is a fantasy epic? Out in a week and already expected to do well."

I nodded, momentarily confused by his Irish lilt and giving myself a moment to run his words through my head and make sure I'd heard them right.

"It's the last one in the series, and each release has really built on the one before," I said, hoping I'd interpreted him correctly. "I've been very fortunate."

Keith smiled and then spent the next few minutes talking about the feedback I'd had on the series and how my career had grown. I answered the questions as matter-of-factly as I could while seeming warm and excited about it.

"Am I right in saying you had the idea a long time ago, as well, but you've only been writing the books in the last few years?" he asked a moment later.

"Yes. I always knew the series would be an important one to me, so I waited until I felt good enough to write it and do the characters and their stories justice."

"Because characters are important to you. And you've stated many times in the past that they feel like real people?"

"Yes. It may sound a little crazy, but they come alive. I often feel like I'm sitting at a laptop or with paper and pen, furiously trying to transcribe their actions as quickly as I can." I smiled, grateful that all the questions so far had been ones I was expecting.

"And speaking of the characters coming alive, I'd like to do something I've never done before and give you all a little surprise," Keith said, almost entirely interrupting me. "I'd like to bring on a second guest!"

The audience erupted again, clearly excited about the idea of the first-ever double on the show.

I exhaled, grateful the focus wasn't on me for the moment, as Keith waited for the cheers to subside so he'd be heard.

"My next guest is in town to record a brand-new album. The lovable rogue and everyone's favorite actor, Jack Starling."

If I'd thought the crowds were loud earlier, they were a hundred times louder when they heard Jack's name. Almost immediately, he appeared out of the same gap I had, and I had the sense to relieve my already painful foot by getting up to move over on the sofa.

Before I could sit down again, however, Jack had finished

greeting Keith and chose to do the same to me, giving me a hug and pecking me on the cheek.

I almost froze, my heart skipping a beat as I inhaled his cologne.

Damn, he smelled good.

As he sat, I managed to persuade my body to follow suit, putting myself on the far edge and immediately feeling a little calmer, doubting that most of the audience would give me a second thought now.

Who would get any attention when they were beside the hottest celebrity on the planet? Not to mention the richest.

I listened as Keith asked him about the new album and the latest film he'd been in. It was one where he'd sung and played his guitar for a scene, and they showed the clip. I hadn't seen the film yet, but I was mesmerized, his deep but somehow gentle voice intoxicating.

"Well, that seems to be a hit with the ladies," Keith said at the end of the clip over lots of feminine cheers and catcalls.

A moment later, our host looked straight at me, and I tried to return my mind to the task of being interviewed.

"And speaking of having an effect on the women, I understand you're a big Jack fan, Juno."

I nodded a little and felt my cheeks instantly heat up, but Keith didn't stop there.

"So much so that you wrote a romance under your pen name based on him?"

I blinked. How the hell did he know about that?

"Is that true, Juno?"

I felt rather than saw Jack shift uncomfortably beside me, turning his body slightly toward me, and I gulped. Was there any way to answer this question that kept my dignity intact? I wasn't sure, but however I answered, I had to do it soon. The room had gone silent while they waited for me to respond.

"I have a billionaire romance or two under my pen name, yes."

"The erotica and dark romance pen name that was revealed in the last year, I understand. And one of those is about Jack?"

"I…" My voice cut out, my cheeks so hot I could barely breathe, let alone think. "It's not one of my very dark stories, but it has elements of suspense."

"And a dominant-and-submissive style relationship, with Jack being the alpha male."

"Yes, well…sort of." I paused, my brain finally catching up. "When I plan a story, it's common for me to take inspiration from the people around me, and then that takes on a life of its own. The characters very quickly become people of their own."

A slight grin crossed my interviewer's face, and I could have sworn he was enjoying my discomfort and my struggle to answer without embarrassing both of us.

"So yes, I started a character from what I knew about Jack, but I always ask myself questions like how would someone meet this person? What would put them off the other main character? And as I build all that up, they morph into something else. Someone else."

This seemed to make Jack relax a little, and relief flooded through me. Maybe I could rescue this. They shouldn't have ever known I'd written about Jack. I'd only told a few people when acting as my pen name.

Someone had been digging, and I had a feeling this question was payback for our insistence that we would both be interviewed. It was embarrassing for both of us.

"And why the submissive-dominant element? I understand the female character was based on you. In essence, it was sort of Jack Starling fan fiction," Keith continued, his eyes full of sparkling delight and the corners of his mouth twitching up farther.

Somewhere on the inside, part of me grew cranky enough that the embarrassment melted away. I was the sort of person who, when intimidated and threatened by a bully, found an inner strength, and it didn't fail me now.

"As I already said," I continued politely but firmly. "The characters soon take on a life of their own, and I don't truly know Jack. We met for the first time today, so they would never be perfect representations of each of us at all. I started a story because I wanted to explore the dynamics in a dominant and submissive relationship that didn't involve the other BDSM elements."

There was a pause, and I expected Keith to jump in. Instead, Jack turned even more toward me.

"You've got me curious now. Go on," the billionaire rock star said, smiling in a much more genuine way. The audience let out little chuckles.

"It wasn't long after your trial against your ex-wife—sorry to bring that up," I said, looking at Jack for the first time properly. "I didn't know what the verdict was, but I knew you had to be innocent of any wrongdoing."

There was silence in the room so intense I felt myself get emotional, but no one else spoke, almost as if they sensed that I hadn't finished explaining.

"My heart broke for you, and I guess when I thought of a story where two broken people came together and healed each other, I thought of you first. I wanted to create a character who genuinely loved you and wanted to see you return to the alpha-male role you belonged in."

There was a collective sigh from the audience and a nod from Jack. I'd done it. I'd won them all over and rescued myself at the same time.

CHAPTER FIVE

"That sounds like a fascinating story," Keith said. "And I understand it's one of your best sellers."

"Under my pen name, yes," I replied, grateful I appeared to be done with that awkward subject.

Again, there was a pause while Keith looked at the little cards he carried in his hands.

"Jack, I understand that you create in other ways, too, and you like to paint as well?"

"Yes. Yes, I do."

"Are you any good?"

"No, not really."

There was laughter at this again, and once more, the attention was no longer on me. I relaxed as the rest of the conversations were far more benign and barely about me.

The host brought the interview to an end, and then we were waiting for the credits to roll, waving at the camera and the audience. As the cameras cut and Keith came back over to us, Jack got to his feet.

Not sure how this was supposed to end, I did the same, and we both hugged our host and all thanked each other.

"Thank you both for coming. That was pure magic. I look forward to having you both back soon," Keith said, but although he smiled with his words, the expression didn't reach his eyes.

I followed Jack offstage, the technician coming forward to collect us. Neither of us spoke until we were both disconnected from the mics and gathering our belongings again.

"Well handled out there," Jack said as the technician walked away. "I'm sorry he put you on the spot like that."

"It must have been embarrassing for you, too," I replied. "I imagine it's not the first time someone has written about you. I… I'm sorry. I would never have brought that up or…well, I probably shouldn't have ever based a character on a real person."

"Why did you do it, really?" he asked, sitting on the arm of the sofa.

I bit down on my lip as I tried to think of the best answer that was still truthful.

"Your case was so awful, and I… I guess I really did want to give you a happy ending. I thought you deserved one."

"Then, please, don't ever let anyone make you feel like you shouldn't have written it. Most fan fiction is written to give the writer a thrill. It's almost a selfish act. You did it because you cared and were moved to feel something deeper and more pure. No matter what kind of story it is, that's a good reason to have written it."

The sincerity in his voice took me by surprise, as did the compliment. It was clearly true when people said he was very kind. He'd been nothing but kind toward me.

"Thank you," I replied, feeling like I wanted to hug him. But I didn't dare move or initiate physical contact when we'd been talking about something so awkward.

"No, thank you," he continued, and then leaned forward and wrapped his strong arms around me in a proper hug, just as I'd wanted to do.

For a moment, I closed my eyes, the warmth and hold perfect

and comfortable in a way I hadn't expected. I didn't take a breath until he pulled away, and then he was picking up his jacket and an umbrella I hadn't noticed until now.

"I've got to get back to the studio for an hour or so and finish something up, but if you're staying in the city tonight, there's going to be a dinner somewhere. About eight of us. Why don't you come and meet the rest of the band? They'd like you."

I blinked again, my mouth falling open. He chuckled, making it clear he'd noticed my shock.

"Assuming you're not busy?"

"Well, it's tempting to stick with my plan of burying my mortified-with-embarrassment self in a pile of blankets while eating ice cream straight out of the tub. And then considering deleting a certain story so no one can ever read it before the show actually airs. But I think coming to meet your band is just slightly more appealing," I threw back, and he laughed again.

"No deleting it, or I'll have to spank you, or, well…whatever it is dominants do in these sorts of stories."

"Spanking would be appropriate," I replied before I could stop my mouth, and Jack grinned even more.

Were we flirting?

I had no idea, but I felt my cheeks flush.

"Right. See you later, then, Mrs. Fernsby." Jack put a hat on his head and turned to go.

"Oh, where do I need to be, and what time?" I asked.

He paused again and looked thoughtful for a moment.

"Come to the studio in an hour? It'll stop the boys from getting carried away, and you can listen to our new sound if you'd like."

"I'd love that," I replied, excited about the idea of meeting the rest of his band, too. With a nod and a slight grin, he grabbed the question sheet I hadn't picked up yet, pulled a pencil from a pocket somewhere, and scribbled down the studio address for me.

As he handed it back to me, he gave me another dazzling smile, and then he swept away. For a moment, I didn't move, not sure I could or where I'd even go for an hour.

Trying not to think about the interview and how difficult it had been, I gathered my belongings back up. Finally, I checked my phone again, noticing I had plenty of messages from the new agent. He'd freaked out over the whole interview fiasco. I listened to a brief voicemail message as the assistant reappeared.

"Do you need me to help you get to the exit? It's quite a maze in here," she asked as I deleted the message asking me to call the agent back and hung up on the phone's automated system.

"That would be great," I replied, wanting to make my way to the studio as soon as I could, even if I saw a few sights along the way.

I tried to smile politely at the brusque woman, but she was already turning on her heel and heading through yet another door. I scurried after her, hearing our shoes clack on the solid floors as we weaved in and out of rooms and through corridors until I finally recognized where I was.

Despite my exclaiming so, the assistant continued heading past a few more doors and down another hallway until I was back at the reception.

"The show will be on late this evening, and Keith would appreciate you letting your fans know," she said before once again turning on the spot and walking away. There was no goodbye or opportunity to exchange polite sentiments of gratitude or well wishes.

I paused for a moment, not sure if she was deliberately being rude or simply busy. Shaking my head, I walked toward the sofa in reception and pulled up the maps on my phone so I could figure out where I needed to go and how far it was from my current location. The studio appeared to be a half-hour walk away at an amble, which would allow me to sight-see along the way.

Given the time that had already passed while I was still in the building, I was sure it was worth walking. It would also give more painkillers time to kick in. Over the last while, the pain had begun to build again, the bruises down my side fresh enough that they were tender to the touch and sore whenever I moved or bent too suddenly.

While I'd managed to hide them for the interview, I was more worried I wouldn't be able to hide them over a whole evening. I didn't plan to let it stop me from going, however. I wanted this fun night out with one of the world's most adorable men.

I'd find some way to continue hiding them and how I'd got them from everyone. I'd managed it so far.

CHAPTER SIX

<u>Jack</u>

The icy wind of the London air hit me as I stepped out of the studio, not a moment too soon. I was making a fool of myself. To top it off, I'd gone and invited the woman to dinner with the band.

"To the studio," I said to Mick as he approached and opened the car door.

Sliding into the back, I relaxed a little. At least in here, I could think without anyone else bugging me. Not that I had long until we'd be at Abbey Road, but it was a start.

The interview had been close to a train wreck. What on earth had I been thinking when I'd insisted they interview us both? It was bound to piss off the host.

I exhaled as I thought about the moment I'd done it. The look on Juno's face. She'd tried to hide it, but she'd been both shocked and grateful. Her face had expressed every little emotion for the observant to see.

The moment I'd set eyes on her, I'd seen this nervous young woman. She'd faced her fears well, standing up for herself as best she could, but she didn't have the clout I did. They almost never did. She'd been denied, about to be thrown out and left with nothing, and she'd known it.

And, of course, I'd done what I always did. Rescued the damsel in distress, even though she was clearly stronger than most. Might even have bounced back and got O'Sullivan to interview her another time. But I'd gone and given her a different option.

Instantly, I'd thought of the moment on the sofa beside her. When she'd been asked about her book. A book about me.

Fuck. That's what I'd thought. *Fuck.*

What a question to be asked in your first interview. Tell us about the fan fiction you wrote about the famous person right beside you.

It had been intended to shame her. Intended to embarrass me. Somehow, she'd found the words to stop it from doing either. *Damn, the girl had a way with words. Not entirely surprising, but...*

No, I wasn't going to follow that thought. It was bad enough I'd invited her to dinner with the band. They weren't going to understand. Especially once they saw the video. They were going to think I wanted to get into her panties. Twenty years ago, I might have wanted to.

Fuck.

There was no way I could undo it now. I didn't have her number. Only thing I could do was neglect to tell the boys at the door to let her through.

Yeah, maybe that would work. She'd get frustrated with them, give up, and go home, and I'd never have to see her again. Wouldn't even need to tell the band.

I let out a growl. Couldn't do it, and I knew it. It would humiliate her. And she'd rescued me from the same thing only half an hour ago.

No, she was coming to dinner, and I would have to tell the band about her. Why was I always so kind to everyone? Rescuing them, inviting them, including them.

Because the world needed more nice people. It needed more people who tried to right the wrongs. Not that the world deserved it. Most people didn't, but that wasn't the point. It made the world a better place, and most people paid it forward where they could.

I'd done the right thing, even if the roadies talked. And I was curious about her. Juno Fernsby. What a name.

This contradiction of a woman. Both a frightened little girl who didn't know what to say or do and a confident young woman who didn't let a disgruntled TV show host intimidate her. She'd found her steel when it mattered.

Part of me wanted to know what she'd be like in front of the band. Wanted to know what she smelled like up close, what her chestnut-brown hair felt like when I ran my fingers through it. What it would feel like to...

No. I couldn't think like that, either.

What I needed most was a cold shower, but all too soon, I was at the studio and being ushered inside. There were crowds of fans outside, and I took a moment to wave and sign autographs, letting them take photos and whatever else they wanted. The fans were great most of the time, and I didn't mind them.

Occasionally, they got overzealous, but most of them just wanted to be able to say something about the music or movies and then go on with their lives feeling like they'd touched the stars.

In a lot of ways, I was lucky. People let me do things others didn't get to. My whole world was like a playground, but it was also full of rules about behavior and a sort of unspoken celebrity code.

The inside of the studio was quieter. Our band was the only one still recording and booked in this late in the day, and it sounded like there must have been a break for a moment as I got closer and everyone was milling around.

"How'd it go?" Kai asked as he noticed me.

"It was different. Don't think O'Sullivan is going to invite me back in a hurry."

"Why? You crap on his sofa?"

"Not exactly. Forced him to interview me and this other chick there. A writer. He'd double-booked us in case I didn't show or couldn't make it and then tried to blow her off."

Kai didn't respond at first, giving me that look of his. He was assessing me, but not in a bad way. Like he didn't want to pry if I didn't want to talk, but he was giving me a moment to continue if I wanted it.

"I told her to swing by in about an hour."

"She cool, then?"

"The interview was…interesting."

"Sounds like meeting her will be fun. And maybe we'll watch that interview, too." Kai grinned, his eyes lighting up, but it was all he would say on the matter. It was time to get on with the job.

Within seconds, I was in the studio, my guitar in my hands. It wasn't my only one, just one of the more comfortable ones. For a moment, I just held it, getting into the mood it brought with it.

Putting on an instrument was a bit like putting on a mask. I slipped into the me who played guitar. I became Jack the rock star. Jack the musician. And it felt right today.

Over the next forty or fifty minutes, we laid down tracks and riffs, tweaking things here and there and playing them again to get the right sort of sound.

"Right, I think we've got everything we need for that part," the main sound engineer said, giving a thumbs-up at the same time.

For a moment, I didn't move, not wanting to take the guitar off and put it down. Taking a deep breath, I did anyway and headed out into the booth.

"I think we should do the last few parts of that song and call it a night. Finish the rest tomorrow," Kai said. "You good with that?"

"Yeah," I replied, my mind already going in one direction.

Juno, with her wide eyes and long hair. She'd turned those bright blue eyes on me and practically begged me to rescue her. How on earth did she seem both so confident and so needy all at the same time?

She was a puzzle, and I wanted to figure her out. But did I really want to do that in front of everyone else? And what would they think of the interview and what she'd said?

Sighing, I excused myself from the group and headed to the front door again. Only then did I find myself wondering, what if she didn't show?

CHAPTER SEVEN

<u>Juno</u>

As cars rushed by and other tourists moved through the busy London streets, I finished my call with my agent. He was calmer now but still a little angry that I almost didn't get interviewed.

I had found my anger disappearing as I thought about what would happen next. I was going to have dinner with Jack Starling and his band, the Vampirates.

Although Keith O'Sullivan, or whoever decided his guests, shouldn't have tried to ditch my interview just to make way for Jack, it had all worked out in the end. Thinking about the interview made me feel embarrassed all over again, however.

I'd been asked about writing a character based on Jack while sitting right beside him. My only relief had been how well he'd taken hearing it. He'd almost deliberately not let it embarrass him, so Keith didn't get the satisfaction of getting to us.

Trying to focus on the city around me for the last few minutes of sightseeing, I pushed it from my mind. I wouldn't ever do another interview on the show again, out of principle, so I could get on with my life.

As I walked the last few hundred meters, I felt my stomach

knot again. I was going to the studio where a famous band was recording, and I'd been invited to hang out with them. It was a little surreal, but there was no way I would pass up the opportunity.

I was still a little early, so I slowed my steps and enjoyed walking across a section of road featured on an old famous album cover. I wasn't the only one doing so. Many people stopped in the middle of the road, despite the traffic, so they could take photos.

It made me smile and helped me relax again before finding the studio nearby. People were milling outside there as well, but I already knew the best way through them was to act like I belonged and needed to get to the front door.

Although they didn't part as easily as I'd hoped, and I had to call 'excuse me' several times, I made it to the door, climbing the majority of the steps alone.

There were a few men just outside the open porch, and the nearest stopped me.

"Sorry, miss, we can't let you inside without some kind of invitation or appointment," he said, his voice holding a slight Southern American twang that made me wonder if this was a personal bodyguard of one of the band members or just a coincidence.

"I know. I was asked to get here about now. I'm the author, Juno Fernsby. I was just recording on the Keith O'Sullivan show with one of the fellas," I said, not wanting to say the name while fans were listening.

The guy frowned almost imperceptibly, his eyebrows flicking closer together for just a moment before he hid it. I waited as if I wasn't worried he'd reject me.

"Do you need to check?" I asked when he simply glanced at his counterpart. "I don't mind waiting if you feel you need to confirm and make sure I'm not yanking your chains."

They still hesitated, but eventually, the guy in front of me shrugged and reached for his radio. Before he could do more than speak a name into it and wait for a response, the door behind him opened. Immediately, the crowd of people behind me, most of them young women, started calling names and screaming.

Jack appeared, and his eyes went wide when he saw me.

"Oh, perfect," he said, reaching for my hand. I placed my fingers in his, grateful I'd wiped any possible sweat off them as I walked up to the building. "I was coming down to tell these two to look out for you, but you're here already. I hope they didn't keep you waiting or try and tell you to get lost."

"No, they were darlings," I replied, smiling and giving the one with the radio a nod.

"What is it?" a voice asked, crackling a little and almost drowned out by a young woman screaming Jack's name at the same time.

"Never mind," the bodyguard said as Jack pulled me into the building and closed the door behind us.

Jack immediately made his way toward the back and right-hand side of the building, weaving through doors and passing others using the space. I looked around at the amazing space, noticing signs that led to studio three and then studio one as we made our way past.

"We're in studio two," Jack continued. "The one the Beatles recorded in. It sounds amazing, but we still have a few bits and pieces to lay down. Want to listen in the control room?"

"I'd love to!" I declared, feeling like I might have died and gone to heaven.

How many people got to listen to one of their favorite bands as they recorded parts of a new album?

Jack took me into a room and gave me a quick introduction to the people inside, although I knew I'd struggle to remember the names. However, everyone was more concerned with what was happening in the studio ahead. We were looking into a reasonable-sized studio space, and the rest of the band were playing various instruments.

I expected him to leave me then, but his part didn't seem to be needed for a moment, and he stayed with me, sitting on the sofa at the back of the room.

A moment later, someone came over to us and offered to get us anything in hushed tones. Jack ordered a soda, so I did the same, delighted to have someone treating me as an equal to the rock star beside me for a moment.

He grinned as the band started playing on the other side of the glass, their music filling the room. Although Jack was sitting beside me and not playing anything or singing, I could hear his distinctive guitar playing on the track and now and then his vocals, his voice backing the lead singer in several places.

It was slightly surreal, but he nodded and seemed to really enjoy listening to it as the band laid down extra sections. At the same time, a cameraman was moving around the recording studio, getting clips of them playing.

"What did you think?" Jack asked as the song finished, and everyone started holding their thumbs up.

"That was amazing. Strange listening to you singing while you were sitting beside me and not singing, though."

"Yeah, it's weird not playing while listening to it, too. But do you think it's a good sound? Like, you get the vibe?"

I nodded, surprised by the seeming desire in his voice to have me approve.

"I really liked the lyrics and the drive it had. And the way it ended. Almost like a plot twist," I elaborated, hoping I sounded as enthusiastic and grateful as I was. How many people got to give feedback on a rock band's song as they were being recorded?

"Fantastic. If we nailed those elements for a storyteller, that makes me happy. Thank you."

"Oh, no, thank you for letting me listen. I feel like I should be pinching myself to see if I'm awake or something."

Jack frowned for a moment and looked thoughtful. The band was finishing up in the recording studio, and the door opened, making me look that way as they came into our room, chatting about how it had gone, too.

A moment later, I thought I felt a sort of tickle to the side of my face. I turned back to Jack to find his face only an inch or two from mine.

"Boo!" he yelled as he did. I jumped, feeling my heart skip a beat and my body tense. A sting of pain shot through my side, but I thought I managed to hide it.

"Nope. You're definitely awake," he said, the corner of his mouth lifting as if he was trying to suppress a laugh. For a moment, I didn't know how to respond, still in a sort of shock, but I began chuckling. As I did, he finally let himself smile, and then I laughed even harder, and he joined me.

CHAPTER EIGHT

"What's got you two in stitches?" the lead singer, Kai, asked.

I looked his way to find the camera on us, and immediately, the laughter seemed to dry up.

"Kai, meet Juno. She's a writer. Was at the interview, too, and has an extremely brilliant mind. The darling loved our lyrics." As Jack said "darling," he elongated the r and emphasized the first syllable in an exaggerated way an English person did, making everyone chuckle again.

At the same time, Kai took my hand and kissed the back of it.

"How do you do, my lady?" he asked, also attempting to speak with the same exaggerated accent.

I tried to stifle my own laughter so I could reply.

"I'm having a capital time, darling," I said, trying to imitate the accent I'd heard from both of them.

This created more amused outbursts as the rest of the band appeared. Although I was a stranger to most of them, they seemed to welcome me with open arms. They included me in their conversations, all of us drinking a variety of soft drinks and eating the snacks that had somehow appeared.

Jack quickly told our tale about O'Sullivan trying to pretend he hadn't double-booked us and how Jack had made sure we were both interviewed, and the indignation spread through the whole band. It made me feel at home until the talk turned to food.

Once again, Jack took my hand as the band and various other people, including some other women who appeared to be partners of band members, all made their way back toward the front of the studio.

When we got there, several cars were waiting. Jack led me over to one, his bodyguards coming with us and parting the smallish crowd. One of the bodyguards opened the doors, and Jack motioned for me to get inside.

The leather interior had a warm, inviting scent that I couldn't place in any other way than to say it was clean, and some kind of polish or air fragrance had been used on it.

The passenger space was also generous and contained a small fridge and yet more snacks of different varieties. I was looking around at it all when I realized Jack hadn't followed right away. He stood by the door, talking in hushed voices to the bodyguard.

In the background, I could hear more fans calling his name and shouting various bits of praise or their desires. Some of it was less than appropriate, but Jack barely seemed to react, as if it was a normal backdrop to his life. Before he got into the car, however, he waved, and this made the fans squeal all the more.

It had me wondering what they must all be thinking of me. This random woman they probably didn't recognize, now in the back of Jack's car with him. Would they wish they were me?

"Sorry about that," Jack said. "There's always some sort of decision to make or things to plan. Our schedule is crazy right now."

"I can imagine," I replied. "I don't know how you manage to make so many films each year and do albums and tours at the same time."

"Careful planning and a lot of staff," he replied, still smiling.

"But I don't know how you write so many books each year. You have a lot."

"It's like therapy. I sit in my little study, and I just let the voices in my head tell me their stories. It keeps me sane. Mostly," I said, seeing his eyes light up at the humor.

"The songs are similar for me. I feel like I'm just getting something out there that someone else gave me. It's a relief to have it out."

"Does the acting feel the same?" I said before wondering if I'd asked something he was bored of responding to.

It had come out several years earlier that he preferred to be in a band but thought the movies both paid better and were easier to do.

"The acting is more about having fun and paying the bills. I have amazing fans, and I get paid a lot to do it. I get to live a life where I have all the money I need, and I get to tell people not to be asshats to others. It makes sense, but it doesn't make me feel alive in the same way."

I nodded as he spoke, his voice mesmerizingly gentle but equally expressive. When he finished speaking, neither of us moved for a moment, our eyes locked but the moment somehow not awkward.

Eventually, I looked down, wanting to pinch myself again. He was stunning, and I was that girl who had written a few books and got lucky with them. Not to mention, I'd written smut fan fiction about him. I didn't deserve to be sitting in the back of a fancy car with one of the sweetest and most gorgeous rock stars on the planet.

Thankfully, Jack didn't seem to mind the silence either, but he shifted to look out the window.

"Shouldn't be too much longer before we're there. Then we can get some decent food and wait for the fallout of this interview. It's going to cause quite a fuss, I think."

"Sorry," I replied, pretty sure he meant my fan fiction.

"I told you, don't be ashamed of it. You did it for good reasons. If I need to, I'll tell someone that in one of the next few interviews I do. But if it bothers you, you might want to steer clear of social media for a few days."

"Oh, I don't mind what others think, really. But..." I trailed off as he looked at me again, giving me his attention and distracting me.

He had changed since the interview, now wearing a flannel shirt with the top few buttons undone and open. Several necklaces hung in the gap, but it still gave me a good view of his sculpted chest.

"But?" he asked, and I was pretty sure the corner of his mouth twitched up.

"I don't want to embarrass you or make you think I'm only interested in...well..."

"Getting into my pants," he finished.

"Yeah, that." I looked away again, trying hard not to be embarrassed myself.

"So you're not interested in getting into my pants?" he asked.

Immediately, I looked up, about to protest, before I saw the twinkle in his eyes and the sly grin on his face. I'd almost walked into one of those moments where I'd have dug a very big hole.

"I'm not embarrassed. I feel flattered, as I said. But let's talk about something else before your beautiful cheeks go even darker red. I think they look better with your natural pale color."

I nodded and looked down again. A moment later, he reached out and lifted my chin, so I had to look right into his eyes, his face closer again.

"Blue. I thought so," he said before letting go.

I blinked, not sure how to respond. His eyes were a dark brown and expressed a great deal of emotion. Or at least appeared to.

Of course, he was a famous actor. Who knew what was really going on inside his head? I'd spent about an hour in total with him so far, most of it reeling from one surprise to another.

It didn't take much longer for us to reach our destination, and the car pulled over to the side of the road again. The bodyguard appeared incredibly quickly to open the door and let Jack and me out.

The rest of the group soon joined us as well, some of them in cars ahead and others in the cars behind. It was a little strange, and I was pretty sure we annoyed some of the other drivers in the area, a few beeping to express their annoyance.

The whole time, Jack kept his fingers wrapped around mine and led me into the restaurant. Immediately, the head waiter was there to show us to our seats and hand us menus, even managing to accommodate my awkward diet. I was sort of a celiac, but not. Instead, I had some kind of unexplained auto-immune disease that made me react like a celiac.

CHAPTER NINE

"Looks like the interview is about to air," Kai said and immediately pulled out his phone.

We'd finished eating and were chilling in a small, private area of the restaurant, snacks and drinks continuing to flow. Already, I was blown away by the strange way dinner had been conducted. It hadn't been anything like the eating-out experience I was used to. We had our own waiter, and there was no apparent rush to our meal.

Although we'd all ordered fairly early on, one of the band members had signaled for them to bring out each of the next courses, and it had happened. There had been almost an hour of chatting between the main course and dessert.

"I'm guessing you have no desire to watch it again," Jack said quietly, leaning toward me so only I would hear him.

As several of the other guests got up and went to Kai's side to watch, I nodded. It was bad enough that so many of them were watching it and would want to comment.

Again, Jack took my hand and led me through a set of double doors to a sort of game room. I'd noticed a few of the others head this way earlier, and I saw them playing pool at the far end of the room. At this end were several large game machines, one of them pinball. All of them had a pot with a sort of token inside.

Grabbing one, Jack pointed toward the pinball machine.

"Do you like these sorts of things?" he asked.

I'd never really played one before, but I wasn't about to admit that. Instead, I nodded and moved closer. He'd been heading toward it, and that was enough for me right now.

As he slipped the token in, the machine seemed to come to life, and a ball fell out of somewhere onto the trigger. I watched him pull it back and let it go before moving his hands to the paddles on the side and making sure it didn't come back down too fast.

He managed to catch the first fall with a good flick, sending the shiny object up to bang on lights and start racking up a really good score. Glancing at me a moment later, he waved me closer. As soon as I was near enough, he motioned to the left of the table.

"You take the left flipper," he said, and I happily obliged, looking at the table, our bodies side by side, only inches apart.

We batted it around a few times, neither of us speaking, but both of us clearly trying to make it work. My timing was far from perfect, however, and I reacted too slowly a couple of times, the second time losing us the game.

"Sorry," I said as the game ended.

"Don't worry about it. I've had a lot of practice. You can learn quickly." He grabbed another token as he spoke and shoved it in. Instead of pulling the trigger, he ushered me closer to the center of the table and moved behind me.

"Put your hands on the flippers, and I'll try and show you when to flick."

I did as he suggested, feeling the warmth of his body behind mine, his hands cupping the backs of mine and making me almost freeze for a moment.

"Ready?" he asked.

"I think so," I replied, trying to concentrate on the game and not the attractive man standing so close to me. It wasn't easy. Standing like this, I could smell his cologne again. The slightly citrus-style smell had hints of smoked wood and possibly vanilla. It was hard to tell, but I found myself almost drinking it in.

Jack pulled the trigger again, and then I tried to concentrate, his trigger finger over mine on both sides.

He pressed gently each time he tried to encourage me, not trying to do more than indicate to me to press. It still took me several attempts to get into the same sort of rhythm, but I got there eventually, and then we were pressing it together, each attempt a little better than the one before.

"It's a shame we're not in London for long," he said. "I could show you some of the boys' collections of these things."

"Maybe another time you're around," I replied without missing a beat. It was kinda fun and almost hypnotic, flicking a small metal ball around a machine that lit up and made noises whenever you got something right.

"Definitely." He pulled the trigger again and set us both off, but this time, he gently pulled my hands out of the way. Leaning into me a little more to get a better angle, he took over.

I got the feeling he was showing off a little, but I didn't mind and kept still while he bounced it around and racked up the points on the headboard. Although I'd been getting better, Jack was far more skilled and showed he'd had experience with the game. It just kept giving him more points, and he never missed a flick.

Suddenly, the door opened again, and several more of the group strode in.

"Nice interview," one of the women yelled, although I couldn't remember her name. The group came closer, and I got the impression Jack deliberately let the ball drop so he could back up and put some distance between us.

As he did, he caught the side of my body with his arm, not

hitting me hard but catching one of my larger bruises with enough force that I sucked in my breath and winced.

Immediately, he seemed to notice and came back to me. His eyes fixed on my hand. It had gone instinctively to cover the hurting area. I lowered it and looked away to draw the focus from it.

"Sorry," he said quietly, leaning in a little. "Are you badly hurt? Did I catch you somehow?"

I could see the confusion on his face. After all, we hadn't connected that much, but here I was in pain. However, my brain froze, and I didn't respond or explain, not knowing how.

While the couple at the pool table were finishing their game, the new arrivals appeared to be distracted. Before I could stop him, Jack had come over and swept my blouse out of the way, covering the view from anyone else in the room.

As he got a good look at the yellowing but still very dark bruise, he sucked in his breath.

"That looks like it hurt," he whispered, gently covering it back up again.

"I slipped," I replied without thinking, unable to meet his gaze. "Distracted by an idea in the shower. Stupid thing, really."

"Have you been in pain all day?" he asked.

"Painkillers have taken the edge off, but yeah, it still hurts a little when I sit. I was lucky not to break anything, but I'll be fine in a few days."

Jack paused and studied my face, his doubt and questions lingering in his eyes. Again, I looked away, but he reached for my chin as if he was about to give me a stern but caring lecture.

"What are you two up to over there? Acting out a scene from Miss Writer's book or something?" one of the other women asked, grinning as she did.

I thought I heard Jack sigh as he let go of me and turned, but I couldn't be sure. He put distance between us and asked a question I didn't hear, the pinball machine behind choosing that moment to begin its jingle and remind people it was there to be played.

Trying to look normal, I slipped out of the room and found the nearest ladies' room. Not just to relieve myself but also to check the bruise that had taken another battering.

Although I couldn't be sure how much Jack had seen in the dimmer and mottled light of the games room, checking it now made one thing clear. It was a really nasty-looking bruise.

CHAPTER TEN

Before I could leave the bathroom, still washing my hands, more of the women in the group came in, Kai's partner coming to stand near me and redoing her lipstick.

"Jack seems to have taken a shine to you," she said a moment later.

"He's been very kind," I replied. "Especially after that awful interview."

"Oh, don't be too hard on yourself." She turned to me. "You handled it well. There's likely to be fallout, though. Might want to keep your head down for a few weeks and not make headlines for other reasons. The press'll move on soon enough."

"Thank you," I replied, grateful for what appeared to be genuine care and advice as I moved to the towel dispenser and started to rub the moisture off my hands.

"You looked like you really meant it when you said you wanted our Jack to have a happy ending. You've got a sweet heart, but anyway, let's not keep the guys alone for long. They get strange ideas and up to all sorts of mischief."

Before I could do anything but finish drying my hands, she

slipped her arm through mine, thankfully on my less bruised side, and tugged me out of the bathroom with her.

The other women who had come in with her were left behind, making me wonder if this had been a bit of a setup or if I'd been pursued with the purpose of bringing me out again.

Whatever the reason, I wasn't about to ask. But I was going to be wary. It was already clear there were plenty of people watching Jack and his social life, and the last thing I wanted right now was to be in the spotlight or to be judged by other women. I was in the middle of a separation and a divorce.

It was lucky enough that I hadn't been asked about it during the interview. I didn't need to open myself up to prying eyes here or attract jealousy from others.

As I emerged, I spotted Jack again, the man clutching another soda as he and Kai stood talking about something off to one side of the group. Although I glanced his way, I was pulled in another, my companion keeping my arm pinned at her side and leading me back to the snacks.

"This is Emily," she said. "And because there's been so many names that you've probably been overwhelmed already, I'm Alma. We were just talking about how strange this business can be for women, especially when the media likes to make us look like bitchy money-grabbers hanging onto men with loads of money and heads easily turned by pretty women."

"Deep subject," I replied, surprised but also grateful for the courtesy and warmth I was being shown.

"Very, but we face it every day, and it takes a brave woman to walk into it with an idea of what she's getting herself into."

I lifted an eyebrow. Was this a warning of sorts? Was I being told not to expect much of Jack? My body wasn't in the best shape. Some of the women here had perfect figures, flat stomachs, manicured nails, and spotless makeup. I was still wearing the makeup the TV stylists had put on me, and I was far from perfectly formed around the middle.

I noticed Alma was less of the ideal shape, but she had an amazing dress sense. Her trousers were loose but styled enough to show off curvy legs, and a well-cut blouse showed she had plenty to offer on the top half as well.

For a while, I listened as Emily moaned about a recent tabloid article on her dress at one of the band's events and how it had apparently made her thighs look fat.

It reminded me that Jack lived in a very different world, and I wasn't a great fit for it. Or at least, as Alma had suggested, I would be walking into it blind.

Maybe it was a good thing I wasn't very famous yet. I'd wanted a movie deal for as long as I could remember, and I was so close to having my books sell well enough for that. A TV series was possibly enough, but equally, I knew of many other authors who had climbed this high and been gone from everything five years later.

Was this why? Was fame a double-edged sword?

"We've got to go, babes. Need to sort out an issue with one of the plans for the music video tomorrow. It's making Jack antsy. You know what he's like. Won't rest 'til he knows it's fixed," Kai said, interrupting us.

I looked behind him to see Jack already hurrying out the door, his bodyguards following. Kai strode off after them, and a couple of the band members left too until the room was a lot emptier.

Involuntarily, I shivered and looked back at the group of women I was with.

"Oh, didn't he say goodbye?" Elsie said, coming up beside Alma and grinning just a little too much to look sincere.

"Leave her alone, Elsie," Alma replied for me. "She's Jack's guest, and even if she wasn't, I like her. Knows how to write a story and works hard, from what I hear."

"Yeah, well, at least she's got that going for her." Elsie flicked her gaze up and down my clothes and body.

Before I could even think of a response, let alone say it, Elsie turned and walked away, the ice in her glass clinking and the liquid almost sloshing over the side.

"Sorry," Alma replied. "She's had her eyes on Jack for some time. Never particularly happy about anyone new joining the group if it might threaten her attempts to bed him. Or have him bed her. Not sure which she's after."

"Oh, she's welcome to him if it makes him happy. I'm not interested in another relationship right now," I said, knowing I meant it.

Jack had been lovely, and maybe he'd make a great friend, but that was all I needed right now.

With this in mind, I turned back to the conversation with Alma and Emily, the topic having moved to great Christmas movies. There were always lots of feel-good romances, and it seemed even the wealthier women of the world swooned over the happy endings and the handsome men who ended up with the heroines.

However, the conversation didn't have the same feel to it, and I soon found myself both bored and tired. It was time to leave.

After letting Alma know I was pleased to meet her and making sure she knew it wasn't just a British pleasantry in her case, I made my way out to the street and looked for the telltale sign of a black London cab.

Thankfully, we were in a busy enough part of the city that, even late at night, one arrived within only a minute or so, and I was soon on my way to the hotel.

As soon as I sat in the back, my hotel destination in the driver's possession, I found my mind turning to the last time I'd been in a car. The way Jack leaned closer just to lift my chin and check the color of my eyes.

Exhaling, I stared into the busy night, car lights and street lights illuminating the many people still out and about in the city.

"You look a little familiar, love," the cabbie said a moment later, glancing in the mirror at me.

"Must just be a similarity," I replied, as I usually did. "Unless you like to read fantasy."

"Yes, you're her. That author who was on O'Sullivan's this evening," he said, the excitement of discovering someone slightly famous in the back of his car making his eyes light up.

For a moment, I wanted to shake my head and deny it, but I hesitated just a fraction too long and missed the polite window to deny it.

I forced a smile and listened, knowing that all most people wanted was to be acknowledged and listened to for a few minutes. And it wasn't like I was going anywhere.

CHAPTER ELEVEN

Jack

When Kai came over, I knew he didn't have good news. He never looked so surly or walked so purposefully past people who wanted his attention unless he needed to. And he was coming straight for me.

"What's wrong?" I asked.

"Simon said there's a problem with the production schedule. Something about the gig next month and having shit ready in time. I think they need us to figure it out."

"All right. Let me just grab my coat."

Although Kai didn't say much more, I could tell it was serious. He wasn't going to give me all the details while others could hear, that much was clear. As he walked past the rest of the band and gathered them, too, I followed.

It was only as I got into the car that I remembered Juno.

Fuck.

I'd just walked out on her. And she'd have no idea why. I also still didn't have her number.

Letting out a sigh, I tried to tell myself it would be fine. She wasn't that into me anyway. And it hadn't been a great idea to invite her along. Besides, the band needed me, and they came first. What else would I have done? Gone up to her and said, "Hey, sorry I invited you to dinner, hurt you, and now I've got to go. See you around, sweetheart."

Yeah, it wouldn't look good, no matter how I played it. Either way, I'd just blown it.

In some ways, it was a comforting thought. I could put her out of my head and get on with fixing whatever shit had just hit the fan.

The car pulled up at our hotel, and we all went inside, coming together in the lobby before heading to Kai's suite. It wasn't long before Kai sat on one of the chairs and let out a deep sigh.

"So, that gig we're supposed to be doing in New York next month. It looks like we might have to cancel it," Kai said.

"But we've sold out the tickets," I replied. "The fans are going to be pissed."

"The folks supplying the gear for the gig didn't block off our slot. They've just informed us it's all double-booked. When we added the extra dates, it got missed or something."

"So we'll get different gear," I said, knowing it wouldn't be quite that simple but refusing to give up without at least trying a few different avenues.

"Yeah, I've got Derek on it now, but there's a chance we won't find anything this short notice. At least, not anything decent. We might have to decide between doing a gig on old, worn-out gear and not doing it."

I nodded, sitting back and letting the others say their piece. It was a crap position to be in and made me more than a little angry, but it wouldn't be solved with emotion.

While they talked and threw around ideas, I listened. Several of the team came and went, Derek and Simon both appearing and sticking around to help work through it. More than once, phone numbers were found and used, all of us looking for an alternative to canceling the gig.

Everything ended up in a negative way. No one seemed to have what we needed.

"What if we ship it in from another state, or heck, even another country? There's got to be one of the large arenas with some gear." I looked between them all as they stared at me, but Derek pulled his cell out again and started dialing someone.

I relaxed a little as, once more, everyone else tried to fix the problem, and I tried to think of anything but my guilt. How could I have walked out on Juno after I'd asked her to join us?

Even if I wasn't looking for a relationship right now, it was still unkind of me, and I'd had more than enough bad press lately. Sighing, I grabbed one of the soda cans off the mini bar and moved toward the window. Down below, the London hotel cars moved in a hurry, their lights bright in the night air.

A moment later, Kai was by my side. He stared at me again, that knowing look on his face.

"Got a message from Alma. Said she likes your new girl."

"She's not my girl."

"She likes you, though," he replied, the corner of his mouth twitching up.

"Yeah, that much was evident by the smut story. But she's still not my girl. I felt sorry for her. Even if I wanted something more, I just walked out on her. She'll think I'm a jerk by now."

"Maybe. Want me to see if Alma can get her number, or do you have it already?" Kai asked, now grinning.

"I don't have it, and I'm sure she wouldn't hand it over now anyway," I replied, not sure I wanted to discuss her any longer but equally not sure what else to talk about.

"It's a shame we had to stop and sort this out. Looks like we've probably fixed it. It's going to cost some to grease the wheels, but it's settled. We should all get some sleep so we can finish the recording tomorrow."

"Aye, mate. We'll need to be fresh enough. Swing by my room in the morning, and we'll get breakfast, okay?"

"Yeah. Alma will be sleeping in, no doubt. She's still out with the other gals. You'd best not stay up reading, either. I know what you're like when you get a good book."

I laughed, knowing he meant the book I'd been up reading only a few nights earlier.

"I've finished it. Don't worry."

"Well, don't go starting another one, especially this book Juno wrote. You can read it when we're done." Kai smiled as he walked away, and I shook my head, finding myself grinning at the tease. But as I made my way to my own hotel room, I couldn't shake the idea. She hadn't allowed O'Sullivan to embarrass her with the book, but she hadn't denied it was about me.

She'd even mentioned giving me a happy ending. Maybe a happy ending and the hope for one would help lift me out of my funk.

Or it could make me worse, the disconnect between what she'd written and my reality ground into my face.

As I walked into my room, the empty silence only made me feel worse. I was such a loser. I'd become such a loser. All this money and fame, and here I was alone in a hotel, no woman to share it with and a world full of rumors and allegations. I'd lost so much in the past to women who wanted nothing more than my money or fame.

Now and then, Kai and other bandmates tried to encourage me to get serious about someone again, but none of them made me want to take the risk. None of them made me feel.

Until today. Today, I'd wanted someone. The moment I'd seen Juno, like a deer in headlights. And then she'd not only stood up to our host but given her explanation with such care. She had a heart. That much was clear. And she believed me. That also meant a lot.

But there was so much to her I didn't understand. Her own recent breakup. The bruises she'd hidden until I'd actually hurt her.

As I lay on the bed, still fully dressed, I thought back to our moment playing pinball together. I'd been so close to those bruises, and she hadn't even thought to warn me. They must have hurt. Must have been hurting all day. And then there was the book itself. It had apparently been some kind of darker romance. Were they linked somehow? Was her world far darker than it appeared?

Reaching for my tablet, I found myself opening the ebook store and searching for her name. An entire library of books popped up before I remembered she had this fan fiction of sorts under a pen name.

For a moment, I almost put the tablet back down, but I paused, the device in my hands and my fingers poised to open the internet browser and search for it.

Would it be easy to find? She'd acted like it had been something people knew.

Curiosity got the better of me, and before I knew it, I had the book before me. I stared at the cover a moment, the couple on it in a suggestive pose, the man clearly in control, dominant, and then I swiped to begin reading.

CHAPTER TWELVE

<u>Juno</u>

As the driver continued talking about seeing me on TV and recognizing me, I was already zoning out. I almost growled out loud. Why was I always so passive and polite? Why couldn't I think of responses fast enough to get myself out of situations I didn't want?

I sighed. I couldn't be so passive anymore. I just couldn't. I had to grow a spine. Assert myself. I was confident in who I was, but now I needed other people to know it, too.

"I guess you must need to find lots of inspiration for writing those pen name books they mentioned," the driver said, bringing my attention back to him, my heart rate instantly picking up.

"Not really," I replied. "I actually swing the other way."

It was the answer I always gave when someone I didn't know asked about my books. It was maybe a little disrespectful to women who were genuinely queer, but it was the best answer for getting men to leave me alone most of the time.

Of course, it didn't work on everyone, but most of the time, it gave me the relief I needed.

Thankfully, today was no different. We rode the rest of the

way in silence, and I could finally relax, even if I did detect a little frostiness from the cabbie when he asked me to hand over the final fare.

Eventually, I was in my hotel room and alone. The first time I had been since leaving my house that morning. I sighed, relieved and more than a little tired.

I slipped out of my boots, noticing I had a fresh blister, took some more painkillers, and slowly unpacked what I'd need for the night while the drugs kicked in.

Once I was done, I switched my clothes, trying to be careful as I revealed bruise after bruise. Most of them were on the right-hand side of my body, some little more than yellow marks now, but at least three larger, more purple ones showed, ugly and still swollen. One was on my thigh, the least painful because of the extra padding I had there.

There was another bad one just under one breast and across my lowest ribs. The worst sat above my hip, the one Jack had seen.

I tried not to look at them for too long, the memories of how I got them something I didn't want playing across my mind. It had been almost a week now, and it would never happen again. I couldn't let it happen again.

Still in pain, I tried to look for something else to distract me and help me unwind. Immediately, I reached for my phone. I hadn't checked anything but texts and voicemails all day, but I had tons of messages on social media, my Discord server, and even missed phone calls and texts. I started reading through everything in a sort of stunned disbelief.

Although it hadn't been a great secret that I had a pen name, the darker erotic romance I wrote under it was unknown to many people. At least it had been until today. Just as O'Sullivan's team had found the pen name and therefore the books under it, so had the rest of the internet now.

Responses ranged from understanding and interest to vilification that I would write such books when I gave the impression I was a clean and wholesome person. I rolled my eyes at the latter. To a large degree, I'd expected this sort of reaction when it finally came out into the public arena that I was writing dark erotic romance.

It made me sigh, however. Why did people judge others so much without understanding what was truly going on in their heads and hearts?

The worst part was the missed calls. They included my mother, my agent, and a few of my best friends.

I considered calling my friends first, but I knew I'd probably want to leave those until last to help me recover from the other two calls. My agent would be up for hours, so I called my mom. Might as well get the worst one over and done with.

"What were you thinking?" she asked as soon as I was on the phone. "Telling a man you wrote one of *those* books about him live on TV."

The extra emphasis on those didn't escape my notice, and I sat back and rolled my eyes as she continued her tirade.

"Why were you writing those kinds of books in the first place?"

"They were stories I needed to tell for one reason or another," I said, shrugging. "We'd be here all night if I gave you the reasons behind every single one of them."

"Yes, well. I hope that's the last of them now. You need to focus on your cleaner books and the opportunity you have with them."

"As always, I'll write the stories I feel are most important at any given moment. I've never been able to do anything else. The characters scream in my head until I write their story."

I heard her sigh in the background. I imagined her pursing her lips and frowning, possibly even pacing. It was clear I wasn't off the hook for the pen name yet, but it could have been worse. She'd let me off lightly so far. I hadn't been informed I needed to cleanse my soul or atone for anything yet. That was a small victory.

"And what is this about everyone saying you're separated? I've corrected Marge, of course, when she declared it, but honestly, why on Earth could they think you and Greg aren't together anymore?"

I winced, trying to sit up again but making the bruises hurt too much. Giving up, I tried to think of the best way to tell her.

"Well? I thought you'd at least be indignant. How does Greg feel about everyone reporting that you're not together? He must be livid after he's taken such good care of you."

"We *are* separated," I blurted out as much to stop my mother talking as to finally tell her the truth.

"What?" she demanded. "But he has kept that roof over your head for almost a decade while you try and make yourself a career. Now you get some success, and you leave him? What is going on in your head, child?"

"For one, Mother, I'm not a child any longer, and two, Greg is the reason we're separated. And three, while I was very grateful that he believed in me enough at the beginning of my career to pay the bills while I wrote, by the end, he was anything but supportive of my career choice. Our relationship was never going to continue. There was nothing I could do to save it."

And four, you're not in a position to talk, I thought, but didn't say. I might have been arguing with my mother, but I wasn't suicidal.

My mother didn't reply at first, and the silence only made me more worried that another discussion of my moral failings was coming, but in the end, she just sighed.

"I'm going to go to bed and hope we can all make sense of this in the morning. But you're not to do anything drastic. Greg was good to you. I refuse to believe your relationship can't be salvaged. Do you have any more interviews coming up?"

"No, that was the only one," I replied, suspecting where this was going.

"Good. Maybe if he doesn't see you flirting with that rock star, you'll have a chance to put things right. Goodnight, dear. Try to get a good night's sleep."

I responded in kind, not bothering to argue further. It wasn't worth it. At least the worst conversation was out of the way. My mother would have to get over her dislike of me leaving Greg. I'd already begun divorce proceedings. We were over, and I was taking little with me but my clothes, books, and a few small items of furniture. With any luck, it would all be over before anyone could try and truly stop me.

Sighing, I looked at my phone and tried to decide if I had the energy to call anyone else. I wasn't sure I did. It had been a long and eventful day, and I wanted nothing more than to go to sleep and dream of handsome men sweeping me off my feet and plucking me out of my mess.

CHAPTER THIRTEEN

<u>Jack</u>

Taking a deep breath, I tried to calm my frantic heart. Thoughts raced through my head as I pictured the words I was reading, the story unfolding in my head while I raced through the book.

Finally, I reached the last page. A large "The End" was staring me in the face. I sat back, unable to think of anything else but the book I'd just finished. It was over a week since I'd met Juno, and I'd finally finished reading the book she'd written. The book about me.

I was still sitting there, not sure how to react or feel, when Kai reappeared, coming up the plane's aisle and sitting down opposite me.

"Finished it, then?" he said, an amused grin on his face.

"Yeah. It was…not what I expected."

"More lewd?"

"No, less so. More…emotion, heart, passion. More just everything. She can write."

"That where this new song came from?" he asked. "Mickey just played me the demo track you recorded this morning."

I considered telling him it hadn't, not wanting to admit she'd gotten under my skin and made me feel something I hadn't expected to feel, but I found myself nodding anyway.

"It's a good song, but it should have some lyrics."

"Yeah, that's why I gave it to the rest of you. We should put some lyrics to it."

"Any idea where you want to begin?" Kai asked. "It has some real passion to it and heart, but unless we all read that book or you can figure out what made you feel so strongly, we're not going to be able to do it justice."

I exhaled, not sure I wanted the rest of the band reading what I just had. Part of me didn't want them to see into her capture of my soul. Although she'd declared the hero in her book had taken on a life of his own, he'd been enough like me that I'd been able to imagine myself in his shoes with ease.

"Let me see if I can summarize it in a way that works," I replied eventually.

"All right," Kai said, reaching into a nearby bag and pulling out a notepad and pen. "Do it while it's still fresh, and we'll see what lyrics we can pull out of it, 'cause right now I'm not sure it's something I'm up to."

You and me both, I thought as I stared at the blank page. How did I sum up what had happened while I read this book? How did I talk about an emotional journey a character had gone through when I was still feeling it and being changed by it?

Kai got up and moved back down the plane, leaving me to the task and giving me some space, something I appreciated. Right now, I didn't need the pressure of someone looking over my shoulder or sitting there waiting for me to produce something.

Sighing, I tried to begin, to just focus on how it had started. But by the time half an hour had gone by, I just had a pile of balled-up paper and two words on a page. *Fucked up.*

The character started so messed up in the head and heart, and she gently opened him up, slowly offered him love, acceptance, and healing until he could trust and love again. She did it all out of her own pain and fear, her own worry that he'd crush her entirely. The characters needed each other so desperately and so completely, and somehow, they found a way through that pain together.

But no matter how much the thoughts made sense in my heart and head, I couldn't get anything out on the paper.

A few minutes later, I threw the pad of paper across the area of the plane with a growl and got up. I paced a few times before Kai reappeared.

"Struggling, then," he said more than asked. "Wasn't sure you'd find it easy, either. Maybe we should get outside help on this one. Someone better at putting this sort of thing into words."

"Got someone in mind?" I demanded, knowing he didn't deserve me sounding angry at him but unable to help from snapping anyway.

"Yeah. The writer. She's already put it into words once. Figure she'd have a good chance of doing it again."

I growled again, both hating the idea and liking the possibility of legitimately reaching out to her about something. I'd considered it ever since the book had hooked me. Thought about finding some kind of communication for her and letting her know I thought she'd done a good job of capturing me. But how did I do that?

Especially after I'd walked out on her.

"She got to you that bad?" Kai asked as I continued to pace in front of him.

"No. Yes, I… Maybe. It's more that it was difficult to start with, you know? I swooped in and rescued her without thinking, and then I was this hero."

"And you don't want to fall off another pedestal," Kai finished.

"Something like that. I think we all know I can't afford any more bad press."

"And you're worried she will be?"

"Bad press? Yeah, a little. Or just bad in general. I mean, I'm just not sure someone else is a good idea right now."

I exhaled and tried to stop pacing. I felt like a caged animal, and I had to calm down. Thankfully, Kai stuck around and sat down again after getting us both something else to drink.

"Want me to message her and sort something out? Doesn't even have to involve you. I can find her agent or something."

"Her email address is in the back of her books," I replied, not even thinking about it.

"That's bold. Do you think she monitors it?"

"Seems to. The fans say she does." I sighed again and finally sat as well. Could I message her? Would it be so bad? If we were talking lyrics, I could keep it professional and all business.

"Tell me about the book," Kai said a moment later. "Tell me what sticks in your head most."

"How broken the characters were but how passionate they both were about seeing the other healed and safe. They found a way through their mess together, and it made them so much more…human. Like, all these sappy Christmas movies and fluffy romance films have these almost perfect couples whose only flaw is that they don't communicate well enough, or one of them has been offered a job somewhere else. They're so unrealistic for people like us."

"Tell me about it. Alma loves them, but I can't stand watching more than about ten minutes."

"This book was realistic. It made me feel what it was to want that same happy ending but being so messed up by the world that it's so much farther away. Yet they get it anyway. They find a way through the shit and trust each other."

"If all that's true, email her. She sounds like the kind of writer who's going to understand that you're not perfect, who won't create a mountain out of the things that are less important. We had shit hit the fan when you were with her last. Ask her for help, see if she'll give you a chance to say, 'Crap, babe, didn't mean to walk out on you, but I had to take care of band stuff, and I screwed it up.'" Kai picked up my tablet and handed it over.

Taking it, I nodded. Maybe I could email her, and it wouldn't be so bad.

CHAPTER FOURTEEN

<u>Juno</u>

Sitting down with my tea at the cafe table, I exhaled and felt my body relax. It had been over a week since the TV interview and I was finally getting some relief from all the hounding and questions upon questions about it all. I'd also finally got to the point where my body no longer hurt so much when I moved or sat.

Most of the bruises were gone, and the rest didn't hurt so much. It was a relief all of its own.

"There you are," Kit, one of my best friends, said. She beamed as she spotted the drink I'd also ordered for her and sat down. She took a sip and let out an approving moan. "No one else makes tea like they do here."

I grinned, pleased to see her.

"So, tell me all," she said a moment later. "What's up with all these major changes? This isn't like you."

"I..." I trailed off, feeling my emotions rise, my throat restricting and my eyes moistening.

Turning my head, I looked out the window and found something to focus on. A mother trying to wrestle a toddler into a winter jacket, the rain getting heavier and the child wanting none of it. While I watched, I pushed the emotions back down. I couldn't show them all right now. Not yet.

"Things with Greg had been getting worse and worse. I couldn't take it anymore. This is better, but…" Kit was a close friend, but I hadn't been able to bring myself to tell anyone properly yet what had been happening.

"No one else is seeing it that way," she replied, her eyes full of warmth.

I nodded, emotions threatening to overwhelm me again, but this time full of gratitude. Here was someone who wasn't judging me. Someone who accepted it when I said it was better to be over than to keep fighting.

"Anyone with sense has been seeing the cracks. If this is what you want, I won't tell you not to do it. I am worried about you, though. Rick said you missed the last writing evening, and you've not done much else."

"No," I said as I looked at her again, preparing to lie as naturally as I could. "I needed to get the new little flat organized and get paperwork done, that kind of thing."

"And you really won't tell anyone where it is?" she asked.

I shook my head. "I don't want Greg to know where I am, and if none of you knows, then you can honestly tell him that. It's easier for now. Once it's all over, you can all come over for a little housewarming if you like."

"That sounds more like you."

We slipped into silence, sipping our teas some more before I remembered to ask her how she was doing. She grinned and spent the next ten minutes telling me about the latest comic book she was illustrating, clearly enjoying the process.

Listening to her helped relax me even further. I'd missed this. Missed just chatting to someone about what mattered to them and creating beautiful art.

Eventually, she ran out of things to say, our tea gone but

neither of us eager to move. It was good to catch up, and my conscience wasn't completely comfortable with not telling her more about what was going on with my life, but it didn't feel like I could go back to it now.

With the lull in conversation, I took a bathroom break and suggested we get another round.

"Cake this time?" she asked, her eyes lighting up.

"Only if they've got that gorgeous, gluten-free carrot cake," I replied, grateful for a friend who understood.

I wasn't gone long but by the time I came back, Kit had two more teas on the table and a slice of cake each. She was also scrolling through something on her phone, her eyes wide.

As I sat down, I pulled one of the cake plates toward myself, wondering if I should ask what was so interesting, but she soon turned the phone to me.

"When were you going to tell me you hooked up with one of the most amazing men on the planet?"

On her phone was a picture of Jack leading me out of his car and into the restaurant, my fingers entwined in his and his bodyguards at our sides.

I frowned, noticing the headline over it was speculating that we were a thing. We were very much not a thing.

"It was just dinner with his band and groupies. He grabbed my hand to help me through the crowds, I think," I explained.

"So what happened afterward?" she asked.

"He left. The whole band did, and I talked to Alma, Kai's wife, for a while. She was lovely, by the way."

Kit sighed and sat back, but she got the point.

"Really, nothing happened?"

"I've only just separated from Greg, and honestly, I wasn't sure what to make of him. He was…confusing." I shrugged. I didn't have the words to tell her he wasn't someone I was interested in right now, even if he might have been in the past. I didn't need an alpha male in my life. Not until I'd healed and figured out who I was again.

Of course, another set of news reports and all this extra attention was enough to set my phone going again, my mother the first to call me. I hung up on her, not wanting to go through another argument about my life choices, but my agent called again as soon as I'd finished my cake.

I gave Kit an apologetic look and answered.

"When were you going to tell me you'd hooked up with one of the most eligible bachelors in all of history?" my agent demanded.

"We didn't hook up," I immediately protested, rolling my eyes and already aware I was likely to be sick of saying this before I'd managed to convince everyone that nothing had happened.

I spent the next few minutes repeating what I'd told Kit.

"Such a shame. That would have been so good for your career. Might have given you a lot more leverage with this TV series and made it even easier for me to get you a decent movie deal. Hmmm… Promise me you won't publicly deny it just yet?"

I rolled my eyes, already knowing what my agent was thinking. If everyone thought it was true and I hadn't denied it, it might allow a quick deal to go through under the assumption.

"What if he comes out and denies it? Or he's seen with another woman tomorrow? Hell, I don't even know where he is."

"You let me worry about that, sweetheart. Now, if anyone else comes along and takes an interest, don't blow it this time. Give them your number at least, or, I dunno, get in their pants quicker."

"I'm not seducing someone just because it's good for my career," I replied, firm even though he hadn't sounded entirely serious.

"Pity, but either way, I'll work with what I've got now. Photos of you with Jack Starling? I feel like it's Christmas."

He hung up, and I shook my head, not sure whether I wanted

to laugh or cry. On the one hand, I was angry at even the idea that I might choose to have a relationship with a person based on how much money they could make me, but equally amused at my agent's delight in me being a big story.

"You've got to admit, there's a certain ring to Juno Starling," Kit said a moment later, grinning, a twinkle in her eyes.

"Stop right there," I replied. "We're not together, and I have no intention of trying to make it happen. I'm grieving a past relationship, and I'm busy making a TV series work."

"Not to mention all those deliciously dark romance novels people are now reading in droves."

"Exactly," I responded. Sales on all of them were up after the pen name had finally been fully outed as me, and there were clamors for me to write more of them. Of course, I'd had another in the planning stage for a while, but no one else had needed to know that.

"Right, I really better get back to work. See you for games and dinner tomorrow?" she asked.

I nodded, already off in my own head, trying to reach for my new characters and get to know them a little better. It was time for both of us to get back to work.

CHAPTER FIFTEEN

As I closed the door to my little apartment, I looked around. It was tiny and mostly bare, but for now, it was home.

I carried the laptop bag to the sofa and plopped it down before heading to the kitchen to prepare a meal. Now that it was just me, I cooked a few times a week in larger batches and froze multiple portions. Then, I could pull out whatever I felt like eating for a while until I needed to cook again.

It worked well enough, but today was a day I needed to cook properly.

After getting all the vegetables out and setting the meat to defrost in the microwave, I started to chop. However, the regular *clink* of the knife on the glass chopping board soon irritated me. And the place was too quiet.

Pausing for a moment, I grabbed my laptop and brought it to the kitchen counter.

Within seconds, some of my favorite tunes were blasting into the room. The speakers weren't great, but the sound took away the oppressive silence and helped mask the irritating noises I was making.

I was just finishing the chopping and trying to choose another song when a notification popped up in the bottom corner of my laptop. It was for the email address I put in the back of my dark romance books. Over the last week, I'd seen a slight increase in emails, but I had a few subjects filtered out elsewhere to make sure I didn't miss them.

This subject immediately caught my interest.

After wiping my fingers, I clicked to my email.

Subject: I wrote a song about your book

From: jackthepinballwizard

I blinked, not sure who could have sent it at first until my mind put two and two together. Was this Jack Starling?

Without delay, I clicked to open it and read the contents.

Hey there, Juno. (Or should I use your pen name while emailing this address?)

Kai told me to check out your book after the interview and stuck a copy in front of me the day after. I read it and could barely put it down. Woke up the next day with some music in my head, and we arranged a song. Still needs some lyrics, but Kai suggested you should be involved since it was inspired by your story.

We've recorded a rough version and thought you might want to have a listen.

Jack

I didn't move as I read the email three times and then finally looked at the attached file. Did one of the biggest rock stars in my lifetime just write me a song based on a book I wrote about him? Was this really happening?

Not sure what else to do, I opened the audio file and pressed play. I was met by an almost haunting tune, the old-school style rock combined with what might have been strings.

While I listened, I tried to imagine the book I'd written. The way the story progressed and how someone like Jack might have felt reading it, knowing it was about him. It was hard to do, but I continued making dinner, the music on repeat for a while.

More than a few times, I remembered a scene in the book and

blushed at the thought of Jack reading it, knowing I'd imagined him. It was almost as bad as the idea of my mother reading the sex scenes I'd written.

Eventually, I went back to the computer and considered the implied request. Was I being asked to help write lyrics, or just give them more info so they could?

With no way to know for sure, I hit the reply button and stared at a blank box for a few minutes.

Hi Jack,

Juno is fine unless you want to call me something else.

Thank you for your email. I'm so glad my story inspired you and you didn't think it was too strange or weird to read it. Did you have anything in mind lyrics-wise? I have no experience at all writing lyrics, but you've made me curious about the process for sure.

Let me know what you need me to provide, and I'll see what I can do.

Juno

As soon as I'd sent the email, I wished I could delete it. What had I been thinking? "Unless you want to call me something else." What else was he going to call me?

Trying not to think about my utter lack of coolness, I finished preparing my stew and started it cooking. Within seconds, I was sitting on the sofa with my laptop and a drink to do some work.

Before I could get into plotting my next book, another email popped up.

Cupcake,

Fantastic. It was a great book, so no more blushing. I'm sure you were already.

Honestly, I have tons of questions, but they're not all useful for the song. Kai wants to write something that encompasses the raw emotion of it all and the interesting power and control dynamic. They're two very passionate characters.

You mentioned somewhere that you have an emotional outline for your romance books. Could we have a copy for this story?

What did you think of the music?
Jack

I frowned, ready to hit myself. I'd forgotten to say that I thought the music was cool. So smooth of me. Definitely wasn't impressed by the cupcake bit, though.

Hi, Cookie,

The song was amazing. I totally loved it. I got a passionate power dynamic vibe from it. Made me think of quite a few different scenes from the book. I've attached the outline. If you need me to explain anything, let me know.

Feel free to ask me any questions you have about the story, especially if it will help. Also, would I get to see the lyrics before you start recording any vocals?

And cupcake? Seriously? You could have picked anything, and you chose cupcake?

Juno

I bit my lip as I sent the email, not sure if I'd come across quite as planned. The downside of being a writer was that I overthought every word I used. And I still didn't know this man very well. I also still couldn't completely believe I was talking to Jack Starling. And he was asking me to help him with something work-related.

Calm, I told myself. *Take some deep breaths and think about it like he probably is. The band wants to write a song about a fictional romance that inspired them. That's it.*

I'm not being chatted up or flirted with. Jack was clearly just an intense person. Someone who could approach anyone and strike up a conversation. Normally, I was confident enough to do the same.

I sighed. My confidence had been knocked down, and I already missed it. But I couldn't let fear stop me. I needed to be braver. Maybe working with Jack would help me regain some of that? With this in mind, I tried to focus on my own book again, beginning to flesh out a female character while I waited for my stew to cook.

I'd just finished eating it when the *bing* of another email took me back to my laptop. I flicked it open, noticing my stomach flutter with anticipation.

Kitten (an improvement?),

I thought cupcake was appropriate. You're both sweet and dainty, but there's something hiding on the inside under all those layers of sugary icing. Something that can both surprise and delight or repel the wrong connoisseur.

Thank you for the outline. That's going to really help. And of course you can see the lyrics. Kai is also eager to include you in creating them. We're still darting around various places for the next few days, but I'm sure we'll get back to you about a good time to talk in another way.

Don't call me cookie, and I won't call you cake?

Jack

I laughed aloud at the last line, the quote from a great book. Smiling to myself, I considered my reply. This was clearly becoming a bit of a game. And I loved word games.

CHAPTER SIXTEEN

<u>Jack</u>

Sitting on the hotel bed, I kept refreshing my emails. It was silly of me. She wasn't always going to reply immediately, and we'd been talking about business.

I looked over the last email I'd sent, checking my wording for the hundredth time. The email was almost anything but business. What had possessed me to call her kitten? It was one of the nicknames her characters had used for each other. A way for the dominant alpha male in her books to feel protective of the kitten he now had to take care of.

And I'd just referred to her as a kitten, too. What had I been thinking? I also wasn't sure she'd get the book reference, but she'd possibly led it there.

Taking a deep breath, I put the tablet down and went to get a drink. No sooner had I walked away than the device let out a *beep* to let me know I had an email.

Rolling my eyes, I made my way back to it.

Hi, Falcon,

That sounds great. You've made me very intrigued about your process now.

And thank you for the compliment, I think! I'd like to think most people would find me adorable, though.

You seem to dart around a lot. How did the rest of the album recording go?

Kitten.

I sat back, taking a moment to realize I was grinning like a Cheshire cat. We were flirting. I knew it, and she knew it. We were using the nicknames from her book. And it felt good—right, somehow.

I also hadn't missed her subtle way of mentioning my behavior. If I was going to apologize for walking out on her, now was the time. But did I want to open this up again? No part of me wanted a relationship right now. But flirting was harmless, right? For a little while, I could pretend to be her character. The man I was writing a song about.

Kitten,

Life on the road is often chaos, and the band has to come first. I hope you weren't stranded the other night when I had to leave.

How's the writing going?

And yes, I think you're very adorable, but apparently not in the same way as a cupcake.

Falcon.

I hit send and then immediately could have hit myself. What was I doing? I hadn't even apologized properly. She was going to think I was a total jerk. Or a playboy. Sighing, I tried to decide what to do. I had a few hours to kill before I was needed for a rehearsal for a new film. And then I had to fly back to London.

For a moment, I contemplated telling Juno I would be in her part of the country, but I couldn't bring myself to do it. I didn't want to make it sound like I was only interested in talking to her again because I was going to be nearby, and it was simply convenient.

I'd let the band know she was up for helping with the lyrics, though. Kai could worry about that part. That was more his section of things, anyway.

While I was lying there, I found myself looking up her social media. What was she likely to say to people if I flirted more? Was she likely to air it in public?

It took me a moment to find her, nothing for her name on quite a few of the current social media platforms, but eventually, I found one with her photo as the profile picture. She wore a fancy dress and had made herself look like an elf. Instantly, I felt my groin stir. Fuck, was she hot in the almost hippy-like dress, her long hair cascading down one side.

Trying to focus on why I was there and not the way I was heating up, I looked through her posts, the pictures almost entirely work-focused. There were writing memes and tons of posts about dragons, walks in nature, and the imagination. The rest were book covers, release information, and word count goals and achievements. She was even more prolific than I'd realized but still seemed pretty down-to-earth about it all.

It was clear she wrote because she liked the act of writing and telling a story. This was who she was, through and through.

I found all sorts of other details as I continued, but I was soon interrupted by the *ping* of another email from her.

Hi, Falcon.

Definitely not in a cupcake sort of way. I'm not sure exactly what kind of cute I really am. It's kind of a mix between fluffy animal with big eyes, petite elf, and hapless writer in need of reminding to eat, drink, and generally remember the basics of self-care.

Writing is going okay, but I admit I'm a little distracted. Someone keeps emailing me about very interesting things, and I find myself ignoring my book world for a while.

I got home okay after you left the other night, don't worry. Alma was really lovely to me. I can see why Kai adores her so much and why they've been together so long. She mentioned there was a hiccup with something, and you had to go take care of it. Did you manage to fix whatever had broken?

Kitten.

Grinning, I immediately replied.

Kitten,

Sounds like you need someone in your life to remind you and make sure you behave yourself. I can stop emailing if you'd prefer. Don't want to make you feel divided between your characters and me, especially when I've been one of them.

Alma said she liked you, too. Glad you weren't alone after I left. We've mostly fixed the problem. Had to fly some gear in from London for a gig in New York. Not ideal, but it means the show goes on.

Falcon

As soon as I had sent the message, I growled at myself. It was just information. Nothing witty, or really flirtatious, or clever. And nothing she truly needed to reply to. That would be the end of the conversation until Kai got back to me, and they decided on a date.

It had been so long since I'd flirted with someone, it was as if I'd forgotten how. Somehow, I had to put it from my mind, however. I had a rehearsal to do, and it was time for me to become someone else for a while. If nothing else, it made me feel like I could escape the life I led. One day maybe I wouldn't want to, but for now, who knew?

I was about to leave the room and head to the studio when I heard another *bing*. Without thinking, I darted back and pulled my emails open.

Falcon,

You offering to keep me in line? I can imagine you as a firm hand but also very protective. I guess you probably knew that already, though. I've made that plain in writing.

Anyway, you said you had questions. What can I help you with? I'm all yours.

Kitten.

Although I had to go work for a while, I grinned and thought about the response I could give her as soon as I had the chance. I was still smiling to myself and imagining all sorts of responses, from clear acceptance of a dominant role to a more gentle but, as she'd suggested, protective part as I walked into the rehearsal room.

"Something has put you on top of the world," Ken said when he spotted me. He was the director of the film and was sitting on the edge of a table with the script in hand.

I pulled mine out but didn't respond. I definitely wasn't telling him that I was planning on flirting with an author who'd written smut about me.

"Come on, you're like the cat with the cream. Haven't seen you like this since before we last worked together. Who is she?"

"Who said there's a she?" I replied, trying to focus on the script.

"He, then?"

"No, it would be a she, but…" I trailed off, not sure I could lie exactly. Had she really made me feel so much better just by emailing?

I had no idea, but nothing could happen between us. She'd just come out of a difficult relationship, and I wasn't looking to be a rebound—or worse, someone else's road to fame and money. Unfortunately, she just wasn't famous enough in her own right.

CHAPTER SEVENTEEN

<u>Juno</u>

Biting my lip, I tried to focus on the story I was planning. Again, I was stuck, and nothing I did seemed to be helping. I just wasn't feeling these new characters at all.

I'd even tried going to my favorite writing cafe, my life still flying under the radar of celebrity enough that I could get away with going there and still be left alone to write. It helped that I knew the staff really well.

Yet here I was, my usual favorite hot chocolate beside me and my paper and notes all around my laptop. And I still couldn't seem to get anywhere.

Of course, I knew why. The emails and meeting Jack Starling himself were still at the forefront of my mind, even if I knew an actual relationship with him wouldn't work. After all, I'd just separated from my husband, and I wasn't ready to trust another man with my heart yet.

But the thought of it and the flirting in the last few emails had woken my imagination to it once more. I was more than a little curious about where things might go.

And the story I was trying to write kept trying to morph. The male lead kept becoming a little bit more rock star and the same sort of dominant that Jack was, and the heroine…

It didn't help that Jack had emailed and flirted briefly one day, then hadn't replied again for ages except to tell me he was waiting on the band to organize another date, and he was knee-deep in rehearsals for another film.

Pushing those thoughts from my mind, I looked back at my notes and tried to picture the hero I'd initially been planning, a rich Russian mafia don who would be the perfect dominant for my female lead.

I sighed. This wasn't working.

I was just considering getting up and going home when someone sat in front of me. I looked up to see a man wearing a bandanna over his lower face and a hat pulled down over eyes covered with sunglasses.

He wore a plaid shirt unbuttoned, with a T-shirt underneath, and jeans, and it only took me a second to place him.

Jack Starling had just sat in front of me.

"Hi. Is this seat taken?" he asked, lowering the bandanna.

I lifted an eyebrow. Was he acting like he didn't know me?

"I'm looking for a seat out of the way. I find it's nicer sitting on the side of the room where people are less likely to notice me, but I can see them. I like to people-watch," he said, his husky accent making me want him to say my name or call me anything, really.

"Feel free, then," I said. "I like to do the same, although you'll find me knee-deep in work."

"Work? In a place like this? Surely, in such a delightful café, everyone should be doing something delightful. Drinking tea. Eating…scones, or whatever it is you British have with your tea."

I grinned at the sweet and funny way he talked about it.

"I do like a good carrot cake," I replied.

"Ah, then, my dear, let me order us both some, and you can

forgive an old man for interrupting you from your work just to have the best seat in the house."

"It is a very cheeky thing for a stranger to do," I replied.

"Well, let me not be a stranger. My name is Hunter," he said, using his name from my story.

"I'm Ella," I replied, grinning, giving him the other name from my book. If he was going to introduce himself as the character I'd based on him, I would pretend to be his romantic interest and see what happened.

He gave me a quick smirk before looking around for the waitress, but she was already on her way over to clear away my empty cup and plate from my lunch earlier. She stared at him for a moment, clearly suspicious, but he gave our order quickly, asking for a pot of tea and two helpings of cake.

"I'll bring it all over in a moment. Do you want some kind of tab?" she asked.

"I'll come over to the bar in a second," I replied, not wanting to embarrass Jack when he'd assumed it was table service.

The waitress smiled and walked off, and Jack raised his eyebrow just a fraction. I saw the question in his look.

"It's normally an order at the bar," I explained, reaching for my bag and pulling my purse out.

"Oh, how unobservant of me. I'll go," he said, moving his chair back to get up again, but I was already on my feet. "Or I could pay you back."

"I can buy some cake without needing to worry," I replied before heading to the bar, where the waitress was already preparing the tray.

"Here you go, lovely," she said when it was all done and I was paying. "This might sound a little weird, but I recognize your friend. Is he someone…well, is he who I think he is?"

"Don't breathe a word of it to anyone. Not until he's gone." I met her gaze, studying her reaction to see if she'd freak out. Instead, she leaned across the bar.

"Are you serious? It's actually Jack Starling?"

"Yes, but I didn't just confirm it. I don't think he likes crowds, and I'd like to talk to him before he's bombarded by strangers asking for autographs. Please don't say anything 'til we're going?"

Her eyes went wide, and she kept glancing over at him, but she nodded and gave me my receipt.

"All right, lovely, but I want to hear about how you know him the next time you're in. Deal?"

I nodded and took the tray, more than eager to return to Jack.

"So, Mr. Hunter," I said as I put the tray down and sat. "What brings you to this neck of the woods?"

"Boredom," he replied without missing a beat. "But, please, no need for the mister."

"Boredom?" I asked. "Perhaps I can help with that."

"Oh, you already are, sweetheart. You already are." He gave me a cheeky grin, and for a moment, his eyes wandered, not even trying to hide how much he was checking me out.

It made my body heat up, and I involuntarily squeezed my legs together, imagining just how interesting things could get.

"Let me pour us some tea," he said a moment later, reaching for the teapot. "And you can tell me what you're working on."

"I can, can I? What if I don't want to?"

"I'd find that quite…disappointing. And I'm not the kind of man who is often disappointed."

"This might be one of those rare occasions when you are," I replied, giving Ella's response to his line from the book and feeling the heat pool between my legs, grateful that my arousal was hidden from everyone but me.

Damn, he could flirt, and I didn't know if I wanted him to stop. I should, but he was bringing one of my characters to life, and I'd dreamed of him saying that line a thousand times.

"I don't think so. You might need a little…persuading, but I'll have my way."

"So persuade me, Mr. Hunter."

I saw the corner of his mouth twitch up as he tried not to laugh. In the story I'd written, Hunter had strode over to Ella and pinned her up against a wall before claiming a kiss that melted her into a puddle of desire and submission. That wasn't going to work in a busy cafe.

"How did you find me?" I asked, relaxing a little and focusing on my cake, breaking the flirtatious moment. I couldn't let him under my skin. Couldn't let him seduce me.

CHAPTER EIGHTEEN

<u>Jack</u>

Picking up my fork, I focused on the cake for a moment to try and cool my body down. Although pretending to be Hunter had been spontaneous, it had instantly made me hotter than I wanted to be. If we weren't in public, I could easily have pinned her beneath me and claimed every inch of her.

Seeing her again after reading her book made me hunger for her in a way I hadn't expected.

It helped that she was wearing a much more relaxed but flattering outfit, her hair simply out and draped over her shoulders.

"Earth to Jack," she said a moment later before eating a mouthful of carrot cake. I watched her lips move, imagining her wrapping them around my hard cock.

Damn it, Jack, get your mind out of the gutter. She's just flirting with you. No way she's going to want you for any reason you want her to.

"Sorry," I said, trying to drag my gaze up to her eyes. "What was the question?"

"How did you find me?"

"Oh, it wasn't hard. You posted that you were stuck writing at a cafe on your social media and couldn't get the characters to do what you wanted. And when I asked my driver if he knew where it was, he told me he could find out, and then he drove me here."

"You got someone else to find out my favorite place to write, and then you had them drive you here? That has to be the laziest form of stalking I've ever heard of."

"I was bored," I replied, noticing that she grinned even though she was shaking her head.

"How's the lyric writing going?" she asked. "You still haven't given me an idea of when and what you want from me."

What I want from you? I want your hot body at my mercy, I thought but didn't dare say.

"Kitten got your tongue?" she asked as she smirked.

"Something like that. So, tell me, kitten, can I help you make your characters behave?"

"Do you have a talent for making people behave?"

"I've tried my hand at it a few times," I replied, fighting back the schoolboy grin that wanted to spread across my face.

She smiled and looked away, and I could have sworn her cheeks flushed. The waitress chose that moment to come and collect our empty plates. I caught the look she gave Juno and was pretty sure she'd figured out who I was.

"It might not be long before we're interrupted if we stay here," I said.

"Oh, she promised me she wouldn't say anything," Juno replied. "She figured out who you were when I got the cakes."

Both of us calmed as we talked about something more normal, but I noticed that she still didn't let me see her plot notes or talk about her book.

"Come on. Spit it out," I said a moment later. "What's wrong with the characters? I'm not easily embarrassed."

"Aren't you? Perhaps I am," she replied.

"You weren't too badly embarrassed on the talk show. What could be worse than that?"

"Good point," she replied before looking at her notes.

"I can make it a command if that makes it any easier?" I asked, the words coming tumbling out before I could stop myself.

"A command. Well, I'd better talk then, hadn't I? Or who knows what the Falcon will do to his kitten?" She paused, taking a deep breath before turning her notes around and pushing the paper toward me. "The main hero is supposed to be a Russian mafia lord, but he keeps wanting to be more...rock star."

"More rock star. I see. Could he be both?"

She let out a delighted laugh. "I don't know. You tell me. Can you be both?"

I thought for a moment, imagining a Russian version of the Godfather before looking her in the face.

"Nobody disobeys me. Everything around here belongs to me, including the women," I said, my accent mostly Russian, but a hint of Italian crept in. It made Juno smile and then laugh again.

"I guess that answers that question. Although I'm not sure it will help me write him the way I originally intended."

"Does he have to stay the same?"

"The fans might get a little upset if I deliver two books with the same main character."

"You already have a Russian rock star?" I asked, although I already knew she had meant me.

"No..." She averted her gaze again, although she didn't look down. Without thinking, I reached across the table and pulled her chin around to face me.

"No, what?"

"No, sir?" she responded, her eyes wide for a moment. Immediately, I let her go and chuckled.

"Not quite what I meant," I said, but I felt my groin stir. Did I want to hear her say those two words to me?

"No, I don't already have a Russian rock star. Just a rock star. I'm not sure I like you Russian."

"So, make him an Italian mafia don?" I suggested before doing my best impression of an over-the-top Italian.

Within seconds, she was laughing again but shaking her head.

"I'm not sure I'd call this helping," she said when she had calmed again.

"Okay, so tell me about his submissive. I assume he's going to have a kitten of his own?" I asked, leaning forward, not even looking at the words on the paper.

"I think so, but she's being even less accommodating. What sort of kitten do you think an Italian, Russian, mafia don, rock star would want?" she asked.

Chuckling again and finding myself unable to hold her gaze, I looked down. I was pretty sure "you" wasn't the right answer.

As I looked up again, our eyes locked, and I knew she'd read my mind.

"Why did you come to visit me today?" she asked, her voice suddenly serious. I appreciated the blunt directness, yet I knew she was also asking more than she'd implied.

"I was in London again. We've got this gig tomorrow evening. I didn't want to just wait around in London for it," I replied, trying to figure out exactly why I'd come as I told her.

"So you came to find me?" she asked, beginning to smile.

"So I came to find you and talk about kittens and their protective falcons," I replied.

I watched her inhale before she quickly stacked up her notebooks and shoved them into her bag, followed by her laptop. A moment later, she got up and took my hand, practically pulling me out of my seat.

Making sure my face was still mostly obscured, I let her lead me from the cafe, pretty sure this was a bold move for a submissive. If that was what she even wanted to be in real life.

When we got outside, however, she faltered.

"I walked here," she said and looked at me, almost like she expected me to suggest something.

Tightening my grip on her fingers, I pulled her toward the parking lot and the sleek black car she'd failed to notice. We were only a few feet away when my bodyguards got out and opened the back door.

"Oh, you brought the whole team, then," she said before greeting them.

They smiled at her, and Mick offered his hand to help her into the vehicle. She accepted, giving me a moment to appreciate the beauty of her body as she slipped into my car. Now, she was in my domain, and I was going to make sure she knew it.

"Hotel," I said quietly to Mick. "But take your time."

I followed Juno into the car, hearing rather than seeing Mick shut the door behind us. She was already sitting on the opposite side of the car, but rather than sitting beside or across from her, I went straight to her. Before she could move or act, I pushed her back against the seat and plunged my mouth down on hers, my lips claiming her softness.

She gasped against me but yielded, her whole body tasting and smelling heavenly. Instantly, my cock hardened and made it clear which way he wanted this to go.

As the car pulled off and I eased back a moment, Juno reached up and pressed her hands against my chest. Without hesitation, I took them in mine and pushed them above her head as I pulled her sideways and laid her down on the back seat.

Her eyes went wide, but she didn't fight my dominance, yielding to me as I pushed her legs open and settled myself over her. She was my kitten now, and I was going to make sure she knew it.

CHAPTER NINETEEN

<u>Juno</u>

I could barely breathe as Jack took control and pushed me beneath him, my body betraying any protests in my head. All I could think of was the obvious hardness in his pants, his body poised over me already.

The thought of having him inside me made my torso heat up and wetness form between my legs. I wanted him to take me and could think of nothing else as his mouth came crashing down on me again. Although I felt a little fear, there was something about him and the way he'd been so considerate so far that pushed past all the objections. Not to mention the chemistry. I wanted him, whether it was good for me or not.

As his free hand wandered and cupped my breast, I moaned into his passionate kiss. Immediately, he plunged his tongue past my lips and claimed me even further.

I instinctively tried to reach for him and explore him, too, wanting to run my hands along his muscular chest, but he kept my arms pinned above my head, refusing me the option. Entirely at his mercy, I felt a hint of panic ripple through me. Before it overwhelmed me, his free hand moved lower, pushing my skirt up and reaching for my pussy.

Already slick, I knew he'd find me ready for him. I tried to squeeze my thighs together, but he was already between them, holding them open.

Pushing my panties to the side, he slid his fingers deep into my wet folds. I groaned against him, the penetration taking me by surprise but feeling so good.

"Damn, you're wet for me, kitten," he said as he pulled away from our kiss. "Do you want me in you?"

I nodded without thinking, too caught up in how this felt and how hot this powerful man was. While I looked into his deep brown eyes, I heard him undo his zipper.

Not daring to look anywhere but his face, I felt his fingers withdraw, leaving me empty and hungry.

Again, I tried to move my arms, wanting to reach up and pull him deep inside me, to be full of nothing but his hard cock. He held me still, but he brought himself to my entrance, pressing against my wet folds but denying me the satisfying fullness I yearned for.

"Ask me, kitten," he said. "Ask me to take you."

"Please, Falcon," I replied, the words coming out of me without hesitation. I bucked my hips at the same time, trying to push myself onto him, but he pulled back and growled.

"Lie still. I'll take you when I'm ready," he said, his face stern.

Exhaling, I fought to do as I was bid, but I didn't have to fight my desire for long before he thrust into me. Again, I moaned, but it was muffled against his lips as he claimed my mouth once more.

For a moment, he stilled within me, his body entwined with mine, every inch of him in control. Slowly, he eased back and forth, pulling out only to fill me once more.

I tried to thrust against his pace, wanting him deeper and

faster, but he denied me every attempt to speed things up, forcing me to give him control.

As I yielded and shifted my legs and hips to give him a better angle, he thrust harder, driving deep into me. I felt my pleasure building, tightening my slick pussy around his hard cock until the pressure tipped me over the edge, moans and shudders of orgasmic heaven rippling through me.

He peaked a moment later, pushing deeper one last time and holding himself there while he filled me with his cum.

Slowly, we came down together, our bodies remaining entwined until he finally let go of me and pulled back.

I tried to make myself a little more decent again, aware that my panties were probably ruined but not daring to do more than just pull my skirt back into place and try to fix my hair.

He looked at me as I sat back. Slowly, he smirked.

"What?" I asked, trying to appear stern and not to smile back.

"You look even more gorgeous with an 'I've just been fucked' redness to your cheeks."

I gasped that he'd dare say something like that, but it only made him grin even wider at me.

"That's not the sort of thing you say to a lady," I said.

"Then it's a good thing you're a kitten and not a lady," he replied without missing a beat. At the same time, the car pulled to a halt outside a large hotel. He took my hand as his bodyguard opened the door for us. At the same time, a doorman opened the hotel door, and we were ushered inside.

I tried not to stare as I took in the insides of the hotel lobby. It was stunning, everything a combination of old stonework, new glass, and modern metalwork.

Jack merely waved at the receptionist and headed for a large, sweeping staircase to one side.

"I'll check Juno in for you, boss," one of the bodyguards said as he peeled off toward reception. The other led the way to the hotel room, making sure the coast was clear before we walked down the hallway on the second floor.

He also produced the key to Jack's room, admitting us both.

"Next door if you need us," the burly man said as Jack pulled me into his hotel suite.

For a moment, I didn't know what to do but stand in the middle of the room and look around. It was a living room of sorts with a small bar at one end, a large sofa, a TV, and a coffee table taking up most of the rest of the room. Two doors led off to the left, one of them wide open to reveal a plush bedroom, a suit laid out on the covers.

"Oh, good, housekeeping has my suit ready for tomorrow," Jack said when he noticed it.

I raised an eyebrow as he went over to it and moved it to hang from the still wide-open door. It was a charcoal-gray three-piece, and I tried to imagine him in something so smart.

Before I could ask what it was for, he came back over to me and put an arm around my waist while lifting my chin.

"Now, where was I? Ah, yes, enjoying the kitten I've brought back to my den."

My breath hitched in my throat as he gazed down at me, his eyes the hungry ones of a predator. I was caught in his web, and the thought alone made me wet again. As he plunged his mouth down on mine, claiming me once more, I let out the smallest moan, my voice betraying my desire.

I yielded to him instinctively, wanting to feel his hands on my skin. And this time, I was also free to explore. Reaching for him, I ran my hands over his chest, the muscles beneath his shirt firm and warm.

He pulled me into the bedroom, his powerful arms wrapping around me and practically carrying me. Heat rushed through me in anticipation of what was to come. This man was everything I'd ever wanted, wrapped in spice and strength.

This time, his hands explored me properly, taking the time to remove my clothing and reveal every inch of my skin. I slowly did the same to him, undoing each button of his shirt and running my hands across the chest beneath.

I moaned as he cupped my breasts, running a thumb across each nipple until they were hard nubs, and then he moved onto my skirt, pulling it down and helping me step out of it.

When I reached for his pants, he stopped me, taking my hands in his.

"Not yet," he said. "I want to see you first."

I paused, suddenly feeling self-conscious and aware of his gaze on my body. As his fingers slipped under the edge of my panties, I felt a ripple of desire and fear head up my spine, making me shudder.

"Relax," he said. "I won't bite hard."

My eyes went wide at the extra word he'd added to the common saying. People said they didn't bite. Did that mean he liked it rough?

He smirked and slipped my panties down and off my body while I was distracted. A moment later, I stood before him, naked and wet.

CHAPTER TWENTY

<u>Jack</u>

My cock throbbed as I stared at her hot little body. She curved everywhere she was supposed to, two sweet breasts sitting perky and full above it all.

I stepped forward, wrapping my arms around her as she looked away and down. She was a bundle of nerves, but she was still reacting to my touch and submitting to my desire.

Once she was laid on the bed, I settled beside her, still drinking in her soft, smooth skin with my eyes. She was thin but not so skinny that she looked like she might break, and she had a mole on her left hip and several on her arms.

There were a few stretch marks on her thighs, but they were faded and old, and they seemed to add to her appeal. She had a past.

I also noticed the faded but not quite gone bruises on her side, a large one over her hip and several smaller ones down the same side.

"These look like they were painful," I said, gently running one hand over the largest. She looked away but didn't flinch or stop me.

"They were, but they're almost healed now," she replied.

I gently bent down and pressed my lips to the first one before moving on to the next I saw and the next until there was only the worst one left. I had to shift down the bed slightly, but I was even more gentle as I pressed a kiss to it.

"There," I said as I moved back up the bed and wrapped an arm around her.

She didn't say anything at first, but her eyes said it all, her gratitude there in the way they lit up and fixed on my face.

"Thank you," she said a moment later. As she opened her mouth to speak again, I pressed my finger to her lips.

"Nothing should mar such beautiful skin," I said before kissing her, my hand reaching around to cradle her neck and stroke her cheek.

She yielded to me, pressing her body closer and making her desire obvious. And I didn't plan on disappointing her. Pushing her legs apart, I shifted my weight until I was between them and over her, every inch of her mine to claim.

I trailed kisses down her neck, wanting to taste her skin, to take her nipples into my mouth and make her mine. She moaned as I cupped her breasts and rubbed my fingers across her rosy pink buds.

As I took the first one into my mouth, she shuddered and bucked her hips upward toward my groin.

I chuckled at her eagerness, but I had no plan to rush this time. She'd lie beneath me and let me do as I pleased with her body first.

Her hands came up to run across my chest, but I pushed them away again, pinning them above her head. Then I brought my mouth down on her second nipple, hearing her gasp at the sudden roughness after how gentle I'd been. Still, she yielded, not even fighting my grip on her and my shift in attitude.

I took her nipple between my teeth and bit gently while my

free hand twisted the other, making her whimper and mewl. *My little kitten.*

As she shuddered again, I returned my mouth to hers and slid my hand between her legs, cupping her pussy and finding her hot and slick, her folds parting with little effort.

"I'm going to take you again soon," I said, as much a promise as a declaration that she was going to be mine.

"Please," she replied, her eyes wide and her breathing ragged.

"When I'm ready and not before."

She opened her mouth to object, but I kissed her again before she could speak, thrusting my tongue between her lips as my fingers did the same to her pussy. Groaning against me, she opened up and let me claim her even further.

When I pulled my fingers back out, slick with her juices, she whimpered, her eyes fixed on me as if she was pleading with me not to leave her empty.

I couldn't help but smile at how much she was being my little kitten. She was delicious. Lifting my fingers, I touched them to her lips before sliding them into her open mouth for her to taste.

She sucked on them, and for a moment, I imagined pushing my cock into her mouth and as deep down her throat as she could take it. But that could wait. She wasn't leaving this hotel room until I'd had her in so many ways, but I wanted her pussy first. I wanted to claim her slowly.

As she sucked on my fingers, I shifted myself and brought my cock to her entrance. Her eyes went wide as I took my time sliding inside and pushing myself down as deep as I could get. Moaning, she tilted her hips and let me push even further.

She was mine, completely mine.

I pulled slowly out only to slide in again, the feel of her hot pussy wrapped tightly around my cock so perfect that it took all my control not to ravage her again. It helped that I'd already had her once. That had been to satiate a need. This was to enjoy and savor every moment.

Her body quickly responded, her cunt growing tighter and tighter as she reached her orgasm and cried out, her body tensing underneath me and shuddering with each wave.

I almost lost control again, her pleasure bringing me close to my edge, but I wasn't done with her. I slowed, tightening my grip on her wrists to keep her still beneath me as I wove my other hand into her hair.

Pulling back her head, I exposed her smooth, graceful neck and trailed kisses down it while I stilled inside her for a moment. She was going to cum for me again before I was done.

As she came back down a little, I stoked the fire once more, rubbing her nipples with my thumbs and gently easing in and out of her again. Closing her eyes, she moaned and surrendered to me.

I gently picked up the pace as she thrust back, eager for me as much as I was for her. Our bodies moved in harmony, each stroke bringing me closer to heaven. Just as I tipped over the edge, too, I heard her cry my name and tense beneath me, her tight pussy rippling with a second orgasm as I pushed as deep as I could get and filled her with my seed.

Resting my forehead against hers, I met her gaze as we cooled together, our bodies still entwined. I tried not to think about anything but how good it had felt to claim her the same way her character had.

Slowly, I slipped beside her, keeping her in my arms and kissing her again and again, almost as much to convince myself she was genuinely there as to taste her again.

Neither of us spoke. Neither of us needed to. Our bodies had said everything we wanted to say.

CHAPTER TWENTY-ONE

<u>Juno</u>

The sun streamed into the hotel window, waking me from sleep. As I opened my eyes, I saw Jack beside me, his sleeping body peaceful in a way I instantly adored. Without thinking, I reached out and stroked his cheek.

He opened his eyes and met my gaze. I smiled, already almost lost in the emotion of those deep hazel eyes. He was beautiful, but I saw the flicker of uncertainty as he reached for me.

"Good morning," I said, wanting to reassure him but not sure how.

I'd willingly given myself to him, but I was already feeling a little worried myself. This was one of the most famous men on the planet, and I wasn't ready to have my heart broken again. Had we leaped too soon?

He didn't respond, but he cupped my cheek and smiled. I leaned forward and kissed his lips again, wanting to know he was truly there and still wanted me.

"I'd love to spend all day in bed with you, but I'm needed in London," he said as we broke away. I can be back tomorrow until I have to go to New York for a few days."

"That sounds wonderful," I replied. "I should probably finish planning this new book anyway."

He chuckled and kissed me again before slipping out of the bed, every inch of his body toned and making me want to try and seduce him again. However, I ached, and I knew he needed to get on with work.

I sighed as he entered the bathroom and left me alone in the bed. No part of me wanted to think or to worry, but doubts immediately niggled. I looked down at myself. A man like him could have someone far better-looking than me.

Trying not to think about that either, I sat up and checked my emails, quickly replying to some fan mail on my phone, grateful they were all enthusiastic readers loving my stories.

There were often a few from people who thought they knew better about my books and wanted me to write them a different way. They always got a polite thank you, but after a lot of thought, I decided to write it the way I did.

If they were polite, I might explain, but too many were simply demanding, and I didn't have time for that. If I changed every story to suit every email I received that suggested a different direction, each book would become a mess.

It took my mind off things for a while, and as Jack came back out half-dressed, jeans on his bottom half, his bare chest on display, I paused and took him in. As he came closer, he smirked, clearly amused that I was staring at him.

I kissed him again, fighting the urge to reach out and touch him. As much as I wanted him to have his way with me some more, I was also aware he needed to go, and so did I.

"Mind if I use your shower before I head out?" I asked.

"Feel free. Just don't get lost in there."

"I'll do my best. Although, maybe you could give me your number, and if I do get lost, I can call you to come find me," I replied, biting my lip as I tried to subtly point out that I had no way of contacting him.

He chuckled and reached for the phone.

"Go shower. I've got to gather the stuff I need for later. If you're quick enough, I'll get Mick to drop you off at your place," he said as he started adding his number to my phone.

Not wanting to waste the opportunity to spend a little more time with him, even if it was only while he took me to my little apartment, I hurried to the bathroom.

I could immediately see why he'd told me not to get lost. The shower was huge, a large, rectangular shower head sitting in the middle of it. I turned it on and adjusted the heat control until it was almost burning.

The whole experience was bliss, but I didn't want to keep Jack waiting, so I was quick to scrub myself clean as best I could and use the little bottles of hotel shampoo and conditioner to wash my hair while I was at it.

I was just wrapping a large soft white towel around myself when Jack came back in. He sighed as he looked at me.

"What?" I asked, wondering if something was wrong.

"If I didn't have to go to London, I'd be unwrapping you from that and enjoying you again," he said.

I felt myself smiling as I walked closer, the corner of his mouth twitching up in his characteristic smirk.

"I guess you'll just have to come back to see me soon," I replied before I kissed him.

He grinned and wrapped his arms around me for a moment before he pulled back.

"Want me to order some breakfast while you get dressed? Probably won't have long to eat it. I need to leave in about forty minutes, but…I feel like I should at least offer you something to eat after putting you through your paces like that."

"Breakfast sounds wonderful," I replied as I slipped back into the bedroom. I didn't have anything to dress in except the clothes I'd worn the previous day, but I didn't think they smelled too bad.

After slipping into them, I tried to fix my hair using the small travel brush I always carried. It wasn't great, and it took me a while to do something with it that looked half decent.

Sighing, I gave up when breakfast arrived, and Jack admitted a waiter with a small trolley. He came in and placed everything on the coffee table before heading back out, cash from Jack in his hand.

I grinned at the sweet way Americans tipped everyone and made my way over to see what he'd ordered.

There were four different plates of food laid out.

"Didn't know what you wanted, so I took a leaf out of *Pretty Woman's* book and ordered several different things. It's all gluten-free for you," he stated with a grin. There was a plate of mini-pastries complete with pain au chocolat, so I reached for one of those and then heaped some scrambled eggs and toast beside. It was a bit of an odd combination, but I wouldn't say no to good food.

Jack chose the bacon sandwich and poured us both a glass of juice.

"Do you often eat in hotel rooms?" I asked, wondering what this man's life was like.

"Sometimes. It beats the cleanup, and I don't have to cook. Also means I can eat in peace. Not everywhere we go to eat can seat us out of the way, you know. Or keep the fans from noticing we're there until after we've eaten."

I nodded, not sure I entirely understood how difficult that must be, but feeling like being famous wasn't as glamorous as people implied.

As soon as we'd finished eating, Jack took my hand and led me to the hotel entrance again. I gave his driver my address, noticing that Jack was listening intently as I did.

It made me realize how cavalier I was being. Although I knew everything the general population did about Jack Starling, I'd still given a relative stranger, and a powerful one at that, knowledge of where I lived. Did I really want that?

I looked at him as he sat beside me, holding my hand and looking stunning in the morning light. He was so perfect, and I was… I wasn't even sure who I was anymore.

Trying not to worry and to enjoy the moment, I thought of how my friends would react if they knew I'd spent the night with Jack Starling. I didn't plan on telling any of them. At least, not yet. If something happened after today, I didn't want to endanger it by having everyone know about it before we were ready for them to.

And if it was only one night, the world didn't ever need to know about it.

CHAPTER TWENTY-TWO

My apartment felt empty and too quiet as I strolled inside. It wasn't really. At least, no more so than it had been the day before.

I'd left it the day before to get on with what I'd felt was my life as normal, but spending the night elsewhere had changed how it felt. I'd enjoyed having a few hours where I was living in one of the most amazing bedrooms on the planet with one of the sexiest men alive.

It was strange how one night had made me feel. Normally, I'd never have jumped into bed so soon with someone, but he'd been intoxicating, and I'd never found the words to refuse.

As I sat and tried to distract myself with the mail on my front doormat, I thought about how good it had felt and how much he'd made me feel like I was his.

I shuddered, both with the desire for more and the fear of where it might lead.

No, I thought as I got up again. I couldn't worry. There was no guarantee he'd even be back in the morning. He might not. I could just be another notch on his bedpost, and then he'd be gone from my life forever, the book I wrote about him the only reminder we'd ever even met.

And that interview.

I sighed, wondering how my mother was explaining it to the people she knew. Once more, I was the disappointing daughter.

We hadn't spoken since she'd seen the interview, and I didn't want to bring it up again, so I'd avoided calling her. I also hadn't spoken to my agent recently, although he was at least far happier about my decision-making skills lately.

Then there was my ex-husband. Or, at least, my soon-to-be ex-husband. I didn't want to see him, but we'd agreed to go over the divorce papers and sign them. Thankfully, I'd had the sense to suggest a neutral public location. There was no way I was letting him see where I'd moved into.

I put a hand to my side and ran it over the bruises there. I'd expected fear to fill me as I did. And memories of how it happened. Instead, I thought of how tenderly Jack had kissed each one. He'd been so sweet and almost protective.

But then, so had my ex when I first met him.

Sighing, I fetched my laptop and settled into some work. I had a few hours before lunch, and I needed to make the most of them. My book wouldn't write itself.

Time slipped past, the plot finally coming to me and falling in line while I frantically wrote notes and tried to keep up with my muse. It felt good, exciting even, and I lost track of everything else.

Only as my phone rang, my agent's number coming up, did I realize I'd worked through most of lunchtime.

I answered as I made my way to the kitchen to grab a snack.

"Juno! Why didn't you tell me that you and Jack hooked up? Do you have any idea how good this is for PR?"

I growled in response, pretty sure we'd already had this conversation.

"We haven't hooked up. We're...possibly working together," I lied. "There's no way you're saying anything to anyone until I have something more firm. Do you hear me?"

I heard him loudly exhale as I grabbed an apple from the fridge, deciding it would have to do, and I'd eat it on the way out.

"I know a brush-off when I hear one, but...I know you've been through it lately. And you are clearly a private person. If you really don't want me to use this, I won't yet."

"Yet?" I asked as I grabbed my jacket and keys and headed for the door.

"Yes, yet. I'm your agent, not your friend. At some point, if you're dating Jack Starling or working with him, you need to let me use it. I can do so tactfully. It could seriously boost your career."

"I am going to say this only once, James, so you better listen carefully," I replied. "My relationships, and even my friendships, will never be fodder to earn me more money. I expressly forbid you from using it. Do you understand?"

"Of course, but it's a shame. I really could be tactful, you know."

"No. The answer is no, and it always will be."

"All right. Message received. If you work with him?"

"If I work with him, you'll be the first to know as soon as I feel like I can tell anyone."

"That will have to suffice. But you don't make an agent's job easy," he replied, and I could imagine him pouting as he did.

"You're not getting such a large chunk of my income to have an easy life."

"Good point, my dear. All right. I shall concede this one, but tell me there's more romance coming soon and that we can discuss smoothing out some wrinkles with this TV series."

"Of course. I'll call you later. I have a meeting now, and I was so busy with that romance book you want that I almost forgot about lunch."

"I interrupted you, didn't I?" he asked. I rolled my eyes at the hint of delight he didn't manage to hide.

"You interrupted me, but don't do it again. I'll call you later."

I hung up before he could get me involved in further discussion and quickly hurried to the cafe. I was taking a bit of a roundabout route, not wanting to come from the right direction, and I wasn't driving.

As I walked, I ate the apple and tried not to feel too anxious. I hadn't seen Greg since I'd walked out of my marital home with nothing but a small suitcase full of clothes and toiletries.

One of my friends had picked up the few other belongings that mattered to me after I'd made a list. It sucked, but I didn't care about the stuff as much as I thought I would. If anything, it was a reminder of happier times I didn't need.

Plenty of people were baffled, but I didn't care much about that, either. I had no intention of explaining what happened. They didn't need to know how quickly our relationship had unraveled once I'd started earning more than he did.

I was several minutes late by the time I arrived at the café, and I quickly spotted Greg sitting at one of the small tables near the side of the room. I was grateful he'd picked one a little more out of the way, but not that he sat facing the door. It meant I would have to sit with my back to the door, and he knew I hated that.

I walked up and sat down anyway.

"Sorry I'm late. My agent called as I was getting ready to leave."

"And you couldn't tell him to call back?" Greg demanded before shaking his head. "You know, it won't matter much longer. Here."

He pushed the papers and a pen across to me.

I knew he hoped I'd sign them then and there, but I wasn't about to sign something I hadn't read. After ordering a drink, I sat back and started to read.

It felt a little odd since I knew his eyes were on me as I did so, but I was determined to ignore him until I was done. Quickly, I slipped into a world of lawyer language and the catch-all sentences about little details.

We'd discussed the details, of course. He wasn't pleased that I was trying to get it pushed through so quickly, and we had to state that the relationship had gotten violent as a way to get it done, with no particular finger-pointing. The alternative had been for one of us to confess to an affair, but neither of us had, and it had gotten violent. Even if it had been only him hitting me.

Everything else was split as we'd already hashed out. Thankfully, he wasn't trying to grab my new income. In truth, I wasn't sure he knew how well I was doing, and I didn't plan on telling him.

CHAPTER TWENTY-THREE

"You've not signed it," I said as I reached the end of the consent order.

"Didn't see the point until I knew you would."

I handed it back to him along with the pen, not sure I wanted to be the first signature. It was maybe a little petty of me, but it felt vindicating to make him sign it. After all, it was his actions that were ending us.

For a moment, he looked as if he might object. Instead, he picked up the pen and held it over the signature box.

"And you're definitely sure this is what you want?" he asked.

"Yes," I replied. "There's no going back from what happened. Don't get me wrong. I'm grateful you're handling this and not causing any more conflict than necessary, but there's no second chance on this one."

With a resigned sigh, he signed in the box and then pushed it my way.

A moment later, my phone rang again. I frowned as I checked it to find it was my agent again. Greg sighed and sat back before crossing his arms.

"Go on, you might as well answer it. You always used to."

I glared at Greg as I picked up and stood.

"Oh, my dear. Have you seen the papers?" he asked.

"No. What's in the papers?" I asked, aware I didn't want to be doing this now but knowing there could be only one thing. Trying not to panic, I walked out of the cafe.

"Only your little tryst last night. I knew you met up with him yesterday and had some kind of afternoon tea or something, but I didn't know you went back to his hotel room."

I groaned, wishing no one had seen that. It wasn't something I wanted the public to know about, and I had a feeling Jack wouldn't be particularly happy, either.

"Well, do what you can to downplay it, okay? I asked. "I'm not interested in a fuss. It's too soon."

I heard him sigh, but before he could respond, I hung up. Would there ever be an easier time?

As I walked back inside, I saw Greg on his phone, the frown on his face getting deeper until he looked up and glared at me.

"Didn't take you long, did it? Is this what you always wanted? Let me pay for the roof over your head while you were a starving artist, and then the second you became successful, you ditch me and go for someone really famous?"

I took a deep breath, feeling fear grip at my insides. We were in a public setting, and heads were beginning to turn our way. I was safe. Or at least, I was pretty sure I was.

Bending down lower, I reached for the divorce papers.

"My reasons are the same as they have always been. I don't think you need me to repeat them. We've been over since then. What I do now is none of your business." As I spoke the last word, I signed. I then took the phone out of my pocket and snapped a quick photo in case he decided to act like I hadn't signed it.

"Goodbye, Greg," I said and walked out of the cafe, leaving him with the papers and the bill. It was perhaps a little petty of me, but I wasn't walking back to pay it after his accusation.

Shaking and wondering if it was too soon to call Jack or message him, I strode home, stopping at a convenience store I passed on the way to grab a chocolate bar.

It took me several more minutes to completely calm down, and then I felt more than a little stupid. Jack was used to the media. He hadn't tried to hide our relationship, and he was likely beyond caring what they thought of him, anyway.

And everything with Greg was over now. All we had to do was wait for the rest of the legal process to happen. I could do that.

Trying not to worry, I walked the last few streets to my apartment block and climbed the few steps to the main building entrance. For a moment, I fumbled for my keys, the damn things having buried themselves in my handbag somewhere.

Eventually, I had the door open and walked into the large hallway. It stretched back to admit entrance to the four ground-floor apartments, and off to the side was the staircase. I turned to head up, my apartment on the top floor, the one with the best view. Partway up, I heard the sound of footsteps on the stairs somewhere below me and wondered which of the neighbors had also just returned.

Most of them were friendly, but a few liked to play music a little louder than most. If it was one of them, I could be heading out again swiftly.

I reached the top, feeling a little out of breath, and paused for a moment. Wondering what Jack would think of the place when he came the next day, I turned to head to my apartment at the back on the right. I'd only taken a single step when I heard someone come up the steps right behind me, their pace increasing.

As I looked back, intending to be friendly, I noticed Greg.

"What the hell are you doing in here?" I asked as my brain tried to process that he must have followed me and somehow got into the building. He still had the divorce documents in his hands, and he shook them at me.

"You would live on the top bloody floor, wouldn't you?" he said, panting worse than I had been. I frowned and stood my ground at the top of the steps, almost hoping one of the neighbors would open their doors to see what the fuss was.

My hands began to shake, and my heart pounded, but I didn't intend to let Greg see how much he was scaring me. I folded my arms and took a deep breath.

"I have nothing else to say to you, and you're not welcome here," I said. "Please leave."

"I'm not leaving until I've spoken to him. I want to know—"

"He's not here. He's in London, and you don't need to speak to my work colleague about anything."

Greg faltered for a moment before he shook his head.

"No, Juno, you can't fool me. He's got in your knickers. Men like him do. And I'm not having it. You're my wife." Greg came forward and tried to grab my arm, but I backed off and tried to push him away.

He wobbled at the top of the stairs before lunging at me.

I yelped as he knocked me back into the wall.

"I'm not your wife anymore!" I yelled as I recovered and shoved him again. Fear tore through me, making me quake, but there was enough anger that he thought he could act like this that somehow, I stood my ground.

"I'm not letting a man like that have what's mine. You're coming back to the house with me, and we're going to make a new start of things." Greg grabbed my arm again, this time getting a good grip. I struggled and tried to stop him, but he was far stronger than I was. Slowly, he dragged me toward the stairs and then took a step down himself.

I reached for the wall at the top of the stairs and grabbed on with my free hand. It helped stall him for a moment as I yelled and tried to defend myself.

Inside, I wanted to sob and curl up in a ball, but I fought the urge.

Suddenly, the pressure eased, and I fell backward onto the top of the steps.

"What the—" Greg said before he was cut off, Jack grabbing him by the shirt and lifting him physically off the ground.

"She clearly doesn't want to go anywhere with you. I suggest you take the hint and leave without her," Jack said, his voice deep and firm but controlled.

Greg's eyes were wide and full of fear, but he had enough sense to nod.

Jack let go of him and waited for him to walk away, standing on the stairs like some powerful guardian. I had no idea where his bodyguards were. I could only stare at him, stunned.

CHAPTER TWENTY-FOUR

As I calmed, Jack finally relaxed and came up the last few steps, helping me back to my feet as he did.

"You okay?" he asked.

I shivered against him but nodded.

"Thank you. For showing up when you did. I don't know what—"

"Shhh, it's all right," he replied, cutting me off and helping me along the hallway. "I got here. And you're safe now."

He helped me open my door, my hands shaking too much to grip my keys and get them in the lock. Immediately, he escorted me over to the sofa and sat us down together.

"Do we need to call the police or something?" he asked.

I shook my head.

"No. I'm pretty sure it won't happen again. He was only being shitty because the papers got wind of me staying at your hotel last night. And…" I trailed off as I realized I wasn't supposed to be seeing him until the following morning.

"You came back early," I said.

"Yeah. We were done, and I was about to check into a hotel

there when I realized I could still drive here in time. Just because my agent had booked a hotel in London didn't mean I had to stay in London. That okay?" he asked, his gaze searching my face for reassurance.

"Of course," I replied as I nodded. "You pretty much just became my knight in shining armor. I'm more than okay with you coming back early."

"Fantastic." Jack stroked a stray lock of hair off my face and smiled.

I couldn't bring myself to relax, my body still tense. I shuddered as I thought about what might have happened if Jack hadn't arrived when he did. I had a bunch of questions and so many things I wanted to talk to him about, but I couldn't think about anything but how scared I'd felt as Greg had tried to haul me down the stairs.

"Do you want to go somewhere else?" Jack asked a moment later, putting his arm around me. "Is he going to be a problem? I guess you knew him."

"He's my ex."

"Your ex. Your husband?"

"I'd just signed the divorce papers and come back here. Thought it was all over. He must have followed me. I… I don't know what would have happened if you hadn't turned up when you did."

Jack frowned, shifting so he could get a better look at me.

"I thought you and your ex had drifted apart over time."

"Yes, that's—"

"No. That's not the reaction of a man you've drifted apart from. And…he didn't know where you lived. You're hiding from him, aren't you?"

I nodded, suddenly unable to look at Jack. Shame filled me, making me feel awful. This was exactly what I hadn't wanted anyone to know. Men who knew about this sort of thing could take advantage of it, too. Or judge me. I wasn't an abused wife. I was stronger than that.

Jack got up and walked away for a moment, putting distance between us and confirming my suspicions.

"It was only one time," I said. "I wasn't going to stay in a relationship where he thought he could bash me around."

"Those bruises?" Jack turned to face me again but kept the distance between us. "The day we met. He gave you those bruises, didn't he? They weren't because you fell and hurt yourself."

"No, they weren't. I just... I didn't want anyone to know. It's not even cited in the divorce. Not properly. It was just once."

"You shouldn't make excuses for him."

"It's not an excuse, and it's not for his sake," I replied instantly, indignant at the accusation in Jack's tone and looks. His face was dark, and his jaw clenched as he stared at me.

"I don't like being lied to," he said. "And I don't like being dragged into a marital dispute that hasn't been dealt with properly."

My mouth fell open, not sure how to respond. Before I could form my thoughts into words, Jack grabbed the jacket he must have slung over the arm of the chair at some point and started putting it on.

"I'm sorry, Juno, I can't do this. I'm glad you're not hurt and I could prevent your ex from assaulting you, but I've had more than enough of women lying to me. You're no better than any of the rest."

I got to my feet, still stunned by his words, my brain frantically trying to figure out how I could respond to such an accusation. I'd barely met him when he'd noticed the bruises. Being abused wasn't the kind of thing you told someone when you'd barely met them.

Before I could stop him or come up with any kind of defense, my body and mouth frozen even while my mind raced, he walked out of my apartment and slammed the door behind him. I hurried after him, but it was as if my body didn't work properly. I fumbled with the door, trying to get it open.

As I hurried down the hallway, I could hear Jack's feet tapping down the stairs. I called his name a few times. He didn't stop, getting into his car and having his driver pull off a few seconds before I could get out of the building and onto the street.

I had just enough presence of mind not to let the door slam shut behind me, but I stood there for some time, panting and wanting to cry. How had my day started so well and then come to this?

Shaking, feeling a strange mix of exhausted and emotional, I slowly made my way back inside and up to my apartment. I slipped into the living room and sank onto my sofa. A moment later, I noticed I was hugging a cushion, my arms wishing something larger was between them.

When I'd first moved out of my marital home after living there for well over a decade, I'd assumed I'd feel lonely. But I hadn't. We'd already drifted so far apart that it had been freeing, if odd, living somewhere else.

This was the first time I felt lonely. I wanted to call out and just have anyone answer me. My life had fallen apart in only a few short months, and it felt like I would never be able to put it back together. All I had left were books and a TV series my agent cared about far more than I did.

Sighing and not sure what else to do, I called my agent and spent over an hour letting him talk my ear off about the TV series problems and what I could do to fix most of them. At first, it was something to do to keep me occupied. My agent was someone I could talk to, but over the hour, he somehow managed to pull me out of my emotional state and remind me of the stories I loved to write and how much my characters meant to me.

There were still a few details to work out when I finally hung up, but I felt better and less abandoned. I reheated one of the dinner portions I'd made on a previous night, stuck the TV on a Christmas movie channel, and settled in to make my heart feel in the mood for romance. Maybe after that, I'd be able to write my own again.

CHAPTER TWENTY-FIVE

<u>Jack</u>

Getting to my feet, I ran a hand through my hair and walked to the nearest window, as much for something to do as a way of exiting the current conversation. The band and I were waiting for the jet to be ready to leave and were talking about the new songs. Right now, the last thing I wanted to do was think about Juno and if she'd be involved.

A moment later, Kai appeared at my side, a can of diet soda in his hand.

"Want to talk about it?" he asked. "Or just brood until one of us decides for you?"

"Is the latter an option?" I replied, smiling at the bluntness of it. He grinned back.

"If you leave it to me, I'll get her in anyway and see if you can solve whatever it was that upset things."

"She wasn't who I thought she was," I said, watching someone load luggage onto a conveyor into the cargo hold of the large plane.

"You'd only just met her. Of course you didn't have everything right about her. But the big question is, was this new piece of information a deal-breaker?"

"She…" I sighed, not wanting to tell him what she was clearly keeping a secret. "There's more to the breakup with her ex-husband than she's telling people."

"Of course there is. No one leaves a fifteen-year marriage without a good reason. The more important thing is, why didn't she tell the truth?"

"To protect him. And I think a misguided feeling of shame on her part. The usual reasons for something like that."

Kai nodded and took another gulp, also staring at the luggage handlers. They'd almost finished, but they weren't in any kind of hurry. Again, I considered telling Kai what had actually happened but found I couldn't. It wasn't my place to tell someone what she clearly didn't want people to know.

"You know, that's a pretty good reason not to tell someone something. Or at least an incredibly understandable one. It doesn't make her a monster. If anything, it makes her a lot like you. I think I remember you telling a fib or two to hide someone else's flaws out of loyalty. Misplaced or not, it shows she cares about people as much as you do."

I sighed. Why did Kai have to be so right?

"It's too late for anything now. She'll hate me for walking out on this one."

Kai shrugged. "You never know. You said you'd already blown it with her, and then you seemed to fix it. Maybe reach out?"

I shook my head. Not this time. I wasn't going to pursue anything. We'd had some fun, and I liked her, but I wasn't ready for another relationship. I didn't trust myself, and I wasn't ready to trust anyone else, either.

Somehow, I would have to find a way to put her from my head and think about work or something else instead. It was time I stopped thinking about her and what had gone wrong. I never should have read her book.

With any luck, I'd never see her again. It wasn't like writers and musicians moved in similar circles. She'd stay in England, and I'd continue traveling around, and within days, I'd forget about her entirely.

This resolution made me feel better, despite my mind's nagging reminder that I had tried the same thing the last time I'd met up with her and only found I thought of her more. This time needed to be different.

Thankfully, our plane was finally ready, and the band was taken through the last section of the airport and onto the jet. It didn't take us long to get comfortable, all of us used to this part of the process.

I sat near the back and pulled out my sketchbook, trying to think of something, anything, to draw to take my mind off life. We were heading back to New York, so it wouldn't be the longest flight, but I hated being bored.

Most of the band settled down to get some sleep, but Kai pulled a notebook out, too, making notes and jotting down lyric ideas. I drew several different sketches, none of them seeming quite right. An elephant, a dog, and then I decided to tackle a person.

Only when Kai got up and came to sit beside me did I realize time had even passed.

"You're just going to forget her, are you?" he asked, looking at what I'd sketched.

I frowned as I realized I'd drawn someone very similar to her. Putting down my pen, I ran a hand across my chin and sighed. Kai chuckled and put down the pad of paper he'd been holding.

"Is it going to make things awkward if I tell you I think we really need her involved in these lyrics if we're going to use the music?" Kai asked a moment later.

"We could just not use it."

"Yeah, that's possible. But it's the best thing you've put together."

I frowned again. This wasn't an ideal situation or set of

choices. On one hand, would it be so awful to see if she wanted to keep going with the lyrics? I could always excuse myself from that part of the process. But then she might think I was deliberately avoiding her, and I didn't think I could be that disrespectful.

"Think about it," Kai said. "But if the rest of the band wants to get the lyrics done for this song, I'll probably arrange something with her. She's got an agent, right?"

"Yeah. Probably having a field day over the media attention she's getting."

Kai let out a quiet laugh again, and I found myself smiling as well. It made me worry, though. It wouldn't be the first time someone had tried to worm their way into the affections of one of the band members to gain fame for themselves.

By the time we arrived in New York, I had more than one sketch of Juno, and I'd given up trying to fight the desire to do so. Maybe I could sketch her out of my head.

Maybe even writing the lyrics and finishing the song would help close that chapter of my life. It would give her a way to gain a bit of fame without needing to date one of us if that was truly something she wanted, and it would allow me to feel like something was done.

It was worth a shot. Anything to get her out of my head and get my concentration back. I couldn't afford to be distracted. I didn't want to be distracted. I'd had enough of women and being committed to anyone. They weren't worth it. Love wasn't worth it.

CHAPTER TWENTY-SIX

<u>**Juno**</u>

The buzzing of my phone on the nightstand dragged me out of sleep and made me groan. I saw my agent's name and almost hung up on him, but he'd never called me so late before. Or early, I thought, as I noticed it was after two in the morning.

I reached for the phone and picked up.

"Do you know what time of night it is here?" I asked before he could say anything.

"Yes, but I knew you'd want me to wake you up for this," he replied, sounding smug.

"What is it?" I sat up and pulled the duvet tighter around me to keep warm.

"I knew you'd want to do it, so I've accepted on your behalf already and let the media know it's happening. You know that business opportunity you were talking about with a certain handsome rock star? His band made it official."

My blood ran cold, and confusion rendered me mute.

"Okay, I was expecting squeals of excitement, like when I told you that you had the TV deal last year. What's wrong?"

"Uhhh…" I didn't know how to respond. I thought Jack hated

me. Why was his band offering to officially get me involved in the lyrics? This made no sense.

"What did I miss?" my agent asked, pressing me for an answer again.

"I don't know. I guess I just didn't expect it. You say you've already accepted. How does that work? Don't you need me to sign stuff?"

"Well, yes and no. With music, sometimes there's a sort of good faith element. How much you'll get paid will depend on your actual contribution. So we'll hash out the final details of the contract after you've begun. It's a little unconventional. You'll need to sign an NDA, and we'll get them to sign something to say you'll be remunerated sufficiently for any help you give."

I frowned. It sounded like something I could get out of, but how on Earth was I going to explain that to my agent? He would want me to see it through now that he'd agreed to it, and had he said something about media involvement?

I asked him what he'd meant, beginning to panic.

"I was discreet with my little nudge to the media. They'll report that it's rumored you're working with the band on some kind of song, but with those photos of you with Jack circulating, it's got enough weight that the media will lap it up. This is going to be so good for your career. Not to mention the constant trickle of royalties it will bring in."

"Right," I replied, feeling like I should say something. It didn't sound like I could refuse this anyway.

Or did I just not want to? Did I want the chance to see Jack again and explain myself? I had no idea, but while my agent babbled on about details and possible career opportunities this might lead to, I considered what I might say to Jack if I got the chance.

"You still awake, darling?" he asked a moment later. "I haven't put you to sleep, have I? 'Cause I'd have thought you'd be excited about the idea of growing your income fourfold."

"While more money can make the world an easier place to live in, you know full well that making money isn't my main focus. I want to get to work on lots of projects and see my stories evolve beyond me."

"That still doesn't explain why you're not excited about this one. This is literally all that, as well. The song is inspired by one of your books. They want you involved in the song because of that."

"I know, and that's cool. I guess…it's a huge thing. The band is huge."

"You feeling nervous?" he asked, his voice gentle now, as if he felt we'd got to the real matter. It was why I'd picked him over other agents. He clearly cared about the money, but he'd appeared to care about me just as much, if not more. He knew his job was to make me money, but he still listened to my thoughts on the matter.

"Nervous is one word for it," I replied, knowing I couldn't explain exactly why I was nervous. He could assume it was because they were so famous, and I'd never written song lyrics before. He didn't need to know it was because I was worried Jack would be difficult to work with.

Of course, there was a chance I wouldn't even be working with Jack. I might be working with some of the others, and he wouldn't be as involved. He'd said it was Kai who had been interested in me helping in the first place.

"You shouldn't let nerves stop you. You're always telling me that when fear wins, opportunities are lost, and sometimes forever. You've always faced your fears. I'd be an awful person if I let you say no to this—if that's the only reason you can give me."

"It's the only reason I can give you," I said, knowing he had a point. My fear of how Jack would react wasn't a good reason not to try something new and exciting that I'd love to do under any other circumstances.

"That's my girl. I'll let you go back to sleep and forward you the details. You'll need to fly out there for a while, I think. They're busy, so I said you'd go to them. You can write anywhere, and we don't have anything else on your schedule for another three weeks."

I shook my head and smiled as my agent continued to talk about the details, having already forgotten he'd told me to go back to sleep. It was clear he was excited for me, too.

Eventually, I managed to get him to promise to put all the details in an email and get off the phone, but even when I lay back down, I couldn't sleep. My mind kept focusing on the one part of this that didn't add up. Why did the band now want me to hang out again when Jack didn't like me anymore? Or whatever he felt.

I'd blown it with him, so why was he okay with this? Was this his way of apologizing? Was this him trying to make amends? Or had he tried to stop it? Was it the rest of the band that wanted it and not him?

As I thought about these questions and more, I tossed and turned. I'd always been the sort of person to lie awake at night and wonder if I'd offended someone or said something I shouldn't have. Now, I was lying awake at night wondering if a boy liked me.

I was far too old for such nonsense. Or at least I felt too old to have my heart tugged around in this way. I was done with high school crushes and will-he, won't-he romances.

Despite my desire to let it go, it seemed my heart wasn't going to play ball, and my mind was quite happy to indulge in its whims.

Sighing, I got up again and made my way to the small living room. I sat on the sofa with a blanket and a hot chocolate and tried to figure out what I was going to do and what I'd say to him. Before I knew what I was doing, I'd pulled open my emails and found the email address he'd used before.

Jack,

Just got a call from my agent about coming to New York to try and write that song. He said yes before asking me. Happy to come anyway, but wanted to make sure you wanted me there. Don't want it to be awkward or to come if you don't truly want it. Let me know what you think.

Juno

I hit send almost by accident, my finger hovering over the trackpad in just the wrong way, so the computer seemed convinced I'd double-tapped it. For a moment, I panicked. Had I really just sent that to him? Over the next few minutes, I reread it at least a thousand times, trying to figure out what I could have said differently. I hadn't done a bad job, but I knew there were a bunch of better ways I could have phrased it.

Trying to put it from my mind, I put the laptop down and picked up a book. I'd read until I felt sleepy again. It was my only hope.

CHAPTER TWENTY-SEVEN

<u>Jack</u>

Sitting on the bed and sipping a drink, I was sketching some more, unwinding before I got some shuteye. I was in an apartment I had in the city, propped up by pillows and using the lamp-light to cast shadows onto a wall in a particular shape.

As my tablet let out the *bing* of an incoming important email, I considered ignoring it, but I had a few particular addresses it notified me of for a reason.

I put aside my sketches and picked up the tablet, wondering what it could be. The moment I spotted the sender, I almost put it down again.

Juno.

Fuck.

Instead, I opened it and quickly read. I sighed. Kai hadn't wasted any time in getting things moving and organizing everything to bring her in.

Was I really ready to have her in my face every day? It looked like she was offering me a way out, but there was also a good chance she was letting me know she'd really like to get the opportunity without me making it awkward.

There was nothing manipulative about it at face value, which was something. More like an olive branch and recognition that it might be uncomfortable. It wouldn't take away all my doubts, however. I wasn't going to let myself be played again.

After thinking a little longer and noticing the time, I decided to respond and put her mind at ease. She was clearly up late over it.

Juno,

Come. The band wants you there, and I'd hope we could be civil if nothing else. It'll be a good song, but we want to make sure it's the best. Kai wants to pick your brains about it some more, and it's easier to create in the same space.

Jack

I sent it and sat back, trying to get the memory of her sweet face and how her eyes had lit up when she saw me again out of my head. She was a beautiful woman, but I didn't want her under my skin. It would take all my resolve not to let her worm her way in.

Before I could move, she'd replied.

Jack,

Thank you. I'd hope we could be more than civil, perhaps even friends. I don't think I was truly ready for anything more, and I'm sorry. It wasn't fair for me to invite you into my world when I was still getting my shit straight after the breakup with Greg. As you can probably imagine, it's been an emotional few weeks.

I'm glad you don't mind. I was really looking forward to the idea of coming to New York. It might sound crazy, but I've never been to the big city before, and I've always wanted to.

Juno.

I raised an eyebrow, but the email made me feel better. She was at least appearing to be mature about the whole thing. It was a start.

Juno,

Friends sounds good. I'll show you around my favorite places while you're here if you like? There's a few amazing restaurants you need to eat at. I think Alma is looking forward to getting to know you better, too. Kai said she had good things to say after you came to hang out with the band.

I hope you're not up late worrying about any of this. I won't get in the way of your career or anything just because we had a thing, but it didn't work. That would be a pretty shitty thing to do to someone who clearly already has enough shit to deal with.

Or, if it's your ex making you scared or something, I can recommend a bodyguard company. I've had to hire some UK-specific ones a few times.

Jack

This time, I didn't put the tablet down. Now that I knew she was up and responding quickly, I wanted to make sure she wasn't awake because she was scared before I stopped responding. I thought back to the tussle on the stairs a few times. She'd been terrified, and even now, just the thought of what her ex might have done to her made me want to fly back and be some kind of guardian angel.

It must have been even scarier for her. She hadn't known I was coming back so soon. Until I'd shown up, she'd have thought she was alone. And then I'd taken offense at her secrecy and rushed out, too. More than once, I'd felt guilty about abandoning her like that, but the thought of having someone lie to me again, whatever the reason, made me want to run a million miles.

The chime of the next email pulled me from my guilty thoughts.

Jack,

My agent was so excited about getting to work with your band and thought I would be, too, so he woke me. I was a little worried about my ex, but he doesn't know exactly which apartment I'm in, only the floor of the building. I also think you scared him pretty well. Sometimes, that's all a bully needs to make him back off.

I was a little worried you wouldn't want me working with you, which is why I emailed, but it was more that I didn't want you to be forced into this, either. I'm honestly just over the moon that reading one of my books inspired someone to write a song and create something of their own.

Juno

I grinned at the sweetness of her response and found myself tapping away in reply.

Juno,

I'm also flattered you were inspired to write such a beautiful story of love and healing out of my characters and music. It feels like it's a full circle. I inspired you, and then you inspired me. It's fitting. You're clearly a beautiful person.

Jack

As I hit the send button, I realized what I'd said. It was definitely going too far. I swore and got up. What was I thinking? I was going to make her think I wanted something more again when I just wanted to get through this songwriting thing and move on. But she *had* inspired me, and I was stunned by the book she'd created from her own inspiration.

Growling my frustration, I threw myself back on the bed and tried to think about anything else. This was no good. I was going to tie myself in knots. Another *bing* disturbed me once more.

Jack,

You're a very beautiful soul as well. I'm very glad you feel the way you do about my story and Hunter and that we can be friends. You're a good man.

I should try and go back to sleep. Looking forward to talking more about it all when I'm there with you and the rest of the band. Hope your shows go well in the meantime.

Juno

I exhaled, feeling both relieved and as if I wanted to message her again and catch her before she slept. I wanted to get her attention back and ask her something. Anything.

It could be lonely on the road, and for a moment, we'd

connected, and not just in a sexual way. We had something to talk about, and I felt protective of her.

As I lay back, I pictured the bruises on her side. They'd haunted me since the moment I'd first set eyes on them, and she'd hastily covered them back up. How had any man done those to her, such a sweet little thing?

My hands clenched into fists as I thought of her ex and what he might have done if I hadn't arrived when I did. If nothing else, it made me glad I'd been in her life as little as I had. My actions had prevented her from facing more of his abuse, even if they'd done nothing to help either of our hearts.

With this thought, I also decided to get some sleep. I had shows to perform, and it wouldn't be long before she was here in New York with us. Whatever it brought, I knew I needed to be ready. Ready to resist and keep us level.

CHAPTER TWENTY-EIGHT

<u>Juno</u>

I stared out the window as the plane touched down on the runway. I was in first class for the first time, having enjoyed the special treatment. I'd never been able to afford it before, and even if I'd been paying this time, I'd have gone coach. But Kai had apparently insisted, and my agent hadn't dreamed of refusing.

Despite all the warmth and the attention the hostess lavished on me, however, I was a mess. I was about to see Jack again after a week of waiting. I hadn't dared to email him again after we'd cleared up where we were at. It didn't feel like something I could get away with despite wanting to.

It took forever to get through all the security checks and grab my bag from the luggage carousel, but eventually, I was heading out of the main doors and into the lobby, where I was supposed to see someone waiting for me.

I wasn't sure who I'd see, but I recognized Jack's driver holding up a placard with my name on it almost immediately. As I walked over, I smiled and let him take the bag from me.

Part of me had hoped to see Jack there as well, but the bigger part of me was relieved. He clearly cared enough to send his own car but felt relaxed enough to not have to be there, too.

"Is it a long drive?" I asked as we walked out to the car.

"It'll be about half an hour. That okay, ma'am?" he replied.

"Sure, but please, call me Juno. I'm not sure I'm old enough to be a ma'am."

The driver smiled and nodded before getting the door for me. Only then did I wonder if Jack had waited in the car. Of course, he was famous, so he wouldn't be waiting out in the lobby.

Inside, I sighed with relief. I was alone, and Jack had stayed behind, sending just the car and his driver for me.

"I'll just let them know we're on our way," the driver said through a pane of glass between the back and front of the car.

"Thank you," I replied, feeling my stomach flip over at the thought of seeing the whole band again. The first time I'd met them, I hadn't been too worried about what they thought of me, interested in only Jack. This time, it felt as if I needed them all to like me.

And on top of that, I had to attempt to be creative in a way I never had before. No pressure.

Moving through the traffic in New York helped calm me a little, although it took a while to get anywhere. I looked out the window at everything that passed us by, marveling at how many yellow cabs there were and how many different places to get food.

Finally, the car stopped outside a large apartment block, and the doorman rushed forward to open the car door for me. I got out and smiled, knowing this was it.

"Ms. Fernsby?" the man asked, looking sharp in his dark gray uniform.

"Yes. I'm here to work with the Vampirates," I replied.

"Fantastic. I believe most of them are here already. Top floor, penthouse three. Would you like me to escort you up?" he asked as he opened the building door for me.

"I think I can find it," I replied, grateful for a moment alone to try and compose myself.

As I found the elevator and pressed the up button, I was keenly aware I was so nervous I was beginning to shake.

Keep it together, I thought to myself. *You've seen Jack before, and the rest of the band only asked you to be here to talk about your book and characters.*

Thankfully, I'd had the good sense to reread the story on the plane on the way over. I'd written so many books in my decade or so as a writer that I couldn't remember all the details of each of them anymore.

The elevator let out a little *bing* when I reached the top floor, and the doors opened to reveal Jack himself. His eyes widened as I stood there feeling like a deer in headlights.

He stepped back, his gaze roaming my body, and still, I didn't move. I'd planned to take a few deep breaths before I knocked on a door somewhere. I'd wanted to think about what I'd say. Not to find him right in front of me.

"Come on in. I can show you the view," he said as if we'd ridden up the elevator together. It helped me finally get my feet to work, and I hurried out of the contraption just as the doors were going to close and slice me in half.

He immediately reached out a hand and stopped them, rescuing me once again. I still couldn't think of anything to say, but thankfully, Jack's door was only a few steps away, and it was already open.

"She's here," he called, and immediately Kai came around a corner.

"Juno, I feel like I'm finally going to get to meet you," he said.

"It does feel a bit like a first meeting, doesn't it?" I replied, finding my voice finally working.

"We didn't exactly have long the last time, and Jack seemed eager to have you to himself. Now, come on in, let me get you a drink, and tell us all about your writing. I find authors fascinating. And Jack's had more than a few authors as friends."

Kai took my hand and almost tugged me into the main sitting area of the apartment, making me feel much more at home. I noticed that Jack hung back and let Kai take the lead, but I wouldn't complain when it instantly helped calm my nerves and made me feel less on the spot.

I moved over to a small seat at one end of the pair of sofas and immediately perched in it, a little too near the edge to be able to sit back. I put my small bag down beside my feet before I realized I didn't have my main luggage, nor did I know exactly where I'd be staying while I was here. I'd simply been told to come and given plane tickets.

Trying not to worry about that detail for the moment, I took the soda can I was offered, not thinking about what was in it so much as giving my hands something to hold to stop them from shaking so obviously. Kai sat on the sofa nearest me, and Jack sat at the farthest point from me.

For a moment, I looked between them, wondering where the others were. There were instruments dotted around the living room, and it looked as if at least Jack and Kai had been playing before I'd arrived. I didn't know what I'd expected on my arrival, but this wasn't it. I'd assumed we'd work in a studio, but these guys seemed pretty comfortable in a simple living room.

And that made me wonder why I was there. Surely, if they could have done this anywhere, I could have been brought in on a video call or something?

"Now, tell me about your process," Kai said. "Where do you begin with your ideas? What gets you excited about a story?"

I frowned, surprised by the questions and not sure what they had to do with us writing a song, but it was something to talk about and focus on.

"My ideas, especially my dark romance, come to me in one of two ways. I want to explore a relationship dynamic. An imbalance or power struggle between two conflicting personalities and see if it's possible for two people like that to have a happy ending together. Or I have a character or person come to mind, and I almost instinctively start coming up with what I think would be a good partner for them to help them grow and move into a better life."

"So it sounds like it's all about the characters. That's what Jack said it felt like. I confess I haven't read much, but Jack has told me a lot. Why don't you tell me about the characters and what makes them special in this story?"

Exhaling, I thought about Hunter and decided to begin there. As I opened my mouth and started talking about him, all my anxiety and worries melted away. I was in my zone now, and it felt good.

CHAPTER TWENTY-NINE

<u>Jack</u>

The rest of the band had arrived while Juno was answering Kai's questions. Sitting on the other side of the room, I could still feel the pull. As Juno described Hunter, and therefore described me in a frightening way, considering we'd never met before she wrote the story, I felt equally vulnerable and seen in a way I hadn't been in a long time. She talked about me and her character with fondness and a lack of judgment that made me feel okay being me.

It was strange. Almost liberating, and I hadn't said a word. Occasionally, Kai glanced my way, but only when Juno looked down to think for a moment. Her hands clutched the soda can he'd given her as if it was some kind of lifeline, but she relaxed as she spoke. This was her opening up in a way I hadn't seen before.

As she moved on to talking about the woman she'd created for Hunter, I listened even more intently. Her telling began almost hesitantly after talking about Hunter so easily.

"I wanted someone both gentle and firm for him. Someone he'd need to tame a little, but not someone brash or rude. She needed empathy to see his scars and an appreciation of how long the road might be for him to walk into a better space, but the understanding that he'd be worth it if he'd just let her in and on that journey with him."

"So you gave her a…difficult history."

"Yes. I gave her mine." Juno spoke as if it was a normal thing to do for her characters and explained everything, but it made my body tense. Her character's past had been worse than difficult. Kai had put it politely when he'd said it was difficult.

"Wow," Kai said. "That couldn't have been easy to write."

"It wasn't at some points. I think I put on a few pounds in chocolate," she replied, grinning at her own words. "It made for a more believable character, though, and it remains one of my best dark romances to date."

I exhaled, not sure how to respond, and I could see Kai wasn't either. No wonder it had felt so true and so real. It was a combination of two very real people.

"Just like Hunter took on a life of his own, so did Ella. She wasn't entirely me by the end."

She continued talking about the characters a little longer as if she realized she'd put us both into a state of shock and needed to help us out of it. It was astute of her and made me like her even more. Which wouldn't have been a problem if I hadn't been trying to like her less.

The fondness for the characters came through again and again as the others arrived, making themselves at home, grabbing drinks, and settling in to listen. Kai encouraged her to keep going each time she stopped, and eventually, she reached the end of her download of information.

"I cried when they finally got their happy ending, and he swept her into his arms," she said to wrap things up.

"Properly cried?" Kai asked.

"Yeah. I cry all the time when I'm writing. Anyway, is there anything else I can tell you?" she asked.

Kai looked around the group, and I nodded at him to let him

know I'd heard enough. The lyrics weren't my main area, but she'd explained so many elements I hadn't been sure of. It made the characters even more alive in my head.

I reached for the paper pad near me and immediately jotted down a few things that came to mind, some snatches of things she'd said. I played with the phrases, then I handed it to Kai.

He read them aloud to the room, and then we all started throwing in ideas. Although Juno didn't offer any whole lines, she was good at picking out words that could be changed and tweaking things we'd suggested to make it better.

At the same time, I played the music we had already arranged, and we started to fit the words to the rhythm and beat, picking out a melody for the lyrics to follow. Kai started to sing it first, but no sooner had I attempted to sing another few lines than he passed what we had back to me and got me to sing the rest.

Time seemed to fly by, the magic of creating happening quickly and in a way that all of us got into easily. We ordered takeout, and before long, I found myself sitting closer to Juno as she sat on a cushion on the floor and wrote down a final version of the lyrics.

As she put down the last word, we all seemed to collectively sigh, and silence fell.

"Wow," she said. "Is that what it's always like?"

"No," Kai replied. "That's what it's like when it goes well. It's not entirely finished yet, either, but it's a good start. We'll need to get everything recorded. Make sure it really works when we sing and perform everything together, but that will take a few days, maybe even weeks, to get settled."

She nodded and glanced around at us, although she looked down when our eyes met.

"Come on," Kai said, getting up and glancing between Juno and me. "Let's get some air and a decent meal. The ladies can join us, and we can chill out for a bit. Then we can get started on the next part tomorrow."

I smiled and nodded, needing no more persuading. If I was going to put space between Juno and me, I needed other people there. It wasn't going well so far, but she'd been nothing but professional. My problem was in the subject matter.

Every time I thought about the book, I thought about showing up at that cafe, pretending to be Hunter while she pretended to be Ella, and then taking her back to my hotel and screwing her brains out.

And it hadn't helped to hear her talk about Hunter the way she had. It had both been me and not me while she was talking.

As we gathered some stuff to leave, she grabbed her bag again and looked my way, and I couldn't help but smile. She had that slightly nervous, wide-eyed look about her again. She'd looked that way when I'd met her outside the elevator. It made me want to scoop her up, pin her against a wall, and claim that hot little mouth of hers.

Mind out of the gutter, I thought again, tensing and looking away from her, trying to find anything else to focus on. Thankfully, Kai seemed to take her under his wing, telling her where we were going and asking if she wanted to see any sights along the way.

I listened rather than talked, letting her clear English accent break through my thoughts as she responded.

"Oh, I don't really know what there is to see here. I spent all my research time making sure I remembered everything about Hunter and Ella. I didn't know if there would be time to see anything."

"There will be time. And I insist on it. Jack knows the place best. Don't you, Jack?" Kai asked, reaching for my arm.

I had no choice but to look at her, but as I did, she looked down, fiddling with her purse handle and looking as awkward as I felt.

"I'm sure I can show you a thing or two," I said before mentally kicking myself at the innuendo.

I caught Kai's amused look before I rolled my eyes and looked away. The rest of the band was finally ready, and we trooped out, relief flooding through me at the break in contact and the escape.

Just four more days and she'd be gone, and we'd be done. Four more days.

CHAPTER THIRTY

<u>Juno</u>

As we finished eating, I exhaled with satisfaction. I was stuffed, and the food had been delicious. I was sandwiched between Alma and another lady named Eve, who hadn't been to London. She was a makeup artist and dating one of the other band members. It was apparently a new thing, and it made me feel a little calmer. If Jack and I had been together, I still wouldn't have been the new girl in the group.

Although Jack was sitting across from Eve and glanced my way often enough that I couldn't ignore him entirely, there hadn't been any more awkwardness. I was still aware of him, and I hoped we could grow more comfortable together at some point, but I didn't doubt it would take time.

If I thought about it too much, I wanted to cry for how quickly he'd decided he didn't want me in his life as anything more than work colleagues, but it was probably for the best. I'd been through so much in the last few months. I wasn't sure I could trust myself around him, either, and I didn't know how much I could trust him.

To distract myself, I asked Alma and Eve about them, listening as they told me about all the celebrities they'd met and whether they'd truly been as they presented themselves to the general public. They soon had me laughing and feeling more relaxed.

With everyone having eaten and the drinks finished, we opted to make our way back to the penthouse apartment to chill before heading to bed earlier than I was expecting.

I'd heard of infamous parties and late-night drinking, and it seemed I wasn't getting that this evening. Not wanting to rock the boat or register any kind of complaint, I headed back to the apartment with everyone else. I found myself in the car with Jack, Eve, and Ed, and I tried not to show the instant tense feeling.

"Is this what every day is like?" I asked, knowing it was a stupid question as soon as it came out of my mouth. Eve grinned and shook her head.

"Enough of them to make it worth doing," Jack replied, rescuing me and answering the question at the same time. "There's a lot of days of rehearsing for gigs, doing promos, and just getting stuff done, but plenty of weeks like this where we just create for a while. They're like this on good days, and there can be a lot of heated conversations on the bad days."

"Like, disagreements and stuff?" I asked, the frankness taking me by surprise.

"Sometimes. Mostly frustration if we can't work out a melody that makes the song come alive, or someone is struggling to play what we need or whatever. We're all in it together, and sometimes we have to figure out how to get everyone on the same page."

I nodded, aware it was a whole different dynamic to writing a novel. I had the final say in everything, even when my editor looked it over and made suggestions. I could decide whether to change something or not, and the skill was all up to me and my use of words.

Eve asked a question next, letting Ed know she had work of

her own to do over the next few days and asking how many days we were all planning on working on the song.

It felt a little like they were all talking another language as they used music-related jargon, and Jack and Ed discussed the plan for the next day. They were still discussing parts and which instruments they were thinking of using when the car pulled up outside the apartment block again. Jack immediately sent the driver back out to get some munchies and drinks, and then we all went inside.

Kai, Alma, and the rest of the band arrived at almost the exact same time, and there were too many of us to fit in the elevator at once. I hung back, offering to take the stairs.

Several of them looked at me as if I'd grown two heads, but Jack stepped back as well.

"I'll show you where they are," he said as he let the elevator shut on most of the others. Kai and Alma were also left behind, but both of them clearly intended to wait for the elevator to come back down.

I felt a little silly but equally committed now I'd suggested it. What had I been thinking?

Jack led me past the elevator to a small door set into the wall behind it and used a tag on his keys to open it.

"Thanks," I said, heading toward the stairs I could see. "I assume it goes all the way to the top?"

"Yeah, all twelve floors. You sure you don't want to wait?"

"The exercise will do me good," I replied, catching the scent of his cologne as he held the door open for me. I needed to put some distance between us.

To my surprise, however, he followed me.

"You don't have to come, too," I said as I started to climb.

"Nah, it's okay. I think you're weird, but I've never actually been up them. Might actually do me some good, too." He smiled at me, his deep brown eyes so full of warmth it took all my willpower to look away and keep climbing.

My brain kept trying to think of something to say. No matter what I tried, however, nothing came out.

"Thank you for today," he said a moment later. "You didn't have to open up the way you did. It means a lot to all of us that you could be so vulnerable. I know it's not easy."

"You're welcome," I replied, stunned by his gentleness and appreciation.

No matter what kind of conversation we seemed to be having, Jack kept taking me by surprise, and this was after he'd told me I'd done a good job of painting a picture of him with Hunter. How did I seem to know him so well yet feel so off-balance around him all the time?

I was a writer. I understood people on a level some didn't even understand themselves, yet here I was in front of one of the most mysterious and complicated men I'd ever met.

All of me wanted to get to know him better and figure him out as if he were some great puzzle, but I also knew he was a delicate puzzle, someone I couldn't and would never want to force to open up to me.

"I hope I didn't make the song too dark," I said a moment later, thinking of all the difficult elements that had gone into it.

"Oh, no, it's no darker than it should be. It's tackling a tough subject. It's a beautiful song." He looked at me as we walked up.

I was starting to get a little winded, the numbers on each wall reminding me I wasn't quite halfway there yet. This had been a bad idea.

Beside me, Jack wasn't even slightly out of breath, and he seemed to be loping up the stairs with easy strides, not even needing to hold onto the railing.

"Okay, maybe the elevator would have been a better idea," I said as we reached the seventh floor, and I stopped for a moment. Jack chuckled.

"Twelve floors is a lot more steps than you'd think."

"Sorry," I said, daring to finally look at him properly.

"I didn't have to come with you." He smiled, the corner of his mouth twitching up. I didn't know whether to kiss him, slap him, or do something else entirely.

All my emotions felt confused, so I focused on the steps, counting up the sets of eight and the pairs that made each floor. Sixteen steps per floor and twelve floors. No wonder I was exhausted.

Finally, we reached the top, and I noticed Kai standing on the landing waiting for us.

"None of us could get in," he pointed out. "Not without you and the keys."

Immediately, I felt my cheeks flush. They'd been standing out in the hallway because I'd opted to take the stairs. And it had clearly been enough time for the elevator to go up and down again and fetch the second part of the group.

"Sorry," I mumbled as Jack handed Kai the keys. However, none of them looked my way as they hurried to let everyone in, and Jack left my side to get everyone settled with a drink.

I exhaled, feeling like a total idiot.

CHAPTER THIRTY-ONE

As the night wore on, more and more of the band and their partners left, and even I began to yawn. More than ready to hit the sack, I tried to figure out where I could go and who I needed to talk to about getting somewhere to sleep for the night. I still didn't even know where my luggage was.

"All right, I'm going to get some sleep," Kai said a moment later, making me even more worried. "Alma will tell me I'm keeping her from her beauty sleep if I stay up much longer."

Alma rolled her eyes as he smiled at her, and the pair headed to the door. The last of the band quickly followed while I was still sitting on a cushion near the TV, a third of a can of soda in my hands.

More than once, I'd noticed no one really drank alcohol, one or two of the partners having a glass of wine, but no one else really taking an interest. Now, it seemed they were also turning in for earlier nights than I was expecting.

"We're all more reserved when we're creating," Jack said with only the two of us left.

I took a final gulp of my soda and stood, not intending to keep him up, and pretty sure he'd just asked me to leave.

"So…where am I being sent off to for some shuteye?" I asked, hoping it sounded casual enough.

"I thought you'd want a room with a view, so I had one of the other penthouses prepared for you," Jack replied.

I blinked, not sure of what I'd just heard. Had he just told me I was staying in another of the penthouses?

"Come on," he said, heading toward the door and the rack of keys on hooks near it. Only then did I notice a row of five keys, all labeled from one to five, each on its own little fob. He took number five off the hook and motioned for me to follow him.

I expected him to go toward the other end of the floor, but instead, he literally crossed the hall and opened the door.

"Here you go," he said as I spotted my luggage, the case having been wheeled a few feet into the apartment and left there. "I had the guys stock the fridge with some drinks and snacks. Not sure exactly what you'd want, but I took a guess." Jack grinned again, and I felt myself beginning to melt, every inch of me wanting to invite him into the apartment with me and take him to bed.

The last thing I wanted was to be alone. But I knew nothing was going to happen between us. Instead of inviting him in, I smiled and thanked him, and he handed me the key.

"All yours for the week."

"Do I even want to know how much this cost?" I asked a moment later.

"Oh, technically nothing. I own the whole floor."

I lifted my eyebrows, and he chuckled at me.

"Don't worry, you'll get used to it. Kai owns an entire block in another city somewhere. Didn't want people snooping into his garden or something."

"Oh, so it's a way to have privacy," I said aloud, thinking that made more sense.

"Yeah, sorta. But it also means we can do this. Everyone is crashing in an apartment instead of us forking out for hotel rooms." Jack leaned against the edge of the door as he spoke, almost as if he was planning on staying there.

I looked down, suddenly feeling self-conscious again.

"Anyway, I should let you sleep," he said a moment later and backed up. "Let me know if you need anything. I usually hear it if someone knocks on my door."

"It sounds like I'm going to be just fine. Thank you."

He turned and left, almost as if he was suddenly running away, and I sighed. Why was everything so tense between us? And why didn't my brain want to work? I'd been such a dork all day.

Trying not to worry and instead focus on how the good things had gone, I shut the door and looked around the apartment. It was almost identical to what I'd seen of Jack's but a mirror image. Nothing prepared me for the view from the bedroom, however. It looked out over New York. Plenty of buildings were taller, but enough weren't so I could see off into the distance.

I stood in the dark, looking out at all the lit-up windows for a while, taking it all in and starting to like how the rest of the world appeared to live.

It was late, and I should have been tired, but possibly from the caffeine in the soda or just because of the day I'd been having, I was more than a little wired. I tried to lie down and get some sleep, but the second I was in bed and cozy, my eyes wanted to be wide open. It wasn't going to work.

Sighing, I tried rolling over several times. Eventually, I drifted off, but I dreamed of Jack and what might happen on subsequent days as the band worked on the song.

A few times, I thought I heard a noise as if someone was opening the apartment door while I was dozing. Both times, I sat up and listened closely, not daring to breathe.

Telling myself I was just being silly, I tried to settle down again. I needed sleep, or I was going to struggle the next day, and

I wanted to make the most of it. But another noise, sounding like someone shutting a door, soon had my eyes wide open again. It was no good.

Pulling on my dressing gown and slippers, I made my way to the apartment door and listened. I couldn't hear anything outside, but as I was about to move, I thought I heard someone else shut their door. Had someone else been spooked, or was someone else awake?

A moment later, I thought I heard footsteps approach my door. I looked around for something to defend myself with, instantly terrified but making sure I didn't make a sound.

As I found the end of an umbrella, whoever was out there stopped moving. I lifted it and waited, listening. Slowly, the footsteps shuffled off again, but I wasn't sure what direction they'd gone in. Taking several deep breaths to try and calm myself down, I moved back to my apartment door again and tucked the little key into my dressing gown pocket.

It made a clinking noise, but it was quiet enough that I was pretty sure no one else would have heard it. I then pulled the door open as quietly as I could, the umbrella still held in one hand and ready to defend myself.

Immediately, I noticed Jack standing in his own doorway, looking toward my door as if I'd startled him. He wore nothing but a pair of pants, his muscular chest bare.

"I heard a noise," I said, feeling as if I wanted the floor to swallow me whole, my cheeks flushing as I lowered the umbrella.

"Yeah, me too," he replied. "You couldn't sleep either?"

I shook my head and sighed. I hadn't been sleeping well since Greg had physically assaulted me. The moment haunted my dreams, and my body still hadn't fully healed.

"You want to come in and have a hot chocolate?" he asked a moment later. "I don't think you'll need the umbrella though." A grin spread across his face, but it was a sweet look.

Immediately, I nodded and put it down. I was halfway across

the hall before I remembered what I was wearing. It wasn't exactly the sexiest of material.

However, Jack already had his back turned, the door propped open enough to admit me while he made his way to the kitchen. I shut the door behind us, hearing it click and feeling a strange sort of finality, and then I followed him to the kitchen.

CHAPTER THIRTY-TWO

<u>Jack</u>

As I handed Juno a mug of hot chocolate and picked up my own, I tried not to stare. She was wearing some kind of pajamas underneath a robe, and I was still in nothing but my pants.

I wanted to unwrap her. To find out what her breasts looked like in her pajama top. Instead, I looked down and noticed her toes. She had painted her toenails, but a few days ago, the lilac metallic varnish having chipped just a little here and there.

Her gaze followed mine until she realized what I was staring at. Immediately, she curled her toes up, almost as if trying to hide the imperfection. It was cute in a way I liked, and it made my groin stir.

"Want to talk about whatever was keeping you up?" I asked, desperate for something to put some distance between us. I should never have invited her in, but I'd been unable to resist those wide, scared eyes. She'd needed reassurance. Needed something to make her feel calmer again.

"It's nothing you don't already know. My asshole of an ex did a number on me, and now every little noise I hear while I'm alone practically gives me a heart attack. I'd begun to get used to the new apartment near Bath, but…" She trailed off and sipped her drink.

Leaning against the counter, I studied her. She looked so fragile and vulnerable, yet equally feminine and beautiful.

Her hair was loose, chestnut locks tumbled around her head and down her back, and despite the lack of makeup, she had soft-looking cheeks.

I wanted to stride over to her, scoop her up in my arms, and show her what real men did to women like her. How a man should take care of his woman. How he should make her feel.

And I wanted to take her, to claim her, to make her submit to me and give me everything her ex didn't deserve to have claimed of her. I wanted to earn it and take it all. To make her want to yield to me and give me every inch of her to taste and screw as I desired.

Focusing on the hot chocolate in my hands to try and get my mind off fucking her where she stood, I took a gulp without remembering it was still hot. Immediately, I had to spit it back out again and almost splashed it all over the floor.

She looked up, her eyes going wider questioningly.

"Hotter than I thought it would be," I said, not sure if I was talking about the drink or her.

She smirked slightly and took another sip of hers. I watched her mouth move, immediately imagining her lips wrapped around me instead, those wide eyes looking up as I pulled her hair back and made her take as much of me as she could.

"So, what's got you up?" she asked, her eyes alight, almost as if she knew.

I faltered, not sure how to answer. *Hot dreams of fucking your deliciously submissive body. Dreams of pinning you down and driving my hard throbbing cock as deep as I could get it into your tight, wet pussy.* No, I couldn't say that. What should I say?

"You don't have to talk about it if you don't want to," she said, but the light went out in her eyes, and she looked down. *Damn it,*

I didn't want her to think I was a dick either, especially after she'd just opened up to me.

"It's complicated," I said, not helping myself. "I mean, my life. Everything about it. How careful I have to be. I can't let my guard down around the wrong people, and…"

"You've been hurt too many times before," she finished.

I nodded, but I felt as if I'd just erected a wall between us. Maybe that was for the best.

We continued to drink in silence, my eyes wandering over her as I thought back to the dreams I'd been having. Why had she gotten under my skin so deep? She wasn't anything particularly special to look at.

But as she looked at me again, noticing my gaze was on her, I saw her awareness of being stared at. I expected her to shy away. To make some excuse about why she had to go, but she didn't. Instead, she put her mug down and closed the distance between us.

"Thank you," she said, her eyes on my face, seeming to study me, almost checking for permission as she moved into my personal space. "You've been there for me so much already. You're…"

I found myself putting my own mug down, too, my hand brushing hers as I did. The contact between us broke the last of my reserve.

Letting out a growl of desire, I closed the last of the gap, wrapping my arms around her and bringing my mouth down upon hers. My tongue plunged between her lips, the surprise parting them as I shoved her back against the pantry door.

She moaned as I slipped one hand between the layers of her gown and cupped her breast. The fabric of her pajama top was thin enough I could find her nipple and give it a rough pinch.

Her hands lifted to my chest, running across me as I pushed my hardening cock against her. I couldn't think, my hands automatically acting as I pulled her robe the rest of the way open and yanked her pajama pants and panties down with one rough motion.

Squeaking against me, she tried to push me away a moment, but I resisted, holding her there and bringing my hands back to her breasts while she adjusted to the idea of her pussy being bare and exposed to me.

I was going to fuck her, and I wasn't completely sure I could have stopped myself if she'd asked me to. Thankfully, she calmed again, my tongue still exploring her mouth, tasting the hot chocolate we'd both just drunk.

Still tugging on one nipple through her top, not even trying to be gentle, I unbuttoned my jeans and shifted them down, exposing my erection. The cold night air washed over it, but it was almost a balm, giving me enough cool to check she was ready for me before I claimed her pussy.

Sliding my fingers between her legs, I parted her lips and found her core wet and dripping. It was all the encouragement I needed and all the restraint I could show.

Grabbing her hips, I lifted her and drove my cock deep into her pussy. She let out another gasp as I pushed her into the pantry door, getting as deep as I could.

Her arms wrapped around me, her feet off the floor as I pinned her between me and the hard surface and pounded into her tight, hot little pussy again and again. It was even better than my dreams were, each stroke perfection, each thrust taking me closer to my peak.

The pleasure built as my mind focused on only how good it felt to take her and make her mine. I groaned as I reached my peak and drove as deep as I could, my cum filling her in the waves of my orgasm.

As I came down, I let her slip back to the floor, her wide, doe-like eyes looking up at me, hazy but unsatisfied.

I took her hand and wordlessly led her to my bedroom. I wasn't done with her.

CHAPTER THIRTY-THREE

<u>Juno</u>

I shivered as Jack put some distance between us, his fingers wrapped around mine, a promise of what was to come. He'd just given me one heck of a screwing, but he'd left me wanting, his cum dripping down my thighs while my pussy throbbed with desire and need.

Wanting him more than ever but unable to speak, I let him lead me to his bedroom. It seemed no matter what he did and no matter how many mixed signals he gave me, he only had to touch me, and my body gave in.

It had been a long time since anyone had made me desire to submit to them and give them everything they wanted, but somehow, Jack only had to look at me, and my body yearned for his firm hands and demanding commands.

As soon as we were in the bedroom, he tipped me over onto the bed and came down on top of me. I moaned as his mouth found mine again, and his hands pulled every last inch of clothing I had off me.

I tried to reach for his pants to shove them into the pile already at the edge of the bed, but he stopped my hands and pushed them above my head. I exhaled, desire making me clench my thighs.

His body between my legs prevented me from doing anything other than revealing my frustration. He chuckled against me before sliding one hand down my torso until he cupped my pussy in his hands.

Pulling back from our kissing to study my face, he thrust his fingers down and into me, filling me as his thumb ran over my clit.

"Do you want my cock?" he asked.

I nodded without hesitation. He'd felt so good inside me that even with three fingers pushing deep inside and his thumb running over my sensitive nub, I wanted more. I wanted his throbbing manhood buried in my core.

"Come for me, then, sweetheart. Come for me, and I'll stick my cock in you again."

His words washed over me, making me eager to please and, at the same time, finally feeling like I could desire my own pleasure. It was as if he'd given me permission to want him and what he was doing to me.

Still pinned down beneath him, I could only shift my hips against the motion of his fingers and try to press my clit harder against his thumb. Suddenly, he pulled out of me, leaving me empty and wet. I mewled, desire making me shake. Twice now, he'd pulled out and left me wanting.

"Lie still," he said. "Yield to me. Will you be a good girl, kitten?"

I nodded. "Yes, please. Please let me come."

The words tumbled out in a desperate pleading rush, and for a moment, I felt like a whimpering mess, but it seemed to please him. His mouth closed over mine as I moaned, and his fingers slipped between my legs again, claiming my depths and making me want to buck against him.

Instead, I fought to keep still, pretty sure I'd be denied any kind of release if I failed. It was almost torture to fight my own body as he touched, rubbed, and impaled me as he pleased.

Slowly, I neared my peak, each circle of his thumb and each thrust taking me further and showing me that I belonged to him entirely. I yelled into him as the first shudder of ecstasy rolled through me, his motions continuing, dragging out the waves until I thought I might burst.

I panted as I slowly calmed, his body still on top of mine and pinning my arms above my head.

"Now, about that cock," he said a moment later, but instead of revealing his hard penis and plunging it into the pussy he'd just assaulted with his fingers, he shifted up the bed until he was crouched over my head. "Open up those sweet lips of yours and wrap them around this. Taste every last inch."

It hadn't been what I had in mind when I said I wanted his cock, but there was no way I planned to disappoint him. Immediately, I opened my mouth and let him move forward, pushing his manhood so deep I almost choked on him.

As he pulled back, I ran my tongue over his hard tip, tasting the combination of precum and juices from my own pussy. He moaned and pushed deeper again.

My arms still pinned above me, and with him in full control of the rhythm and depth, all I could do was work my mouth to please him, taking delight in hearing his breathing quicken and feel his cock throb with desire.

Slowly, he pulled out of my mouth again.

"Good girl," he said before moving back down and pushing my legs apart again. Without any warning, he thrust his manhood deep into my pussy again, his shaft still slick and filling me with ease.

I closed my eyes and tipped my head back in ecstasy at the perfect feeling of fullness.

He chuckled and kissed my neck but kept himself still within me for a moment, almost as if he was savoring how it felt to be deep inside me. As one hand traveled to my breasts and he rolled his thumb over a nipple, I groaned and gently bucked my hips.

"You're not very good at laying still and letting yourself be taken, are you?" he asked as he brought his mouth near my ear.

"I haven't had as much practice as I'd like," I retorted. It earned me another chuckle, and then he kissed my neck again.

"You'd better get perfect at it and fast, or you'll be mewling as I pull out of you and leave you wanting."

"Yes, sir," I said, once again trying to fight my natural desire to thrust against him.

He kept the pace slow, almost gentle compared to the previous time he'd been inside me, and I wanted to beg him to go faster, but instead, I focused on keeping as still as I could and enjoying being full of him.

It felt perfect having him deep inside me, and knowing I was giving him exactly what he wanted only made it feel better. Slowly, he rocked his hips back and forth, each agonizing loss as he pulled out, sweetened by the pleasure as he filled me again.

Looking into his eyes, I yielded to him and let him have me however he wanted. As he neared his own orgasm again, he sped up a little. Every stroke stirred the fire within me along with him until I was panting hard and close to my peak.

He cried out and thrust deep one last time, his cock filling me with his orgasm and tipping me over the edge once more. Slowly, I returned to Earth in his arms, his body warm and comforting over mine.

Slipping to one side, he held me close and pressed gentler kisses to my lips. It made me wonder if he was looking for more from me, but he relaxed beside me and stroked his hand gently down my side, my body warmed by the touch.

"We really should sleep, or we'll never be able to function tomorrow," he said. "Do you want to stay or go back to the other apartment?"

I considered offering to go back, but the thought of being

alone in a strange place made me instantly want to stay right there with him. For whatever reason, he made me feel safe, and I needed that right now.

"Can I stay?" I asked. "I don't think I'll sleep as much or as well if I go back."

"Even after the screwing I gave you?" he asked with a grin, but he pulled me closer again and kissed my forehead.

I smiled but didn't reply, instead getting comfortable in his arms. There were a lot worse places to sleep than in the arms of Jack Starling.

CHAPTER THIRTY-FOUR

The sound of someone talking in the background woke me up. I opened my eyes and looked around, taking a moment to remember where I was.

Jack's voice came to me from somewhere outside the room. Sitting up, I looked around and took in the messy bed. My nightgown and pajamas had been folded and laid neatly on a chair in one corner of the room.

For a moment, I merely listened, my body aching, until the conversation ended, and there was a tap on the door. Immediately, Jack came in. He was carrying a tray with breakfast and a glass of orange juice.

"Wow. Breakfast in bed, too," I said as I smiled.

"I wondered if I'd still find you asleep. Most of the band went to a studio nearby to lay down some of the stuff officially. Alma and Kai stuck behind to wait for us."

I swallowed, aware that probably meant everyone knew Jack and I had slept together. Was it good they knew? Would it somehow help us? Or would it make things worse?

Without knowing for sure, I tried to focus on what was in front of me. Food, a good-looking man who appeared to be recently showered and dressed himself, and a song to help his band finish.

It was surreal in so many ways, but I couldn't believe I'd slept through so much.

"Do you often sleep so deeply or just when you're with me?" Jack asked a moment later. "I showered, and the whole band was in the room next door, and you still didn't wake up."

"I don't normally sleep very deeply at all," I replied without thinking about what I was confessing.

Had I just admitted that something about having him around made me feel safe and relaxed? I knew my ex had once made me feel like that, however. I wasn't sure I believed my own feelings on it just yet.

As I ate, Jack went back outside, and I heard him tell Kai that we'd meet them at the studio soon. It made me wonder how long I had been asleep, but I ate the scrambled eggs and toast he'd brought me, amused that he'd made me the same thing I'd tucked into at the hotel. I guessed it was a pretty safe bet to give me something he'd seen me eating.

It tasted wonderful, my body starving after the late-night adventure we'd had.

I didn't realize how much I ached and how sore I was until I tried to get out of bed. Jack took the tray and then tried to help me up. Only then did I register how naked I was.

My cheeks grew hot and went pink as I looked for something to cover my nakedness with, but he and the breakfast tray were between me and my clothing. His eyes roved as he smirked.

"If you want to shower, you'd best hurry," he said. "I don't know how long they'll want to wait for us. They're used to me being late, but I think they were hoping you'd be more on time."

I frowned, but it helped refocus me, and I hurried away. The bathroom was so clean I felt as if I might have been staying at a hotel, although the shower wasn't as insanely huge as the one at the hotel he'd stayed at while visiting me. It was strange how much fancier everything was than I was used to, but I tried to push all the anxiety that it brought with it out of my mind and get myself clean.

There were a couple of fresh bruises on my sides near the backs of my hips, and I was pretty sure they happened when Jack had pushed me into the kitchen cupboards at some point, but they didn't hurt.

The rest of my bruises were almost entirely gone, my body mostly healed again after everything Greg had done. There was just one patch on my side that still showed a faint mark, and the area under the skin was still a little tender. It was an improvement.

I hurried through my shower as quickly as I could, Jack bringing me a towel just as I was turning the jet of water off.

"I'll gather my things. How long do you need to get dressed and be ready to go?" he asked.

"Give me half an hour?" I replied, hoping that was enough time.

He nodded, but his gaze wandered again, and I could see him considering something else. Before he could reach for me, his phone started to buzz. Walking away from me, he answered it.

"Yeah, I know. She's up now," he said, his voice getting quieter as he moved farther away.

I dried myself as I listened to him tell whoever was on the other end of the phone not to worry and that there was still plenty of time.

Rushing the rest of the process, I quickly pulled my dressing gown on and grabbed my PJs. It was only as I practically ran back to the apartment he'd assigned me that I noticed the time. It was a little after eleven.

No wonder everyone was waiting for me, and he'd asked if I normally slept so much. It was an insane amount of time to have been late. We would be lucky to get half a day of my input into their process at this rate.

Feeling incredibly guilty and as if this was so unlike me, I tried to get dressed and brush my hair as swiftly as possible. It took me a moment to tame the strands, a large portion at the back tangled from all the screwing. And then, I quickly put on the most basic makeup in about three minutes flat.

When I saw that I'd only taken about twenty minutes in total to get ready, it made me grateful I wasn't one of those women who took ages to get ready because I couldn't leave the house without flawless skin or makeup.

I hurried back to Jack's apartment with my handbag to find him sitting on his sofa, drawing. As soon as he saw me, he put the pencil and paper down and grabbed his phone.

"Come on," he said. "The car's waiting for us already. We'll take the elevator."

I grinned as he did, not minding the subtle dig at my choice to take the stairs the day before.

A part of me felt like I was on cloud nine as we descended. Jack reached for my fingers and entwined them in his, and it only made me feel even better. He was claiming me in ways that made it easier to give in to the needs and desires he clearly had. I could just accept it and let him have what he wanted.

He'd blown my mind the night before, but every time I thought about it, I felt my cheeks heating up. I'd been so hungry for him to be inside me that it was all I could think about. His very touch made me react in ways I hadn't expected.

The elevator reached the bottom all too soon, but Jack didn't let go of me as he walked me out to the car, and we got inside. I noticed it was parked somewhere it shouldn't have been, but no one really said or did anything about it. I guessed it was easy not to worry about a parking ticket when the cost of one was the amount of money you earned in only a few minutes.

Once I was inside the back of the car again with Jack, he pulled me into his arms and kissed me. My eyes widened as I wondered what he intended to do with me. Was he going to screw me on the way to the studio?

No sooner had I thought this than he settled back and let me do the same beside him. A moment later, he pulled out his cell phone and sent a message to the rest of the band, letting them know we were on our way.

CHAPTER THIRTY-FIVE

Jack

I exhaled while we drove and focused on the guitar resting to one side of me. I picked it up, trying not to think about the gaze looking my way. Juno was under my skin, there was no doubt about it. After bedding her the way I had, I'd partially hoped she wouldn't be anymore.

But I kept thinking about Hunter and Ella in her books and how they'd developed this interesting dominant and submissive relationship, and it called to me like some kind of siren song.

I wanted her. To claim her the way Hunter did Ella. But I couldn't shake this unease I felt at the same time. Was I being a fool to think she wanted this, too?

More than once, she'd said Ella was based on her, but it was a book. Fiction. Did she truly want a relationship like that? Did I?

I kept coming back to these thoughts, but I didn't have answers to many of them. Not yet.

For now, I tried to switch off my mind. Tried not to worry about what might be.

I had to start trusting someone again sometime. Maybe if she wanted to be the Ella to my Hunter, it would mean I was always in charge. Always in control. What I said would happen and nothing else.

Just the thought of being able to have her sweet body whenever I wanted made my cock harden, but I knew it wasn't that simple.

I lived in New York most of the year and on my island in the Bahamas for the rest. She lived in the UK. But as a writer, she could move anywhere, couldn't she?

"You're deep in thought," she said, looking at me. "You keep frowning, and your grip is getting tighter."

She lifted her hand, her fingers entwined in mine. Immediately, I loosened my grip. I hadn't even realized I was hurting her.

"Sorry," I said.

"What's bothering you?" Her wide eyes looked up at me, searching my face, a hint of worry making her bite the edge of her lip. Without thinking, I let go of the guitar, leaned in, and kissed her, wanting the anxiety to leave her face and unable to think of another good way to reassure her.

I wrapped my arms around her and pulled her closer, the worried thoughts leaving my head as I tried to make her feel better, too. While she was in my arms, I didn't worry about anything anymore. She felt good. Right.

Slowly, she pulled back.

"Please...tell me what's worrying you. It's the second time you've suddenly looked like you might throw something or cry, and you're not sure which."

"It's complicated," I replied, knowing it was a copout.

"Life's complicated. Maybe we can simplify it together."

"You live a long way away. And I..." Words failed me, and I wasn't sure I even wanted to say everything I was thinking anyway. How did I tell her what was going through my head? I was sure at least some of it was too soon.

"Are you already asking if I'll move in with you?"

"No. Well, yes, but no. I mean. Not…" I panicked until I saw the smirk on her face.

"It's okay," she replied. "It's just occurred to you, and you have no idea how it will actually play out, but it's still early days, and we aren't even at that bridge, let alone thinking about crossing it."

"Yeah." I ran my hand through my hair, grateful she'd put what I couldn't into words. "That."

"Well. Would you consider moving to another country for the right woman?" she asked.

I thought about the question and almost nodded, thinking anyone would for the right person, but then I thought about the band.

The right woman would know how much the Vampirates meant to me, but the kind of woman who'd be willing to follow me wherever I wanted to be career-wise should have me reciprocate that.

"It's complicated," I said and exhaled again.

"Because of the band and your friends and stuff," she replied as if she understood.

"Yeah. I think the right woman would be someone who came here. I just…can't."

She nodded and looked away, and immediately, I felt an ache in my chest. It was clear she didn't want to leave her home either. No doubt she must have many similar things she was tied to. It would be a sacrifice for either of us to move in with the other, and it wasn't going to happen.

Her fingers squeezed mine a moment later.

"I don't think we're there yet," she replied. "But don't assume it wouldn't work without asking me, okay?"

"Okay," I said, not sure how else to respond.

It hadn't been what I expected of her.

The pain inside me receded a little, helping me to think more rationally. She was right. We weren't there yet. This was just a great week with the band and her.

She was fun, a distraction, and it felt good to stick my cock in her. Anything after that didn't matter right now.

"Is the studio far?" she asked a moment later.

"No. We're almost there," I replied, wondering what else to say.

"Pity."

"You want to be in the car?"

"The last time I was alone in the car with you, and we had a decent journey ahead of us, I'm pretty sure you screwed me senseless," she replied, her eyes lighting up with an amused twinkle.

I laughed and pulled her closer to kiss her again.

"I'd love to bed you again, but it will have to wait until later."

"Then later can't get here soon enough," she replied, pressing her lips against mine again. I lost myself in the moment, the desire she was reciprocating making me more than a little turned on.

Taking a few deep, slow breaths, I pulled back. I couldn't show up at the studio with a hard cock, throbbing with the desire to be driven deep into her cunt.

She smirked again and gave me some space, and I almost pulled her back and fucked her anyway. Damn, she was so tempting.

Instead, I looked out the window, desperate to find something normal and mundane to focus on. A random person on the street, another car. Anything that would allow my mind to move to calmer subjects.

We'd only gone a few miles from the penthouse, but the journey had been a roller coaster ride of emotion. Everything with Juno was a roller coaster ride of emotion.

Thankfully, she didn't push me for anything more as we made our way to the studio, and the car pulled up by the sidewalk.

Unlike at the studio in London, there weren't any fans milling around here. We'd booked it so last minute that not even our most fanatical groupies had managed to figure out where we were going to be. There would probably be a few by the time we finished, but that would be hours away.

I led Juno out, keeping her hand in mine. Her soft, slender fingers felt good in mine, and they helped calm me. Something there for me to hold onto reminded me that she was there, I wasn't alone, and I could keep going.

Kai gave me a slightly exasperated look when he saw us coming in together, our fingers still entwined, but he said nothing, and neither did the rest of the band. I felt a stab of guilt. If I hadn't invited her in, then maybe we'd have been on time.

Immediately, I thought of the scared look on her face and how she'd tried to hide the umbrella in her hand. I thought of the bruises on her body and what I'd seen her ex attempting. If anything, she'd slept better because of me. No, I couldn't feel guilty for making her feel safe enough to finally sleep as much as she needed.

Thankfully, Juno seemed to sense the band's desire to get on and got stuck in, asking them what progress they'd made. For a moment, I could sit back and recover. It was time to be creative and trust her experience and the band's skill once more.

CHAPTER THIRTY-SIX

<u>**Juno**</u>

As the band packed up their instruments and finished up for the day, I sat on the nearest chair and waited for whatever was going to follow. I was exhausted. Happy but completely exhausted.

It felt good. Although I hadn't done much besides give my opinions on differences in riffs and melodies, I felt as if I was being given a window into a creative process so different from writing a story that I was honored and more than a little grateful.

On top of that, Jack had been a darling to me all day. I felt as if everything was perfect. A part of me wanted to take some kind of snapshot of it all, but I was aware any recording of what we were doing wouldn't capture how wonderful it truly was.

After Greg and the sudden outward physical abuse, I felt like my life was over. I'd dedicated years of my life to the home and life we'd made together. At first, I'd thought it had gone violent and toxic so quickly. I still didn't quite understand how I'd got from there to here.

If I looked back on when I'd last been happy, however, it had been several years earlier, with plenty of little red flags since. I'd had momentary bursts of excitement now and then, but nothing that came close to the contentment and satisfaction I felt right now, at the end of the day, with the Vampirates and their friends.

It was still strange to be included in all this, and I couldn't quite believe the string of events that had led me to meet Jack and then have him find out about the book I'd written.

"Come on, sweetheart," Jack said. "We're going to get some food and chill out this evening. We're making good progress, and I think we should all probably head to bed early tonight."

"Is that a promise?" I asked, keeping my voice quiet and grinning.

He smirked in response, clearly understanding what I was asking. A few seconds later, he wrapped his arms around me to give me a hug and leaned near my ear.

"You can bet it's a promise. I want to find out what it's like to be your dominant."

My eyes widened at his response, and my core flushed with heat and anticipation at what that might mean. I really liked the idea. More than I'd expected to. It had been a long time since I'd been in a dom-sub relationship, but Jack and his desire for one made me shudder with anticipation. Could it be exactly what I needed?

Before I could say anything else, Kai and Alma came our way.

"Come on, you two love birds. The rest of the band is already heading out. Apparently, we've drawn a bit of a crowd. Someone saw one of us coming in and then phoned to see if the studio was free. The receptionist didn't think to stay tight-lipped about who was here."

I blinked as Jack swore and sighed. With no idea what to expect, it made me nervous, but Jack let go of me only a moment later. Did he not want to be seen with me? He'd held my hand a few times in public, and people had been suspicious after I'd been at the same hotel as him, but no one had caught a picture of anything definite or made a clear connection.

Of course, my agent would be over the moon if they did. I was pretty sure he thought all publicity was good publicity. Yet another reason I'd kept Greg's abuse to myself.

Following on with the others, I let Kai lead the last of us out of the recording area and down the stairs to the front door. It was clear people were outside, some very loud women chanting the names of the band members and occasionally the band name. Suddenly tense and uneasy, I tried my best to keep up with Eve as she walked near the back of the group, Jack no longer at my side.

Jack and Kai's bodyguards stood on both sides of the door as Alma stepped to one side and let the band members through.

The bodyguards formed up around them, working as a group to get the band through the screaming and heaving crowds to the cars while we watched from inside, and before my eyes, Jack's car drove off, leaving me with Alma, Eve and a session drummer they'd pulled in to help with the recording.

"You look scared half to death," Alma said, slipping her arm through mine. "Don't worry. They'll disperse a bit now that the boys have gone. They're not anywhere near as interested in us. We'll give it a few minutes and head to the second car."

"Do you think we'll have to wait long?" Eve asked. "I'm starving, and they already look like they're slipping back a bit."

Not answering yet, Alma looked through the gap in the door and pursed her lips.

"They're getting less dense, but you know some of them can get a bit out of line if we go too soon, and there's not enough room to cut through."

"Out of line?" I asked, having not expected any of this and feeling more and more sick as we waited.

"Yeah, it varies. We're in a better part of New York, so it's not as bad as it can be, but sometimes we have to wait for the body-guards to return for us. The fans want the boys, and we're in the way. I don't get as much stick as I used to now that Kai and I have been together so long, but Eve and you are newer. They take a while to adjust to that."

I frowned even more. That sounded worse.

"I don't care about them. They're all talk, and they aren't the ones with the boys. We are," Eve replied. "It's just jealousy."

Alma shrugged, and Eve moved up beside her to look herself.

"Come on, let's go. It's not as bad at all."

Without another word or any warning, the two women swept into the crowd. Immediately, there were more shouts, and I felt my body tense up and my heart race. I couldn't move at first, watching the mob of mostly female fans react to the presence of Alma and Eve, and then some of them spotted me.

Alma looked back, already several feet between us and people closing the gap she'd created. The shouts brought the groups pressing back closer, and some of them mistook the fuss to be about more famous people and not just their partners.

"Come on, Juno," Alma called, reaching back for me although she kept moving forward.

It was the call I needed to get my feet moving. I locked my gaze on her as she followed Eve through the crowds, pretty much having to push through the crush.

I could feel my mind panicking, aware my breathing was already erratic and my body tense.

Just focus on Alma, I tried to tell myself, but a shout to one side almost made me flinch, and Alma continued to get farther ahead as I met the resistance of the mass of bodies.

It was almost painful, and I wobbled as someone pushed from one side.

"Who is this one with?" someone yelled near my ear. At the same time, they jabbed toward me, and I flinched. Continuing to push forward, I managed to keep my feet, but I was starting to get a tingling feeling in my temples, not enough oxygen getting into my body.

I could barely breathe, and for a moment, I didn't move,

swaying with the crowds. I couldn't see Alma at all, and I couldn't hear the road or any of the cars above the yelling and laughing near me.

Still, I knew I couldn't stay where I was, so I pushed forward.

"Is she with Jack?" someone else yelled.

"Nah, look at her. She's far too ugly for Jack. He's got standards."

"I dunno. She looks like that stan from the British talk show."

I almost froze, my vision blurring. They'd recognized me. Was that good or bad?

Taking one last step, I finally spotted Alma, the confident woman coming back for me and grabbing my hand.

Through the gap she'd created, she pulled me toward the car, and I practically fell into it.

"Paper bag. She's hyperventilating," Alma said as my vision started to darken.

CHAPTER THIRTY-SEVEN

"Breathe, Juno. You're safe now," I heard Alma say, a strong arm around my back as the car we were in started up and drove off.

"Damn, they were… I'm so sorry," Eve said. "I thought they'd be more chill than that."

"No point worrying about it now. We're through it. Come on, Juno. Count your breaths or something. Whatever helps you calm it down. You're through and in the car. Ain't no one going to hurt you. It was just some shouting and crowd movement."

Alma's words slowly got through to me. It had felt a lot worse than she was saying, but she was right. I needed to calm down.

Closing my eyes, I tried to think of anything else and focused only on taking slow, deep breaths before exhaling them steadily. It felt like it took forever, but I calmed, and my vision cleared.

I could still feel the prickle around my eyes that accompanied any form of panic attack, but I felt steadier as the car drove us off.

"I guess you don't like crowds," Alma said.

"No," I replied, not sure what else to say.

"Want to talk about it? Or pretend it didn't happen?"

I opened my mouth to confirm the latter, but I hesitated partway.

"I had something shit happen recently, and I'm still not over it. The crowds and all the shouting brought it back to me. I don't want to talk about that, but I'm not normally like this."

"Got it. We'll wait a little longer next time or ask Jack to leave Mick behind. The majority of the fans know not to get in his way." Alma patted my hand and offered me some painkillers from a bottle she pulled out of her purse.

I shook my head and exhaled. Inside, I was still incredibly shaken. What bothered me most now that I was calming, however, was how Jack had just walked out with the band and left me to cope on my own. Had he not even considered how scary that would have been for someone not used to it?

As we were driven to the restaurant, I felt myself getting angrier and angrier. Jack had told me he wanted to be a dominant in my life and then abandoned me the moment I could have used the protective presence he represented.

Alma and Eve started talking about something, neither of them making me join in but filling the silence so we didn't feel uncomfortable and awkward. I appreciated it and let myself become distracted by the talk about makeup and whether the color and style of Eve's eyeshadow and liner worked for her.

It was a safe subject, even if I knew less about it than they clearly did. Twenty minutes later, we were getting out of the car again. This time, only a few people waited out on the sidewalk for the band. The fact that there were already a few people made me feel instantly on edge again. Would there be more later?

Alma slipped her arm through mine and led me inside, flipping me a wink as the front door was opened for us by none other than Mick.

"They're up on the top floor already," he said as he let us through.

"Thank you, darling," she replied, smiling and patting his shoulder as she went past.

I was more than a little grateful she was around as she led me through one corner of the restaurant where normal people were dining, and waiters and waitresses scurried back and forth. A waiter looked as if he was going to come and stop me until he noticed Alma on my arm, and instead, he moved to a staff door and tapped in a code.

Opening it for us, he motioned to the stairs and smiled.

Alma once again greeted them by name, and then we were sweeping past, our shoes clattering on the stairs as we climbed to the third floor.

It opened across the whole building, a seating area with a few tables on the nearest side and then a pool table, some bar stools, and even a small dance floor and disco area on the other side.

The band were all sitting on stools and had drinks in hand. A waitress was already laying the table for the group and passing out menus.

I didn't stop Alma as we trooped over to join the men, feeling as if everyone's eyes were on us. Jack immediately took my other arm, and Alma gave me a quick squeeze before heading to Kai.

She glanced at Jack and then at me before she retreated, making it clear something had happened. I wasn't sure I was grateful for it, as he immediately studied me. I looked down, not sure how I felt yet but worried I was too angry to talk about it rationally.

"Did something happen?" he asked. "Are you okay?"

While he spoke, he guided me over to some seats a little more out of the way, and I felt even more glances coming our way. I looked back over to see Alma talking quietly to Kai. Was she telling him what had just happened? Would they think I was a total flake?

I sighed and looked away again. Immediately, I felt silly. They were used to the fans.

"Juno?" Jack asked again. "What happened?"

"It was just the crowds," I said. "They stuck around for a while after you left, and I wasn't expecting it. Took me by surprise, and I got separated from Alma and Eve."

Jack frowned but didn't say anything, so I felt like I had to explain further, my anger already gone and leaving nothing but embarrassment at my reaction.

"Alma said waiting meant they were usually easier to get through, but Eve thought we'd be fine. I froze, and…it's all fine now. Just wasn't prepared for it. I'll know what to expect next time, and I'll make sure I keep with the others."

"I'll let Eve know to be more careful," Jack said as he got up again. I immediately grabbed his arm.

"No. It's okay. It wasn't her fault. I… After… The shouting made me freeze up. It won't be so bad another time."

Jack slipped his arms around me and pulled me up and into a hug. Almost immediately, I felt like I might cry, his strong arms making me feel safer instantly. I fought back the emotion, not wanting to be so vulnerable in front of the rest of the group.

"I'm sorry," he said as he pulled back and saw the emotion I was battling. "I'm so used to everyone coping with the fans. I didn't even…"

"It's okay," I replied. "Really. Just…"

"What?"

"I don't know. I guess I'm tired of having scary things happen. Of feeling scared. Of not coping very well with it."

Jack exhaled and sat back down again, bringing me down beside him.

"It's understandable. And if you want to talk about it, we can later." As he spoke, he reached up and tucked a stray lock of hair behind my ear. "I'm sorry it was so scary, and you weren't ready for it."

My anger melted under the tender apology, but I still found myself biting my lip and feeling less secure than before. Were we really a good match for each other? Or was I completely out of my depth?

CHAPTER THIRTY-EIGHT

<u>Jack</u>

I watched Juno as she chatted with Alma and Eve. Dinner was done, and everyone was chilling. They were talking about going shopping together after they'd discovered Juno didn't have something they thought she should have.

All through dinner, I'd been tense, aware she didn't seem herself, more subdued. I got the impression she'd not told me everything about what had happened earlier and was trying to put some kind of brave face on it.

"You're not yourself," Kai said as he plonked down beside me. "What's got you so serious?"

"I keep wondering if I'm screwing this up," I replied without hesitating.

"Screwing it up? Already? I'm pretty sure it hasn't even been twenty-four hours yet. You can't be doing that badly." Kai smiled at me, and I couldn't help but smirk back.

It was obvious I'd bedded her last night, and I appreciated him not being obvious about it. It didn't make it any easier to figure Juno out, however.

"Alma said she panicked in the crowd and seemed to react

badly to all the shouting." Kai glanced my way as he spoke. "Wasn't used to it like some of the other girls around us."

"Yeah, I should have known she would. She's a tough cookie in some respects, but she's been through a lot. I feel like I should have hung back and made sure she was okay. Or at least have left Mick behind to help her."

"So say sorry to her and make sure you do better when we leave here tonight. Looks like there's a bunch gathering outside now."

I sighed. Most of the time, I was used to being famous and everything it came with, but on nights like tonight, I just wished I was a normal person out for dinner in a normal way. It sucked to always have to rush from one place to the next.

Before I could dwell on it for too long, Alma came over.

"I'm exhausted, and I think you all probably need a bit more sleep before tomorrow. We should get ready to go," she said.

"You're right, my dear. As always." Kai finished his drink and gave me a pointed look. It was still a little early, but the look in Alma's eyes made it clear she wanted to take her man home for more than just some sleep.

I grinned to myself as they walked away. They'd been together a long time, but it was great to see them still very much in love with each other.

Wishing I'd found myself someone as steady and devoted as Alma, I also got to my feet and finished my drink. Almost as if she'd sensed the change in mood, Juno was by my side before I could put the glass down, her jacket in her hands.

"Time to go," I said as I put my own jacket on.

"Eve said there's a crowd outside again," she replied as she copied my actions.

I almost winced at the hint of fear in her voice, the pitch just a fraction higher. I was an idiot for not knowing how frightened she would be. It had scared me the first few times, and I still didn't like it or feel comfortable with it after all this time.

I pulled her into a hug immediately and lifted her chin until our eyes met.

"It'll be all right this time. I promise. Mick and Gary are going to take us both out together, and I'm going to be right behind you, guiding you after Mick."

She nodded, her eyes wide but her jaw setting in determination.

"That's my girl," I said, slipping back but keeping a good grip on her hands.

I didn't let go of her as we made our way back down the stairs and waited by the staff door. A waiter came through only a few seconds later and opened the door for us.

Leading Juno through the restaurant, I got Mick's attention, the bodyguard having come in. He lingered by the door, Gary coming in after helping Kai and Alma to their car.

"Just a moment, boss. They're still bringing your car around," Mick said, moving his fingers to an earpiece as if he was also being talked to.

I nodded and shifted Juno so she stood in front of me.

"We're going out together," I said a moment later, discussing with Mick and Gary how best to do it.

They both agreed that having her right after Mick would be best, and then Gary right after me. Gary tried to suggest getting one of Ed's bodyguards to go between Juno and me, but I refused and wrapped my arms tighter around her waist.

"We're going together," I reiterated, making sure my voice was as determined as I felt.

The guards nodded, and then Mick gave the go-ahead.

A waitress came up to open the door for us, and then, before Juno could freeze again, I gently nudged her toward the door after Mick. The bodyguard didn't lean back for her, but he was built with a wide enough frame that he'd naturally clear a space for her to follow, and I'd be forcing it to stay clear as I came up right behind her.

The crowds screamed my name as we emerged, but Juno kept going, her body shaking against me but taking hurried steps and pushing through as we did.

Thankfully, the fans weren't quite so pushy, and the sidewalk wasn't as wide, so we were soon through, the driver already standing by the open door. Juno ducked under his arm and slipped into the car, and I easily followed.

Immediately, I went to her side and pulled her into a hug again. Her breathing was rapid, and she continued to shake, but she was otherwise okay.

She leaned into me, but it was clear she was trying to pull herself together.

"You can be scared," I said. "It's not a pleasant experience."

"I know," she replied, not looking at me. "But it shouldn't be quite this bad."

"You've been through a lot, but I'd like to make you feel safer. If you'll let me. I want…"

"To be my dominant," she finished for me.

"Yes. I think. I still don't understand everything it means. You make me feel protective of you. As if I want to claim you and keep you safe."

She took a few more slow, gentle breaths and slid a little closer so she was more upright.

"The dominants and submissives I usually write about, and Hunter and Ella, are all about being there for each other. Love and acceptance, protection and obedience. Trust and safety."

"Is that what you want?" I asked, a part of me barely daring to breathe as I asked it.

"I think so. I… In the stories, it's simpler in so many ways, but the submissive wants to please her dom. She wants to make him happy and meet his needs. And she often doesn't want to make all the decisions. Some only want that in the bedroom, others want it in every area of life."

"And what does the dom want?" I had some ideas, but I wanted to hear her opinion.

"To feel in control. To protect. The dom practically worships the ground the submissive walks on as much as she endeavors to give him everything he wants and needs and to please him. And then the dom rewards the sub for doing a good job. Some punish submissives for behavior they don't want, but I think I like that less." Juno lowered her gaze again, and I quickly lifted her chin back up.

"So the dom feels in control and has his needs and desires met, and the sub is kept safe and happy, the dom taking care of her."

"Mostly. It's a little more complicated, but that's the basic premise. In a lot of ways, they're just words used to describe a relationship where one partner does most of the decision-making and provides safe boundaries for the other to be themselves. And in return, they can expect to enjoy that control."

As she spoke, my cock hardened.

That was exactly what I wanted.

CHAPTER THIRTY-NINE

<u>Juno</u>

I felt my body calm far quicker than it had after my first run through the crowds, Jack's arms wrapped tightly around me. I could feel his eyes on me, and the bulge in his pants had made it clear he liked the description I'd given him of a typical dom-sub relationship.

He was staring at me, and I could feel him studying me, but he hadn't spoken, and I didn't want to break the silence. The idea of submitting to him so completely made me more than a little hot, too. I imagined him telling me I'd been a good girl. That I'd pleased him with my obedience, and I grew wetter as I did.

Slowly, his hand shifted from propping up my chin as he tried to get me to look at him to gripping it more tightly.

"Look at me," he said, his voice husky.

I exhaled, the change in his tone both making me a little frightened and burning with desire. Doing as he bid, I met his gaze. There was a fierce hunger in his eyes, the way a wolf might look at their prey before they devoured them. And I was caught in his embrace, one arm tight around me and the other holding my head in place.

"You belong to me now," he said.

I gulped but didn't refuse.

"You're going to submit to me, and I'm going to take care of you."

With that, he plunged his mouth down on mine, his actions following his words as if they cemented them in our minds.

I yielded to him, my body hot and hungry to be his in so many ways. My heart raced in my chest, and my skin tingled where he brushed against it.

Every inch of me wanted to be his, and I wasn't going to get in the way.

Somehow he managed to keep himself at bay, doing nothing more than passionately kissing me until the car pulled up outside his apartment block. He grabbed my hand and pulled me out of the car behind him, then strode toward the front door, not even softening his grip.

I went eagerly after him, wanting him to know I was as willing as possible.

The wait for the elevator seemed to drag out, every second almost torture that made me glance toward the stairs. Despite the desire to run up them, I kept my mouth shut and waited by his side.

With the night late enough that the building was quiet, and the band returning in staggered groups, we were the only ones in the elevator. The second the doors were closed, Jack pushed me up against the back wall, lifting my hands above my head and pinning me in place.

One hand cupped a breast, rubbing across my nipple and making me moan into the mouth that claimed mine once again.

Heat flushed through me, running deep until I was wet and involuntarily squeezing my legs around the thigh he'd jammed between them.

We stayed like that until the elevator dinged to let us know we were at the top. Immediately, he pulled back, but he didn't let go of my wrist. Striding like a wolf on the prowl, he headed straight for his apartment and fished out the keys.

He opened the door with practiced ease and only turned to shut it behind me.

Without another word, he led me to the bedroom and swept me off my feet and onto the bed, pushing me forward. Before I could move or turn, he reached for my pants and pulled them off.

I managed to get my hands underneath me before my panties followed. It pulled my legs out from underneath me, and then he was over me, pinning me beneath him.

Pushing my legs wide, he moved between them, and then he grabbed a pillow. Before I could ask what he intended to do with it, he slid a hand underneath my stomach and lifted off me enough to pull the pillow through the gap sideways and underneath me.

Anticipating what was to come, I grew even wetter, my own juices reaching my thighs. I wanted him, but I didn't dare speak, his strong body still keeping me beneath him, even if I hadn't asked for this.

I heard rather than saw the jangle of his belt buckle and the zipper that followed, and a moment later, I felt his throbbing cock near my entrance. He groaned as he pushed me down even farther and my legs even wider.

With no more warning, he drove himself hard and deep into me. I gasped, the sting and pleasure of his hardness everything I'd hoped it would be. He stilled for a moment before reaching forward, grabbing my hair, and pulling my head back.

At the same time, he brought his mouth to my ear. I couldn't move, trapped against him.

"I'm going to fuck you now," he whispered.

I mewled in response, trying to shift, to encourage him to thrust into me, but he remained still, deep inside.

"Lie still and take your fucking, kitten," he commanded, almost growling the last word.

Instantly, I fought to obey and give him what he wanted, but I was hungry for him, and it wasn't easy. Moving agonizingly slowly, he pulled back out of me, going almost all the way before he paused. With no warning, he drove deep again, making me gasp.

After letting out a short chuckle, he did it again and again.

I closed my eyes, my body enjoying every moment of the dominant way he was claiming me, giving myself over to him entirely and letting him pleasure us both.

With every thrust, Jack brought us both closer to our peak and made me his a little bit more. I let out a deep moan as I fell into heaven, and only a few seconds later, he joined me, impaling me and filling me with his cum.

As he came down, he shifted to the side, wrapping me in his arms and pulling me close against his chest. We cooled together, and at some point, he swept the covers around us.

Neither of us fell asleep, but we didn't speak, nothing left to say. In his arms I felt safe and warm, wanted and cared for. It was one of those perfect moments when the world feels right, and you never want it to end.

Occasionally, we kissed, or he stroked my cheek. It was perfect.

Eventually, he pressed his mouth against mine a little more firmly.

"We should sleep," he said. "As much as I don't want today to end, we need to be fresh tomorrow, or Kai will never forgive me."

"I'm sure he would forgive you, but I'll behave and do as I'm told," I replied, smirking.

"I should hope so," Jack said with a little growl before rolling back slightly.

I snuggled into him more but finally closed my eyes and let sleep steal over me.

CHAPTER FORTY

Once again, Jack was gone from the bed when I woke up, but I could hear the shower running. Grinning, I slipped out of the bed and padded over to the bathroom.

The door was unlocked, so I slid inside, making as little noise as possible. A moment later, I was stepping into the shower as well, reaching for Jack. The second he noticed me, he roamed his gaze over me and reached to pull me under the spray, too.

Hot spray hit me, making me gasp.

"Sorry," he said. "I like it really hot. Want me to turn it down a bit?"

"No, it's okay," I replied. "I like it that hot, too. It's… There's something about knowing you're clean when you get out."

A look of understanding passed between us. We both knew what drove the need to feel that clean, and neither of us had to speak of it.

Moving closer to him, I ran my hands up his smooth chest, feeling the contours of his muscles. I wanted to do more, but I wasn't sure I dared initiate something like that without some kind of signal from him that it was okay.

A moment later, he grabbed the sponge and turned back to me.

"Hold still," he said, the corner of his mouth twitching up.

I exhaled with anticipation as he ran it over my shoulders and down my arms and slowly cleaned me, starting with my limbs. He then took an extra-long time to wash my torso, being careful with my most sensitive areas.

As he finished, I reached to take the sponge and return the offer, but he stayed my hand.

"Although I like the idea, I'm already clean, and I'm supposed to be taking care of my little submissive, remember?" he said. "Time for us to get dressed. I'll screw you more later."

I couldn't speak, part of me wishing it was already later and another part excited about getting involved in more of the band's process. However, I wasn't going to argue with anything Jack said.

We quickly toweled dry and got dressed before Jack took my hand and offered to pick us up some breakfast on the way.

There was no argument from me. Breakfast sounded great, and I was as eager to get back in the studio again as I was to spend more time with Jack.

Although I almost didn't come to New York at all, I was extremely grateful that my agent had accepted the arrangement for me. Of course, if I'd really wanted to refuse, I was sure he'd have let me. But it was harder to argue for not doing something when a plan was already made.

As we stepped out of the main door of the apartment block, Mick and Gerry appeared immediately, and the car pulled up by the sidewalk. Before we could get inside, some men came up carrying large cameras. They quickly snapped shots of me and Jack, his arm around me as we walked to the car.

Immediately Jack growled and sped up. I tried not to react, surprised more than anything else. He quickly bundled me into the car and followed before the car door was shut behind us.

Mick and Gerry got in the front, and then we were off. A moment later, Jack ran his hands through his hair and swore.

"Were they paparazzi?" I asked a moment later.

"Yes. Within hours, those pictures will be all over the internet and in magazines and…" He sighed and shook his head as he trailed off, his hands bunched into fists.

Instantly, I reached for him and tried to help calm him, fear making my words catch in my throat. I couldn't cope with the anger. It was too similar to how Greg had been before he'd eventually taken it out on me.

Jack pulled out of my grasp and shook his head before sliding farther away on the back bench.

I gulped and felt myself shrinking back as well. This wasn't how I'd imagined everything to go. We rode in silence, me not daring to say anything and Jack so angry he was clearly fighting to calm himself down.

Every bit of my body tensed up until my muscles ached, and I was relieved when the car stopped at the side of the road in front of a small diner. I shifted instinctively, expecting us all to get out, but Mick was the only one who did, never opening the door but heading into the diner for us.

I lifted an eyebrow but otherwise didn't move. What was I meant to do? Was Mick fetching us breakfast? Once again, I considered reaching out to Jack, but he was still rigid and staring out the window.

Mick came back out again a minute or so later with a box in his hands. Instead of opening the car door at the back and handing it to Jack, he got in the front, and they lowered the partition.

At first, neither Jack nor I moved, and I looked between the two men, not sure if I should take the box off Mick and rescue him or wait for Jack to do so.

"Want me to keep hold of it until you're at the studio, boss?" Mick asked.

Jack frowned but shook his head and finally shifted to take it off him. I felt myself relax as I exhaled a little, and Jack brought the box back to the section of the car we were in. He dropped it on the seat as Mick gave us our privacy back.

"Dig in. I'm not feeling hungry right now, but you should eat. It's going to be a long day."

"You should probably eat too," I said, gently reaching for the box but not opening it yet. I tried to keep my voice even, but I wasn't sure I'd done a good job.

"No. I'll eat later. I'll be fine." Once again, he turned away from me.

For a moment, I couldn't move. I felt trapped, as if at any moment I could do the wrong thing. As if by not eating at all, he could be aggressive and angry at me for wasting it, and if I did eat, I would potentially face his wrath for doing so without him and being insensitive.

In the end, I chose to try and eat a little, even if I couldn't stomach a lot with the bad atmosphere. I didn't entirely understand Jack's reaction when I'd been seen with him a few times already.

Had it been how much closer we'd appeared? Was it the way it had taken him by surprise? I had no idea, but I tucked into one of the gluten-free breakfast biscuits in the bag and tried to think of something to break the silence.

I was still struggling when we pulled up outside the studio, however.

There were already fans there, although not as many as the evening before, and I froze, only just having finished eating. Jack looked my way, holding out his hand to take mine, but then he saw my face.

"Do you want to wait to go in and get Mick to guide you?" Jack asked as he leaned over and picked up a napkin. He wiped the edge of my mouth and gave me a brief look-over.

"I think I'd rather come with you if that's okay?" I replied, grateful he was being civil even if he wasn't in a great mood.

Without hesitation, he grasped my hand and entwined our fingers. I grabbed the breakfast box, grateful I'd had the sense to close it back up again, and held it between us, cradled against me. It provided something for me to focus on and helped me ignore the crowds as Jack, Mick, and Gerry formed a group and carved a path through the band's screaming horde of fans.

I didn't relax until I was inside, and the door was shut behind us.

I'd made it through the crowds yet again, and it hadn't been so bad it gave me a panic attack.

CHAPTER FORTY-ONE

<u>Jack</u>

I tried not to let the anger inside me show as we walked deeper into the studio. Sometimes, I just wanted the chance to get to know someone and explore a relationship without it being plastered all over the news. I didn't always get that luxury, however.

Sighing, I led Juno deeper, noticing she'd brought breakfast with her. I was glad she was eating, even though I didn't feel like it anymore. At least she wasn't being stubborn or crazy or anything else I didn't have the capacity for.

Thankfully, the rest of the band was there, although it looked like most of them had only just arrived, and I didn't get any extra glares from Kai this time.

Within minutes, we were at work, and I could focus on the music and guitar and forget about the paparazzi and the way they hounded everything I did. Once again, Juno was a sweetheart, providing encouragement and ideas if we needed them without getting attached to anything.

It was a relief that she seemed to have her head screwed on, but I still didn't feel entirely at ease. My heart had betrayed me in the past, falling for someone who wasn't real and had appeared to be something far better than the truth had revealed.

Shuddering, I tried to push that thought away as well. I didn't need to dwell on gold-digging ex-partners. I wanted to be in the here and now, making good music and enjoying the company.

Only Alma had come to the studio today out of the band's partners, but she kept Juno company while we laid down a few more parts of the song and tweaked a few others. We discussed a lot, and the two women bore it admirably, letting us interrupt them and then going back to their own conversations without a pause as if the two were facets of the same conversation.

I felt myself relax as the day went by, and then we all sat around to listen to what was a pretty decent raw recording. It would need some tweaks in post, and the mastering would need to polish off some rough edges, but by the time the day was over, we had a track.

"Wow," Juno said a little while later, her hand in mine again. "I can't believe it's all done on our part. It's amazing."

I looked at her, seeing the delighted light in her eyes. She looked like a kid on Christmas morning.

"It was a good session. We've laid it down quicker than we allowed for. Gives us a couple of days together. I mean...if you want to stay in New York now that it's done."

She smiled and looked up at me.

"I'd love to stay longer if you'll have me. I mean, I'm not needed anywhere and..." She trailed off, not saying something that was clearly on her mind.

I almost blurted out right then and there that I wanted her to stay permanently, but I couldn't bring myself to do it. It was too soon. Had that been what she'd also held back on? Or was there something else?

She'd only offered to stay a little longer, not for a long time.

Did that mean she planned to go after we'd had some fun? Or that she wanted to see how things went?

"Come on, let's celebrate a job well done," Kai said. "Back to my place. We'll invite the usuals and have some actual fun."

"I hope you'll also get someone else in to clean up after it all," Alma replied. "The last time everyone came to our place to celebrate, we had to replace the carpets in the dining room and the studio."

"This song'll pay for it, I'm sure," Kai replied.

There were chuckles all around, and then Alma looked at me.

"Welcome to the celebrity life, where you spend money you don't have yet and hope the creative stuff you just crapped out makes enough to pay for it." She rolled her eyes as she spoke and grinned, but Juno blinked in shock, only making everyone else laugh.

"Don't mind Alma. She doesn't really think the song is crap," Kai said a moment later. "Just that I'm not careful enough with money."

"No, to be fair, this one definitely isn't crap. Juno's made sure of that." Alma slipped her arm through Juno's and started leading her away. "Come on, love, let's go get an overnight bag for you and get there early to get ready. You can even tell that agent of yours to get the paperwork ready to sign and finalize with a writer credit for you. Don't you let these boys stiff you for your fair share of the readies it makes."

Juno glanced my way, and I frowned at the advice Alma had just given her. We hadn't discussed exactly what role Juno would be credited with. Had she been expecting a full writing credit and everything that came with it?

Before I could say anything or think more about it, Kai was handing me my guitar so we could pack up the rest of our gear and leave as well.

"What did you actually say to her agent?" I asked Kai a short while later when I was sure the rest of the band wouldn't hear.

"That we wanted her to come help us write a song about one of her books and that she already knew what song and what book because you'd told her."

"Nothing about money?"

"Not directly. I told him we usually attributed the exact credits and union standard royalties after, and that if she was okay with that, to come to New York. Told him we'd cover costs if nothing else." Kai continued to clean up, and I helped, hoping Alma wasn't making Juno think she could earn tons from the song.

While songs could earn a decent amount, there had been at least six people involved in the writing, and she hadn't played a major part. In this instance, she was unlikely to even have her name down as being credited. If she did, it would only go against the lyrics.

Had she expected more?

"Come on, man, you don't need to worry about it. I'm sure her agents explained it to her, and she appears to have her head screwed on straight. If we have a problem, we'll deal with it when it happens," Kai said a moment later.

I exhaled and nodded. He had a good point. There was no big sign trouble was coming, and I didn't need to try and find some. For now, I just needed to focus on getting to know Juno and enjoying the way she submitted to me whenever I demanded.

With all the instruments gathered and taken down to the van, Mick and Gerry helping to load, the band was finally ready to leave. We all headed for one car, none of us heading back to the apartment. I'd already had my PA pick up the things I needed, and Juno would have gotten everything she wanted with Alma.

Settling into the car, Kai broke out the snacks and sodas, and I sat back and tried not to think about it all. It was an hour or so to get to Kai and Alma's place out in the suburbs, but it would be worth it to chill out somewhere big enough for all of us and a few friends.

As we drove along, I found myself thinking about all the people who would be there and how Juno would react. I was pretty sure they'd like her—everyone seemed to—but I was curious what she'd think of some of them, too.

It made me feel a little more relaxed. I could handle this.

CHAPTER FORTY-TWO

<u>**Juno**</u>

Feeling both apprehensive and excited, I rode with Alma toward her main home. We had picked up Eve as well. She'd been to the spa, and then clothes shopping, and part of me wondered what it was like going to the more expensive places, but I'd enjoyed the day I'd had anyway.

We'd stopped by the apartment so I could stuff a change of clothes and my toothbrush in a bag, and then we'd made our way out again, grabbing more food along the way.

Alma seemed in high spirits, and she carried the majority of the conversation, telling us stories of old parties and some of the things the band had gotten up to while on tours.

It sounded like most of them got to be big children and live an amazing life, but they also took care of each other like some kind of slightly dysfunctional nomadic family.

On top of that, Alma made all the locations they'd visited sound so glamorous. I was seriously envious.

"I need to travel more," I said with a sigh.

Eve nodded, and Alma chuckled.

"It's not all glitter and fun, but it beats being stuck in one place all the time." Alma patted my hand, and then Eve changed the subject, moving it on before I could ask anything else about where to go and places to avoid.

Although the journey passed quickly, and I felt like I was making some new friends, even if we were in different worlds, I worried about how things were going with Jack. He'd been lovely to me in every way, but I still didn't feel at home in his world, and his declaration that he wanted me to submit to him and become his submissive kept coming back to mind.

Most of me was fine with the idea, excited even, curious, and a whole heap of other positive feelings and emotions, but a part of me was terrified. What if I was just getting into bed with another Greg? Someone who made me feel great sometimes but who secretly just wanted me around to make themselves feel good. How would Jack react if I continued to grow more successful?

It was a question I knew would always be at the back of my mind, and I'd have to either trust and let it go or pull back and not take the risk at all.

I also couldn't decide exactly how I felt about the sleeping arrangements. It appeared the band was used to sleeping wherever, no one attached to a particular location and everyone traveling whenever needed. I was used to a single home and being there all the time, but I was also used to the safety of that home.

When Greg took his fists to me, the first thing I did was go and find somewhere else to live, somewhere he didn't know about. And in the short time since, I'd done everything I could to make it feel safe.

Now, here I was, having almost slept one night in an apartment Jack owned and then the rest of that night and another in Jack's apartment with him. I hadn't been too worried because I'd been able to run away to the other apartment if I needed to. Or I felt like I could, anyway.

Tonight, I would be sleeping in Kai's house, and it seemed everyone else would be as well.

The whole thing had been decided around me without anyone asking me if I was all right with that, and I didn't feel as if I could easily say I objected. Not without potentially excluding Jack from the fun if he wanted to spend time with me.

I felt torn but helpless, and my stomach was twisting itself in knots the more I thought about it. It wasn't necessarily Jack's fault, and there was no indication that anything dangerous could happen to me, but I was putting a lot of trust in people I didn't know well.

Without thinking, I reached for my phone and messaged a friend, asking them how they were doing and telling them I was still alive.

It was possibly a little rude while in a car with others, but I felt the overwhelming need to tell someone else where I was going and what I was doing so if anything happened to me, they'd know where I had been last.

Part of me wanted to laugh at my level of paranoia, but I was a writer. My imagination was overactive. It was one of the reasons I could write stories for a living in the first place.

Trying not to worry, I put my phone away again and focused on Alma and Eve's conversation until the driver took us into the New York suburbs. Eventually, we ended up down a small road full of large wooden houses. They were gorgeously maintained, and they all had large, gated driveways. The central one at the end of the road swung open for us as we arrived.

We were still getting out of the car, and Alma was pointing out that she and Kai owned the houses on either side, as well as the two behind, when another car pulled up.

Assuming these were the houses Jack had told me about, I marveled at them. It must have cost an extraordinary amount of money to do something like that, and I found it hard to imagine spending so much on houses just because I could.

Of course, I'd never had that much money before.

"And who've we got here?" a voice said behind me, a Southern twang to the words. I whirled to see a guy striding up wearing jeans, cowboy-style boots, and a flannel shirt.

He looked me over, not even trying to be subtle about it.

"This is Juno. Jack's sweet on her, and she helped write the most recent song," Alma said as she came closer to my side and looped her arm around mine almost possessively.

"Of course Jack's sweet on her. He always gets to the hot ones first."

"I'm also standing right here," I snapped back, instantly taking a dislike to whoever this was.

Alma grinned and squeezed my arm.

"That you are, my dear. Forgive my rudeness." He took his hat off and flicked his eyes down to my chest for a second time. "I'm Logan, and I'm an old friend of the band's."

"As I already said, this is Juno," Alma said for me as I tried to decide whether I should be glaring at this man a while longer. "And you had better be nice to her. Kai and I like her, and we want her to stick around. Got it?"

"Of course, my gorgeous hostess. Your house, your rules. I'll behave and do what I usually do, enjoy the view."

Alma rolled her eyes, turned, and walked me toward the house. I tried not to show how I felt on the outside, but although Logan hadn't so much as touched me, I felt as if someone had covered me in a layer of slime.

"Don't mind him too much," she said once we were in the hallway of the house and temporarily alone. "He's terrified of Jack and won't touch you while you're with him."

I exhaled and nodded, still not sure I trusted my voice. The knot in my stomach grew tighter, and I found myself longing for Jack and the safety he appeared to now represent.

CHAPTER FORTY-THREE

It was another hour before Jack and the rest of the band appeared, having made several stops on the way and also gotten changed. By then, the house was full of people, none of whom I knew. Although Alma had introduced me to many of them, and some had been polite, the reactions I'd received had been mixed.

There were clearly a few people who didn't like something about me and didn't have a problem showing it. Since Alma was busy hosting, I started to feel like the uncool kid who gets invited to the party in high school just to be obviously ignored—or worse, bullied—by all the much cooler and more expensively dressed people.

Already, I was trying to think of excuses to leave and go somewhere else. I considered pretending to be sick or actually making myself sick, but somehow, I held out, desperately hoping that when Jack arrived, everything would be better.

When his car first pulled up, there seemed to be a movement of people in the house toward the front. I found myself near the back, unable to get any closer. I tried not to let it get to me, but on top of everything else, it was almost too much.

To make matters worse, everyone seemed to want to talk to the band on their way past. Twenty minutes later, Jack was still lost in the throng somewhere, and I was still standing in the kitchen with a drink in one hand and no one to talk to.

I was trying to psych up the courage to push through to Jack when Logan appeared, coming to get a refill.

"Juno, what's got your pretty face out here?" he said, striding over to me with a fresh beer bottle in his hand. I immediately tried to walk past him, but he blocked my path and put his arm out to wrap around my waist.

Backing up, I tried to move around, but he followed and maneuvered me against the kitchen counter, then stood in front of me.

"Get out of my way. I'm going to find Jack," I said immediately, trying to sound more confident than I felt.

"If you were going to Jack, you'd have done it already. We both know he's been here half an hour or more and hasn't even tried to come find you." Logan reached out and tried to stroke my hair.

I flinched back and tried to move away again, but his grip on my waist only tightened.

"You know, I don't think he's as sweet on you as Alma reckons. Not surprised he tried to get into your pants. You've got a good shape, and those big eyes of yours can draw a man in, but come on. Why don't you come have some fun with me?"

"No. I'd like to go find Jack now. Let me go." I spoke more firmly, holding his gaze and tensing so I didn't shudder. I was starting to feel sick.

"Come on, now. I know we don't know each other very well yet, but we both know you must be willing to get it on with someone you've just met, or Jack wouldn't have—"

"I said no. I mean it," I hissed, pushing back at him and fighting to get away.

His grip only tightened, but he didn't say anything. I was trapped, and we both knew it.

A moment later, Jack walked in. I froze, and Logan looked his way.

Jack strode up to us.

"Let her go. She's with me."

"Doesn't look like it. She was in here by herself and making eyes at—"

"She's with me. Don't make me say it again," Jack replied, his voice lower and darker, his fists beginning to clench. For a moment, I didn't think Logan was going to move. I couldn't speak, my heart racing, pretty sure Jack's anger was about to be turned on me as well.

I exhaled with at least some relief when Logan finally unhooked his arm from my waist and backed up. Both Jack and I watched him walk out.

When he'd left, Jack looked right at me.

"I'm… That wasn't. I didn't…" I trailed off, the words refusing to come out as Jack relaxed.

"It's okay, Juno. We all know what he's like. Alma let me know he'd taken an interest in you just now. I came to find you as soon as I realized neither of you were nearby."

I nodded and took a deep breath, looking away from him as I did. He moved away, getting himself a drink, and I noticed he didn't go for a soda as he normally would. Instead, he picked up a beer and took a large gulp.

Shivering, I wrapped my arms around myself, still feeling a sick knot in my stomach. I had so many things I wanted to say.

"It took you a while to come find me. You've been here at least half an hour," I said, my voice coming out whinier than I'd wanted it to. I was scared, but it wasn't his fault.

He took another gulp as he fixed his gaze on me.

"You could have come to find me as well. I assumed you were somewhere talking or whatever. Were you really in here alone?"

"Yeah," I replied, looking away again, feeling like a complete idiot. I was the loser girlfriend who didn't fit in, and I'd just proved it.

Jack walked closer, his booted feet pounding a rhythm I couldn't ignore until he was standing right in front of me. He put a finger under my chin and lifted it, so I had to look at him.

"You're not having fun?" he asked.

I shrugged.

"That's not an answer."

"I don't know. I really like Alma, but I don't know anyone else, and not everyone seems to want to get to know me. You took a lot longer to get here than I expected, and..." I trailed off as I tried to stem the flow before I started to feel too deeply and cry. My emotions were still on edge after everything Logan had done.

"I'm here now," he said, putting his arms around me. "And I won't let Logan anywhere near you."

"Thank you," I replied, leaning into him. "He's a complete douche-canoe."

"Yeah. But he does a lot for the band. He sucks with women, but he gets how to promote us and market us like no one else I know. And we have to keep him at least mostly happy." Jack spoke quietly, as if he was almost ashamed of it. I got the impression he'd change it if he felt like he could.

"Alma tried to warn him off. Tell him I was yours, but I guess when you'd been here a while and didn't find me, he thought you'd just screwed me once and were done with me."

"Well, you are mine, and they'll all know it by the end of tonight." Without warning, Jack pulled me closer and brought his mouth down on mine.

Instantly, I could taste the beer he'd been drinking, and then he was thrusting his tongue between my lips, exploring me.

The intensity and passion stirred my core, making me heat up and desire more, but he pulled back a moment later. Taking my hand, he led me back to the main rooms of the house, his grip tight enough that I knew I wouldn't get my fingers back anytime soon.

209

CHAPTER FORTY-FOUR

<u>Jack</u>

I watched Juno as she slowly relaxed, Alma and Kai keeping an eye on her with me. It had only taken a whispered word to get Kai to realize she needed the extra watchfulness, and Alma already knew the threat.

It had taken all my control not to clock Logan when I'd walked into the kitchen and seen his arm around Juno. At first, I'd thought she had been happily getting to know him, but then I'd seen the fear in her eyes, that wide-eyed look, and the relief that had passed over her face the second she'd spotted me.

Either she was a very good actress, or she had been terrified. And I'd been angry either way. Now that I'd calmed down a little, I didn't feel like I could relax. I didn't want anyone else to have her or go near her. The very thought made me want to break something. Or someone.

Of course, I couldn't show that at a party for the band. It wouldn't be right for me to show my anger, but Kai had picked up on it anyway and asked me what had happened when I'd finally let go of Juno and let her sit with Alma and Eve to talk over girl stuff.

I'd mentioned Logan's interest and gained another ally and a promise that we'd all keep her away from Logan or Logan away from her as best we could.

It didn't make me feel much better, but it was a start. Logan wasn't always easily dissuaded. And there were rumors. Rumors he'd used drugs to get what he wanted out of women in the past. Of course, we would never have allowed something like that if we'd had proof, but there wasn't always a way for us to prevent it.

Sometimes, the predators slipped through, careful enough not to get caught. And for the first time in a long time, the thought terrified me. He was now interested in Juno, and she'd been through enough. She didn't need a man like Logan making her feel even worse or putting her through more hell.

Trying to relax, I focused on the conversations around me, but they weren't interesting, most of the groupies talking about another gig they'd been to recently.

I got up and moved closer to Juno again, Alma also moving off and glancing my way to see if I'd noticed. Before anyone else could do so, I sat beside Juno and put my arm over the back of the chair near her shoulders.

Immediately, she leaned into me, and I noticed she held her drink in one hand with the other over the top of it. It made me feel a little better to see her clearly being careful, but I still couldn't quite relax.

I'd noticed how a lot of the women were avoiding her, too. Were they being catty, or had something happened before I arrived? I had no way of knowing, and I wasn't going to ask when we were in the middle of the party.

"You seem preoccupied," she whispered as she leaned closer, almost resting her head on my shoulder.

Instantly, I felt a little better. I wrapped my arm around her and looked into her blue eyes.

"I wanted to make sure you were okay after..." I trailed off, also keeping my voice down and not wanting to say anything too derogatory about Logan while others could hear.

"I'm a lot better now you're with me again. You make me feel safe."

Without thinking, I pressed my lips to hers, my groin stirring with the desire to screw her brains out right then and there. I heard murmurs around us, our kiss the first time anyone had directly seen what was happening between us.

It almost made me pull away, but she relaxed into me, either oblivious to the reaction we were beginning to get or not caring that we'd been noticed.

"Get a room," someone yelled a moment later, finally making her pull back a little, looking toward whoever had yelled it. I didn't as she looked back at me again, her eyes searching mine as if she didn't know what to do and wanted my opinion.

I pulled back just enough that it was clear I didn't plan to go any further or kiss her again, and she settled her head onto my shoulder, letting out a small sigh as she did.

For a moment, I could almost believe we'd been a couple for a while and this was the comfortable way she'd feel near me whenever we were at social gatherings together, but then I spotted Logan again, and it all came flooding back.

A part of me wanted to have him slung out and to make a scene just to make sure everyone knew that Juno was mine, but I also knew we hadn't known each other long, and what little we'd done together had been fraught with problems and setbacks.

Thankfully, the night wore on, and Juno didn't appear to even want to leave my side or talk much to anyone else. I didn't encourage her to. It felt good not to be alone, and it gave me a way out of awkward conversations.

Juno seemed to enjoy conversing with others and made me envious of her ability to steer a topic more than once. Still, I noticed that not everyone was interacting with her, some going out of their way to avoid her entirely.

If she noticed it, she ignored it and kept talking to whoever would be civil to her. However, it made me angry, and as the last of the evening passed, I felt more and more on edge. It had been a shitty party, and by the time people started leaving, finding places to sleep or some private time with others they were hooking up with, I was more than ready to go find somewhere quiet with Juno.

Kai found us near the front door as I slipped my shoes back on my feet.

"Here," he said. "The keys to the one around the back. It's the quietest out there. Pop back for brunch when the pair of you are up in the morning. Or afternoon. You know, whatever."

I grinned as Juno's eyes went wide.

"Have fun," Alma added as she took Kai's hand and led him away.

"They're an interesting couple," Juno whispered as they went up the stairs, going around a couple with their lips locked together on the bottom step.

"They're still in love. And they have no problem showing it. But he's always gone home to her and no one else. It works for them," I said as I helped her put her jacket on and then opened the door.

No one appeared to notice us leaving, and it made me feel relieved. I wanted Juno. And in that moment, I'd have given anything for what Kai and Alma had. To know there was always someone on your side. Someone who accepted you the way you were. I tried not to be too eager as I strode around the side of the house and looked for the alleyway that led to the house at the back.

I was just about to go down it and lead Juno with me when she stopped and patted her pockets.

"Fuck," she said a moment later. "I've left my phone there."

I let out a growl, unable to help it, but she'd already turned.

"I'm pretty sure I know where I left it," she added. "I'll catch up to you. Do I just follow this path to the other house?"

"Yeah, but…"

"Turn the light on and get comfy. I won't be long." Without another word, she walked off and left me standing there.

I growled again, more than a little pissed off but not wanting to be too angry at her. She'd be back, but I found myself staying on the spot to wait despite what she'd suggested.

CHAPTER FORTY-FIVE

<u>Juno</u>

I shivered while walking back up the driveway to Alma's house and tried to remember exactly where I'd left my phone. It was stupid of me to have forgotten it, but there was nothing I could do about it now.

When I told Jack, I got the impression he was a lot more annoyed than he'd let on, so I didn't waste time going up to the front door. Thankfully, it was unlocked, and I could still get in, but it took me a moment to orientate myself again. The couple had left the bottom of the stairs, but there were still people up, and music was still playing somewhere, a classic rock song I recognized but didn't know the words to.

I moved to the living room, looking by the sofa where I'd sat with Jack for some of the evening. Not only was my phone not there, but another couple was making out, too stoned or drunk to care that the rest of the room could see them screwing on the section of the sofa.

Trying not to blush at the strange world I'd entered and thinking how different this was from the other parties I'd been to, I moved toward the kitchen.

Eventually, I found it in a pile of cell phones on the kitchen table. It seemed I wasn't the only one who had left their phone lying around, and for a moment, I was amused that someone had decided to collect them all and leave them somewhere where people could come get them. Maybe I wasn't the odd one out after all.

Grinning to myself and feeling a little better, I walked back to the front door. At least I wouldn't keep Jack waiting too long.

Before I could get to the door, however, Logan seemed to appear from nowhere. He immediately blocked my way, leaning across the hallway.

"Juno, what's your hot body doing here again? And without Jack once more. I'm starting to think your little thing isn't as much of a thing as the others say. I mean, sure, yeah, he likes you. Who wouldn't want to fuck your delicious-looking body? But it doesn't have to be him, you know."

"I'm leaving. Let me by," I said, feeling sick once more. There would be no rescue this time.

Logan reached for me and grabbed my wrist before he grabbed my breast with the other hand. I tried to twist away and lash out at the same time. My hand connected with his face and made a loud slapping noise, but he also slammed me into the wall and pinned me against it.

"Get off me," I said and growled as he continued to grope. I reached up, but he grabbed my other hand. I pushed back, determined not to get caught a second time. It was as if something inside me snapped. I'd had enough of being screwed around by men who wouldn't respect what I had to say for myself.

Without hesitation, I brought my knee up, connecting with Logan's balls. He dropped like a sack, and I immediately moved to the side to find Jack coming back into the house. He took one look at Logan and then at my face.

"You okay?" he asked.

"I am now," I replied. "Let's get out of here."

Jack took my hand again, and we left for the second time. Neither of us spoke until we were in the next house, the back patio doors shut behind us and the lights on. Our bags were by the door, someone having already brought them over for us.

Although it was a similar size to Alma and Kai's main house, it had an entirely different layout, and we found ourselves in a dining room. Jack led me to the kitchen as if he knew the place well and dropped the keys on the kitchen countertop.

I quickly looked around, feeling awkward in the same way I often did when I first went on vacation. This was both mine for the night and not mine, and I didn't know what to say to Jack, either.

My stomach was still tense, my pulse rapid after running into Logan again. Just the thought of his hands on my body made me want to throw up.

"Hey," Jack said, coming to me and wrapping his arms around me. It was only then I realized I'd done something similar, hugging myself once again. "Did he hurt you?"

"No. He groped a little, but no more." I exhaled as I spoke, my voice breaking and betraying the emotion I felt.

Jack wrapped his arms even tighter around me. I leaned into his chest, inhaling the scent of his shirt and skin, the combination of tobacco, cologne, and him making me feel warmer and safer almost instantly.

"I almost hit him the first time. If you hadn't given him a good kick to the nuts, I think I'd have gone crazy on him." Jack's voice added to the soothing atmosphere despite the anger in it.

"I'm not sure where I found the fight. Normally, I freeze or want to run when something shitty happens."

"It's okay, you know. You can feel scared. But you're safe now. I won't ever force you to do anything," he said, pulling back and lifting my chin so our eyes met.

"I know," I replied, realizing I meant it.

I'd felt safe with Jack from the moment I'd met him, and

although sometimes my brain decided to present me with irrational fears, I still loved how it felt to be close to him.

"Come on, let's go find a bedroom and have some fun to end this party with. Replace those bad thoughts of yours with good ones." Jack didn't wait for me to answer but took my arm and guided me to the stairs. They creaked slightly as we went up, making me feel like I should be quieter despite being alone in the house.

I noticed several bedrooms, each one neat and ready to use, but Jack led us straight to the back of the house and a large master suite, the bed in the middle of the room so large I was worried I'd get lost in it.

As soon as the door shut behind us, Jack came to me again and took my hands in his, his gaze wandering over me.

Feeling self-conscious, I didn't move and merely looked back over him. I wasn't sure how much he wanted from me, and I didn't know how I felt after the evening we'd had.

On the one hand, I was livid at the so-called friends who'd been at the party and the strange culture everyone else appeared to be okay with. On the other hand, I was standing before Jack Starling once more, and it was clear he wanted me there.

"I want to do so many things to you," he said, his tone dark and a slight smirk on his face, reaching out to grab my body.

I gulped.

He cupped my chin and ran a thumb across my bottom lip. My mouth parted at the slight pressure, his gaze locked on me. More than once, I wondered what he was thinking, but I didn't dare ask. I'd promised to be his however he wanted me. To submit to him.

"Will you trust me?" he asked a moment later.

I looked into his eyes, a ripple of fear running down my spine. The intensity of his expression as he looked for my answer made me feel a little braver. After everything that happened with Logan, I had a feeling he needed me to show him I knew he was better. That I wasn't scared of him abusing me the way others had.

Despite that, I couldn't speak. I was terrified, and I had no idea what he was going to ask of me.

"Juno, I want you to trust me," he said, a hint of anxiety coming through as his arm tightened around me.

"I trust you," I replied, the words coming out in a rush of emotion and breath.

Immediately, he relaxed and kissed me before pulling back, smirking once more.

"Good," he said as his eyes roamed downwards. "Now strip for me, kitten."

CHAPTER FORTY-SIX

My heart raced as I pulled my top off and revealed my bra and torso. Jack's eyes were locked on my body, but he'd given me a command, and I had a feeling this was one I was supposed to obey.

On top of that, he'd asked me to trust him, and I knew saying I did was only half the answer. Now, he needed me to show it, too.

Fear still rippled through me, but I had something to focus on. Reaching for my pants, I slipped them down as well. Although I wasn't stripping in the sexiest way possible, I noticed the bulge in his pants as he enjoyed the view.

Once I was standing before him in nothing but my underwear, I paused and exhaled, looking at him again. His gaze was quite clearly on my torso, drinking me in, hungry for me.

"Keep going," he commanded. "I want you completely exposed."

I noticed he hadn't just asked me to get naked. He wanted me to feel vulnerable. To feel as if every inch of me was bare before him and at his mercy. And as wetness formed between my thighs, I was pretty sure I wanted it as well.

Slowly, I reached up behind my back and unhooked my bra. I couldn't look at him, feeling too nervous as I slid the straps off my shoulders and revealed my breasts. I knew he'd seen them before, but we'd always been in bed together already, our bodies close and entwined.

Now, my chest drew his gaze, and he almost stepped closer, holding himself back at the last minute.

While my pert breasts and hardening nipples had his attention, I slipped a thumb into each side of my panties and pushed them downwards. They fell to the floor, revealing the final part of me.

Not sure what to do with my hands now, I took them behind my back and clasped them together, and then I lowered my gaze, doing my best to look as submissive as possible.

My heart continued to race as neither of us moved, and I could only imagine where he might be looking. Time slipped by, feeling like each second was a vulnerable lifetime until he stepped forward and reached for me, his hands going to my hips.

He lifted my chin again until I was looking at him before claiming my mouth hungrily with his. A moment later, his other hand reached up and cupped one breast, his thumb rubbing across my nipple and making me moan against him.

I instantly felt calmer, more used to this sort of approach from him, but he pulled back again a little while later.

"Lie on the bed," he commanded. "On your front."

Trying not to show my surprise at such a command, I turned and moved to get on the bed. I heard him follow, and the rattle of his belt buckle came with it.

Another ripple of fear ran through me, but I pushed it away and carried on, equally wet and hungry for him. I wanted to be his, wanted to have him deep inside me.

It took me a moment to get comfortable, but as soon as I was, I tilted my head to the side and tried to look back at him. The bed shifted as he knelt at the end of it and pushed my legs farther open.

Trying to keep calm, I exhaled slowly and focused on my breathing, but as soon as his hands touched my back, I jumped.

"Nervous?" he asked.

I nodded without hesitation.

He kissed my shoulder as he settled over the back of me.

"Try and relax. I don't want this to hurt you."

I knew his words were supposed to calm me, but as his hands slipped down my arms and up to my wrists, pushing them up to the top of the bed, fear gripped me even further.

He'd pinned me before, but he had his belt in one hand, and it was clear he intended to bind my hands to the top of the bed. Instantly, I resisted, my heart racing and my mouth going dry.

Being tied up wasn't something I wanted. Being that trapped.

Immediately, I shook my head and tried to pull back. Far stronger than me, Jack continued, pushing my wrists the rest of the way and placing the belt against one of them.

"Please, stop," I managed to say, the words coming out high-pitched and unlike my usual voice.

Thankfully, Jack paused, still over me and holding onto my arms. For a moment, neither of us said anything as my breathing grew even more rapid.

He kissed my cheek and neck a few times, his movements gentle and soft, helping me relax against him until I sighed and closed my eyes. The second he continued to try and tie my arms, I panicked and shook my head again.

"No, please. I can't." Pushing up against him, I tried to get out of his grip.

He let me go and shifted to one side. Immediately, I shifted to the edge of the bed and curled up, my back to him. I felt awful, every breath ragged and my body shaking.

Gently, Jack came closer and put his arms around me.

"You don't trust me?" he asked, the hurt in his voice clear.

"I..." The words wouldn't come out of my mouth.

I didn't have a good answer. I had so many awful memories of men trying to force me to do what they wanted. Of being helpless and hurting. While it was clear Jack wasn't one of those men, it didn't make those images leave my head or my body feel much calmer.

"I thought you wanted this?" he asked a moment later, the bite to his words clear as his hurt turned to anger.

"I do," I replied. "But I'm not sure how ready I am. I thought I was. I want to be. But Logan has brought up tons of old memories, and I'm struggling not to think of them."

The words weren't perfectly true. Logan hadn't brought up anything that wasn't already on my mind, but the sentiment was. I wanted to give myself to Jack entirely. To know that no matter how much I was at his mercy, I was safe, but I was too scared and too nervous.

Jack pulled back again and sat on the other side of the bed, his belt in his hands.

Tears threatened to fall at how I'd clearly hurt him and how there seemed to be nothing I could do about it. Wanting to try anyway, I shifted across the bed, aware of how naked I still was.

Sitting beside him, I reached for his hand.

"Maybe we could work up to it over a few days?" I asked, trying to offer him a way we could both get what we needed.

He looked at me, his eyes only flicking briefly to my exposed breasts. I slipped my hand in his as I searched his face for some kind of sign that I was helping him or he could forgive me.

When he looked away again, I only wanted to cry all the more. I fought back the emotion, however. It wouldn't help Jack feel like I truly trusted him. But could I, right now? I had no idea.

"Let's sleep," he said a moment later, squeezing my hand. "Maybe in the morning, we'll feel differently."

I watched him turn away from me, his eyes full of sadness and pain. Every part of my mind screamed at me to reach out to him again, to tell him I wanted to try again right then and there, but my body wouldn't move.

Before I could do anything else, Jack had the light off and was lying in the bed beside me. I slid in next to him, grateful when he at least reached out for me and pulled me into his arms. He seemed to close his eyes and drift off, but I lay awake beside him for some time. This hadn't gone according to plan at all.

CHAPTER FORTY-SEVEN

<u>Jack</u>

The sun was up and streaming into the room before either of us woke up. I opened my eyes and immediately noticed Juno's sleeping form beside me. I'd enjoyed waking up to her every day since she'd arrived in New York, and in a lot of ways, today was no different. But I felt a pang of sadness as I remembered the night before.

It had been a disaster from one moment to the next, Logan beginning a chain of events that had snowballed.

And there hadn't appeared to be any way I could have prevented it. I had felt fixed to rails, reacting emotionally to each moment and being caught up in everything. In the clear light of morning, with a rested mind and calmer emotions, I knew it had been a bad idea for me to have asked Juno to trust me when and how I had.

But that hadn't stopped me from wanting it. I wanted to know that she could tell the difference between what Logan wanted from her and what I wanted and needed.

Asleep beside me, naked under the covers, I was tempted to

reach out and touch her, but I knew that might make the problem even worse. Her trust was something I wanted. I needed her to know I wasn't going to abuse her. I wanted her to be mine, to give herself over to me for my pleasure and know that I intended her to enjoy every minute of it.

After all the past issues with my ex, all the slander and gossip, everything I'd been accused of, I needed to know she didn't believe any of it.

Her eyelids fluttered briefly, her mind lost in some sort of dream. I could only hope it was a good one as I watched over her. I considered getting up several times, but every time I did, my gaze was drawn back to the peaceful look on her face and the sweet way her slightly mussed hair framed it.

I made up my mind then, however, that I wanted more time with her. She was due to go home the following day, late in the evening, but I already knew I wanted her to come to the island with me. When we'd had an intense period of promotion and creativity, I often went to the island to rest and be away from the public eye for a while.

Alone wasn't what I wanted right now, however. But would she come if it was just me? She'd be alone on an island with me. Would that make her scared?

The more I thought about it, the more I knew I needed to see if some of the others would come, too. At least for a few days. I could keep it a band thing. Invite Alma and Kai.

Lying back, I reached for my phone and checked the band schedule. They were all free for the next few days, the rest of the band needing the downtime as much as I did.

It made me feel even better about the idea and I quickly zapped a message to Kai to ask him if he wanted to invite the others and Alma. Although I didn't expect a reply right away, I held onto my phone a little longer.

Was I doing the right thing?

I'd only known Juno a few weeks. Did I really want her on my island with me? Did I truly want to include her in a place I normally kept reserved for the people I cared about most?

I exhaled and looked over at her again. In truth, I didn't think I'd ever be sure, but there was something about her. She stilled a part of me that was almost never calm. And she made me yearn and hope for a feeling I'd thought might be lost forever.

Looking at her again, I forgot about anything but that moment and how much I wanted her.

As her eyes flickered open, she saw me, and I smiled at her, determined to have a better day.

"Good morning, beautiful," I said and reached out an arm to scoop it around her waist and pull her closer.

I couldn't help it. As soon as her skin touched mine and I was aware of her nakedness again, my cock grew hard, close enough to her that she'd feel it, too.

She gave me a smirk, leaning into me and shifting so she was pressed even more firmly against my body.

"Someone's pleased to see me this morning," she said.

"I'm pretty sure he's always pleased to see you, especially naked."

She chuckled and reached out to hug me back. Immediately, I kissed her, wanting to taste her again and knowing my desire to be inside her was only going to grow.

Yielding to me, she kissed back and tilted her body so I could push her onto her back. The subtle invite was more than enough encouragement, and I was soon on top of her, pinning her beneath me, one of my legs between hers.

She was already heating up, her nipples hardening with a single brush from my thumb. Breaking off from her lips, I trailed more kisses down her neck and toward one breast before taking her nipple into my mouth. After giving it a gentle bite and making her moan, I did the same to the other.

Arching her back, she closed her eyes as I continued, both pleasing her and getting her ready to be screwed and showing her that I was in control of her body.

My cock continued to harden until it was throbbing by her entrance, almost demanding to be driven deep into her hot, wet pussy. Without giving her any warning, I did just that.

She gasped and groaned as I set a fast, hard rhythm right away. All the pent-up frustration from the night before and the desire I'd felt that morning drove my hips as I thrust deep again and again. Every inch of her was mine, and she would know it by the time I was done.

Slick and pulsing with desire, she seemed to pull me deeper and encourage me faster and faster. Pleasure built between us as I sped up and thrust even harder. Fighting the orgasm that was soon threatening to tip me into heaven, I plunged my mouth down on hers, desperate to focus on something else.

She moaned into me, ripples of pleasure tearing through her body as she shuddered. Her orgasm and the tightness that gripped my cock finished me off, and I pushed as deep as I could get as I spurted cum and groaned with sated need.

We lay entwined, my body connected to hers in so many ways that I felt like she was part of me. My heart raced, and my mind felt clear for the first time in days. I wanted nothing as much as I wanted to be fucking Juno.

Although I considered letting her get up then, I soon found myself kissing her some more and stroking her cheek. Kai had told us to take our time, and I fully intended to. Juno was going to take my cock at least once more before I let her out of the bed we were in. And I would make her beg me to give it to her.

Slowly, I reached for her breast and cupped it, her nipple hard and tight against my palm.

Her eyes widened at the stimulation, but she made no protest at being touched and explored. A moment later, I pinched her nipple hard enough that she gasped. Inside her still, my cock began to harden again. Unable to help it, I smirked at her.

Yes, I was going to fuck her again, and it was going to be even better than anything else we'd done yet.

CHAPTER FORTY-EIGHT

<u>Juno</u>

Still trapped beneath Jack, I tried not to panic as he grew hard again and made it plain he wasn't done with me. He'd already screwed me hard once, and while I'd very much enjoyed it after the night before and the way we'd ended it, Jack was so dark and brooding sometimes that I didn't know how to feel around him.

It was clear he wanted me, but he was also as reluctant to trust as I was. Could we find a way to open up to each other?

I had no idea. But I wanted to try. And it made me feel better to know he hadn't given up on me either.

Exhaling, I persuaded my body to relax and enjoy being his; after all, he'd saved me twice now. What could be so bad about giving in to his desires again and again?

His mouth pressing against mine took my focus off me, and his hands ran over my body, stoking the fire deep inside. Instantly, desire rippled through me, his manhood almost entirely hard, filling me still.

Not sure how he could be so still inside me and so turned on. I marveled at his calm. It was taking all my self-control not to buck my hips against him and encourage him to begin thrusting into me again.

Shifting one of his hands, he wound it into my hair and tugged my head back, exposing my neck.

Trailing kisses down my skin, he heated me up again before slowly beginning to move within me. I moaned, totally vulnerable in a way I would normally have been terrified of but desperate for him to keep going.

I wanted him so completely that I tried to reach for him again. A smirk flickered across his face as he held my hands still and made it clear he was in control.

"Relax, Juno," he whispered before kissing my neck again. "You just need to give in and let me take you with me."

Closing my eyes for a moment, I exhaled and tried to will my body to do what he asked, each muscle fighting me. No sooner had a part of me relaxed than Jack shifted and claimed the advantage to pin me further.

At the same time, he thrust even deeper, reminding me he was already claiming me completely. I could be no more vulnerable, not truly.

Slowly, we moved together, taking our time, his hardness making me feel full and hungry for more. His powerful body made me feel both safe and nervous at the same time, the combination adding to the emotions until I was so wet and nearing my peak that I would have given him anything.

Before I could orgasm, he pulled out of me. I mewled, trying to reach for him and pull him back toward me.

"Not yet," he said. "I don't want you to come yet. Not until I tell you that you can."

No words would come out of my mouth. I'd never been deliberately denied before. My pussy felt wet and hungry for him, the emptiness worse with having had his hard cock deep inside me.

Gently, he brought himself back to my entrance, the slight pressure of his manhood making me mewl again.

"Ask me to fuck you," Jack said a few seconds later, one hand still pinning my arms and the other pulling my head back farther. "Beg me to finish what I've started."

"Please," I said without hesitation. "I want you in me."

"All the way?" His gaze met mine, and I saw the deep desire in his eyes.

"As deep as you can," I replied. "Please, Jack. Take me."

Smug, grinning, and completely in control, he thrust down and back into me. I moaned, the pleasure so intense and everything I wanted from it that I almost tipped straight into the perfect oblivion of an orgasm.

He stilled a moment and I remembered that he had told me to wait until I had permission. It took all my self-control to stay in this limbo state, waiting for him to give me his command.

"Come for me, sweetheart," he whispered, thrusting deep inside me at the same time.

I couldn't have disobeyed him if I'd wanted to, waves of pleasure tearing through me and making me groan his name. While I came down, Jack thrust hard and fast to finish himself off.

Letting out a moan of his own, he thrust deep one last time and filled me with his cum.

Slowly, we returned to Earth together, his grip on me relaxing until I was cradled in his arms, our mouths finding each other and kissing again and again.

As he rolled to one side, I followed, keeping my body close to his. A moment later, my stomach rumbled, and he chuckled.

"We should make ourselves decent and get breakfast. Although I'm pretty sure Alma and Kai are going to know what we have been up to in here," Jack said, not letting go of me despite his words.

"I'm pretty sure they already knew what we were going to get up to," I replied, smiling. I didn't care, and I knew they wouldn't, but I looked around the room and realized we'd trashed the bed.

My glance seemed to break whatever spell had kept us

entwined. Jack slipped away from me, and we got up. He didn't leave me by myself for long, however. Within another second, he had me on my feet.

I let him lead me to the shower, where we washed each other, taking our time on that as well.

It felt good not to need to rush anywhere, every other morning we'd been together cut short by something one of us needed to do or somewhere we needed to be.

But no matter how good it felt or how much he was there with me, I felt as if I'd let him down the night before. Let myself down, too. Fear had got the better of me.

If Jack was still bothered by it, he didn't show it as we went to join Alma and Kai, Jack only pausing to check his phone and reply to messages a few times while we dressed.

More than a little grateful that we'd brought overnight bags with us, I put on fresh clothes and brushed my teeth before I slipped my hand into Jack's again.

"Please tell me not everyone who was at the party is staying for brunch," I said as we made our way down the stairs, leaving the bedroom and bed in the 'we'd just been seriously fucking' state we'd created over the morning.

Jack chuckled and shook his head.

"It'll just be some of the band. Everyone else will have gone home already or still be in one of the other houses."

I exhaled, relieved that I wouldn't be seeing Logan again. He'd made me feel so sick, and I didn't want the reminder that he could be trying to push me for something I wasn't willing to give him. He'd not appeared to understand the word no, and I knew the fear he'd made me feel had translated into my night with Jack.

Maybe another time, I'd be able to say yes to Jack's request, but I already feared I wouldn't be asked again. The look on Jack's face had implied that it meant a lot, and he'd been hurt by my lack of trust in him.

"There you two are. I was beginning to consider sending Kai

over to find out if you were lost in that bed over there or just each other," Alma said as we walked into the main house.

I felt my cheeks flush, but the warmth in her smile as she looked me over briefly made me feel less self-conscious.

"Come on, I've got plenty of brunch left, even if the two of you are the last to come looking."

Relaxing at the familiar way I slotted into the group and finding several of the other band members still in the dining room, I decided to try and trust that, for now, I was in a good place. I'd been accepted as one of the band's partners. And everyone was treating me like I was here to stay for a while.

CHAPTER FORTY-NINE

After I finished stuffing my face, I sat back and sighed, content and happy for the first time in a long time. Around me, the band and their partners chatted as if this was a normal way to spend the morning.

Every time I looked at Jack, he was smiling or talking about something that had him fully engrossed, and he appeared more relaxed and at ease than at any other point that I'd seen him.

"Right, if you lot are all done, I want my house back so I can start packing for the island. I hear we're all going tomorrow for some chill-out time," Alma said, collecting some of the plates.

I lifted my eyebrows, aware that was when I was also supposed to be flying home.

"Please tell us you're coming," Eve said, reaching out to gently touch my arm. "You have invited her, Jack, haven't you?"

"I hadn't yet," he replied, breaking off the conversation he'd already been having to look our way. "But Juno is very welcome."

"The island?" I asked as much to buy myself more time as to express my curiosity.

"Jack owns an island in the Bahamas. It's amazing. He likes to unwind there. and sometimes the rest of the band goes with him." Eve grinned. "Say you'll come?"

I frowned, feeling so put on the spot that I didn't know what to say. Fear made my stomach churn. What kind of island was it?

"At least give the girl a chance to check her schedule," Alma said, rescuing me. "And on that note, I want your opinion on an outfit, my dear. Let's let these guys clean up, and you can tell me what you think."

Although I was pretty sure Alma didn't need my opinion on her clothing, and it was a cover for something, I nodded and got to my feet. I felt Jack's gaze follow me, but I tried not to be freaked out or bothered by it. Alma had been a darling to me so far, and I was fairly confident I was about to receive some piece of advice or be asked a question.

She led me upstairs and then pulled me into her bedroom. For a moment, I stood near the doorway, letting her go past me to open the door to one of the largest walk-in closets I'd ever seen.

As she pulled out clothes, I wondered if I was wrong about her intentions entirely, but she soon placed some on the bed and grabbed a suitcase.

"Now, you looked like Logan had just invited you to his island down there," Alma said a moment later. "Not our Jack. So something about the idea hooked you, I'm guessing."

After biting my lip, I nodded and looked away.

"All right. I won't make you explain it to me if you don't want to, but I want you to know you'll be far safer on that island than most other places in the world. Everything poisonous has been exterminated. There's a small chance of a tornado, but it's remote, and we'd get some warning. No earthquakes. And you don't have to go out on the water or anything."

I tried to smile as Alma listed all the normal things people would be afraid of. It wasn't any of those, but could I tell her that?

A moment later, she sat on the bed, ignoring her suitcase and clothes. She patted the blanket beside her.

"Come on, chica. Sit, and let's see if we can help you get past it. I like you, and even if I didn't, Jack does. I'd do anything to see his heart in good hands again."

"Thank you," I said, pretty sure she'd just told me she really liked me.

"So, what is it about the island that scares you? There won't be any crowds, that's for sure."

I chuckled, knowing she was referring to the fear I'd already shown her.

"It's the feeling of being trapped. On a small island, I might not be able to get away if I wanted to. Here in New York, I can be back in London in less than twelve hours. I can get anywhere."

"You mean you can run away if you need to?" she asked.

"Something like that. More that I can get safe if I need to. I try not to run away unless I have no other option. But..." I trailed off, not sure I could tell her what happened between Greg and me. It was something I'd only told Jack because he'd seen the bruises and walked in on Greg trying to do something even worse.

"Someone once made you feel trapped and did something they shouldn't, and now you find it hard to trust that you'll be safe. I can understand that. But you won't be alone. I promise you, at any point, you can come running to me, and nothing will happen to you. Even if it was Jack you were running from."

"I don't think he would do anything to hurt me," I said. "But fear isn't rational."

Alma shook her head. "No, it ain't at all. I'd love to promise you Jack wouldn't hurt you, despite all the rumors about him. They're all crap. But I don't think that's the kind of promise you need. So. Let's have a code word or two. You say it, and I won't leave your side until you give me the safe word again. Got it?"

I couldn't speak, Alma's kindness overwhelming me. She was doing everything she could to make sure I felt safe and not even demanding an explanation for why it was necessary. But what on earth could we use for code words?

"What about one of your books? Or characters from something? We could talk about your books in some way, and I'd know you mean something else." Alma smiled as if she'd just had a brainstorm, and I quickly nodded.

"There's some characters of mine that help each other in a difficult situation. Lucy and Laura. They call themselves the little Ls."

"Perfect. Lucy for trouble, and Laura for 'I'm safe.' Mention them together if you're not sure, but you want me to be aware that you're worried."

I nodded, feeling my eyes water up at the kindness she was displaying. Immediately, she reached out and hugged me.

"Oh, you're such a gentle soul. I can see why he likes you. Now, you'd better go downstairs and put him out of his misery. He'll be terrified you're going to refuse, and having to check your schedule isn't much of an excuse. I assume you're actually free?"

I laughed as I nodded, immediately feeling a lot better. After wiping away the only tear that had managed to fall, I got back up again.

"I'm not very famous or much of a socialite. Us writers tend to spend a lot of time locked in small rooms by ourselves so we can talk to our characters without being disturbed," I said as I pulled my phone out and opened my calendar anyway.

It was Alma's turn to laugh, but she returned to her packing, and I went back downstairs.

The second I walked into the kitchen, I spotted Jack leaning against the kitchen counter, his arms folded and a frown fixed on his face. Kai was near him, and they were talking too quietly for me to understand what they were saying. I couldn't see anyone else from the band at all.

As soon as Jack saw me, he looked up, and Kai trailed off, turning to me and then glancing at Jack as well.

"Oh, sorry," I said. "I didn't mean to interrupt. I can come back later."

"No," Kai replied. "We were talking of unimportant things. Is my wife happy with her clothing choices now?"

"I believe so." Walking closer to Jack, I lifted my phone. "And I checked my schedule. I'm free to come to the island too if you still want me to."

"Yeah," Jack said, exhaling a big breath. Almost instantly, he relaxed, and I felt my body doing the same.

For now, we were going to be together a little longer, but I was beginning to get the impression that at some point we needed to start trusting each other. Or this whole thing was going to explode.

CHAPTER FIFTY

Jack's arms slipped around my waist, both of us still standing in the kitchen with Kai and Alma. We'd stuck around when Alma returned and started talking about all sorts of things.

It felt good to be in his arms and be doing something chilled. It was clear he had a good relationship with Kai and was as relaxed around them as Alma made me feel with her.

We'd talked a little more about the island, too, which had helped me calm even further. We'd be essentially stranded on it with nothing but a yacht to get off it with, but the yacht would still be there, and it had a crew who would sail me back to a bigger island with an airport at a moment's notice.

I'd also been assured the band would be there with us, and the house on the island was incredibly comfortable, with plenty of space for everyone and a gorgeous view for miles.

It sounded heavenly, and part of me was excited. From the moment I met Jack, I'd been sucked into a life full of wonderful houses, plenty of money, and someone to do pretty much everything they wanted for them.

And on top of that, they played music whenever they wanted and spent the rest of the time hanging out and chatting.

If I hadn't seen the level of work that also went into their songs and music, I'd have thought they had the laziest, easiest lives possible. It was clear they loved making music, however, and they were willing to work at something until they felt they'd got it right.

"Come on, we should let these two have some peace and quiet, and I should make sure the island will be ready," Jack said.

There was no way I was going to argue with Jack. Either he knew his friends wanted and needed some space, or he wanted me to himself elsewhere. I was good with either.

After promising to see the couple the next day and fly out to the island together, Jack led me to his waiting car, his men already there. Once again, it made me wonder if they were always there or if Jack was really good at summoning them without making it obvious.

Either way, I found myself grateful as I slipped into the back of the car, and Jack followed. It was just the two of us again and we were returning to the more familiar territory of his penthouses.

Although I hadn't been there for many days, they felt safer and more like a home than Kai and Alma's had. Possibly because I hadn't been threatened in either of the penthouses so far. Having one to go back to when I wanted also made me feel like I had some way to put distance between us if I needed to. It was a safety net.

Jack didn't say anything at first, staring off into space, his face serious, a frown playing at the corners of his mouth. I wanted to reach for him and bring him back to where I was, but I wasn't sure I dared.

Instead, I tried to distract myself with something else, worried that he was withdrawing from me after everything that had happened the night before and not sure what I could do about it.

"Do you truly want to come to the island tomorrow?" Jack asked a few minutes later, his words taking me by surprise.

"Of course," I replied. "I've never been to the Bahamas before."

"And that's your reason for saying yes?" He finally looked at me and studied me, his gaze laser-focused, his jaw snapped shut with a force that made me instantly feel scared. Was he about to lose his temper with me?"

"No. I mean, of course that's a reason." I closed my mouth and gulped. What were my exact reasons? Why had I said yes?

Jack shifted to look my way even more, but he crossed his arms, and I got the feeling this wasn't going well. Not sure what else to do, I decided to be honest.

"I want to come to be with you, but honestly, I'm also scared. It hasn't been long since Greg hurt me. And I haven't known you long."

"So you don't trust me?" he asked, almost interrupting me.

"I want to trust you."

"They're not the same thing."

"I know." Again, I looked away, feeling his hurt and not sure what to do about it.

"I won't make you come. You can go back to England if you'd rather. If I'm not what you want, then just say it, and we'll—"

"No, I don't want to go back to England at all. I want to come. I want to be with you and give us a chance. But I'm… The memories of what Greg did in the past are still just below the surface. And Logan yesterday really didn't help. It's not that I don't trust you so much as I wouldn't trust anyone right now."

"Then maybe you shouldn't come at all. I don't want to walk on eggshells the whole time, even if I can understand why you're scared. I'm not your ex."

I sighed, feeling the indignance in his voice like a punch to the stomach. He wasn't wrong, but at the same time, could I push myself past this? Was I being unfair to Jack by making him accommodate this fear? Did I just need to decide to trust him anyway?

"I talked to Alma about it. We agreed that I should come anyway. That trying to trust you in as safe a way as I could was the best I could offer. I'm sorry if that's not enough. I'm trying to get past the fear, but I can't just magic it away, either."

Jack seemed to freeze as I finished this sentence, only a few blinks showing me he was still alive and functioning.

"If you don't want me to come, I'll understand, but I'd like to. I want to give you my trust. Will you give me a chance to work up to it?"

Jack exhaled and then nodded.

"Yes. I want you there. I just…" He trailed off as he ran a hand through his hair. "I don't want you to fear me."

I scooted across the back seat so I could take his hand.

"I don't directly. The idea of no safety net scares me more than what you might do to me. So far, everything you've done to me has been…amazing."

Smirking, I thought of all the hot sex we'd been having. It had been phenomenal, and my words brought a light back into Jack's eyes.

He reached out for me and pulled me into his arms. Instantly, everything felt right again. Being safe in his arms made everything feel better.

However, despite the gentle way he held me close and kissed me, I kept imagining the look in his eyes as I told him I couldn't let him tie me up. Something inside him was desperate to be trusted. But could I give him that?

I had no idea.

CHAPTER FIFTY-ONE

<u>Jack</u>

Inside, my emotions churned. I wanted Juno to trust me so badly. It still hurt that she seemed reluctant to, but I was already falling for her. The way she felt in my arms, the soft skin as I ran my hands over her.

Even the look in her eyes as she looked around and spotted me. I wanted her in so many ways.

Most of the time, I could remind myself that she was still hurting. That all she needed was a little time, but I was hurting too. So many people had stopped trusting me after all the rumors and slander. So many people gave my words and actions no chance to prove those rumors wrong. And there was also the money and fame.

So many women had come along just for that. That was all they'd wanted. My money or to be famous. It was clear Juno liked certain aspects of the life we led as a band. So far, she hadn't appeared too hungry for money, but Kai had mentioned her agent pushing for writing accreditation for the song. Pushing for her to get a significant percentage of the royalties.

And while she had helped, even deserved some of them, she

was one of many on the project and had played only a small part overall. Kai said he was taking care of it, but it had made me wary. I wasn't sure I could handle another woman who was only with me to make herself richer.

Money made so many people ugly on the inside.

Trying to focus on the positive, I thought about the near future. Juno was coming to the island for a few days with the band, and that meant she wasn't leaving yet. I kissed her again. She always tasted so amazing, and today was no different.

"So, what's the plan for the rest of today?" she asked as we broke off again.

I smiled, unable to help it as she looked up at me, her eyes full of hope and warmth. Several thoughts ran through my head, thoughts of taking her back to my apartment and bedding her some more, but I also knew it would be a good idea to actually do something with her somehow.

"We should pack, and if you want anything washed, we can get it done before going to the island," I said, choosing the most practical option. "Do you have everything you'd need for somewhere like that?"

"That didn't even occur to me. I don't have anything summery. How hot will it be?"

"Not very warm, but summer."

"I might need some different clothes, then," she said, looking wide-eyed at the idea.

"Shopping it is, then."

"Shopping?" she asked, looking away and sitting back.

"You appear scared," I replied, slightly surprised by her reaction. Most women loved the idea of shopping for more clothes.

"I don't really like shopping. Clothing stores are scary places full of clothes that either make you feel fat or out of fashion because they're all cut wrong, or you don't like them all."

For a moment, I didn't know how to respond. She had a point, but I was still surprised. Surely, she could find some clothes she liked out there.

"We could try and go for the *Pretty Woman* approach," I replied. "I'll wave my best credit card around, order pizza, and make sure everyone helps out."

She chuckled but shook her head. "As sweet as that would be, I think the attention would be worse. Besides, I don't think you should be buying me clothes yet."

I lifted an eyebrow, knowing most others would have simply accepted that offer. Yet here she was, saying she'd pay herself. Did she mean it?

With no way to know, I let the matter drop for now. Although I was aware she'd be buying more clothes simply because of me, I was also hopeful she wanted to be more financially independent. It would allay the fears Kai had raised if she was okay with paying her way.

The rest of the journey passed quickly, Juno talking about past vacations and asking questions about the island that revealed a train of thought more in line with planning to come.

She grew more animated as I told her about the beaches, houses, and everything we could do on the island.

"It sounds amazing," she said when the topic ended. "Thank you for inviting me to join all of you. I... I don't normally get to spend so much time in such amazing places."

"You haven't been as successful as you are for long, right?" I asked.

She shook her head but didn't seem bothered by the admission.

"It's harder to get famous as a creative than some people think. Especially as a writer. So few writers earn a living, even when they write amazing books."

I noticed a hint of sadness in her eyes and wondered what she meant exactly, but I wasn't sure now was the time to pry. We were almost back at the penthouse, and I wanted to get packed and on the island as soon as possible. While I still had worries, I was excited to see Juno's reaction to the island and the house I'd built on it.

A few fans were lingering outside the apartment building, and yet more paparazzi, but no one who would get into our faces. After telling Juno to focus on the building and come straight inside with me, I got out.

Although she came quickly after me, I didn't take her hand this time, and I moved right after Mick, another of my men falling in behind Juno.

I didn't relax until we were in the elevator and heading upward. As soon as I was alone with Juno again, I took her hand and pulled her into my arms. She smiled up at me, and for a moment, the world seemed to fade into the background.

"You seem happier, more relaxed than you were in London," I said, hoping it was true and wanting confirmation.

"I've really loved being here. Everything with the song, being with you. You have an amazing band and some great friends," she replied before the elevator stopped and let us out.

She was right, and for a moment, I focused on the gratitude I felt for both them and her. In a lot of ways, I had an amazing life, and I was aware I had things easier than the average person. But that didn't change how much a broken heart could shatter everything.

I held onto Juno for a little longer, standing in the hallway. She needed to go to the second apartment to pack her suitcase, but I didn't want to let her go. The more time I spent with her, the more I wanted to spend every second at her side.

After giving her a brief kiss, I backed up and went into my main apartment to pack as well.

Some of what I needed was already at the island, the place prepped with basic clothes, instruments, and all sorts of other stuff there for me whenever I showed up, but there were always a bunch of clothes and other things I wanted to take with me. I hated packing, however.

Sighing at the empty bed in front of me and remembering the last time I'd been in it, Juno beside me, I tried to focus on the positive. We were trying to make something work between us, and I had to hope that was enough.

<h1 style="text-align:center">CHAPTER FIFTY-TWO</h1>

<u>Juno</u>

I quickly shoved all my clothes back into my suitcase, thanking one of Jack's men when he brought my overnight bag in from Alma and Kai's. It was a little weird having someone keep track of all my luggage for me, but I was grateful to have one of them there. Before he could leave, I asked him what type of luggage arrangement we'd have.

I'd arrived with just one suitcase and a small carry-on bag, aware there were limits on commercial flights, but if I was going to buy extra clothes that suited the climate on an island in the Bahamas, they weren't going to fit in my case. I'd only just realized that.

I had the overnight bag, but they weren't all going to fit in it.

"Oh, it's all right, ma'am. We'll be going to the island by private jet and then a yacht. We can provide a spare suitcase if that would help, and it can all be loaded as usual."

I blinked, not entirely surprised, but beginning to feel like this was something no one else would have worried about.

"An extra suitcase would be great. If it's not needed for anyone else," I replied as I tried to recover.

Thankfully, this ended the awkward moment as the burly bodyguard hurried away to either let someone else know I needed a suitcase or get it for me. I exhaled and sat for a moment.

This whole world Jack and his band lived in was so unlike anything I was used to. It felt like there was always someone there to fetch whatever was needed or make sure every desire was granted. And everyone else clearly felt this was normal.

While Jack was always polite to his staff, and it was clear they got along well with him, it felt so alien. A part of me liked how much easier it made life, but I already knew it came with a price. The paparazzi, the legions of fans who weren't always great with boundaries, and having to be careful where you were going were pretty hefty downsides sometimes.

Experiencing the celebrity world firsthand made it clear there was a lot more to being famous than people realized. I could finally see it wasn't everything it was cracked up to be.

I wasn't sure it was what I wanted, not that I'd ever pursued it hard, but it was easier as a writer to be less of a celebrity and still have everyone know your name. In many ways, I was extremely grateful for my career choice.

By the time I'd finished packing again, I was already wondering what it would be like after the TV series was complete. Would more people know me then? I had no idea, but I wasn't going to push for it, either. My name could be far more famous than my face.

Once I finished, and I was sure I wasn't leaving anything in the apartment, I made my way back to Jack's and knocked on his door. For a moment, I wasn't sure if I should go in, but I soon heard Jack.

"That you, Juno?" he called.

"Yeah. I'm done. Definitely going to need to buy some summer clothes, but everything else is packed up," I said as I pushed the door open and went inside, feeling I had permission to.

It was strange having several apartments on the same floor owned by one person, almost like they were elaborate dormitory rooms in some kind of college or youth camp.

I tried not to look out of place as I padded to his bedroom, his large suitcase open on the bed. With him was his PA, the man helping him pack by pulling out clothes, hats, and boots from the large closet for Jack to decide whether or not he wanted them.

For a moment, I watched from the doorway, as amused by the process as I was surprised. I'd never seen anyone go through something like this before. Jack's PA knew where everything Jack might want was and everything about his preferences, and it made them a very efficient packing team.

Once one suitcase was full, I expected Jack to be done, but his PA simply grabbed the bag and wheeled it away before bringing a second into the room. It made me wonder if that had been the first, but it also explained the lack of a reaction I'd had for requesting a second suitcase. It appeared Jack needed more than one, too.

"Almost done," Jack said a few minutes later when I yawned. "I thought you'd take longer."

"I only brought one suitcase with me," I replied. "And I didn't unpack all of it while I was here."

"Smart. Most women I know have at least four, and they insist on unpacking it all, even if we're only somewhere for a night."

"Far too much bother," I replied. "Even with help."

Jack finally looked at me and then glanced at his PA. I fought back a smile, not sure how he'd take my remark.

"Neil here makes himself invaluable. And why pack alone if you can have good company?" Jack replied, sounding a little defensive."

"I'm not knocking it. I love the idea," I replied. "You have me more than a little envious."

"You don't have a PA?" Jack asked as he put yet another hat in a box and added it to the pile on the bed.

"Nope. I have a VA for some of my author admin, but no PA." I decided to help speed things up, so I grabbed some of the hat boxes Neil didn't have room to carry and followed him with them.

The PA left the apartment and went down the hallway to the one next to me. There, he revealed a pile of suitcases, luggage boxes, and full-length suit bags.

For a moment, I gaped, and Neil laughed.

"It's not all Jack's, but it helps us organize it like this. We add our own stuff to the mix when we're ready, too."

I gave him the last of the boxes, letting him place them where he wanted, suspecting there was a sort of system. As I did, I spotted my full suitcase in the pile. It was almost amusing knowing my contribution was so tiny. I definitely didn't have to worry about having two suitcases.

Before we could return to Jack's apartment, he appeared, pulling along the wheeled suitcase he'd just finished with.

"That's the last one," he said as he pushed it toward Neil. There's two more hat boxes on the bed and another suit I want."

I watched as Neil didn't react at all to the request. It seemed this was a normal amount of luggage.

Considering we were going by private jet, I could see why someone might not be as restrained, but this seemed more than a little excessive. It was far more than I ever hoped I'd get into the habit of taking everywhere with me.

"Ready to shop?" Jack asked me as he took my hand.

I grinned and nodded, beginning to like the idea. I'd seen some of the clothes Jack had packed, and it gave me an idea for some cute outfits that might go well with them. Maybe I could grab a few and make up for the feeling of unnecessary spending when I had perfectly good summer clothes back home by treating myself to clothes I could use for another purpose later on.

I tried not to think beyond that. Although I had ideas, I had no clue what the shops in New York were like.

"So, where do you normally go to shop?" I asked, knowing Jack had an eclectic style and wondering where he'd get his clothes.

"I don't normally. Neil gets stuff that he knows I'll like."

Again, I had no idea how to respond, and Jack immediately chuckled.

"Beginning to think a PA sounds like a good idea?" he asked.

"Oh, very much so," I replied. "Someone who goes clothes shopping for me sounds amazing."

"It's also necessary sometimes when you're... Well, if the crowds know I'm there, they can get a little …"

"Yeah, I can imagine," I said as I slipped my hand in his.

For a moment, he looked a little sad, almost like he would have liked to live normally sometimes. And I couldn't blame him.

CHAPTER FIFTY-THREE

Being driven around New York had its benefits. Jack pointed out more sights for me as we were taken toward Manhattan and Central Park.

The streets were busy, but there were also fewer pedestrians than I expected. A lot of taxis flowed, many folks getting in them and then sometimes only traveling a few blocks before they'd get out again.

As cars pulled in and out, it was clear this was what slowed the majority of the traffic as well. It was a sort of chaos I didn't think I was capable of getting used to. It made me grateful I wasn't the one driving.

Along the way, we'd stopped to grab a late lunch-to-go from a small cafe Jack liked and had already polished it off before the driver finally pulled us over right outside a grand building.

I blinked at the large single word over the double door.

Dior.

Jack had taken me to shop at Dior.

Trying not to show my nerves, I let him pull me out of the car and into the store. Immediately, a smartly dressed woman approached us, her eyes taking in Jack and lighting up before they switched to me. I was appraised with a single look, and it was obvious the assistant tried not to show her distaste for the cheaper clothes I was currently wearing.

Although I gave her credit for trying, it didn't make me feel any better about the experience.

After looking me over again, she refocused on Jack.

"Can I help you both today? Men's wear?" she asked, almost sounding hopeful.

"No, nothing for me today. Juno needs some clothes to wear on the island. At least seven outfits and some sandals, hats, and accessories. The whole works."

"Right. Of course. Follow me, then, and we'll see what we can find. You look to be about a size six, ma'am. Is that correct?"

"I'm sorry. I'm not familiar with American sizes," I replied, feeling so far out of my depth I wanted to cry already.

Almost immediately, the woman's expression softened, and she seemed to turn into a warm, comforting aunt or matron.

"Well, there's no need to fret on that count. It's my job to help you find some clothes you love, and I'm sure we can do just that."

Feeling a little better but aware I was so obviously out of my depth that Jack might decide I didn't belong in his world, I let myself be led along to a section of the store.

Immediately, the associate started pulling items of clothing off the displays, and I noticed the shop was very different from the cheap ones I was used to. Instead of twenty different styles of jeans and racks and racks of tops, there was a greater variety and far less on display.

But the store seemed to make up for the lack of over-whelming quantity that was supposed to cater to many tastes by having some stunning outfits and matching sets designed to flatter thin people far more than anything else.

I'd only been in the shop for a few more minutes before I found myself eternally grateful that I was at least relatively slender, although I noticed I was on the upper end of the sizes they stocked.

Trying not to worry about it, I allowed the assistant to keep going a little longer and even looked at a few things myself, picking out a summer dress with a matching hat and sandals I liked the look of. As I did, I tried to look for a tag or some kind of price sticker, but there was just the brand logo on a small card with a barcode on it.

I caught Jack's attention as I held it up again, trying to decide if it was worth spending an unknown amount of money on and guess what it might cost. He came over and took it off me before holding it up against my body and popping the hat on my head.

"I like it. You should definitely get this one," he said.

I saw the assistant look over and immediately smile before hurrying to another section of the store, where she found a matching bathing suit. While she was far enough away, I leaned closer to Jack.

"Where are the prices on these things?" I asked, barely above a whisper.

"They don't put price tags on their clothes," he replied. "They operate under the assumption that if you can afford to buy here, you aren't worried about the differences in costs of one piece of clothing versus another."

"Right," I said, feeling even worse. Why couldn't this be simple to do? And who thought people didn't need price tags? I had absolutely no idea if I could afford just one outfit or twenty new ones.

"You feeling okay?" he asked a moment later.

"Yeah, just…there's a lot that's different in the world of the rich and famous. I guess I'm still getting used to it."

"Okay, but don't worry about the prices, all right? I can get these. You only need them because of me." I saw him studying my face as if he was trying to figure out if that was why I'd reacted the way I had.

"No. It's okay. I'm sure I can pay. It can't be that expensive to buy some material, even if it has been made into something beautiful," I replied, aware the assistant was back and looking between us as if trying to decide whether she should interrupt.

I smiled at her but shook my head at the bikini she'd found in matching print.

"As much as I like the fabric, I think that would be overdoing it," I said.

"Understood," she replied, looking like that answer had been expected and made all the sense in the world before putting it down on a nearby shelf that seemed to be placed exactly to take discarded items.

Feeling a little sorry for her when she was clearly just trying to help me find what I did want, I let her show me the other pieces she'd picked out, and I chose some of them to try on as well.

With about six outfits and all their corresponding accessories, I made my way to the changing rooms. Jack paused outside them, and I noticed he was immediately offered a drink and snacks while he waited. That impressed me.

"Do you want me to show you each outfit as I try it?" I asked. "Or let the ones I buy be a surprise?"

"Whichever you'd prefer. They're going to make sure I'm not bored either way," he replied with a grin.

I couldn't help but smile at the cheeky way he glanced at the assistant, and it seemed to help break some of the awkwardness of the moment.

Still not sure which I'd choose to do, but grateful for Jack's ability to diffuse some tension, I hurried inside, and the assistant immediately showed me into one of the biggest changing rooms I'd ever seen. Rather than the heavy curtains I was used to pulling across gaps, it was a room in and of itself, with another small changing area off that.

It also contained a seat and a rack to hang everything on.

When the assistant handed me the first outfit, I decided to assume she was sticking around and took it into the smaller, curtained area.

"That dress you picked out really is a good color for you," she said as I began to change, clearly trying to make polite conversation. "I'm sure you're going to look amazing in it."

I hoped she was right, but I wasn't sure how to respond to it and merely concentrated on pulling off the less well-designed clothes I already wore.

Immediately, I felt exposed and vulnerable, and I noticed the last few marks of the bruises I had left. The dress would expose more than one of them, its back crisscrossed and more open than I'd originally imagined.

Trying not to let it stop me, I put the dress on anyway.

CHAPTER FIFTY-FOUR

For a moment, I could barely move. There was a long mirror in the small changing cubicle with me, and I was right. The old, fading bruises on my right-hand side could be seen. While none of them looked as bad as they had when Greg had first given them to me, they stood out enough against my pale skin that I wanted to cry.

"Everything all right?" the assistant asked. "Do you need me to help with anything? A zip or... I can be discreet about it."

"No," I called back, my stomach knotting at the idea of her seeing the dress and bruises. I'd done everything I could to hide them. Would she think Jack had given them to me?

I looked amazing from the front, and I felt a pang of pain as I realized I couldn't buy the dress and wear it while on the island if I wanted to keep hiding them.

"Does it fit all right?"

"Yes, but...I'm not sure it's really right for me after all," I finally replied, feeling a little defeated.

"Oh, nonsense," she said. "I'm positive you'll be stunning in it. Let me see."

Once again, I froze as she came to the curtain. She didn't

come in, but I had the feeling she wasn't going to let me off the hook for the dress.

Trying to calm my racing heart and focus on just showing her enough to satisfy her, I faced her and pulled back the curtain just enough so she could see the front.

"Oh, my. Yes, it suits you so well. It makes you look a little less pale and brings out that gorgeous blue in your eyes. You have to get this one."

"I'm really not sure," I said immediately, finding her enthusiasm made me feel worse.

"I'll get Jack. I'm sure he can help me convince you. You're a dream in this."

Before I could stop her, she strode out to the door and waved to him. I gulped and tried to decide how rude I could be and if I could simply pull the curtain back over and pretend I was so certain of my decision I didn't want Jack's opinion.

No sooner had I thought this than the moment passed, and he walked into the room, a glass of iced tea in one hand.

His eyes widened as he looked over the dress.

"Where's Juno, and what have you done with her?" he asked the assistant a moment later.

"It's gorgeous, isn't it?" she replied to him and ignored me.

"Come and do a twirl for me, angel," Jack said, going over to the sofa and sitting down. I gulped again and didn't move, but the assistant also motioned for me to do so.

I still didn't move. Both of them stared at me.

"I'm really not sure I like it," I said, hearing the tremor in my voice.

Jack gave me a look as if he'd picked up on my reluctance, but instead of saying anything or giving in, he held his hands out to me, trying to encourage me to go to him.

Taking a deep breath and trying to act as if I wasn't sure about the dress and not my bruises, I went over to him and put my hands in his.

The dress flowed behind me like silk, like I was some sort of summer nymph, making me feel even more sure he would insist I buy it.

I'd just reached Jack, going past the assistant, when I heard her intake of breath. Although it was subtle, both Jack and I looked her way. She was staring at the right-hand side of my back, and I knew she'd seen the fading bruises there.

This seemed to be enough that understanding dawned on Jack's face.

"It shows off the bruises," he said, uttering what I hadn't been able to.

I nodded, feeling my eyes water.

Immediately, he put his arms around me and pulled me into a warm, strong hug. It broke the dam, and I felt the first sob hitch in my breathing before I buried my face in his shoulder and tried not to cry.

"It's okay to be upset, Juno, but they'll fade. One day, they won't be there anymore. And he can't hurt you anymore. Okay? You're safe from him now."

The soothing, gentle tone to Jack's words helped calm me, and I pulled back, aware I'd smudged my makeup a little.

If Jack even noticed, he didn't seem to care as he gently kissed me, his arms still holding me close, making me feel safer than I had in months.

"I'll go get some tissues and water. Would you like some iced tea as well, my dear?" the assistant asked.

I nodded, not sure I did, but willing to say anything to get some privacy for a moment.

"Will she tell anyone?" I asked a moment later, fear gripping at me.

"No. We'll ask her not to, and I'm sure she'll understand." Jack kissed me again.

I leaned into him and felt the tension leave me. He knew now. There was a strange relief in not having to hide so much again.

"Do you like the dress?" he asked.

"Yes. I love it. It's just going to show the bruises."

"Get it anyway. Even if you'd rather not wear it on the island this time. You'll be able to wear it in only a week or two more."

It made sense, and part of me didn't know why I'd gotten so upset about it. Of course I'd still be able to wear it. I tried to smile as Jack made me twirl and admired it, seeming to look past the damage my ex had done to my back.

By the time I was in his arms again, the assistant had returned, a tissue box under one arm and a glass in each hand, one with water and the other with the iced tea she'd offered to fetch in the first place.

"There we go, my dear," she said, holding them out to me to let me choose which to pick.

I started with the water. She placed the iced tea on a coaster on a small side table and then pulled out a tissue.

"Why don't we get you cleaned up a little, and you can try on the rest of the clothes? And then, at the end, we'll go over to the makeup department, and we can get you looking amazing again."

I noticed she said 'again' at the end of the sentence and appreciated the vote of confidence on my looks, if nothing else. With Jack's encouragement and some help from the assistant wiping off the worst of the mascara that had run, I soon got back to trying on clothes.

Of the six outfits I tried on, Jack and I agreed on three of them but not all the accessories that went with them. I also liked the top that went with one of the other outfits and thought it went well with the pants I'd already picked out that day.

"You can keep that one on if you like. I hope you don't find it rude of me to say, but it looks better on you than the top you came in wearing."

I didn't disagree with the assistant and decided that if I was going to splurge on clothes, I might as well enjoy it.

With everything settled and all the clothes I wanted in a pile, the assistant gathered them up and took me to the makeup department. Jack excused himself from this part, saying he needed to talk to his PA and sort out some things.

Nodding, I watched him leave, feeling suddenly more apprehensive, but the assistant appeared to pick up on it.

"I promise everyone will be lovely to you," she said and put her arm around me. "I guess you've had a rough ride."

"You could say that," I replied without thinking.

"You've found a good man in Jack. He's one of the sweetest men in the city," she said. "Now, come on, let us make you feel like a princess. And don't worry, I won't tell anyone what I saw. I know it can't be easy to have the world know something like that."

"Thank you," I said, genuinely grateful. Maybe coming to a store like this wasn't so bad after all.

CHAPTER FIFTY-FIVE

As I sat in the seat by one of the makeup stands and let one of the assistants there get a good look at me, I felt a little self-conscious again. It wasn't easy letting other women stare at you and judge what they saw.

Some women used the opportunity to make themselves feel better by putting others down. And while I knew they did it out of their own insecurities and fears, it never helped anyone.

"Oh my, you have such gorgeous long eyelashes, darling. And natural, too. With those big blue eyes of yours, I'm sure we can make you look stunning. Do you mind if I take everything off and start again?"

"No, go for it," I replied, feeling as if it was the expected response.

"Fantastic. I'm Beth. I understand you and Jack came in today to get some summer clothes."

"Yeah," I replied as she started wiping away everything I'd put on that morning. Admittedly, it wasn't much. I didn't apply much makeup on the best of days. It had never been anything I'd wanted to put much effort into, but I knew there was a lot of skill to the art, and it could really change how a person looked.

The makeup artist made small talk with me, and my assistant from before came back, having bagged up all my clothes. I tried to hide the shock I felt at the assumption that I was going to pay for everything and could do so. I still didn't know how much it would be, and I had no idea if I could afford it.

Trying not to worry about it, I looked away again and asked Beth something about the makeup as if I was more interested in it than I was.

She immediately started telling me all about it, making my head spin with details. At the same time, my assistant lined up little boxes and bottles of everything being used so I could see it.

I had a feeling they both hoped it would entice me to buy more from them, and a part of me considered it. If this was the level of effort the women Jack normally associated with went to, maybe I should go to these lengths as well.

While I'd been in Alma's room earlier in the day, I'd also noticed she had a lot more makeup than I did, and there were all sorts of different types to get a particular effect.

On top of that, a part of me was genuinely interested. Inside almost every woman was a little girl who wanted to look stunning. It was almost entirely ingrained in us. Could all these bottles and boxes give me that?

Despite all these thoughts and the advice of the ladies around me, I was still sitting in the chair half an hour later and beginning to feel like it was a lot more time and effort than I normally wanted to spend.

That said, it wasn't like I normally had much else to do. I was either with Jack now or single, and I was only writing. Would it hurt to spend more time on my personal appearance?

It wasn't long before I decided I was too emotional and tying myself in knots by overthinking it. I could see how things went, and if I decided I wanted to spend more time on it and enjoyed doing so, I could. Like anything else in life I did or didn't do.

If nothing else, I knew I didn't want to change me to please anyone else. I'd been doing that for too long with Greg, and he had turned into a monster when I'd stopped trying to fit into the box he had for me.

By the time an hour had passed, the makeup artist was finally done. A minute or so before, my assistant had rushed off, making me wonder if she'd decided to help another customer, but before I could get up, she reappeared with Jack.

He had another glass of iced tea in his hand and took a gulp as he stopped. I tried to smile at him but felt too nervous for it to come across properly, and I was pretty sure I grimaced instead.

"That took a while," Jack said, immediately making me feel even worse.

"Starting from the beginning often does, but I think it's worked wonders," the makeup artist said.

"Oh, it's a definite transformation. I'm not even sure where Juno is." Jack flicked me a wink as he grinned and put what was left of his drink down.

Trying not to worry about their opinions and the unreadableness of Jack's expression, I looked at my reflection in the mirror the assistant had picked up. Jack was right. I didn't look anything like myself. With contouring, they'd managed to make my nose look smaller and my eyes look even more doe-like. My complexion was also a lot smoother, and I looked soft in a way I had no idea how they'd achieved.

It looked strange to see my reflection in the mirror most of the time, but this was a whole new level.

"Do you like it?" the makeup artist asked when I continued to study myself.

"Yes, I think so," I replied, deciding to be honest.

"I can provide you with any elements you want to use in your own routine in the future."

I smiled, amused by the obvious sales tactic as I was interested in the idea.

"What do you think, Jack?" I asked. "Suit me?"

He shrugged, offering me nothing to go on. I looked back at my reflection for a moment, trying to decide what to do. I still didn't know how much the clothes cost, nor did I know if I wanted to look differently.

"I think I'd like a few hours to get used to it. It's very different to how I usually look. Could I get a list of everything?" I asked eventually, feeling a little sorry for her when she also probably worked on commission.

"Of course," the makeup artist said, but I could see her deflate a little.

"Or if you have a number I could call to order it through you later or discuss it further and what might complement my requirements going forward, that would work as well," I added.

Immediately, she wrote down her number and added her name, and she seemed a little less disappointed.

Not sure what to do next, I got off the chair and walked to Jack. I felt strange wearing new clothes and lots of makeup I didn't normally bother with, but Jack took my hand.

"All done?" he asked.

"I think so. And I'm getting hungry."

"Me too," he replied and then looked at our assistant. She immediately held up the bags.

"Do you want me to give these to you, or do you have a car nearby we can have them sent to?"

"Car. Usual one." Jack didn't hesitate with his response and then led me over to a small counter where I could pay for the clothes. I walked to it with trepidation and let her punch the numbers into the checkout system.

A five-figure sum came up, making me freeze in shock. I'd expected it to be four figures and higher than I wanted it to be, but it had an extra zero on the end of what my wildest fears had considered.

There was an awkward moment where the pair looked at me

to resolve the situation and hand a card over, but I simply stared and didn't move.

Almost immediately, Jack reached for his own wallet, pulling a card with a quick precision I hadn't expected.

"No, it's okay. I've got it," I said, putting my hand out to stop him.

I'd told him I'd pay for the clothes, and I knew it would be wrong of me to back out now, but I made a mental note to never shop for designer brands again.

The whole time I reached for my purse and opened it to reveal my cards, I tried to decide if I even had one I could put that kind of money on. I only had one. The credit card I had recently acquired when leaving Greg.

It wasn't ideal. There was no way I was paying off the entire sum in one month's royalties, not with all the other bills I had, but I handed over the card and tried to appear as normal as possible. This had all been one very expensive mistake.

Next time, I'd choose the store I bought my clothes in and insist on knowing the prices before the bags were in the car, and I was on the hook to pay for them all.

CHAPTER FIFTY-SIX

<u>Jack</u>

I strode into the restaurant I'd chosen for dinner, feeling like I'd won the lottery with Juno on my arm. Although I hadn't wanted to make her feel bad about her previous attempts to look good, she was stunning now, the women who had pampered her all afternoon having taken her mind off the bruises.

It had taken all my self-control to keep my emotions in check more than once already today, and I was hoping we'd reached the end of it. Of course, it wasn't Juno's fault that she'd been abused the way she had, but it made it hard to think about her in a perfect way. Her skin was marred, even if it would fade in time.

No part of me could blame her if she didn't want to look so good that she attracted attention to herself, either. Sometimes, it was more appealing to wear plain clothes and no makeup and have the world not realize you were even you.

Now, heads turned, and I nodded at a few other celebrities I recognized before we were shown to a two-person table out of the way. I kept hold of Juno's hand as we sat down, and I took the menus for us both.

"Would you let me order for you tonight?" I asked. "They have a special here that I always get, and I think you'd like it, too."

"Sure," she replied, her eyes going a little wider and making her look even more innocent.

My groin stirred as I thought about how not innocent she'd be once I was done with her. Desire flooded through me at this almost angelic creature before me. She'd promised to be all mine and submit herself to my needs.

While I was still eager to have her tied up and entirely at my mercy, I knew there were plenty of other things I could do to her, and for now, I had most of what I wanted. She'd agreed to come to the island with me and the band, and I had tonight with her and only her before we left.

As soon as I'd ordered for us, I let my gaze wander. The new top showed off the curve of her breasts better, fitting in tight beneath them before flowing out again.

"I'm sorry you were kept waiting so much this afternoon," she said, frowning slightly. "I didn't expect that to take so long."

"It's not a problem. We're about to have several days on the island together, and as soon as we've finished eating, I'm taking you back to the apartment to do as I please with every inch of you."

"Oh, you are, are you?" she asked, smirking lightly.

"I am. And I don't expect to hear a single objection. I've earned every inch of you. Even if I hadn't, looking the way you do now, I'm certain I could persuade you."

"That sounds like you don't plan to take no for an answer. I'm pretty sure you're supposed to if I say it," she replied, her gaze fixing on my face. I could see the nervousness in them.

"Do you plan to say no to me taking you into my bed and enjoying you repeatedly?"

She bit her lip, drawing my attention to it before she shook her head.

"I don't think so," she said with an exhale, her eyes wide again.

I couldn't help but feel smug at the effect I was having on her as my cock hardened some more. If dinner didn't arrive on our plates soon, I was going to screw her right here and now. Or at least demand she wrapped that sweet little mouth around me until she'd eaten my cum as well as her food.

As soon as the thought was in my head, I wasn't sure I could shake it, but here and now wasn't the time or place for making her start a meal with me. On the island. I'd have to save that for on the island.

Juno looked away and down at her drink a moment later, and I found myself wondering what she was thinking. I felt better than I should after spending several hours in a single clothing store, but Juno had paid for everything herself, and it had been a relief that she wouldn't let me pay even when I offered.

Despite that, I was pretty sure the price of the clothes had been higher than she was expecting, the shock on her face not completely masked.

It made me worry that she wasn't ready for a world like mine, where everyone had such high standards. But she seemed to have started adapting already, and Alma and Kai liked her. That was a good sign.

"You seem lost in thought," she said a moment later. "Are you worried about something?"

"No," I replied, mostly truthful. "I was trying not to think about everything I wanted to do to you as soon as we're alone."

Her mouth fell open, and I let out a chuckle, but she quickly recovered, blushing a little and looking down again.

"Seriously. I can't wait to show you the island. I'm glad you said you'd come."

"Me too," she replied. "I was a little nervous at first, but being with you and...coming to New York..."

"Are you struggling with your words?" I asked when she trailed off yet again and shrugged.

"A little. I know. Bad form for a writer not to have the words to express themselves, but...thank you. For everything. I'm happier than I've been in a long time."

She smiled up at me, her eyes alight. I couldn't help but be moved, a warmth spreading through my torso.

Was I falling in love with her?

I wasn't sure, but it was clear something was happening between us.

The food soon came, and I watched Juno take her first bite, a little nervous that I'd ordered for her and she might not like it. But she immediately took another mouthful of the gluten-free pasta dish, letting out a delighted little moan.

Eating happily, we talked about the band, music, and the songs we'd grown up with. Once again, Juno kept the conversation moving, asking questions and offering information about herself with natural ease.

The time passed quickly, dessert and more drinks following our main course until she sat back and grinned.

"In case I forget to say it later," she said, "thank you. I've had an amazing time tonight."

I chuckled again as she smirked slightly, and I motioned to the waiter nearby to get the bill. She immediately reached for her purse again.

"No," I said. "I'll get this."

"Are you sure? I'm happy to pay. Or split it. Or whatever."

"I'm well aware that you've already spent way more than you intended today on the clothes. I'm going to insist on this one."

She exhaled and dropped her purse, and I was pretty sure she was relieved. I also noticed she didn't deny that the clothes had been more expensive than she'd expected.

I made a mental note to be more careful with her in the future and not overestimate how much money she truly had.

As soon as the bill was paid, and I'd added a decent tip, I took her hand and led her back toward the car, my bodyguards falling in around us.

I wanted to get her back to the apartment. And I wasn't waiting any longer.

CHAPTER FIFTY-SEVEN

<u>Juno</u>

The day had brought so many different feelings and emotions, but I'd found myself more than a little happy to be in Jack's arms and heading back to his apartment at the end of the night again.

It had been a wild ride since I'd met him, and I'd never have predicted this turn of events or where I'd be now. And in some ways, I still couldn't really believe it.

New York lit up at night in a way that dazzled me further, and I stared out the window at all the lights until we were near Jack's apartment. As soon as we were close, he grabbed my hand and practically pulled me into his arms.

"I hope you're ready for a night of being entirely mine," he said as the car stopped.

"I'm ready for a whole week of it," I replied and fought to appear serious.

I didn't entirely succeed, but it made Jack smirk, so I clearly hadn't gotten myself in any trouble. At least, not yet.

Jack wasted no time in leading me to the apartment, taking me in his arms in the elevator, and pressing almost frantic, passionate kisses to my lips until I was hot and panting.

I felt the heat rush between my legs, making me wet and hungry for whatever he had in mind. There was just something about the way his arms felt around me and his strong body near mine. It drove all the thoughts out of my head except for how badly I wanted to be full of his cock.

Imagining the feel of his hardness deep inside me, I let him take me into the apartment and to the bedroom.

Immediately, he pulled my top up and over my head, stripping me at a pace I could barely process. His hands worked with practiced dexterity until I was naked before him. Although I reached for him a few times to begin removing his clothing as well, he always pushed my hands away and continued stripping me.

The second I was entirely exposed, wetness slicking the tops of my thighs, Jack lifted me and carried me to the bed. He placed me inside the cool sheets gently and then got in with me, shifting so he was over and on top.

I yielded to him, letting him control and dominate me and what we were doing. His hands quickly wandered, finding my nipples already hard. I moaned as he tugged gently on them before taking each one in his mouth.

His hands roamed even lower, finding my wet folds. Slipping several fingers into me, he almost gave me what I wanted, his thumb stroking over my clit.

"Are you going to submit to me?" he asked, his mouth near my ear and his words almost menacing.

"Yes," I replied, knowing that was what he wanted to hear.

He groaned as he kissed me again, his tongue probing past my lips as he claimed me. I denied him nothing, his thumb stroking back and forth across my clit as he repeatedly thrust with his fingers.

It didn't take long for me to be a shuddering mess, waves of orgasm washing over me. I whimpered as he removed his fingers, leaving me cold but hungry for whatever would follow.

As I came back down, he eased himself between my legs.

Before I could entirely recover, he freed his cock and pushed it deep into me. I gasped at the sudden fullness, but I took him easily. He moved inside me gently, his hands pinning mine to the bed.

Setting the pace, he took his time in bringing us both into heaven together this time, his hard cock pulsing as he filled me with his seed to tip me over into the pleasure of another orgasm.

We moaned together, my body entirely his and my mind more than willing. With him staying over me and in me, we came back down, our arms now wrapped around each other and our fore-heads together while we panted.

"Stay here," he said, almost growling the last word.

Suddenly, he pulled up and away from me, the coldness that came rushing in against my skin where he had been making me shiver.

I watched him go to the closet and rummage for a moment. He came back out a moment later with a bandanna. Folding it into a long strip, he brought it to my face.

"I won't tie you up if you cooperate, but I want to blindfold you," he said.

I got the impression it wasn't a question, but I nodded as if I was consenting anyway. I'd promised to be his and submit. This would require my trust, but it was still a long way from being tied up with no way to get out.

Despite my head knowing all that, I still felt my stomach knot and fear ripple through me. My head wanted to trust Jack with everything, but my emotions and heart were still so bruised by Greg and everything that had happened before Jack. How could I trust someone again?

Trying to focus on how good it had felt submitting to Jack so far, even only five minutes earlier, I held still as he placed the soft, silken fabric over my eyes and tied it behind my head.

I was instantly blind. I inhaled sharply, my body tensing, but

Jack gently cupped my face with his hand and pressed his lips to mine.

"Relax. I won't hurt you. I promise. You're safe with me. No different from a moment ago."

His words were what I needed, and although I'd told myself almost exactly the same thing, something about hearing them in his deep but tender voice helped me calm my racing heart a little and relax into the moment.

He kissed me several times, each one helping to soothe the tenseness away. Slowly, he brought his arms around me, pulling me close until our bodies touched again.

Being just as soothing, he slipped me onto my front and nestled one leg and then the other between mine. I could feel his hardness against my ass, making it clear we were going to have another round, but he made no attempt to enter me yet.

With his body over me, he reached underneath and cupped both breasts, squeezing them before he found each nipple and rolled them between his thumbs and forefingers.

I moaned, feeling heat pool between my legs, arousal growing as he kissed the back of my neck and continued down my spine. The sweet way he took his time and made me feel wanted in so many ways soon had me wet again, hungry for him despite not being able to see properly.

Once more, he slipped his hand between my thighs, feeling how aroused I was without me needing to say anything.

I moaned as he cupped my pussy, rubbing across my clit, and making me really turned on, but as his fingers slid into my depths, I felt him press his other hand between my butt cheeks.

"Lift your knees," he said, the words a clear command.

For a moment, I didn't move.

"Trust me, Juno. I won't hurt you."

I inhaled, the breath hitching in my throat. I wanted to ask him if he was about to do what I imagined, but the words wouldn't leave my panicked mind.

Before I could comply with him, his hand left my ass and pushed one knee up and then the other, parting my cheeks for him. All the while, he continued to run his fingers slowly across my clit.

A moment later, I heard the rip of a condom packet, and it confirmed my thoughts. Jack was about to anal me. While I was blindfolded and horny as hell.

CHAPTER FIFTY-EIGHT

I heard the lid snap off something a moment later, making me tense again. His fingers followed, probing coldness as he slipped his thumb into my anus, pushing what could only have been lubricant with it.

"Relax," he said again as I tensed up around him. "Let me make this good for you too."

I exhaled, closing my eyes so I didn't feel quite so robbed of sight and tried to imagine how good it might feel. I'd never been analed before, and I wasn't sure what it would be like.

I'd heard that it could be amazing, but I'd also heard it could be extremely painful. And I had no idea which was likely to be the case.

The coldness turned to warmth as Jack probed deeper into me with his thumb and then pulled back out. I focused on my breathing and trying to remain calm. I wanted him to have this, to show him I trusted him, but I was nervous.

A moment later, I felt him kiss my spine again, right above my ass, before trailing kisses back up me. It made me arch my back instinctively, bringing my shoulder blades up until his head was beside mine. At the same time, he ran one of his hands up my leg until it was at my hip, holding me steady.

"Focus on relaxing as you exhale," he whispered near my ear.

No sooner had I done as requested than I felt his manhood pressing against my hole. On the very next exhale, he pushed in. I tensed a little, but he paused immediately, my body already feeling the strange sensation. A fullness and pressure that was strange but not entirely unpleasant either. Sort of painful as he stretched me, but also full and different.

On the very next breath out, he pushed deeper again, easing himself into me until, after several breaths, he was deep inside me.

Almost immediately, Jack started to thrust in and out, the lubricant helping the process go smoothly, but his body still matched my breathing, pulling out as I sucked air in and pushing deep again as I exhaled.

It felt strange at first, but I could quickly tell he was enjoying every moment, groans escaping him with each thrust. He grew quicker and rougher, but my body took him, my insides full and pleasure building as he rubbed against something deep in me.

Keeping myself as relaxed as I could, I let him claim me in a whole new way, more focused on yielding to him than my own pleasure until he grew even more frantic, pushing hard and deep in several quick thrusts, both hands holding my hips to help drive me onto his throbbing cock.

I whimpered as pleasure started to build in me, but it was too late. He exploded, roaring as he pushed hard into me and orgasmed. For a moment, I held him up, his body draped over the back of mine, and then he slowly eased up and out.

"Good girl," he said, those two words making me feel smug and satisfied in a way I hadn't expected.

Still blindfolded and feeling like I should stay put, I waited for him to clean himself up and then return to the bed and me.

Gently, he pulled me into his arms again and pressed his mouth against mine.

"You're an angel," he said before slipping the blindfold back off.

For a moment, the light made me blink, but then I could see him again. There was an almost relieved look in his eyes as he gazed at me. I smiled up at him and snuggled into his embrace, hoping he felt more trusted and wondering exactly what had happened in his past to make him feel the need for it.

Of course, I'd heard a few rumors, and I knew the stuff the papers had reported, but everyone knew they speculated and went for headlines. Whatever had happened, it clearly still bothered him.

"I've never done that before," I said, the confession feeling right.

Immediately, his eyes widened, and he gaped, trying to say something, but nothing came out.

"It's okay," I added, worried he was panicking. "I'm glad you're my first. You made me feel safe. And maybe we can do it again at some point. I..." I trailed off, not sure how to admit I had enjoyed it.

"You know, kitten, you're continually full of surprises," he said a moment later, stroking my cheek. "Every time I think I understand you, you go and tell me there's more to you. Thank you for trusting me with being your first. And..."

He shook his head and looked away, almost as if he was ashamed suddenly. It was my turn to place a finger under his chin and lift it again.

"What's wrong?" I asked. "What has upset you?"

"Your first time shouldn't have been taken from you like that. While you were so helpless and—"

I cut off his guilty words with a kiss.

"It was perfect," I said as I pulled back. "I couldn't have given my first to someone in a way I liked more. We agreed to try a dom-sub relationship together. So far, I like it."

Jack pulled me even closer, his eyes shining as if he was momentarily overwhelmed. I kissed him again, knowing this was one of those moments in time that were completely perfect.

Sexually, I was still hungry for more, having been stimulated but not taken to my peak, but I knew what I'd given Jack was worth every moment of frustration I'd feel if we fell asleep then and there.

It seemed Jack wasn't going to forget about me, however. A moment later, he rolled me onto my back again.

"Time for your reward," he said, almost growling the last word.

Another swift kiss followed it, and then Jack shifted downward, trailing kisses down my torso as I went. He deftly pushed my legs open again, his lips pressing against my skin again and again until he reached the top of my pussy.

After a glance up at me and a smirk, he continued, his lips forming an o around my clit. I gasped as he flicked out his tongue and caught the top of the sensitive nub, the pleasure intense and instant.

Slowly, he repeated the movement, spikes of pleasure darting out every time he did. I grew hotter and wetter almost immediately, the sexual tension I'd been feeling pouring into a single mad rush until my body shuddered underneath his assault, an orgasm tearing through me.

I moaned long and deep as the waves rolled over me, but Jack didn't stop until I was unmoving again beneath him, the pleasure so intense I wasn't able to speak for some time.

Grinning slyly, he moved back up the bed and wrapped his arms around me again.

"We should rest now," he said. "We need to travel tomorrow, and then we'll have plenty of time on the island together."

His words sounded like bliss, making me more than a little

grateful I'd agreed to go with him. However, as Jack slipped into a deep sleep, I lay awake in his arms a little longer, marveling at how differently we'd gone to sleep the last two nights.

The previous night, I'd felt as if I'd let him down and made him feel like I didn't care about him as much as I wished I did. This evening, I was going to sleep after feeling I'd given him everything he'd asked for and more.

It had been a whirlwind of a day, and there had been moments where I thought it would go badly, especially over brunch with Alma and Kai and then again at the clothing store.

I'd also spent an obscene amount of money on designer clothes for the first time in my life and had no idea how long it would take me to pay off the credit card, but all in all, I still couldn't feel anything but how good things were between me and Jack.

Content, I finally slipped into a dream world. One full of walks on island beaches and dinners under star-lit skies.

CHAPTER FIFTY-NINE

As the day progressed, my stomach tightened until it was once more in a painful knot. We had three hours until we were flying to the island, and it was almost time to leave for the airport.

I was completely packed and dressed in comfy clothes for flying, but it wasn't until Jack started giving his housekeeper some instructions for managing the apartments while he was away that it sank in that I was actually going.

We'd spent the morning together, but I'd mostly been there while he talked to various people. I'd caught up on messages, responded to emails, and written a little, but it had only taken my mind off things for so long.

Jack was still getting things ready, on the phone with someone about something house-related, when my own phone buzzed. I frowned as I picked it up and noticed it was my agent.

"What's up?" I asked.

"Juno, just wanted to let you know I've almost finished negotiating the new final contract for the song with the band. Are you still in the US?"

"Yes, for now, but I'm having a long weekend away. Maybe a week. But don't worry. I'll write a little each day."

"Oh. You're going to the island too?"

I paused, not sure how to answer that question. How did he know, and why didn't he sound pleased?

"If I am, why aren't you happy about it?"

"I can still make it work if you are. Unless you're forbidding me to use it?"

I rolled my eyes as he reverted to his chirpy self.

"You surprise me, Juno. I'd have thought you wouldn't want to after everything in this negotiation."

"Okay. What's happening that I don't know about?" I asked, the knot in my stomach getting tighter.

"Nothing you don't know about. They're just digging their heels in about putting your name in the songwriting credits, and I have to convince them to do so."

"Oh." I frowned, almost in shock for a moment. Harry was just doing what I'd asked him to. I liked to have my name on everything I did, even if it didn't make me much money.

"I think they're giving in. There's been some talk of unions because you're not in a songwriters' one, but I think we've managed to find something that's a bit of a compromise."

"Okay, so you're handling it?"

"Of course, Juno. I handle everything."

"Then why are you calling?"

"Can't an agent call one of his best clients and make sure she's okay?" Harry replied, sounding mock-hurt. I chuckled.

"I think we both know that you're making sure I'm still alive and writing something that will make you money," I replied.

"I'm wounded by that accusation. It will make us both lots of money, darling. That's my job. To make me rich and you even richer."

Both of us chuckled as I hung up again. My agent was at least honest in a flippant sort of way. And I was grateful for what he did. He'd placed a slight worry at the back of my mind, though. Why was Jack's band not okay with sticking my name in the credits? It wasn't like I was asking for money or anything. I only wanted to be able to say I'd done it.

I'd really enjoyed being involved, and I wanted to prove that I was so I could see about maybe doing something similar in the future. It was a way to keep my options open and create more revenue streams. In short, it was good business.

Something about it made me feel off, though. Were Jack and his band trying to sideline me? It didn't make any sense that they would when I'd been invited to spend more time with them, but…

I sighed, knowing I was probably getting myself tied up in knots for something that didn't matter that much. I made a mental note to ask Jack about it and if he understood what all the negotiating was over in case I was missing something, and then I got back to finishing off the messages I had.

While I was on the island, I wanted to focus on nothing but being there and enjoying it. I hadn't had a vacation I fully enjoyed in a long time. I was determined to make this one different.

Before I could do much else, Jack came into the room.

"Everything's organized. Going to leave in about ten minutes. Are you ready?"

"Just got to finish an email," I replied, typing quicker and focusing.

I tried not to think about how stressed Jack sounded while I finished up and tucked my laptop into my bag as swiftly as I could. In less than ten minutes, Jack was back. I quickly slipped some shoes on and grabbed what I needed.

Being late for anything or the person to hold someone else up was always something I hated, and it was no different in this situation. A moment later, Jack and I were heading out the door, Neil not far behind, bringing the last bag that Jack had packed that morning.

I had my carry-on bag, but that was it, and I took it down to the waiting car, although it was heavier than usual, and I was more than a little relieved when Mick took it off me and stuffed it in the trunk of the car.

As he did, I noticed there were no other bags in there and wondered where all the rest of our luggage was. Had it been taken to the airport already?

Jack didn't give me the opportunity to ask, however. He opened the car door for us and pulled me inside with him.

I sighed as we settled onto the back seat together, his arm around me.

"How long do you think it will take to get there?" I asked, trying not to think about anything else now.

"The flight is about five to six hours. And then we'll take a car to the harbor and a boat to the island, which takes another three or four. We'll get to the island late tonight or early tomorrow. You can sleep on the airplane and the boat if you want."

I blinked, having not understood how long the journey would be but not wanting to complain. I'd still be with Jack, and I'd had more than one late night with him already.

"Sounds great," I replied. "Though I might nap on the plane if it's quiet enough."

"There's a bed and a couple of quieter spaces. I'm sure we can find you somewhere," Jack replied without missing a beat, and immediately, I was reminded about how different life was for a celebrity.

For a moment, I'd been thinking of a commercial flight and having to try to get some sleep on the awkward seats in cattle class.

Of course, Jack knew we were going on a private jet, and I had none of that to worry about.

Feeling as if I still had a lot to get used to and remember, I leaned into him and rested my head against his shoulder. At least I was going to enjoy a vacation with some people I was loving getting to know and one of the most amazing men on the planet.

CHAPTER SIXTY

<u>Jack</u>

It had been a long time since I'd taken anyone to the island with me other than the band. I remembered one of the last visits. I'd been trying to kick an addiction and gone there to do the worst of the rehab process out of the public eye. It had been a mixed bag, but made it clear I was with the wrong woman.

So many years ago, but it made me feel tense just thinking about it. Some memories weren't worth dwelling on again, but the mind wasn't always so easily controlled.

To try and distract myself from the unpleasant direction of my thoughts, I looked over at Juno. She'd cuddled up against my side, and the warmth of her body against mine was soothing and helped me relax again almost immediately.

Every time I thought I had Juno figured out, she surprised me with another element of her personality or thoughts. It was also clear she was still feeling the effects of the abuse her ex had heaped on her.

It made everything that had happened the night before between us seem all the more meaningful. She'd given me a part of her she'd never trusted to anyone else before.

Just thinking about it made my heart swell. I didn't feel I deserved it, and I knew I'd been short with her while we got ready to go.

While I loved going to the island, I normally went alone, and here I was trying to act as if it was normal to have the rest of the band come too. In truth, I liked the solitude. The chance to escape and be in my own head for a while and think.

Even having Juno coming with me was a big thing. I'd been on edge about it every moment. Until last night. Now, I felt as if I owed it to her. But it didn't stop me being worried either.

Thankfully, the journey to the airport was short, and we quickly met up with Alma and Kai. Alma immediately took Juno's arm and led her over to the small check-in desk we got to use to bypass the normal queues.

The advantage of traveling on our own plane was having no one else in our departure area except others also using their private jets.

Kai didn't seem as happy to see me as Alma was to see Juno, however.

"What's wrong?" I asked as soon as the women were far enough ahead that we wouldn't be overheard.

Kai set his jaw as if he was considering not saying anything.

"Having more of a battle with Juno's agent than I was expecting. Has she said anything to you?"

"No," I replied, an old doubt springing to mind.

"It might be him. I'll talk to her about it," Kai said.

"No. I'll do it. Is he pushing the money angle?"

Kai nodded. "I don't think he understands entirely how it works. Or she doesn't. But yeah. Right now, they're pushing the money angle."

"Leave it to me," I said, instantly feeling like a weight had been added to my shoulders. I didn't need another woman in my life who was only after the money I could make her. There had been too many in the past.

I was about to walk past Kai and catch the girls when he reached out and took my arm.

"Go gently, okay? It doesn't match with Juno in any other way. I don't think she's a gold digger. I think it's her agent, okay? Just ask her to tell him to back down a little, or we're going to get nowhere."

For a moment, I didn't know what to say. I was so tired of not being able to trust someone or know whom to believe.

"I'll ask her if she has any idea what's going on and tell her if she doesn't. But if she is trying to push for the money, I'm not letting her get on that jet."

"Understood," Kai said, finally letting go of me.

I hurried through the airport, trying to at least appear patient with the woman checking passports and documents. I found Juno and Alma sitting in the departure area, their bags on seats, and both of them with drinks.

"Juno, can I have a word for a moment?" I said, reaching for her.

She lifted her eyebrows but came straight over to me. Kai appeared a moment later and ushered Alma to the other side of the room.

"What's wrong, darling?" she said, elongating the last r in a mock upper-class English accent.

I tried to smile, knowing it was an attempt to be sweet on her part, but unable to stand it while I didn't know where she was at with the contracts and the song we'd written.

"Kai tells me your agent is digging his heels in about the song contract. I know it's only fair that you're paid for being involved, but he wants too much, Juno. If we give him everything he's asking, we'd have to not pay other band members what they're worth."

"Oh gosh, no, I don't want that at all. I was only telling him an hour or so ago that I didn't want it to be about the money," Juno replied, her eyes wide, the look of shock on her face genuine. "I was going to bring up this subject too, and then we had to leave, and I forgot. Did Kai say when they last spoke to Harry?"

"No," I replied, feeling a little better. "You really told him to give in on the money front?"

"Of course. Let me send him a quick message and reiterate." Juno pulled out her phone and began typing, saying only that and mentioning that Kai and I were concerned about everyone being able to have their fair share.

As soon as I'd seen enough of the message, I went back to Kai and gave him a positive nod. I felt almost foolish as Alma looked between us, clearly not filled in on what was going on.

"She spoke to her agent just before we left and was already telling him to give in. And she's sending another message now to make sure," I said, the tension that had built up in a short time rushing out of me along with the words. Kai clapped me on the shoulder.

"What did I tell you? It's not her. Apparently, her agent is known for being ruthless while negotiating for her, although he is respectful enough about it. He's probably not used to his clients saying 'don't worry about the money.'"

I nodded, hoping Kai was right, but the quick way Juno had not only denied wanting the money but immediately reassured me that she was already trying to make sure the money was distributed fairly made me feel better about the situation.

As I went back to her, I felt more than a little stupid and grateful that only Kai had picked up on how uneasy I had truly been. I'd almost caused a massive argument over what was clearly nothing because I'd been hurt in the past. Juno deserved to be treated better than that. She didn't deserve my suspicions and fears making me angry at her.

By the time I reached her, she'd sent the message and put her phone away again.

"Thank you, kitten," I said. "Sorry it's such a big thing. Hopefully, it can all be sorted soon."

"Don't worry about it. Contracts are always more back-and-forth than you ever expect them to be. They get signed in the end. I'm sure they'll all be done by the time we're at the island."

I smiled as she reached for me and put her arms around my waist. I did the same as she looked up, having to stand on the ends of her toes to kiss me.

"I can't wait until you see it," I said, hoping she'd like the place more desperately than I'd ever have expected to.

CHAPTER SIXTY-ONE

<u>Juno</u>

I tried not to ogle the inside of the plane as Jack led me on, his fingers entwined in mine. Thanks to the earlier conversation about money and contracts, I already felt a little on edge. I was pretty sure Jack had been holding back a lot of stress or anger when he'd first brought it up.

Of course, I didn't want his money at all, but it was clear that he was worried I might. It made me even more glad I'd paid for my own clothes the previous day, even if they'd been a huge expense for me but probably pocket change for him.

Now, I didn't know how to react to the interior of the jet. The softest carpet ran along the floor, far nicer and gentler underfoot than anything I'd felt in a building, let alone a plane. The seats were all cream leather that shone and looked so plush that I wasn't sure I could sit in them.

But the real wealth was clearly in all the gadgets and extras. There was a large TV and sofa arrangement on one side of the jet and a full dining table on the other, the seats around it almost as comfortable and plush.

We had several hostesses on board despite the fact that there were fewer than fifteen of us getting on the plane, including the PAs and security. No sooner were we on board than we were offered drinks, the possibilities seemingly endless and the usual preferences already covered.

Kai was quick to receive his usual brand of soda, and even Jack soon had a drink without even having to mention what he wanted.

I asked for a soda as well, feeling out of place, and then tried to take Jack's lead in deciding where to sit.

He moved toward the back of the plane, so I followed. He went past a small curtain and revealed yet another area. This one had smaller seats arranged on either side of the aisle, some headphones, and a few areas to plug in electronics, such as laptops. There were a few doors behind that, and Jack pointed at them in turn.

"Bathroom and bedroom," he said. "Sometimes Liam likes to take a nap, and he needs it to be super quiet and not in a seat, so we usually give him first crack. If he doesn't want it, feel free to nap. Or nap in here if you think you can. We're quieter back here, and the seats recline."

I nodded, taking it all in while in shock. The plane was so much bigger and more spacious than I'd expected. And it was also well-tailored to the band's requirements.

Jack smirked as I stood in the middle of the aisle a little longer before he sat on one of the seats out of the way. I went to sit beside him, feeling as if quiet and calm might be a great idea after all the chaos of the last few days. I also got the impression this was normal for him when Kai merely poked his head past the curtain, nodded in our direction, and then retreated again.

A moment later, Jack pulled a small sketchbook from his carry-on bag, along with a pen, and paid me little attention. I didn't mind, deciding to pull my e-reader from my purse and read for a while. I'd been so busy for so long that I hadn't had a chance to read in forever, and there were always plenty of books on my device just waiting for me to have a look.

The time slipped by, the staff making us a meal after only an hour or so. I marveled at the numerous options, the menu far more varied than on other flights, especially as they seemed to have anticipated my need for a gluten-free diet.

After eating, Kai and Alma came to the back of the plane as well, the latter curling up on a chair and reclining it so she could get some sleep. Kai also grabbed a book, and we descended into peace and quiet once more.

Not long after that, Liam took the option of using the bedroom. For a moment, I considered joining the others in the front of the plane, just hearing Eve's voice now and then, but instead, I stayed put, beginning to feel dozy as well.

The night sky had darkened while we flew. We were staying in the same time zone, but it was farther south, and that meant the sun set sooner.

I closed my eyes, trying to think of nothing but the hope of a nice vacation with Jack and his band. Of enjoying sandy beaches and starry skies. I drifted awake as a hand ran over my shoulder.

"We're landing," Jack said, his voice gentle as I opened my eyes.

I blinked a few times as my eyes adjusted and sat up. A blanket slipped off my shoulders, someone having put it there while I slept. Immediately, Jack sat back in his own seat, his paper and pen tucked safely away again.

Not sure what else to do, I waited and let my mind feel more awake again. It didn't take long to touch down, and then Jack got up and reached for me. Smiling up at him, I let him lead me out, going down the steps in his wake.

The island we'd landed on was warmer than the New York we'd left, even at night, and I was instantly grateful that I'd bought some clothes for summer conditions.

Despite the late hour, we were quickly inside another car, our passports checked, just me and Jack, with the others following in their own vehicles.

I noticed we didn't pull off right away, as airplane staff and the band's security helped load our luggage into the trunk, some of the smaller items coming in the car with us.

It made me feel a little guilty that we weren't doing anything to help. I noticed Jack was still a lot quieter than normal and tried to think of a way to encourage him to talk.

"When were you last on the island?" I asked. It was the first question that popped into my head, but Jack didn't answer it immediately, instead looking away.

"About six months ago," he said as he looked out the opposite window, the unmoving plane under his gaze.

I frowned, hearing tiredness in his voice. Was he just tired, or was there something else bothering him? I had no way to know. It was late, but he normally sounded like he had plenty of energy.

Before I could think of another question, the luggage was finally loaded, and our driver started the engine.

Leaning toward Jack, I sighed. He put his arm around me in response.

"You okay?" he asked, sounding like himself again.

"I think so. A little nervous about this island of yours, but excited, too. I've never been to the Bahamas," I replied, deciding to be honest. After all, that was what I was asking for from him.

"What makes you nervous?" he asked, turning even more my way.

I exhaled, not sure how to answer the question. Not because I didn't want to tell the truth but because I wasn't entirely sure of the answer myself.

"I think it's a mix of things. A little because it's an unknown place. I also don't feel I know everyone well yet, although everyone has been lovely so far. And because…it's a small island in the middle of nowhere. But it's not just that. I think I always feel a little anxious about unknowns and the expectations of others."

Jack nodded.

"I'm anxious, too," he said a moment later. "I want you to like the place."

"Oh, I'm sure I'll love the island," I replied. "And I'm pretty confident about being on it with you."

At my words, Jack smiled, and then we kissed, the passion he felt clear in the way he pulled me into his arms. Maybe being on his island was going to be all right after all.

CHAPTER SIXTY-TWO

The car journey passed in a blur of passion as Jack's hands roamed my body and held me close. We kissed and talked about little things, like what we wanted to do on the island, what Jack intended to do to me as soon as he had me in his bed, and how much I was going to have to take.

I grew so hot and wet at one point I'd pushed him back and straddled him. A second later, he flipped us around and held me against the seat, breaking all the contact between us.

"No," he said. "Not yet. Once we're on the island and not before."

I pouted, deliberately sticking out my bottom lip. Almost immediately, he chuckled and leaned in to gently bite it. Within seconds we were kissing again until I whimpered beneath him, hungry to have his hard cock deep inside me.

I let out a little squeal as the car came to a stop, and he pulled away, his eyes roaming over me.

"You look like you've been screwed a dozen times," he said, a glint in his eyes that showed he was more amused than bothered.

I frowned and quickly tried to neaten my hair, but this only made him chuckle more. A moment later, he leaned back toward me, gently smoothed my hair down, and helped arrange my clothes.

"How's that?" I asked when he pulled back once more.

"Better. At least it will have to do. Don't worry, some of the others won't look any better."

I fought back my own look of amusement before we got out of the car. As I glanced at Eve getting out of the car behind us and caught a look at her appearance, more disheveled than before, I realized Jack had spoken truthfully. It made me feel a lot better.

Still grinning, I let Jack lead me down toward the dock nearby. There were several boats moored there, only a few lit up in the dark, but Jack appeared to know where he was going and greeted several sailors along the way.

Considering it had been six months since he was last here, it gave the impression his trips had been a lot more frequent in the past, especially when he tapped on the window of a large yacht at the far end. A moment later, a sailor appeared on the deck above.

"Jack, there you are. A little early."

"We had a good run," Jack replied as the guy rushed to the nearby gate on the side of the boat. He swung it open and then lowered a small gangplank to the deck below, the wood having steps carved into it and a rail on one side.

I marveled at the ease and speed at which he'd done all this before looking up at the boat we were boarding.

When Jack said we were heading to the island on a yacht, I'd thought of something with three, maybe four cabins and a wheel-house area. This was a luxury yacht bigger than my entire apartment and most of the rest of the block it was on put together.

It took all my self-control not to gawk as we went up the gangplank, and Jack led me toward some seats on the deck. There was more than enough space for everyone to spread out across the main deck.

"You warm enough?" Jack asked me as they started loading the luggage, and a breeze blew across the side of the boat.

I nodded, although I wasn't completely sure I would be long-term. For now, I didn't want to make a fuss.

Once again, we were offered drinks and food as if we were guests in someone else's very expensive home. Despite the luxury and the way I was being taken care of, I declined and tried to rest, not sure I could ever imagine spending this money on just me traveling between places.

It made me feel a little better that at least ten of the band and partners plus security were with us, but I still felt like it was an almost astronomical expense.

Jack was also quiet, almost brooding, and I wasn't sure I had the capacity or energy to bring him out of it again. Instead, I watched the sailors and other staff as our luggage was brought aboard, so many bags and boxes going back and forth that I wondered how everyone kept track of it.

I watched for what felt like forever before yawning. As soon as I did, Jack took my hand and lifted me to my feet.

"You're tired. Come have another nap. I want one, too."

Suspecting he was in no mood to argue, I let him lead me along the deck. I smiled as we passed Eve and Alma, the two of them deep in conversation.

As we headed toward the front of the boat and another blast of fresh sea air caught me, I found myself grateful we were going inside for a while. Although the air temperature was fairly warm in general, especially with a jacket on, the breeze was cooler. I knew it would be stronger out at sea.

Jack led me to a hatch with stairs leading into a plush saloon, the walls and ceiling a highly polished wood, and the seating covered in a similar cream leather to the plane's. We didn't stop there, however. We headed for another small door and made our way back toward the center of the boat.

We passed several large cabins, and then Jack took a left into one, tugging me in after him before shutting the door.

It was a large room for a boat, complete with a double bed,

small sofa, dresser, and en suite bathroom. I marveled at how shiny the wooden floors and ceiling were for a minute before Jack moved to the bed and unbuttoned his shirt.

Going to him, I smirked as I took over.

"Don't get any ideas," he said. "I'm not ready for that yet."

"Can't I even tempt you a little?" I asked, wondering if it would be a better way to pass the time than sleeping, but a moment later, I found myself yawning again.

Jack chuckled before pulling my jacket off.

As soon as we both had our shoes off, he pulled back the covers and ushered me beneath them.

Within seconds, we were curled up in each other's arms, my head resting against his bare chest. I closed my eyes and inhaled, grateful for the familiar scent and the way I instantly felt calmer and safer. Maybe this was exactly what I needed.

"We'll be at the island in about two hours. It can get a little rough sometimes, but it shouldn't be too bad tonight," he said. "If you start to feel a little sick, head back up on deck."

"I should be fine," I said, looking at him. "I'm not the type to get seasick."

He pulled me a little tighter, and instantly, I saw the strange look in his eyes.

"Do you get seasick?" I asked him.

Instantly, he shook his head, but the haunted look on his face didn't go away. Had something happened at sea? Or was he worried about something coming in our future?

"What are you worried about?" I asked a moment later, keeping my voice gentle and resting my head against his chest so he wouldn't feel like I was studying him directly.

"It's hard to explain. I'm… The island isn't always somewhere I have a lot of people. And…" He trailed off and let out a sigh.

"Bad memories?" I asked.

"Yeah," he replied. "From a while back now, but bad memories is a good way to put it."

"Then we can make some new, better ones in a few hours." I looked up at him again, and he smiled down at me.

"That sounds like a perfect idea. I'll hold you to that promise."

I grinned. It hadn't quite been a promise, but I had no problem having my words taken that way, especially when they banished the pained look he'd worn.

Satisfied that we were beginning to figure out how to make each other happy, I settled down again and closed my eyes.

CHAPTER SIXTY-THREE

<u>Jack</u>

I woke sometime later, and for a moment, I panicked, my heart racing as I came up out of the nightmare I'd been having. My arms tightened around the sleeping form beside me, making her stir. In the faint light of the small bedside lamp, I realized it was Juno beside me and not someone else.

Exhaling, I lay my head back down and gazed at her. Still asleep, she looked like an angel. Compared to the woman in my dreams, I already knew that was exactly what Juno was. Pushing the thoughts of my ex away once more, I tried to focus on more positive thoughts.

Her last words to me before she fell asleep echoed through my head. The promise to make better memories. I could do with a balm like that. Too many of my memories were full of pain, arguments, and loathing for both myself and the woman who had caused it all.

I'd been no saint, often wishing I'd handled something better, but she'd pushed and pushed, and more than once, I couldn't take it anymore.

If things hadn't ended when they had, I didn't know what I'd have done.

Juno stirred some more, finally opening her eyes and turning her gaze on me. Her eyes lit up the second she noticed me, and warmth spread through my chest. It was the balm I needed. To see the pleasure in her eyes at noticing me and to know she genuinely wanted to be with me.

We'd had a few upsets and problems along the way, but nothing major, and it was clear we were both hurting over past issues. I was starting to think we could put each other back together again if we had the chance and the time.

I glanced at the nearby clock and encouraged Juno back up and onto her feet. A moment later, I reached for my shirt. I glanced out of the port hole on the side of the boat and noticed the island was beside us, and we'd slowed. Even in the dark, I knew where we were, the approach a view I'd watched so many times.

"Only a few more minutes. We should go up on the deck so you can see us come in. Even at night, it's beautiful," I said, the view something I never thought would grow old.

Juno didn't object, making herself decent again swiftly and letting me take her hand again. I liked feeling her fingers in mine.

Some of the others had taken the opportunity to get some sleep, too, but we found Alma and Kai on the deck, looking out toward the shore and the island buildings that could just be seen toward the center.

"It's so beautiful," Alma said as she spotted me and Juno.

"That's why Jack bought it," Kai replied, grinning, his arm slipping around Alma's waist.

I took Juno closer to them, and the four of us slipped into silence, watching.

Juno leaned into me again, resting her head against my shoulder. I wrapped my arms around her from behind, feeling her shake slightly. Worried she was more than just cold, I gently stroked the back of her hand with my thumb and kept her cozy against me.

If she was scared, she calmed, her body growing more still as the boat docked, and the island provided us with a small amount of shelter from the wind.

As soon as the boat was made fast and the sailors on board declared it safe for us to disembark, I led Juno off, wanting to know what she thought of the house.

We walked up a sandy, beach-like area toward a dirt track and then up a path to the front door of the house. With only a few staff on the island and no one else for miles, there was no need to lock the front door, so I pushed it open and watched Juno's reaction.

Her eyes went wide, and her mouth fell open. Immediately, I grinned, unable to help but be delighted. I took her hand and led her up to the top of the house, which had a view over the whole island.

She ate in every detail with her gaze, her head darting from one view to the next until we were looking out over the bay we'd just sailed in through. Down below, we could still see the crew and staff bringing our luggage to the house.

I watched her watching it all.

"I feel a little guilty," she said a moment later. "I didn't even think to bring my carry-on bag."

I chuckled. I hadn't grabbed mine either, so intent on showing her the view.

"They won't mind, but I'll make sure I don't distract you so much next time," I replied. "Now, I'm hungry. I want a snack, and then I want you."

She turned as I slipped my arms around her, studying me for a moment before she relaxed against my chest.

"Can I skip the snack and go straight to the being had part?" she asked, fighting back a smirk.

I grinned and kissed her, tempted to drag her into the

bedroom and take her right then and there, but I wanted to do this on my terms. Pulling back, I walked back down the stairs.

She followed, slipping her hand in mine and pouting slightly. Alma caught a glance at us as she and Kai made their way to one of the other bedrooms, and she chuckled while I flicked her a wink.

If Juno noticed the exchange, she didn't say anything, letting me show her some more of the house on the way to the kitchen. The housekeeper, Laura, had already stocked it up, but she appeared with a box from the boat while I was looking in the fridge.

"There were a few things I couldn't get till now," she said, talking to me and then giving Juno a brief smile.

I introduced Juno to Laura as I made a sandwich and offered Juno one, too. She declined the offer but sat nearby on a stool at the kitchen counter while I ate and discussed a few details with Laura.

"Are you staying once the band leaves?" Laura asked. "If so, I'll have more food brought in when the boat takes them back to the mainland."

"Yeah, probably."

"Okay. There's a few weather warnings, but nothing alarming."

"It'll be that time of year soon. We'll be careful. Are all the safe areas prepped?" I asked.

"Of course. No chances taken, as always."

I nodded as Laura finished putting the rest of the cold items in the fridge.

"Leave the rest until morning," I said. "It's late. You've waited up long enough for us."

Laura exhaled, the relief something she didn't try to hide. She was a darling, but it was clear the late nights weren't sitting well with her anymore. I made a mental note to try arriving sooner in the day so she didn't feel as if she had to be up so late in the future.

I quickly ate the sandwich while Juno looked around the kitchen from her seat, and I studied her.

She looked like she belonged where she sat, her long, curved legs on display, closed but not crossed. Unlike a lot of women I was surrounded by, she wasn't stick-thin, but she wasn't fat either, her calves and thighs curved with muscle.

I felt my groin stir at the thought of being between her legs, and it took all my self-control not to walk right over to her, push her legs apart, and take her right where she sat.

There were people in the house, and that meant I couldn't screw her in every room. However, if everything went well, I planned to as soon as they left.

A moment later, she looked back my way, catching me staring at her crotch. She glanced at my pants and bit her lip as our eyes met. Within a second, she was on her feet and coming over to me.

I took the last bite of the sandwich as she put her hand in mine.

CHAPTER SIXTY-FOUR

<u>Juno</u>

I felt my body heat up as I realized Jack was staring at me, his cock hard and his food almost gone. It was clear what he wanted, and I'd been taken in by the view so much I hadn't noticed.

It had clearly pleased him when I'd gone to him, making it obvious I would let him do exactly what he wanted with me. Although I'd felt nervous when we'd been traveling here, I knew I wanted to be his, to feel him inside me and to get to know him deeper.

Although we'd been together quite a few days now, I felt as if I was barely scratching the surface of his personality, and everything we did revealed a little more of him, but first, I would have to earn it.

And that meant giving him whatever he wanted, however he wanted it.

As he led me back up the stairs, I grew hotter and wetter just thinking about it.

Jack didn't look back, his strides confident.

The house was quiet now, everyone else in bed, the bedroom doors shut as we passed them by. Jack took me into the main bedroom, the whole far wall made of windows looking out over the beach and sea.

I wanted to go to it but I didn't dare, instead stopping at the end of the bed. Not even asking Jack what he wanted, I slowly reached up and pulled my top off, revealing my torso.

He stopped, his gaze drinking me in.

"And the rest," he said, his voice deeper, husky, and commanding me to obey.

I'd have done so anyway, but something about being told to show him everything made the moment even more arousing. I was already getting wet, and I couldn't stop thinking about how good he'd feel deep inside me.

Slowly, I slipped my pants off as well, pausing in my underwear and turning away from him for a moment as I unhooked my bra.

He let out a small growl, but I turned again before I revealed my breasts. I let him drink in the view a moment before I finished taking my panties off and stood before him, entirely naked.

Trying to appear calmer than I felt, I tucked my hands behind my back and looked down. When Jack still didn't move, I slowly lowered myself until I was kneeling at the end of the bed, facing him.

He stepped closer, and my heart raced so fast I could hear it in my own ears. I both wanted him to have his way with me and felt terrified at what he might ask of me, but I was completely unable to move.

Reaching down, he cupped my chin with his hand and lifted my face so our gazes met.

"Do you submit to me?" he asked.

"Yes," I replied, the words coming out before my fears could make me hesitate.

He smirked slightly before letting me go. Immediately, I

lowered my gaze again, trying to focus on what I knew I'd enjoy —having him inside me.

It didn't take long for him to lift me to my feet and push me back onto the bed, his powerful body soon positioned over me, giving me no way out. Pushing my hands up, he pinned them down above my head.

I was his now, and I would only be relinquished when he said so.

Holding still, I let him run his hand down from my wrists, stroking across my skin with a slow, deliberate movement that made my skin tingle and come alive everywhere he brushed.

When he reached my breasts, he stopped, taking each one in his hand and teasing my nipples. I moaned, instinctively arching my back to push them into his hands.

He moved his hands away almost instantly, denying me and proving he was in control. I mewled but kept still and tried to focus on the way his mouth caressed my neck, moving gradually lower.

Although he'd let go of my hands, I kept them above my head, closing my eyes and losing myself in the controlled pleasure.

Suddenly, he took a nipple between his teeth, biting just enough to make me hiss in pain. I groaned and fought with my body once more, wetness pooling between my thighs.

He did the same to the other nipple, teasing me and licking at the sensitive nubs to soothe them again.

The deliberate switch between pleasure and pain stole my focus, keeping me from being able to think about anything else. I was entirely his to devour or burn. To take and do with as he wished.

And he knew it.

With almost no warning, he slid back up me, bringing his hard cock to my entrance for only a brief moment before he impaled me, claiming my insides and pushing hard and deep. At the same time, he took both my wrists again, stretching my arms up, the rest of me pinned in place.

I lifted my knees, rocking my hips so he could thrust even farther into my pussy. I wanted him to put every inch into me. To make me take him again and again.

He obliged, pulling out of me only to impale me repeatedly.

It was fast and almost desperate, as if he needed to take me, and each pull back drove him crazy until he was buried inside me once more. Already hot and slick from everything he'd done before, I took him with ease, pleasure building inside me as he moved.

Just as I exploded, ecstasy filling me and making me shudder, he joined me, thrusting one last time as hard as he could, so deep I thought I might burst from that, too. He filled me with his cum, each burst of pleasure making us moan together.

Slowly, we came down, our arms around each other and our mouths locked.

No sooner had we cooled than I knew I wanted him again. My body in his control was nothing but pleasure and heaven, and I didn't want to stop and sleep now.

Jack didn't hesitate, but he pulled back the covers and encouraged me under them before getting in beside me and pulling me close to him. Already his cock was hard again, pressed against my thigh until he pushed me onto my front and mounted me from behind.

I briefly wondered if he was about to take my ass again, but he reached between my legs for my entrance and slid his fingers inside, finding me still wet. Slowly running more of his fingers over my clit, he made me even wetter again before he inserted several fingers into me, stretching me out and making me mewl.

"Are you still mine, kitten?" he asked a moment later.

"Yes, entirely," I replied, desperate for him to claim me again. No part of me wanted anything else at all.

Growling his delight, he removed his fingers and impaled me

with his hard cock again. I groaned with pleasure, full of him, the angle letting him drive even deeper than before.

He moved more slowly this time, taking each thrust deeply into me at a careful pace, making me feel it to my core. Under him, I could do little but brace against the bed and enjoy how full I was.

Pleasure rippled through me as he grew faster and more intense. I orgasmed again, my pussy tightening around his cock as waves of ecstasy made me moan his name.

Jack didn't stop, claiming me harder and faster until he held my hips hard against him. He roared as he thrust deep one last time, his hot seed jetting deep inside me.

I held as still as I could as he came down, both of us panting.

"You're perfect," he said as he wrapped me in his arms and rolled me onto my side.

I sighed and rested my head against his chest. If this was what life would be like on his island, I didn't want to go anywhere else.

CHAPTER SIXTY-FIVE

I woke to the sun streaming into the room. Jack was still asleep beside me, his face calm and gentle. I slipped closer, feeling the warmth of his torso.

Beyond him, I could see the most amazing view. The sun shone on an island of palm trees and sand, and a breeze gently blew the palm fronds back and forth. It looked peaceful, and it soothed the anxiety I'd woken with in no time.

It didn't take long for Jack to stir as well, his gaze fixing on me beside him within seconds.

"Good morning, gorgeous," he said, immediately rolling my way.

His mouth crushed down on mine, and his arms wrapped around my body, pulling me against him and pinning me in place.

I let out a slight squeal, shocked by the suddenness.

A moment later, he growled and flexed his hips. I felt his hard cock brush against my pussy, letting me know we weren't getting out of bed until he'd had his way with me some more.

I felt a ripple of heat run through me, and I involuntarily

clenched my thighs together, my mind remembering how good he had felt impaled in me the night before.

Unable to resist even if I'd wanted to, I yielded as Jack shifted until he was entirely on top of me.

My arms were soon above me, against the headboard, while Jack wound the other hand into my hair and pulled my head back. He rained kisses down on my exposed neck and chest, rough as he sucked and nipped with his teeth at the same time.

I quickly grew wet, my body coming alive under his attention.

"Ask me to fuck you, kitten," he said a moment later, relinquishing my arms so he could grab a nipple and tug on it.

I whimpered, unable to speak for a moment, but I thrust my hips upward toward his cock.

He chuckled, but he reached over and tugged on my other nipple, twisting it just enough to hurt. Mewling, I tried to open my mouth, knowing he wanted me to speak.

"Fuck me, Jack. Fuck me, please."

Grinning, Jack ran his thumb over the body part he'd just assaulted. It was all the interlude I had. A second later, he drove his hips down, thrusting hard inside me. I gasped at the sudden sting, but my pussy was wet enough that it was soon gone.

He set a hard, fast rhythm, making it very clear he was fucking me, and there was no other word for it.

I moaned beneath him, trying to keep up, pleasure building from the fast assault on my depths. Despite his clear need for me, he remained in control, his energy seeming endless as I tipped into oblivion, groaning as my pussy tightened around him in waves, but he didn't give me any relief.

Pounding hard, he continued seeking his own ecstasy until I thought he might split me in two. Just before I thought I might burst or I wouldn't be able to take anymore, he yelled and thrust deep one last time. As he orgasmed, waves of his seed filled me, and he moaned again, his hips jerking.

Slowly he came down, his body shaking and his lips pressing against mine.

"God, you're the perfect cunt to fuck first thing in the morning," he said as he pulled out of me finally.

I didn't move, a little sore but otherwise high on the pleasure he'd both given and taken.

"I'd hope I'm the perfect cunt to fuck in the evening, too," I replied as he rolled onto his side and gazed at me.

He chuckled.

"In the evening, you're the perfect pussy to claim."

I couldn't help but laugh at the logic, amused that he thought there was a difference. I was sure there was in some ways, but I didn't care either way. I was his and it felt so good I didn't want anything else.

We lay together for a while before Jack sat up and took my hand to pull me with him.

"Come on," he said. "Time to get up and make ourselves decent, have brunch, and then I'm going to show you around this place."

I had no intention of arguing, letting Jack lead me to the bathroom and pull me into the shower.

Being in the shower with him, both of us washing each other and then drying each other seemed to be the perfect end to every session in bed together, and today was no different.

We took our time, kissing plenty and lingering in each other's arms, but eventually, we were dressed and heading down the stairs toward the kitchen.

Several of the band were already up and lingering in the room. It was clear most of them had already eaten, and Alma gave me a smirk as she noticed me, although she didn't say anything.

It was the first time it occurred to me that someone might have heard us. We hadn't exactly been trying to be quiet.

I moved over to a stool and sat down, soreness flaring

between my legs for a moment before I managed to find a comfortable position. Jack had well and truly taken me.

Brunch was a fairly simple affair of bagels and various fillings. I quickly ate mine, a lot hungrier than I thought I'd be. Jack glanced over at me a couple of times, but the talk turned to plans for the rest of the day.

Jack offered to give me a tour of the island, and to my surprise, most of the rest of the people with us wanted it, too. I had assumed they'd relax in their own way, already familiar with whatever the island offered, but instead, they seemed as clueless as I was.

I didn't say anything, but it was starting to make me wonder if they had all been invited so I would come as well. If I had been invited alone and hadn't been offered the safety of having Alma there in case I needed some way of retreating, I would never have agreed to come.

And nothing that had followed the party at Alma and Kai's would have happened. None of the time we'd spent together and the growing warmth between us. I had no doubt that we'd have ended up putting distance between us simply because we both knew I was going to go back to England.

However, because of her selfless offer, I'd spent several more wonderful days in Jack's company and learned a lot more about him.

As soon as we'd all eaten and cleaned up, Jack took my hand again and started the tour. We looked around the large main house, Jack revealing secret after secret, including a large game room.

We stopped to play with the pinball machines for a few minutes and had more drinks and snacks before heading out onto the island. There were a few made-up paths that ran between the house and the beaches on the island, as well as a tree house built at one end. Everywhere I looked, there were either more trees, sand, or the ocean as far as the eye could see.

At the two ends of the long thin island, the islands along the strip could be seen, but they were far enough away we still had complete privacy.

It was a beautiful place, and I knew it was somewhere I could come and relax easily. I also found myself wanting a quiet place to curl up and write. That was always a good sign I liked a place and felt safe and calm there.

CHAPTER SIXTY-SIX

<u>Jack</u>

Looking at Juno as she stood on the edge of a beach, her feet in the water and her gaze looking out across the sea, made me feel better. For someone who had been reluctant to come, she seemed to be pleased to be here and I hadn't picked up on any fear.

That said, Alma was clearly keeping an eye on her, the two of them walking arm in arm some of the time.

I wanted Juno to myself already, wishing everyone else was going home, but I couldn't help but be worried she'd run when they left.

As I was thinking this, she turned and came toward me, her eyes lighting up the second she spotted me. I put my arms out to invite her into a hug and held her close, our gazes locked.

"Do you like it?" I asked, wanting her approval more than I'd realized.

She nodded. "I love it. And I think everyone else does as well."

I frowned, noticing her words.

"People don't come here often, do they? Normally, it's just you."

I exhaled as I gave her an affirmative.

"Do you mind?" I asked.

"No. I think it's sweet of you, but we could have talked about it some more."

"Would you have come without them?"

"No, I don't think I would, but I'd have regretted it." She held her breath as she looked up at me, studying me, almost as if she feared I might be angry.

I pulled her in tighter and gave her a quick kiss. Knowing what she was thinking and feeling always made this easier.

"When they leave, will you stay longer?" I asked as I slipped back to get a good look at her.

Immediately, she looked down and away, but I refused to let her go. I needed her with me, and I wasn't about to let her pull away out of fear. Not when she was perfectly safe. I might claim her body, but I'd never force her or make her feel pain just to punish her.

She was someone to be protected and pleasured, as well as enjoyed.

I placed a finger under her chin and lifted it again.

"Think about it," I said. "I won't pressure you, but you're safe with me, and I think you know it."

Juno smiled and nodded, her shoulders relaxing. I kissed her again, being as gentle and tender as I could, but I hurt at the same time. I desperately wanted her to trust me. To know I would never abuse her the way others had.

"Would you mind if I wrote for a bit?" she asked a moment later. "I think it might help me relax here."

"Whatever you wish," I replied, surprised by the request but appreciating the thought behind it.

She slipped out of my arms and went toward the house. For a moment, I didn't know what to do with myself, the calm sound of the waves in the background tugging at my emotions as much as she did.

How was I going to navigate this relationship? It was my first that had lasted more than a night or two in years, and I didn't know if I could handle much more uncertainty.

A moment later, Kai appeared at my side, almost making me jump as he placed a hand on my shoulder.

"Still having trouble?" Kai asked.

"Not trouble, exactly. But..." I trailed off, not sure how to explain everything I felt.

"Give it time. She's adjusting to you and fame at the same time."

"That's one of the reasons I'm concerned," I replied without thinking.

"I don't think she's after your money or status. She seems to be content in herself and with the level of fame and money she already had." Kai started walking toward the house, following in her footsteps, and I responded by going with him.

"I'm worried about the song contract, though."

"Yeah, I won't deny I am a little as well. But if she told her agent to back off, I'm sure he'll back off. She's not given us any reason to doubt her yet. I know you're worried it's what she wants, but if it is, she's far better at hiding it than anyone has been in the past."

"I dunno. I never saw it with—"

"Don't beat yourself up about that anymore, Jack," Kai said, cutting me off. "She had a lot of people fooled."

"But not you or Alma," I said, my hands bunching into fists. *How could I have been so stupid?*

"Alma likes Juno. I like Juno. Deep breaths, man, and give it time. You've got her on your island, which is amazing, by the way, and she's happy here. It's a good start."

I nodded. Kai was right, but despite all the reassurances, I didn't feel I could entirely relax. She was a hard woman to read, and as much as I really liked her, I was still trying to guard my heart.

I didn't know exactly how I felt about her yet, either. Yeah, she was hot, and we had chemistry and some great conversations. I also appreciated the different style of relationship she'd introduced me to, but I was still getting used to it.

It made me feel powerful. In control. As if I could do anything. But it also allowed me the opportunity to care for someone who seemed to appreciate it.

Juno was an interesting mix of confident and capable, yet hopelessly naive about some subjects. I was pretty sure she'd never been in a designer clothing store, but she knew her way around words and the publishing business like no one I'd ever met before.

I found myself smiling as I thought of it and strode inside. After pulling some drinks out of the fridge for Kai and me, we made our way around the front of the building and the view of the beach. As I passed the stairs, I noticed Juno.

She'd sat sideways on the window ledge at the top of the stairs and was leaning against the window so she could both see the view and write. And she was writing by hand, a fountain pen in one hand and a notebook balanced on her folded legs.

For a moment, I couldn't move, mesmerized by the look on her face as she moved her hand across the page. Her hair had slipped down to cover her cheek, and I found myself wanting to climb the steps and stroke it back again.

Before I could do so, Kai reached out and rested his hand on my shoulder again and then motioned with his head for me to continue with him.

I tore my eyes away from the angelic view, and it seemed to break the spell. We were soon sitting on the edge of the jetty. I could still see Juno from the other side, but she was far enough away that she wouldn't be able to hear us talking.

"You know, she looks right at home up there," Kai said, grinning at me as he sipped his drink.

I chuckled, knowing exactly what he meant. I'd already noticed that she had a way of looking at home anywhere.

"I asked her if she'd stick around after you've all gone," I said a moment later, looking out to sea where some fish were jumping and making bubbles on the surface of the otherwise calm water.

"Looked like a deer in headlights?"

"Not quite, but not far off. I wish she'd trust me."

"Give her time. She came here. I'm sure Alma can convince her to stay after we go. That woman can convince anyone of anything." Kai looked proud as he spoke, and once more, it made me ache for something I didn't currently have.

Could I have a long-term relationship with Juno?

CHAPTER SIXTY-SEVEN

<u>Juno</u>

I shut my notebook with a snap and realized I was grinning like a loon. Looking down, I spotted Jack sitting on the edge of the jetty alone, dangling his feet in the water and sipping a drink.

Feeling a lot calmer and at ease in my mind, I hurried to put my notebook and pen away and go down to him. I was being an idiot. Just like the romance stories I wrote, I was letting past hurt stop me from embracing a possible future.

Of course, life wasn't always that simple, but it was a good starting place. I needed to push past my fears and live life anyway.

I couldn't wait to get outside and be with Jack again, but I grabbed a drink from the fridge on the way, wanting to make it clear I was coming to hang out with him and chill.

He was staring out to sea, so lost in thoughts that he didn't notice me approaching until I was only a few feet away. Immediately, I sat beside him, and he reached out to put his arm around me.

Leaning into him, I sighed.

"I like it here," I said.

He chuckled and gave me a squeeze.

"You looked like you found a good spot to write in," he replied a moment later, looking back at the waves.

"Yeah, I could get used to writing with that kind of view." I grinned. "And I thought about what you said. I think I can handle staying a little longer if you want me to. I'd need to go back to England eventually, but I can stick around as long as I get some writing done."

"You can write as much as you like, kitten," he said, beaming as he looked down at me. "And don't worry, I can't stay more than another week anyway. Band commitments will call me back to the mainland, but I can spend a week with you first."

I found myself grinning as he pulled me into his arms and kissed me once more. It was soft and tender, and he settled back again, letting me rest my head on his shoulder. A moment later, I dangled my feet in the water beside his, enjoying the way the water moved and made them sway a little.

The island was peaceful, unlike anywhere else I'd ever been, and I could almost see everyone relaxing while they were there, all the cares and worries dropping away.

While we sat there, talking about our favorite characters in books, several of the others wandered by, but no one disturbed us in any way more than to wave and acknowledge us being there.

"Come on," Jack said a little while later, his drink finished.

Getting up, he took my hand and pulled me to my feet. I let him haul me up but wondered what he had in mind.

"Let's have a barbecue," he added as he walked back toward the house. "It's the perfect day for it."

There were no arguments from me as Jack made his way around the side of the house again to a patio area. Tucked in one corner underneath a cover was a massive gas grill, and he immediately pulled it out and started preparing it as if he'd used it many times.

"I'll make some stuff to go with it," I said before giving him a kiss.

He grinned as I pulled back before watching me walk away, his gaze roaming my body. It was a look that sent heat and desire rippling through me, but any follow-up was going to have to wait. Sighing and already ready for the evening, I went inside.

I found Alma in the kitchen getting herself a snack and immediately grinned at her before telling her Jack's plan.

"Oh, perfect," she replied. "I'll tell Kai to gather the others, and then I'll help you prepare."

Grateful for the offer of help and the chance to talk to her a little, I relaxed and had a look in the fridge and pantry to see what was available to us. I marveled at how well-stocked everything was, given Jack was only here for a few days at a time and wasn't that much into cooking himself.

Admittedly, it was possible that the housekeeper had brought in so much food because, this time, we were a large group. It wasn't as if any of us could make a quick trip to the store to get more supplies in only a few minutes. It was a four-hour round trip, at least.

I managed to find some gluten-free stuff as well, grateful that someone had passed on the information to whoever was in charge of getting food, and then I began preparing a few different sides.

Alma reappeared quickly, and we were soon side by side, chopping up vegetables and making salads.

"Looks like everything is going well so far," she said, smiling at me.

"So far, everything is going amazingly," I replied. "Although I'm a little worried it could go wrong at any minute."

"That's natural," she said as she moved to tip the contents of her chopping board into a wok. "But I'm still here, and if you need me, you know what to say."

I nodded and grinned. It almost felt silly while we were safely in a kitchen together, especially after I'd just agreed to stay after the rest of the band went home.

But the fear wouldn't entirely go away, despite us managing to have a very silly conversation about the band's earliest days and how she'd met Kai.

By the time we were done preparing all the side dishes and had taken them all outside, the rest of the group was there, sitting around and chatting, and the meat was almost cooked.

We all dug in together, the evening drawing in around us while we took our time and ate and drank. I felt more relaxed than I had in a long time and talked more to Liam and Kai, the former giving me beginner tips on picking up a bass guitar and starting to play properly.

I'd played it as a kid because a friend had owned one for a while, but my family had never been able to afford lessons or an instrument for me. I'd had to let go of the idea, but now it was a possibility again. I laughed at how eager Liam was to teach me everything I wanted to know and marveled at how passionate he clearly was about playing well.

"You should hear some of our old heroes play sometime," Kai said a moment later.

Before Liam could say anything else or Kai could suggest a band name or song, Eve appeared and plonked herself on Liam's lap. She put her arms around him and immediately planted a kiss on his lips.

"I'm bored and cold," she said, only looking at him.

I grinned at the not-so-subtle way she was asking him to take her inside, and it made me think of Jack and the look he'd given me earlier. I got up and went to him. Within seconds, I was sitting beside him, his arm around me while he continued his previous conversation.

He smelled like barbecue in a smoky sort of way, having used some kind of wood chip to smoke and flavor the meat, and it was a strangely calming smell.

Feeling as if I was the luckiest woman on Earth at that moment, I rested my head on his shoulder and let the calming, deep tones of the men around me soothe me even further.

CHAPTER SIXTY-EIGHT

By the time it was full dark, it was starting to get a little colder, and everyone retreated inside. The conversations continued, however, and I stuck with Jack. I noticed Eve almost drag Liam away a little later, but no one seemed to mind or object.

It was the perfect way to end the day, sitting and talking about life and past experiences. I did more listening than talking by a long way, but Jack was warm, and being close to him while feeling safe was nice.

About another hour had passed after Liam and Eve had made their way to bed when Jack shifted slightly, looking at me for a moment. The conversation had reached a natural lull, and in the dim light of the living room he looked me up and down.

Without another word to anyone else, he took my hand and got up. I followed, catching another smirk from Alma on my way past, although when I caught her eye, she looked more serious as if she was checking for the possibility I might use our safe word. I gave her a smile to let her know I was okay.

It wasn't a perfect solution. Of course, something could go wrong once I was alone with Jack, but so far, that had never happened.

Jack took me into the bedroom. Immediately, his hands went to my face, cupping my cheeks. I looked up at him, seeing the intense desire in his eyes for just a fraction before he plunged his mouth down on mine.

We kissed for what felt like ages and no time at all, my eyes closing of their own accord. I leaned into him and put my arms around his strong shoulders. The kiss quickly turned into more, his tongue pushing my lips apart and exploring deeper. Passion poured from him to me and back again, heat rushing between my legs.

As he lifted me and carried me over to the bed, I felt him grow hard. I moaned as he lowered me down and pinned me beneath him. For a moment, he paused, his hands entwined in mine, holding them above my head, the rest of his body over mine and between my legs.

I wanted him inside me, wanted him taking me as hard as he could. I grew wet as he gently slipped my clothes off, taking his time and kissing each new bit of exposed skin as he revealed it.

Lying underneath him, I felt as if I wanted to give myself over to him again and again, his desire for me exactly what I wanted.

By the time he was sliding my panties down my legs and revealing my hot, wet pussy I could barely contain my need to have him inside me.

Thankfully, he didn't take long to oblige, his warm hands cupping my breasts and rubbing gently over my hard nipples as he brought his manhood to my entrance.

For a moment, he paused, his gaze meeting mine, his powerful body over me.

"Are you mine?" he asked, his gaze searching me for the answer.

"Completely," I replied, holding the searching look and hoping I was offering him what he wanted.

He moaned into me as he both came in for another kiss and

pushed his hard cock into me. I gasped at the sudden feeling of fullness, claimed by him entirely.

Wasting no time, he set a steady pace, my body his. The pleasure soon built, along with the speed and depth of his thrusts, my body tipping over the edge into oblivion only a few seconds before he did the same.

We cried out together, our arms wrapping around each other as his hard cock jerked cum out into me. I shivered in waves of ecstasy, my body momentarily out of my control.

As we came down together, Jack held me close and stroked my skin, smiling down at me.

"I don't want this to end," he said a moment later.

"It doesn't have to. I'm still right here, where you can do anything you want to me," I replied, smirking as I thought of some of the things he'd gotten me to do in the past."

He chuckled and kissed me again.

"Anything I want?" he asked.

"Anything."

Not missing a beat, he got up and went over to the nearby wardrobe, and then he pulled out a pair of handcuffs.

Immediately, I tensed, realizing the error of my words. Anything but being restrained. Shifting onto my side, I exhaled and tried to stay calm. Could I do this?

His eyes took in my sudden reaction, and his face darkened. For a moment, I thought he was angry with me, but instead, he seemed to exhale and deflate along with it.

Neither of us spoke as he stared at the handcuffs in his hands. A ripple of fear ran through me, and I knew I had to do something to both reassure him and stop myself feeling so cold.

I walked up to him and put my hands on the cuffs and his fingers.

"Can we work up to them?" I asked. "It's still a big thing that I'm here on your island with you and planning to stay when the others leave."

For a moment, I thought Jack would either lose his temper or walk out on me, but eventually, he looked up and met my eyes. He searched my face for a few seconds, and I waited, tense, afraid, but determined not to show him I was afraid of him.

"All right. What do you have in mind?" he asked, sounding defeated.

I bit my lip, confused and conflicted by the emotions pouring through me. What did I want to do? I felt like I ought to offer him something, but I didn't want to do it for the wrong reasons, either.

"Why don't we lock the door?" I asked a moment later. "Lock me in with you."

I glanced at the door to see if it was possible and sighed with relief, although it was a simple bolt on the door, nothing fancy, and something I would be able to undo.

He glanced at it as well, looking thoughtful, but eventually, he nodded. Striding over to it, he flicked the bolt across, and then he turned back to me.

Not sure what else to do but eager to remove the tension between us, I went to him and put my arms around him. As he wrapped his strong arms around me, I felt some of the stiffness leave my body.

"I'm sorry it's not more yet," I said, the words tumbling out. "My mind and heart want to trust you, but my emotions keep getting in the way."

"It's a start. It's something. If you'd just refused, I think I'd feel like you didn't care, but this..." He pressed another kiss to my lips, gentle and tender. "This gives me a chance to show you that you're safe. That you can give yourself to me more and more and know it's going to feel good."

I leaned into him and the kiss, my heart swelling with gratitude and something more, something deeper. As he pulled back and our eyes met once more, I knew.

I loved him. Completely and wholeheartedly. I had fallen in

love with this rich, wealthy, yet troubled rock star. And I was in so deep, I was in danger of getting torn apart.

CHAPTER SIXTY-NINE

Taking me over to the bed, Jack once again slipped me between the sheets and took control. I melted into his arms, yielding and feeling the tension leave me as he ran his hands where he wished.

Lying before him, with the desire clear on his face and in his hard cock, I felt as if I was a goddess. Someone to be adored and worshiped and wanted completely. He drank me in and touched or kissed every inch of me, not rushing a single stroke or caress.

Slowly, I heated back up, wanting him to take me again and give us both the pleasure we needed. I needed him to know I was his, needed for him to feel how much I wanted to be in his life, but no sooner had his body come down over mine than my old fears popped back into my head again.

I tensed, and he pulled back, his gaze searching me for an explanation. As he released a wrist, I reached up and stroked his cheek.

"I love you," I said, the words tumbling out almost apologetically.

He blinked, his eyes going wide.

Instantly, I wished I could take back the words, not sure I should have even said them, but they were out now, and I couldn't erase the moment. My heart raced as the silence dragged out until he settled back down, his arms supporting his body as he leaned over me, my skin against his.

He placed a hand on either side of my head and held it still as he kissed me. Panic filled me. He wasn't saying it back, but his lips pressed against mine were full of passion and care.

I was also his, pinned beneath him, with the door locked. And it didn't feel scary because of that. He was exactly as he promised, caring and considerate. But so had Greg been at the beginning.

Jack brought my focus back to him as he pulled back an inch and rested our foreheads together.

"I love you too," he whispered, his voice catching as he spoke.

It was my turn to be surprised into speechlessness, but he smiled slightly a moment later as if he couldn't quite believe he was saying it as well. I lifted my head off the pillows just enough to kiss him again, and it brought his attention back to my naked body and everything it offered him.

Within seconds, he was trailing kisses down my neck, getting me hot and ready once more. I moaned as he focused on my breasts, nipping with his teeth just enough for me to follow it with a hiss.

He slipped one hand between my thighs, finding me wet and ready for him, and wasted no time claiming my depths with his hard manhood. Gasping at the suddenness, I gave way before him.

Needing him deep inside me, I lifted my knees and gave him a better angle. Jack didn't hesitate to take advantage of it, pushing deeper inside me, rocking as he pulled back and thrust deeper.

I moaned as he picked up the pace, his desire for me driving us both faster and faster. He roared his orgasm a few seconds before I also tipped into oblivion, my body tensing as he filled me with his cum and gave me the last bit of momentum I needed.

Slowly, we came back down again together, his arms wrapping around me as I panted. I leaned into him, feeling safe and warm and complete. I wasn't sure my time with Jack could get any better.

It wasn't long before he pulled me over onto my side, cuddling me up against him. I inhaled his scent, feeling sleepy and finally ready to drift into the land of dreams. Not only had we survived another day together, but we'd grown closer and, once again, Jack had shown me that I could trust him so far.

For now, that was enough.

Once again, I woke up to find Jack still asleep beside me, his face angelic in the morning sunlight. It was a little earlier, the sun only beginning to peek above the palm trees and the birds still singing their dawn chorus.

For a moment, I basked in the beauty of it, but my eyes kept going to Jack until I gave up focusing on anything but him. I thought back to the night before, the words we'd exchanged, and the fears I'd tried to face.

I wanted to believe him, and I felt as if he needed to know how much he was bringing me to life again. It might not have been long after I'd split with Greg, but my ex had slowly killed the passion and desire in me with cold, cruel accusations.

From the moment Jack had come into my life, he'd woken me back up again and made me feel. I'd worried I'd never love again. Never trust someone with me, but here he was, giving me the chance.

And he was being patient.

Gratitude made my heart swell, and passion filled me. I wanted him to know I was his.

While I was thinking about making sure he knew how I felt, I watched him begin to stir, turning my way a little. Almost immediately, a thought popped into my head. A way I could wake him so he knew I was willing to give myself to him even more today than the day before.

Slowly, I slipped farther down the bed, his cock already partially erect in his sleep. I ran my hands down it before taking it into my mouth. He stirred some more, his eyes flicking open as I ran my tongue around his tip.

"Oh, kitten, good morning," he said.

I replied without words, taking him deeper and assuming I had his approval to continue. He tasted salty already and moaned as I started to move back and forth.

Now very hard, I worked his shaft with my hand and lavished the rest of my attention on his head. He quickly reached his peak, jetting hot, salty cum into my mouth.

Swallowing every last drop, I licked around his head to make sure I hadn't missed any while he moaned and returned to earth.

As soon as I finished, I slid back up the bed and into his arms.

"Now, that's a way to wake up," he said as he cupped my chin and gazed into my eyes. "But now it's my turn."

My eyes went wide as he pushed me onto my back.

"Lie still while I have you for breakfast," he commanded, pushing my legs apart as he slid down the bed.

With no more warning, he brought his mouth down on my pussy, his tongue already reaching to assault my clit. I mewled at the sudden sensation, almost immediately overwhelmed, and reached down to try and slow him.

He chuckled and pushed my hands away.

"Relax. Trust me," he added before going back to work.

I felt him dart his tongue out with quick, intense probes on my most sensitive area, my whole body quivering with the sensations. Unable to think, I tried to focus on doing as he asked, relaxing and letting him have his way with me. I was soon moaning as he brought me close to my peak.

Before I could orgasm, he stopped and pulled away a moment. Confused, I whimpered.

"Are you mine?" he asked, his hands resting on my thighs, almost pinning me in place, vulnerable and at his mercy.

I saw no point in denying the truth. I was entirely his to do with as he pleased.

"Completely," I replied as soon as I could speak.

"Then you don't come until I tell you to," he commanded, his face so serious I was pretty sure I'd regret disobeying him.

I nodded, unable to reply, my mind trying to imagine how hard it was going to be to fight against an orgasm. But I'd try. Because that was what he wanted.

Continuing to wait, Jack let me come back down a little before he brought his mouth to me again. This time he also slid two fingers inside me, running them in and out as his mouth worked on my clit.

It didn't take long for him to turn me into a hot, sweaty mess, mewling every time he stopped and made me wait. Several times, he brought me close to the edge of an orgasm and stopped before I could tip over. Each time, I found it harder to keep still.

It was torture, exquisite torture.

"Come for me, kitten," he finally said before clamping his mouth down on my clit and pushing his fingers hard and fast in and out of my pussy. I was so wound up with pleasure that I couldn't have stopped the orgasm breaking over me if I'd wanted to.

Jack slid up the bed to hold me close to him as I came back down a little. Immediately, I felt his erection press against me. We weren't done.

My master was awake, and he was going to claim me even further.

CHAPTER SEVENTY

<u>Jack</u>

Shuddering in my arms, Juno came down from the orgasm I'd just given her. It had been a reward of sorts. It had been a long time since I'd woken up with anyone's mouth on my cock, and it had felt so good.

I'd made sure she was rewarded, pleasured for behaving the way I wanted. A part of me felt manipulative for it, but it also felt good. We were made for each other, her body responding to me. And I wasn't done.

I wanted her tied up and helpless before me, but I knew she was reluctant. That meant working up to it. And I was pretty sure it needed to be approached at least a little before the others left. That meant I had just over twenty-four hours.

When I thought she was calm again but buzzed from the orgasm I'd just given her, I rolled her slowly over onto her front, going with her and pinning her beneath me.

She yielded, giving me control easily enough that I was emboldened. I kissed her neck a few times and slid my hands underneath her, gently stroking her breasts and getting her heated again.

When I felt her relax some more and her nipples grow hard between my fingers, I brought my mouth to her ear.

"I want to blindfold you again," I whispered, not including what I wanted to add next.

She exhaled but gave me a quick nod despite tensing up. I went to the wardrobe, pulled out a bandanna to use as a blindfold again, and quickly robbed her of sight.

"Comfortable?" I asked.

"Yes."

"Good. Now, are you going to yield to me and let me have your body?" I asked, reaching for my shirt from the night before.

"Yes," she replied, and my cock throbbed with anticipation.

Grinning at what I planned to do to her, how I was going to take her a little deeper, I got back on top of her, pushing her legs apart so she was completely vulnerable.

With one hand, I grabbed her wrists and pushed them up above her head. She continued to yield, my cock pressed between her ass cheeks.

For a moment, I hesitated there. This could go wrong if I didn't keep her calm, but I wanted this, and I knew she needed some help getting past her fear.

Gently, I looped the fabric of my shirt around her wrists, twisting it so it was almost rope-like. Instantly, she pulled her arms away, and I let her.

"Trust me," I said. "You'll be able to pull your hands out if you really want to, but it will get you used to the sensation and feel of it."

My words seemed to calm her, and I felt myself relax along with her. I wanted this. I needed her to let me push her further.

Slowly, she reached her wrists back up of her own accord, and I exhaled, fighting to keep my heartbeat slow and my own body calm. She was making me hot and hard, the desire to show she trusted me despite her fears making me want to just fuck her hard while she was so helpless already.

I already knew I could have done anything to her if I wanted to, but she was reluctant to be tied up. I knew I needed to push her for it.

When she was still and her breathing had calmed a little again, I looped the T-shirt around her wrists once more. It was loose, so loose that it wouldn't stop her from moving at all. Bringing the two ends together, I twisted them around each other a little.

Pausing, I waited for her to relax again, each movement making her tense. I added two more twists, knowing it was still loose enough she could have pulled her hands out, and I told her so.

I could feel her starting to shake beneath me and knew I needed to find a way to relax her.

"Pull them out again," I told her, my voice commanding.

She did as she was bid, having to tug a little harder but able to pull her wrists out.

Sighing the tension out of her body, she immediately lifted them back, and as I made it looser again, she slipped them back inside the makeshift rope.

Having her right where I wanted her, I tightened the loop a second time, taking it a little further. At the same time, I reached between her legs, touching her most intimate areas and immediately playing with her clit.

She moaned, wetness forming between her thighs.

With the other hand, I continued to slowly tighten the bonds around her arms until I knew she'd not be able to get out even if she wanted to.

Unaware, she moaned beneath me, her pussy slick and ready for my cock. I twisted the bond a tiny bit more, a part of me hoping she'd notice I'd gone further and put her entirely at my mercy.

She shifted her wrist slightly as I pulled my fingers away from her cunt and prepared to fuck her while she was helpless beneath me.

"Have you made it tighter?" she asked, her voice higher pitched.

Not responding, I thrust my cock into her.

I had made it tighter. She might as well have been wearing the handcuffs, and I was so turned on by it I could think of almost nothing but fucking her as hard as I could.

"Jack?" she said, a hint of fear in her voice despite my pulling out of her and thrusting back inside.

"Does it hurt?" I asked, trying to steer her away from her panic. "Does my cock feel good inside you?"

"It doesn't hurt at all," she replied.

"Good, kitten. Now, shh, and enjoy being mine."

I watched her open her mouth as if she was going to object, but I grabbed her breast with the other hand, twisting her nipple and making her gasp.

Wanting to distract her, to make her know she was supposed to yield and let me continue, I continued to stroke and pinch her nipples, alternating between gentle pleasure and pain.

At the same time, I continued to thrust into her, taking her and enjoying every minute despite having pushed her into it. I could feel her getting wetter and tighter around me as she enjoyed what I was doing, even if she hadn't initially been willing.

She wasn't saying no or trying to get me to stop, and while she was yielding, I was going to enjoy having her at my mercy.

Pushing aside the slight guilt I felt, I enjoyed taking her, her body helpless beneath mine as I picked up the pace. Juno was mine completely, submitted to me and unable to stop me from doing as I pleased.

It felt good to be in such control, and I was soon rising toward my own orgasm. I never got to decide if I wanted to try and hold it back, the enjoyment of having her bound and helpless tipping me over the edge.

I moaned as I came deep inside her, filling her with my cum

and claiming her entirely. Although I couldn't tell if I'd given her an orgasm or not, my own enjoyment having consumed my thoughts, I gently slid out of her and reached for her clit again.

While I was coming back down, I rubbed her sensitive nub, making her moan. She tried to pull her hands from the bonds almost immediately and found that she couldn't.

"Jack?" she said. "Are you going to let me go?"

"That depends," I replied. "I don't want to. Not yet. I like having you helpless."

It was the closest to confirmation I was going to give her that I'd pushed her harder than I'd promised.

For a moment, I watched her, my fingers working her clit and distracting her, making it hard for her to think about anything other than the pleasure. It bypassed her objections as she rose toward another orgasm of her own, and I grinned, my cock already hardening.

It had worked.

Juno was mine to fuck exactly how and when I pleased, and she knew it.

CHAPTER SEVENTY-ONE

<u>**Juno**</u>

Fear made me tense as I confirmed Jack had tied my hands off so tightly I couldn't free them as I'd hoped. At the same time, he was trying to give me an orgasm, his fingers playing with my clit with expert precision, my pussy full of the cum he'd just given it.

I wasn't sure what to do. No part of me had agreed to it, but so far, he'd done nothing but enjoy fucking me. Now, he was making sure I was having a good time as well. My emotions swirled in my body, moving me from scared to grateful and then from irritated to so turned on I just didn't want him to stop.

Blindfolded and tied, I was as helpless as I'd ever been in my life, and it was both a huge turn-on and scary. But I felt violated, too. I hadn't told him I was okay with being this restrained.

Despite the mental confusion, I felt Jack continue to work with his hands until an orgasm exploded through me, making me shudder and moan and momentarily silencing my chaos-filled mind.

"Good girl," he said, whispering it in my ear as he continued to lean over me from behind. "You're an angel. My hot little angel."

His words came out like honey, dripping through my thoughts and coating me with the warmth of his appreciation. There was something about having him pleased with me that made me want to lie still and let him continue as he pleased, but I only had to move slightly to be reminded that he had tied my wrists above my head, and I was helpless and vulnerable.

Thoughts ran through my mind, reminding me that he could do absolutely anything he wanted right now, and there was nothing I could do to stop him.

"I promise I won't hurt you," he whispered, "but we're not done. I'm not done. I'm enjoying this far too much to want to stop now, kitten. Will you yield to me? I want to fuck your ass. I want to bury myself in the one part of you I haven't had yet this morning. And I want to do it while you're like this."

Without thinking, I shook my head. I couldn't do it. I knew he'd been gentle with my ass the last time he'd had it, but he was talking about taking me because I was helpless now. And there was something in his voice. Something in the way he was talking about it. I felt...different.

"Please, let me go, Jack," I asked as his fingers parted my ass cheeks despite me already declining. "Don't do this, please."

"Shhh," he whispered near my ear. "I swear I won't hurt you. I've just fucked your pussy while you were helpless beneath me. This won't be any different. Give yourself to me again, Juno. I—"

"No, Jack," I said, the fear making me more tense. Shaking, I tried to pull farther away, but there was nowhere to go. I was trapped beneath him.

I heard him growl for a moment, and I was afraid he was going to take me anyway, his cock hard and pressed against me, but instead, I felt him reach up and slowly loosen the bonds around my arms.

The second I was free, I yanked the blindfold off, and Jack pulled back so I could get out from under him. I panted as I turned and looked at him.

His expression was unreadable as he looked at me, almost cold and closed. I didn't know what to do, but I felt myself calming. He'd let me go when I'd asked, and he wasn't hurting me. But he wasn't holding me in his arms anymore, either.

I exhaled, my whole body trembling with the emotions that had built inside me. I was no longer terrified, but it felt as if I'd just hurt Jack. Was it really so wrong of me to say no to him?

Jack rolled himself onto his back and put his arms above his head, running one through his hair on the way. I moved closer to him, wanting his arms around me, wanting to know everything was okay between us despite what had happened.

"I'm sorry," I said. "I panicked."

"It's okay," he replied. "I pushed too hard. It… It's not your fault."

His words surprised me, making me feel a little better, but they were also devoid of his usual passion and emotion.

I cuddled beside him, resting my head on his shoulder, his arm wrapping around my back and onto my waist. It was warm physically, but as I lay there, I couldn't help feeling like a wall had gone up between us. Still, he pulled me in close and gently ran his hands down my back, helping to calm my body physically.

The care he showed me helped, and I finally relaxed against him, leaning into him, but he didn't try again or make anything else happen between us.

"I'm sorry," I said again.

"Please, don't apologize. You didn't do a single thing wrong. I did something we hadn't talked about being okay with yet. I pushed you too far, and you let me know that. It's important that I respect your boundaries so you always know I will stop when you ask me to."

His words made me feel better despite my fear. It made me want to reconsider stopping. Me being his and at his mercy was clearly something he wanted, but I had no idea how to give it to him and not be terrified.

We stayed lying together until there was a clatter from the kitchen direction and the brief sound of raised voices as they tried to clean something up.

"We should get up," Jack said a moment later.

He kissed my forehead and pulled away, getting out of the bed and leaving me lying there. I sighed and took my time to follow, tears threatening to fall. Why hadn't I just let him take me and enjoy me?

Not once had Jack hurt me, and he'd even come to my rescue on at least two occasions. So why didn't I feel like I could trust him with this?

I couldn't answer the question. Fear wasn't rational.

But I didn't plan on letting it get the best of me. Somehow, I needed to push past it.

Trying not to worry for now and determined to show Jack I was his in as many other ways as I could, I followed him to the bathroom and joined him in the shower.

As before, we washed each other and dried each other off, taking time and care, but something about it felt off, as if we were doing it because it was what we usually did, not because we wanted to show each other we cared.

I tried to be gentle, submissive, and kissed him a few times, seeing if I could find some kind of passion or spark in him, but he didn't give me anything back, quickly focusing on his clothes and dressing himself.

Hoping things would improve as the day went by, I followed his lead, and we joined the others in the kitchen.

Someone had knocked a plate of food onto the floor, but by the time we'd joined them, it was all cleaned up, and there was just a broken plate that would need replacing.

After Jack made a note for the housekeeper and I started to fix us both something to eat, we sat with the others. I was pretty sure Alma noticed the colder attitude between Jack and me because she soon found a moment to pull me to the side and encouraged the others to leave us to talk about books.

I sighed as they left and wondered how I would explain what had happened.

As soon as it was only the two of us, Alma put her arms around me, and I burst into tears. How did everything with Jack keep going so crazily in one direction or another?

Not saying a word, Alma let me get the flood of emotions out of my system. I didn't take long to calm down, appreciating her being there for me.

"Do you want to talk about it?" she asked when I pulled back and exhaled.

I opened my mouth to tell her we'd just had a small disagreement, but instead, the whole story came out. I started with Greg and everything he'd done, moved on to how I'd met Jack, and he'd stood up for me. How he'd rescued me from Greg but been angry about my story for the bruises, and how no matter how much I pushed myself, my trust never seemed to be enough.

Alma listened, hugging me and even shedding a tear or two herself at points. It was everything I needed.

CHAPTER SEVENTY-TWO

After an hour of sitting with Alma, I felt a lot better. She hadn't said much but explained that Jack had a past of his own and that it was important for me to trust him, considering that past.

I wanted to ask more details, but I got the impression she either didn't think she should say any more or didn't want to. Before I could push for an explanation, Jack came back.

He gave me an almost apologetic smile, and Alma got up and went to find Kai.

"Hi," I said, wondering if it was obvious I'd been upset.

Jack sat beside me and offered me a hug, not saying anything. I didn't hesitate, wanting the warmth of his arms around me. It felt good to slip into his embrace for a moment, neither of us saying anything.

"I want you to trust me," he said a moment later. "But sometimes I forget that trust is earned, not taken. Will you forgive me?"

I blinked, too stunned to respond at first. I knew he felt like it was his fault, but I hadn't expected him to act like I needed to forgive him for it and not give me the chance to say anything myself.

"You're completely forgiven. Will you forgive me as well? I…"

"There's nothing to forgive, kitten," he said before kissing me and cutting off any further words I might have. I relaxed into him, all the tension and fear I'd felt melting away. I was his, and it was all okay again.

Passion consumed us for several minutes, both of us sitting in each other's arms. The rest of the world melted away, and I found myself hungry for him in a whole new way. We'd had something go wrong between us and somehow made our way through it.

I smiled at him as he finally pulled back a little, his gaze drinking me in.

"Come on, let's join the others and enjoy the day. They want to have a little party before they all have to go back to the mainland."

I lifted my eyebrows at the idea of a party, but I wasn't going to object to a happier idea, nor was I against something light-hearted and fun.

We found Eve and Alma in the living room, decorating it with candles and instructing the men to rearrange the furniture so there was a larger open space in the middle. Kai was also working with one of the staff to set up some kind of sound system and lights.

Fascinated, I helped wherever I was directed. Jack did the same, offering solutions to problems or ways to make ideas happen from his knowledge of what he had on the island.

It took a few hours to get everything set up and the food prepared, but by mid-afternoon, there was a dance floor with lights, a small DJ area, and enough snacks and nibbles to keep us all going for the rest of the day.

I grinned at the layout and the way everyone had come together to create the party atmosphere. And given the company present, I was also a lot more excited about it than I had been about the party Alma and Kai held at their house.

There would be no Logan. No one to upset our plans or try to pull me away from the only place I wanted to be—in Jack's arms.

It was the perfect way to end our collective stay on the island.

As soon as Kai started the music and Jack dimmed the lights, the atmosphere changed, and everyone grew more animated. Jack grabbed my hands and hauled me to my feet, giving me no option but to dance around with him.

No one was particularly amazing at dancing, but it didn't matter. We were all having fun, laughing and bopping to the beat of whatever song Kai put on next. He took requests and handed over control to Liam a few times so he could dance with Alma.

At one point, I found myself tight against Jack, rocking back and forth with him to a rock ballad I barely knew, but the band appeared to love. Alma and Kai were only a few feet from us, doing the same, and everyone else was eating or enjoying the music as they played cards at a small table at one end of the room.

"Your friends are awesome," I whispered, having to stand on tiptoes to get close enough to Jack's ear.

He grinned at me and pulled me even closer, and for a moment, I could have forgotten entirely where we were, the lyrics and music seeming almost perfect for the time and place we were in. I felt my heart skip and then begin to race.

I was so head over heels in love with Jack, I knew I was in danger of never recovering, but something about him reeled me in and had from the moment we'd met, and he'd rescued my interview. I was so caught up in his love that I never wanted to be free.

We continued to dance, and I even spent a little time dancing with Eve and Alma and then Kai and Liam before I was back in Jack's arms as the sun disappeared and the stars came out.

As I thanked Liam for the fun and returned to Jack, I noticed Eve looking my way, sitting by the food. I smiled at her, and then Jack led me away from the party for a bit.

The song changed to something I didn't recognize as Jack took me outside under the stars. This far out and away from everything, there was no light pollution, and it made the sky look even more intense.

He led me toward a clearing where there was already a rug spread out, and we lay down beside each other on it.

Looking up beside him, I felt as if I'd died and gone to heaven. We talked for what felt like hours, Jack pointing out constellations, and I told him what I knew of old mythology and how people had worshipped different stars and believed they held power over a person's life.

As the night grew colder, I shuffled closer to Jack, and he put his arms around me. At some point, we ended up facing each other, gazing into each other's eyes, the dim light more romantic than anything we could have planned and prepared inside the house.

We soon kissed, our mouths opening as I tasted him and him, me. I felt heat rush through me, the desire to be his still strong. Passion flared in him, his hands running up my sides before he rolled me onto my back and shifted so he was partially over me.

The feel of his body against mine was like electricity, bringing me to life and making me hot and hungry for him.

He reached down and slipped my pants off without hesitation. For a moment, I froze, aware we were out in the open on his island.

Sensing my tension, he paused, but only for a moment.

"It's okay," he said. "They won't come out here. No one will know what we're doing or disturb us," Jack whispered. "Give yourself to me."

I looked up at him, both turned on by the idea of screwing him out in the open like this and nervous about having sex in such an exposed way. Yet after everything that had happened between us, I nodded and leaned into him again.

We'd already had one upset over me not yielding to him. The

worst that would happen was one of the others might stumble across us. And I was pretty sure all of them knew Jack was screwing me senseless every night as it was.

I moaned as he pushed my shirt up just enough to grab my breasts. He unhooked my bra and moved it out of the way, giving himself access to my nipples, and then he paused a moment.

His gaze met mine, and I exhaled at the beauty of the man before me, the man I was giving everything to. He was perfect.

CHAPTER SEVENTY-THREE

Jack trailed kisses down my exposed torso, his mouth warm on my skin as the breeze blew cold across me. Going lower and lower, he parted my legs until he was entirely between them, his lips around my clit.

I groaned as his tongue flicked out and licked over my sensitive nub. Deep tendrils of pleasure wove through me, making me wetter and hotter. A moment later, he did the same again, getting me ready to be screwed in almost no time at all.

Wet, panting already, and eager to have his cock deep inside me, my orgasm stole over me, coming so quickly his name came unbidden to my lips.

I heard him chuckle as I came down, the rock star already repositioning himself. The sound of his belt and zipper were the only warnings I had before he plunged himself into me, pushing himself deep inside with a grunt.

Pinned underneath him, my body his, I rocked my hips to help him drive deeper, wanting to give him the same pleasure he'd just given me. Clearly needing it, Jack fucked me hard and fast.

Feeling him deep within me, I lost myself in the pleasure of it, matching his rhythm and focusing only on making it good for him. I wanted nothing more than his orgasm and for him to know I was going to give him everything he wanted as often as he wanted it.

He grew more frantic and pushed harder and deeper, building my pleasure again as he mounted toward his own. As he yelled his ecstasy, pushing deep one last time as his cock throbbed and filled me with cum, I was pushed over the brink into another orgasm beneath him.

Panting, sated for now, and wrapping our arms tight around each other, we came down together. Feeling happier than I had in months, I lay by his side. We covered ourselves up again and went back to gazing at the stars, warm together under the velvet sky.

I didn't want to move or go anywhere, but eventually, it grew so cold that my body began to shiver despite Jack's warmth beside me.

As soon as Jack realized, he helped me to my feet and took my hand. Wordlessly, we headed back to the house, my heart light again. If days with Jack always ended with such warmth and care, I wanted to be with him forever.

By the time we reached the house, the party had ended, only Kai and Alma still up, the two of them sharing a snack on the beach on a rug of their own. I could just make them out from the front window of the house, but they didn't notice us. I wasn't planning to disturb them when they were going back to the mainland in the morning.

As I remembered they were leaving, I froze to the spot, fear gripping me.

Jack noticed immediately and turned to pull me into his arms.

"What is it?" he asked, his voice low, almost a whisper but comfortingly deep.

I leaned into him as I tried to push the fear away. "I just remembered everyone else is leaving in the morning."

"I really won't hurt you," Jack said, brushing a stray strand of hair off my cheek, his touch gentle as if backing up his words.

"Part of me knows that, but… it's really hard to explain. I want to feel safe with you, and nothing you've done makes me feel scared, but it's as if Greg put me in this terrified mode, and now, I don't know how to go back to normal."

"You will," Jack said. "Give it time, and keep trying to trust me. I'll help you feel safe again. I promise. Perhaps we could even think about choosing a safe word so you feel like you have the ability to stop me at any point. I would listen to you anyway, but if it's something that will help you know you can trust me, I would be more than willing to use one."

Of everything Jack had ever uttered, these words filled my mind, making me relax in a way no others had before. I exhaled and leaned closer, inhaling his warm scent, and it calmed me further. "I'll be fine. As long as you always stop if I ask you to."

Before I could do or say anything else, Jack lifted me off my feet and carried me up the stairs. Being the perfect gentleman, he carried me to the bed and placed me gently on it.

"Let me show you how well I can take care of you," he said, smirking slightly.

My heart responded, pounding in my chest as warmth spread through me. I felt as if my world couldn't get any better.

Still smiling at me, his eyes aglow with care and desire, he eased me back. Taking his time and being more tender and gentle than I could have imagined, Jack removed all my clothing, taking it off properly this time, in complete contrast to the hurried way he'd done it earlier.

Once I was naked and he came closer, I reached up and unbuttoned his shirt, revealing his muscular chest. I eased his shirt off, running my hands over his skin and enjoying getting the opportunity to explore him more. Normally, he was very much in charge, and I was helpless beneath him.

It felt like we were growing together and as if this might still be a bit of an apology for what happened earlier. He wanted me, but on terms we were both happy with.

Slowly I unbuckled his belt and undid his zipper, pressing just a little harder as I unzipped, feeling his erection underneath. I tensed internally at the thought of having him inside me again. What was it about this man that made me want to be screwed so much?

By the time I was removing his underwear, his manhood was fully erect, and I eased him out of the restrictive material. More than once, I'd marveled at how huge he was, and this time was no different. If I hadn't already had him inside me several times, I'd have felt a little fear.

As it was, I slowly ran a hand down his shaft, rubbing his erect head with my thumb.

He let out a groan as he shuddered in pleasure, but he stopped my hand and took it away.

"I want this to be about you this time," he said, his eyes meeting mine. "I'm not coming again until I'm sure you've been pleasured so much you aren't sure you can take anymore."

My eyes widened at the seriousness in Jack's face. If this was him earning my trust, he was doing a good job so far. Slowly, he reached for me, pulling our bodies closer together but still more tender than he'd ever been.

His fingers ran gently over my skin, making me heat up and relax at the same time. Following it with sweet kisses, he caressed and pressed his lips to every part of me, starting at my neck and working his way down.

I moaned when he reached my nipples, and he gave each one a quick suck before continuing down my stomach. He bypassed my pussy, moving to one side and trailing kisses down one leg and then up the other.

As he reached the top of my thigh, I gasped, anticipating what might follow. He smirked slightly before trailing his way across to my clit. Just as he'd done earlier, he fixed his lips around my clit, but this time, where his tongue had quickly and almost forcefully pleasured me, he gently stroked across me, his sensitivity even more of a turn-on.

At the same time, he reached one hand between my legs, feeling for my opening before he slid several fingers into me. I was already wet from the anticipation, my body responding to his every touch.

Slowly he moved in and out of me at the same time as teasing my clit, taking me to heaven one slow movement at a time. I tilted my head back, enjoying this gentler side despite my surprise.

Jack knew what he was doing, his body making mine shudder with pleasure long before he let me cry out in orgasm. Keeping up the pressure as I rode the waves rippling through me, Jack drew out every last bit of ecstasy he could give me.

Only as I started to come back down did he move again, wrapping his strong arms around me and holding me in his embrace.

CHAPTER SEVENTY-FOUR

<u>Jack</u>

After making Juno orgasm several times, each in a different erotic way, I couldn't take it any longer. My cock was hard, throbbing, and I was pretty sure I was only going to need to slide into her wet, slick, hot pussy to blow my load.

I needed some relief, but I was determined not to screw this up. I'd fucked up enough earlier in the day, pushing her the way I had. Every inch of me was desperate for her to trust me, but it had taken a reminder from Kai that trust was earned before I could see how I'd screwed up.

As Juno came down to earth in my arms for the third time, she shifted slightly and rubbed against my hardness just enough that I involuntarily moaned. It drew her attention, and she glanced down at my throbbing member.

A wicked look appeared on her face before she slid downward.

"I think you've waited long enough," she said before gently running her fingers along the tip.

A moment later, she wrapped her lips around me, and I had to grab the pillow and try to think of anything else not to fill her mouth with cum. Fighting for control, I closed my eyes and started focusing on adding random numbers, not sure what else to do.

She ran her tongue around my head, making it even harder, but I managed to cool slightly, enjoying the sensations as she worked on me as gently as I had on her.

Although this hadn't been what I'd had in mind to finally enjoy her, I wasn't going to say no to the pleasure nor the relief I'd eventually let her bring me.

And she worked me slowly, easing her tongue around my head a few more times before she took me deeper into her mouth, almost as if she knew the struggle I was having and was determined to help me.

I moaned as she took me deep in her mouth and then eased me back out, returning to my head to lick and suck. Although I lasted as long as I could, it was only a few minutes before I was filling her mouth with my salty cum. She swallowed each mouthful as I gave it to her, the motion pleasuring me further.

Coming back down, my mind clearing, I vowed to do whatever it took to make Juno feel safe with me. She was perfect in every way, and I wanted to keep her in my life and in my bed.

With both of us sated yet again, I pulled Juno into my arms, and we slept, everything feeling like it was going in the right direction. As long as she happily stayed when the others left in the morning, I knew we would be together for a while.

***

Juno was still sleeping peacefully when I woke, her body curled up and angelic in every way. Her breathing was calm and steady, clearly still in a deep sleep, so I opted to leave her, pulling on some clothes and heading down to make us some breakfast.

I found Kai in the kitchen, frowning deeply.

"What is it?" I asked, knowing that few things made him look so serious.

"This thing with Juno's agent. He's still digging his heels in. I don't get it. Did Juno really tell him to back off? Because he's telling me that he's only doing what she wants at this point, and if he insists on this, we won't be giving everyone else their usual cut."

I sighed, rubbing my hand along my chin.

"I'll talk to her, but I'm getting to the point where I just want it done," I said. "If he doesn't back down any further, take the cut from me and make sure everyone else gets paid what they're worth."

"Are you sure?" Kai asked, his gaze searching me.

"Yeah. If she did all this for money, it's my fault. I brought her into this. I should be the one to lose out, not the rest of them. Take it off my cut, but I'll try and get her to be reasonable first." I exhaled as I spoke, resigned to the possibility that I'd made another big mistake.

I was still reeling as Kai walked away to finish helping Alma pack, and I focused on preparing Juno and me breakfast. Not sure what else to do, I decided to continue giving her the benefit of the doubt for now. But I wasn't going to put up with lies either.

I was about to go upstairs with a tray of food when Eve appeared.

"I'm glad you're up," she said as she came forward, rubbing her hands as if she was nervous about something.

I lifted an eyebrow and waited for her to explain what she wanted.

"I've been trying to decide if I should say something, but...I think you ought to know."

"Know what?" I asked, immediately putting the tray back down.

"The first full day we were here. Liam didn't want to say anything because nothing ended up happening, but…"

"What?" I demanded, feeling more than a little angry already. I had a feeling I knew where this was going.

"Juno started hitting on Liam when she found him alone a few times. He said he made it clear he wasn't interested while she was yours, and she backed off every time someone else came along, but…" Eve trailed off, looking almost nervous as she spoke.

I tensed and tried to think of a calm, measured response, but it took me a moment to control myself.

"Thank you for telling me," I said. "I'm glad to know."

Eve smiled, a strange light in her eyes as she nodded.

"Sorry," she said as she turned to go. "I know you like her. I only hope someone comes along who doesn't break your heart."

I watched her go, unable to move for a moment. Was she telling the truth? Had Juno really been coming onto Liam when no one else was looking? I wasn't sure, my mind searching through everything I'd seen over the weekend.

There had definitely been times when Juno had talked to Liam, and he'd offered to teach her how to play bass. But had she wanted more?

Feeling like Juno and I had a lot to talk about, I grabbed the tray and made my way upstairs. Most of the others had their room doors open, busy packing up and getting ready to leave. I noticed Eve had returned to the room she was sharing with Liam, but I couldn't see him.

Kai was helping Alma, and the rest were farther along the hallway.

With no other reason to delay, I opened the door to the main bedroom and walked in. I shut it behind me, not sure what state I'd find Juno in. She was still in bed, although she stirred as I came in.

Her gaze took in the breakfast tray, and she beamed at me, no idea what I'd just been told about her.

"Oh, you're a darling," she declared, emphasizing the last word again, her eyes twinkling in delight. "You're going to make me feel spoiled at this rate."

I moved over to the bed and set the tray down beside her. She reached up to me and placed a kiss firmly on my lips.

"Last night was amazing. Thank you so much for understanding and helping me feel safe with you," she said, her words surprising me with their intensity. "I don't feel anywhere near worried about staying with you now."

Her words sent a thrill of delight through me. How could she be anything but genuine when she was being so vulnerable with me? How could anything Kai or Eve said be true? How could this woman be doing anything but slowly giving herself over to me?

I moaned into the kiss, wanting to push her onto the bed, part her legs, and claim her for myself. Instead, I pulled back.

"We should eat breakfast and then say goodbye to the others. After that, we can do whatever we want."

CHAPTER SEVENTY-FIVE

<u>Juno</u>

Not sure what had come over Jack and why he appeared to be putting some distance between us, I ate and quickly dressed, straightening myself as best I could before following him out of the bedroom.

The rest of the band was gathering luggage in the downstairs hallway, the staff and some of the crew from the boat collecting it and taking it out. It felt a little strange not to be one of them, but I'd told Jack I was going to stay, and I meant it. I wanted to go further with him and see what it felt like being his with no way out.

Before they left, Alma came over to me and gave me a big hug.

"Last chance to say that safe word if you want me to rescue you," she whispered.

"I'm all good," I whispered back, grinning at her and grateful for her support.

"Perfect. I didn't think you'd need it. Jack's a sweetheart, really. He'll take good care of you if you let him."

With that, she walked off to the boat, arm in arm with Kai. Liam came up to me next and gave me a brief hug.

"Bass lessons. Next time you're in New York. I insist," he said.

Again, I smiled and nodded, but I noticed Eve looking at me with narrowed eyes.

"Have fun wherever the two of you are off to now," I said to her, trying to smile and break some of the tension that had appeared.

"Don't worry, we will," she said, but she barely even air-kissed my way before walking out the door after him.

After saying goodbye to everyone else, Jack left me in the house to talk to the housekeeper and crew about food to replace what we'd eaten and to figure out when the boat would be back.

I stayed inside, deciding to take the opportunity to write a little, and fetched my laptop. Taking up my position in the window at the front of the house, I lost myself in my writing for a while, waving when the boat finally started to sail away again.

My stomach wasn't entirely calm at the realization that I was now alone on the island with Jack, but he'd been lovely to me so far. I was truly excited about learning to be his. Maybe I could trust him with more? I wasn't entirely sure, but I wanted to try.

Jack came and found me as soon as he was back in the house. He sat on the window seat beside me, also watching the yacht sail away. As it did, I finally noticed some clouds in the sky, large, dark ones moving rapidly in the distance.

"There's a storm coming in," Jack said. "It might delay the boat's return, but not for too long."

I nodded, glancing his way to see if he was worried, but his face was impassive. If he was worried, there was no way to tell.

Shifting closer to him, I put my writing aside.

"Well, now that you have me all to yourself, what do you want to do with me?" I asked, trying to smile at him.

He glanced my way, gazing over me as if he wasn't enthusiastic about doing anything.

"Do you truly want this?" he asked a moment later. "Do you

want to be here with me? Doing what I want? Being my submissive?"

I raised my eyebrows, not sure where this sudden doubt was coming from.

"Of course," I said when I had recovered. "I want to be yours entirely. I know I've been feeling a little scared about some aspects, but everything else has been perfect. I… I think I would be able to give you anything you ask for."

The words tumbled out, completely surprising me, but I was still afraid. Afraid he was going to take advantage of me.

"And what about your actions? Words mean one thing, but if your actions don't line up…"

I sighed, pretty sure he was talking about me trusting him.

"I'm not perfect," I said. "I'm used to protecting myself, fending for myself. And making sure there's a safety net. I am trying to let go of that need, but I'm not entirely there yet."

"That's all it is to you. A safety net?"

"Yes." I reached for him. "It's only about me feeling safe. I trusted Greg with everything and walked away with nothing but a few clothes and more than enough bruises. I can't go through that again."

Jack seemed to soften.

"Okay," he said. "If that's the truth, we'll speak no more of it."

I looked at Jack, his face full of darkness and his fists clenched. Something was upsetting him that I hadn't put my finger on, and I wasn't sure what it was.

"Is something else bothering you?" I asked.

"I don't know. I…" Jack exhaled and seemed to deflate as he did. "I think I've been letting outside stuff influence me. It's fine."

He reached out and took my hand, and electricity ran through my body. I was alone on Jack's island, and I had a feeling he was about to make it very clear he was in charge.

"Can I be yours, please, Jack?" I said, my voice coming out more desperate than I'd intended.

He stood and looked down at me before cupping my chin.

"Sounds like we might need a safe word. What is it you suggested to Alma again? Lucy?"

I blinked as he chuckled.

"She told me. I thought it was sweet, and I noticed you never used it. Not even when I was a beast yesterday." He smiled, almost smug as his gaze wandered my body.

"You never made me feel scared enough to, but that word feels…like something flippant we decided on a whim. Not something I might need to use as you encourage me to push myself and trust you completely."

"Then, if you want me to stop, use Hunter's safe word," Jack replied, reaching down and cupping my chin. I exhaled, his word one I'd made up and decided on a long time ago. Prey. Hunter's prey.

"Okay," I said, watching him smirk at me. "I can do that."

"Good," he said. "Now, come on, kitten. Time for you to take all this clothing off and let me see every inch of you."

I moaned as he pulled me to my feet simply by lifting my chin slowly upward. He had me feeling so hot, I was already starting to get wet with anticipation. Fear added to the combination, just enough that I was a heady mix of emotions and entirely unsure of what to do but let Jack guide me.

Although I expected him to take me back to the bedroom, he didn't, reaching for the top I wore exactly where I stood. He lifted the hem, pulling it up over my head before I could do much more than gasp.

His gaze fixed on my breasts, cupped in my navy blue lace bra, appreciating the view. A moment later, he reached around me and unclasped it, letting it fall to the floor along with my top.

I shivered, feeling exposed, standing in the front window of the house. Even if we were alone on the island, I was right out in the open, and it made me feel very vulnerable.

Jack only glanced at my face for a moment before continuing, not touching any part of me except to remove my clothing.

It didn't take long before I was standing in front of him in nothing but my panties, wet and hungry for him. I could see the bulge in his pants showing his own arousal, and it made me feel even more turned on.

"Do you give yourself to me?" he asked, his eyes locking with mine.

Unable to speak, I nodded. It was enough for Jack. He slipped his thumbs into the sides of my panties and pushed them down.

They fell to the ground, the wet crotch of the material obvious and making me feel both embarrassed and even more turned on.

"Perfect," Jack said. "You're going to stay naked until the boat comes back."

My eyes widened. That hadn't been a command I was expecting.

CHAPTER SEVENTY-SIX

For a moment, Jack did nothing but stare at my naked body, drinking it all in.

"Turn on the spot," he said, his voice commanding, enjoying what he could do to and with me.

I tried not to think about anything but what would follow if I pleased him. My heart was racing at my vulnerability. It was taking all my self-control not to run and put clothes back on, but I'd just told Jack I wanted to trust him, and we'd agreed on a safe word. I had to start to trust somewhere.

The world outside was growing darker, the clouds coming in overhead, making it seem almost brooding and scary. As if I'd been left behind on the island with some creature of the night, someone intent on devouring me. After he claimed me as his, of course.

Not sure if having the overactive imagination of a writer was a good thing or not, I finished my turn, facing Jack again. The bulge in his pants had grown larger, and he came closer to me.

"Do you have any idea what you do to me?" he asked, cupping my chin again.

I found myself grinning as I looked up at him, loving the

words and the way he looked at me. For a moment, I could have forgotten where I was, lost in the warmth and desire in his eyes.

Jack didn't give me a chance, however, pushing me back and up against the window seat until I was tipped back onto it. I gave way beneath him as he spread my legs and made me moan at the sudden pressure against me.

Hungry for him, I yielded, relaxing as he positioned me on the seat and unzipped his pants. Within seconds his cock was inside me, thrusting deep into the slick pussy I'd offered him.

I groaned as he pounded into me hard and fast, making it clear that I was his for the taking. He was everything I wanted, and I soon orgasmed, my body tightening around him even further.

Letting out a moan at the sudden increase in pleasure, he slowed, trying to keep control as I came back down, shuddering under his assault. I closed my eyes as he continued to claim me, letting him do as he pleased and focusing on one thing. How good it felt to be full of him.

It didn't take much longer for him to join me in ecstasy, his yell loud as he thrust one last time and then stilled deep inside me.

We lay together on the long window seat for some time, our bodies still entwined, his over mine. Kissing and caressing we cooled together, and for a moment everything was right in the world.

A brilliant flash of lightning caught our attention dragging us back to the real world. Almost immediately the heavens opened, rain pouring down onto the island and pounding into the sand.

"I guess that's the storm," Jack said, but he was frowning now.

"Is it supposed to last long?" I asked, beginning to feel a little concerned. Not just for us but the others on the boat as well. They had been gone for at least an hour or two now, and it probably meant they were safe on the main island, but there was no way to be sure.

"Not too long," Jack replied as he lifted me into a sitting position beside him.

Cold air made me seek the warmth of his embrace, reaching up to him and bringing my naked body into his arms.

For a moment, I had Jack's attention again, but the loud roll of thunder that followed the lightning drew our attention outside once more.

"It's still a fairly long way off. I should find out how close it's going to come."

I nodded, letting him pull away. Although he'd appeared calm about the storm earlier in the day, he wore a worried expression now and quickly made his way toward a laptop to check the news.

"There's a storm warning now," he said a few minutes later. "It's a little early in the season for a hurricane, but the storms can still be on the rougher side. We should keep an eye on it."

With no idea how concerned I should be and feeling incredibly vulnerable with nothing on, I went over to him. He put his arms around me again, holding me close.

"I'm a little cold," I said, his body warm against mine. "And I'm feeling…anxious, I guess."

Jack studied me for a moment, holding me close to him as if trying to decide whether I could put clothes back on. It felt a little strange to be giving him so much control, and I definitely hadn't decided if I fully trusted him yet, but if I was ever going to, I needed to start somewhere.

"What are you anxious about?" he asked a moment later. "Maybe I can help."

I exhaled, slightly disappointed that I wasn't being told to just get dressed. Was it really fun for me to give myself to Jack like this and let him decide? Or was I just worried about everything?

Without intending to, I looked at the storm as another wave of thunder rolled over.

"I'm worried about that," I said. "I've never seen a storm like that, and the island is so…exposed."

"Yeah, I was pretty nervous with my first storm here, too. The house is sturdy, and the storms look fiercer than they are. We'll keep an eye on the warnings, though. There's a storm shelter underneath the house."

Jack's words helped. He sounded calm again, and it had the same effect on me. It was a relief to know he had taken it into account. I also felt grateful he hadn't mocked my worries but listened and told me he'd felt similar.

"I think I'd like to put clothes on until the storm is over," I said. "It's weird being naked while all this is going on."

Instantly, Jack frowned.

"I won't force you to do anything," he said. "But I'd hoped you'd be comfortable with me. That you'd trust me like this. We could go toward the back of the house where it's more sheltered, and I could try and take your mind off it if you think it would help?"

There was no hesitation as I nodded. He'd thought of a way to help me and listened to me. I was grateful, even if I wasn't entirely calm yet.

Taking my hand, he led me through the house to a gorgeous smaller sitting room and sat himself down on the sofa before pulling me down on his lap. From my position, straddled across his lap, I couldn't see any windows, only hear the wind as it whistled through the trees and around the house. It was also quieter and a little darker.

Almost immediately, I felt both calmer and less exposed.

"Better?" he asked, genuinely sounding like it mattered whether I said yes.

I nodded, feeling as if I'd possibly made a fuss out of nothing, but any more cares and worries I had were banished as he pressed a kiss to my lips and held me close again.

Despite all the sex we'd already had, I started to warm again and leaned into him. A moment later Jack pulled away and reached for a small controller on the stand at the end of the sofa. He flicked some music on, turning it up a little to help mask the noise of the storm even more.

Grinning at the seductive tunes he'd picked, I leaned into him again. It seemed Jack wanted more fun with me as well.

CHAPTER SEVENTY-SEVEN

Jack

I moaned as I orgasmed into Juno again, her body over me, riding me hard. She seemed to shudder in her own pleasure a moment later, the two of us coming down together, panting but sated.

If I'd thought being with Juno would feel good and allow us to enjoy each other's company, I had totally underestimated how good it would feel to have her here and doing as I asked.

She was trying hard to give me what I wanted and let go of her fears, that much was clear, but I was still wary of her anxiety. And although I was putting a brave face on, the storm was making me nervous, too.

Naturally, the island was hit by tropical storms now and then, but this one was picking up in strength, and the warnings were updating frequently.

"Relax and listen to the music," I told Juno as I moved her to one side of me. "I'm going to get us some lunch."

"Lunch sounds good," she replied, turning her large doe-like eyes up at me.

Inside me, something melted. I wanted to protect her and

devour her all at the same time. Instead, I walked away, taking the opportunity to check the latest weather update and my messages and see what was going on generally.

I had several messages from the band and the housekeeper, and the weather forecast had gotten worse over the last hour or so. We were now expecting a full-on tropical storm, and the boat had only just made it to the main island in time for the band and staff to get safe.

The skipper offered to try and come back for us and then sail ahead of the storm to a larger island, but I hadn't seen the message in time. It was already too late to do that safely. I declined and quickly went to the kitchen to fix a quick lunch.

We still had at least an hour before I'd need to take Juno down to the shelter if it was truly going to be so bad. I just needed to keep an eye on it.

While I made us some sandwiches and grabbed some fruit and drinks to go with them, I listened to the wind. I couldn't remember it ever being so loud while I'd been on the island before, but I usually tried to avoid being here during major storms.

Sometimes, however, life had other plans.

When I returned to Juno, I found her sitting up, her arms around herself and a wide-eyed look on her face. Even in the back part of the house, it was getting loud.

"I think a tree must have fallen somewhere," she said as she looked at me. "There was a cracking sound and a *thwump* off to the right somewhere."

I frowned and handed her a plate of food. It definitely sounded like we might need the storm shelter.

"Do you have anything you don't want to get broken or destroyed?" I asked her.

With even wider eyes, she looked up at me, her mind going elsewhere as she tried to think.

"I've got some notebooks with ideas and things, and I don't have a backup laptop," she said.

"Okay, go get them quickly. Put them in something waterproof and bring them back here."

She gulped but set her plate down and did as she was asked. I thought for a moment and then went to fetch a few items of my own. I also made sure we had our phones, chargers, and some flashlights.

There were emergency supplies in the shelter as well, but it was always good to be cautious. And there was no harm in heading there earlier than I thought necessary and finding we could come out again without a problem only a couple of hours later. It was better for us to be careful.

It didn't take me long to gather what I needed, getting an update on the weather and from the mainland before I rejoined Juno. She was shivering, but she'd also put her clothes back on.

Although I hadn't officially said that was okay, I didn't say anything then and there and merely guided her to the shelter down in the basement of the house. It wasn't a very large space, given the number of people I could house on the island in total, but it would be more than enough for the two of us.

Juno plopped herself down on the edge of a camp bed, and after stowing the supplies and checking the batteries and food supplies, I joined her.

"It'll be okay," I said as I hugged her a moment. "We're safe down here and the house is sturdy. Chances are we'll be going back upstairs again in only a few hours."

She nodded, but I could tell she wasn't convinced.

I had no choice but to leave her for a few minutes, anyway. There were still a few checks I had to make and parts of the house I needed to try and secure before we hunkered down together to wait.

"I'll be back as soon as I can. Stay here no matter what, okay?"

I saw her take several deep breaths, her eyes wide, but she

appeared to hold herself together and continued to sit where she was. Every part of me wanted to sweep her in my arms and promise her we'd be safe, but I knew I couldn't.

Leaving her behind with far more reluctance than I'd experienced in a long time, I made my way to the main floor again, checked the backup generator, and made sure the grill had been returned to the storage shed and nothing else was loose.

The wind was blowing so strongly that I couldn't stray far from the house. Debris from the trees was already blowing around.

The waves were also getting higher, but the house was built on the highest section of the island, and the storm shelter in the basement had water pumps. It also had masks and air tanks for the worst-case scenario. It wasn't perfect, but it was as likely to keep us alive as any other option.

After checking all the doors were locked and bolted, their frames sturdy, I went around dropping all the shutters over the windows and making sure they were secure as well.

It took so long that the wind was even stronger by the time I was done, and I was more than a little grateful to be back inside with Juno again. The look of relief on her face as she saw me again was almost heartbreaking.

I went to her and wrapped my arms around her, feeling her tremble. She'd been scared. So beyond scared I felt like a monster for leaving her.

"Is everything secure?" she asked, making it obvious she was worried I'd leave her again.

"All secure," I replied. "And I'll stay down here with you until it's calmer out there again, okay?"

She nodded, and I felt her relax against me a little.

I guided her back over to the camp bed and kept her close as we sat together. Down here, it didn't sound as bad as it had on the floor above, but I knew how bad it had gotten before I came down, and it was clear Juno had enough of an imagination to fill in the gaps in her knowledge.

Over the next few minutes, I held her close, slowly rubbing a hand down her back, anything to soothe her a little. She leaned into me, and we waited for the storm to do whatever it was going to do.

"We shouldn't just sit here," she said a moment later. "We should do something to take our minds off it."

I looked at her again, and I was pretty sure she was asking if I had something in mind.

Not sure what else to do, I kissed her. I wanted her body close to mine, wanted to make her feel good and screw her hard. Not because I was turned on but because I wanted her to feel like she was mine and I could keep her safe and cared for. I wanted to pleasure her and make her forget her fears.

CHAPTER SEVENTY-EIGHT

<u>Juno</u>

As Jack looked at me, there seemed to be a change in his eyes. He went from worried to an intensity I only saw when he wanted to take me and make me his.

I blinked a few times, surprised by the sudden change. How could he be so turned on during a storm like this? I had spent the last half-hour imagining Jack dead in several storm-related ways when I finally had the courage to leave the shelter.

Of course, all of them had been unfounded and he'd come back to me, but that didn't make me any less afraid for our lives.

Seemingly oblivious to my fear, Jack leaned down and kissed me. Electricity ran through me despite my anxiety, but I didn't relax into him the way I usually would.

I didn't resist either as he pushed me back. Maybe he needed this. Maybe this was his way of not being afraid. I felt his hands slowly wander over my body and it made me feel warmer, more secure, but every time another gust of wind shook something or there was another *thwump* from either a tree going over or something else, I tensed right up again.

"Relax," he whispered when it happened a third time. "The

wind can't get in here and you'll feel so much better with my cock in you."

I tried to do as he suggested and hid my surprise that he was being so bold about sex being something worth doing right now.

My body seemed to agree with him, even if my mind was less sure, however, and I grew hotter and wetter as he pushed his hands down my pants and between my legs. He cupped my pussy, the pressure enough to distract me.

"That's my girl," he whispered as I let out a small moan. "Let me have you entirely."

His words came out deeply, an interesting mix of soothing and a turn-on. Maybe this wasn't such a bad way to pass the time.

I reached down and pushed my pants out of the way for him, and he grinned at me. Immediately, I also pulled my top off. I hadn't bothered with a bra or panties and I could tell he appreciated the lack of any other clothing.

Every inch of me felt vulnerable again, my body tensing for a moment, but he ran his thumb across the top of my clit, bringing my attention back to what he was doing.

Slowly, I relaxed and he wasted no more time before he undid his trousers and revealed his cock. He was already hard and standing erect.

"You're going to do exactly as I say, Juno, aren't you?" he said immediately.

For a moment, I wasn't sure what to say. Did he have something else in mind for me?

"Juno, answer me. Are you going to submit and be a good girl?" The aggression in his tone surprised me into nodding.

"Good. Open your mouth. You're going to taste me before I let you have a full pussy."

His words both sent a thrill of desire through me as well as a jolt of fear. I wanted him in my pussy, and on any ordinary day I'd have been happy to earn it, but this was different.

Before I could think anymore, however, he had moved up the

bed and brought himself to me. As soon as I parted my lips even slightly, he reached a hand behind my head, weaving his fingers through my hair, and held me still while he pushed his cock into my mouth.

"Suck me, Juno. Earn yourself a fucking."

I did as he bid, running my tongue over his head every time he pulled back and then taking him as deep as I could every time he thrust forward. Although it hadn't been something I'd have chosen to do, it was something I could concentrate on, and I took delight in his moans.

His breathing grew rapid as he picked up the pace until he stilled, cumming over my tongue and into my throat.

After swallowing so I wouldn't choke, I ran my tongue around his tip and licked off every drop.

He moaned and pulled out of me. As my eyes met his, I saw the haze of satisfaction in them and felt a rush of pride, and I grew even wetter. He'd promised to screw me if I pleased him and I was pretty sure I'd delivered my end of the bargain.

Moving down the bed, Jack focused on my breasts, taking one in his mouth and sucking on it and then the other. I gasped and moaned at the sudden assault on such a sensitive part of me, but he didn't stop there, his fingers heading between my legs.

Finding me wet enough, he slid two fingers straight into my pussy while he continued to suck and gently bite a nipple. The sudden sensations stole all my focus, pushing me toward heaven.

Working with his fingers, he found my g-spot like an expert. I groaned at the pressure and the repeated motions until I was hot and sweaty in a way I'd never been before.

Jack never stopped, seeming to delight as I came undone, moaning and whimpering beneath him. An explosion hit me as I cried out, my mind overwhelmed by the pleasure tearing through me.

Within seconds Jack removed his fingers and thrust his cock deep inside me, sending another wave crashing over me.

I moaned, wanting to ask him to give me a moment, but no words came out. He seemed to sense my distress, however, and stilled within me, waiting for me to calm and my breathing to even out.

As soon as I stopped shaking, he continued, his mouth crushing down on mine before I could ask him to stop anything.

Fear tore through me. He wasn't hurting me, my pussy slick, but a part of me wanted to stop this. I was too scared, and my body started to tense. Still, no words came out of my mouth.

A moment later, there was a loud crash, and even Jack looked up.

"What was that?" I demanded, pulling away until we separated. Then, I took the opportunity to put some distance between us.

"Nothing we can do anything about from here. It could have been anything," Jack said, clearly irritated but not yanking me back to him, although he followed me a little way.

I sat up and exhaled, my body shaking again.

Jack seemed to realize I wasn't about to let him continue screwing me. He put an arm around me and pulled me against him again.

"We're safe in here," he said, looking into my eyes. "Try to relax and let us have fun. We'll be through the worst of it soon, and then the boat can come back. We'll get anything broken fixed and enjoy the rest of our time on the island."

I wanted to be soothed by his words, but there was another *thwump* of something falling, and another crashing sound. A moment later the lights flickered out.

Although I didn't squeal, I froze to the spot, able to hear nothing but the sound of the wind whistling past the house and the shaking of something metallic as the wind moved it around.

Jack moved away from me, and it took all my restraint not to reach out, grab him, and pull him back. I was naked in the dark with the worst storm I'd ever been in raging outside. When I'd agreed to stay on the island with Jack and feared certain things happening, something like this had never even been part of my imagination.

And somehow, this felt a thousand times worse than anything I could have thought of. I was trapped in the dark with no way out.

CHAPTER SEVENTY-NINE

I jumped as Jack turned on a flashlight, lighting himself up, and me. Without hesitation, I then grabbed my clothes again and pulled them on. He glanced my way but if he was going to object to me getting dressed again, he decided not to, and instead he found a second flashlight and turned it on as well.

"We should get the backup generator on and have it power this room. It can keep going for some time, but if we're down here for a while, we might need to run it in phases."

I had no intention of arguing with Jack. I was just grateful he appeared to know what he was doing. After taking the second flashlight, I helped him shine it around the small room so he could find the controls for the generator and get us lit up again.

It seemed to take several minutes as Jack checked a bunch of things first and went through a short checklist. He then powered it on.

Almost immediately, lights flicked back on again, although they were dimmer than before. I shivered, pretty sure it was getting colder in the room.

Jack came back to me and wrapped his arms around me.

"Now, where were we?" he said, trying to press his lips against mine again.

I pulled back and out of his arms, almost tripping over the edge of the camp bed behind. He reached out and grabbed my arm, helping to steady me, and then came closer again. A moment later he lifted my chin with his finger.

"We'll be okay," he said. "I promise we'll be fine."

"Can you really promise that?" I asked, sounding angrier than I truly felt.

"Juno. This shelter was built with exactly this situation in mind. It's got everything in it experts could think of. It's designed to keep us alive no matter what."

I exhaled, knowing my fear was getting the better of me, but men had promised me things in the past, and we hadn't been fine. Jack wrapped his arms around me again, but this time, it was the hug of someone trying to comfort the other, not seduce them.

Not sure what else to do, I let him hold me, but I knew the damage was done. There was no way I could handle this. I'd grown up in a safe country where this kind of thing didn't happen. And I wanted to stay that way.

There were so many reasons not to be with Jack, and I knew I'd had enough of trying. I didn't have enough money, had already maxed out one of my credit cards just buying a few outfits. I'd been hit on by a sleazy bottom-feeder, and now I was stuck in a shelter in the middle of a tropical storm and terrified for my life.

No. Jack and his life aren't for me.

I sat down again, but I made sure Jack didn't get the impression that I was interested in anything else. I just wanted to survive, to get out of here and go home as soon as the boat came back.

If Jack realized how closed-off I was to him, he didn't say anything about it, instead grabbing one of the books on the shelf.

"Why don't I read this to both of us? See if it helps."

Nodding, I settled back a little and tried to get comfy. Maybe it would help.

Jack read for what felt like forever as we tried to ignore the hell outside. There was more noise, but Jack did his best to read through it, and I tried to focus on his voice.

Eventually, it seemed to grow quieter outside, and there was a long period without any loud noises or the crack and *thwump* of more trees breaking.

Even with the lack of noise, Jack didn't stop reading for some time longer, waiting until we couldn't hear much of anything. Although I couldn't be sure, it seemed as if it was quieter than when we'd first come into the shelter by the time Jack closed the book and put it back on the shelf.

"Stay here," he said as he got up.

There was no way I was venturing out of the shelter until I was completely sure it was safe, but Jack moved cautiously to the thick, heavy door he'd sealed shut and turned the handle to open it.

It took some effort on his part, but the weather stripping slowly came away, and then he shoved against the door. Almost immediately water rushed into the shelter, pushing him back and the door shut again.

"Shit," he said as I pulled my feet back up onto the bed, my heart racing again.

"All right. We're going to have to do this differently," Jack added, reaching for me.

At first, I didn't move, not sure I liked the idea of getting off the camp bed and into the water, but equally aware that if this room was going to flood, then I didn't want to stay in here either.

"It's okay, Juno. It's shallow up there, but we've got to get out. The pumps in here might not cope with this much water."

I gritted my teeth and forced my body to move and go to him, trusting him one last time. He took my hand and helped me through the water and toward the door.

He then encouraged me onto the steps and stood close behind me.

"Hold on as best you can when I open the door, and then we'll both try and get up the steps together. It will be easier on us, but we'll have to fight the water a little."

I nodded despite the tightness in my chest and the way my legs shook. My mind couldn't offer me a better solution, and I knew I didn't want to drown.

Jack paused for a moment, almost as if he was steeling himself for the challenge as well, before he reached past me, holding on with one hand near mine.

As the door came open this time, he kept his weight against it, letting the water rush in. Able to finally see out myself, I could tell that he was right. The water was less than a foot high inside the house, but it was enough to create some serious force against our legs.

I almost lost my footing, but Jack's weight behind me kept me from shifting too far. Putting all my strength into it, I managed to climb a step and Jack kept close behind, his body pressed up against my back and helping to push me forward as well.

Behind us, the room began to fill up until I heard a strange clunking noise, and some kind of machine kicked in.

"Pumps," Jack said as I hesitated and tried to glance back. "They won't save the room from filling up, but they'll clear all this water out better and quicker."

Not responding but aware I couldn't delay it any longer, I took another step and another, each one taking effort until the water caught up to us, the room filling up while I was still waist-deep.

It was only then that I remembered my laptop, phone, and everything else that was important to me were in the shelter, now underwater. Instantly, I stopped and tried to turn back.

"My notebooks," I said, my soul destroyed.

"They'll be okay," Jack replied, blocking my way and making it clear he intended to keep doing so. "They're in waterproof compartments. I made sure of that. And I can bring them up as soon as the water level is low enough to wade through."

I exhaled, still wanting to push past him and get them now. They were the most important thing in my life. All my ideas and thoughts. My publishing journey and all its ups and downs were in those notebooks.

"You can't get them now. You'll drown trying," he said, his voice hard and his gaze fixed on me.

Wanting to scream but somehow managing not to, I relented. Jack turned me back and encouraged me up the last of the steps and out of the door.

CHAPTER EIGHTY

Already, the water level in the ground floor of the house was lower, enough of it having gone down into the shelter that it had made an impact.

I noticed that the shutters had torn off a couple of the windows, and the glass was smashed higher up the house. It seemed the bottom floor was intact, however. I had no idea what had happened to the glass, but I was glad it didn't seem to be in the water that had rushed down at us.

Wading farther in, I went toward the stairs, but Jack put his arm out and stopped me.

"The structure might not be safe enough," he explained as he slowly made his way to the kitchen.

Not sure what else to do, I followed. Other than the water, there wasn't much damage to the inside of the house on this floor, and Jack quickly decided to get us both something to eat.

"We'll need to keep our strength up. It might be a long night," he said as he handed me some snacks and a bottle of water.

Again, I didn't argue, but I didn't feel like I could relax either. I felt adrift, as if the storm had tossed me about directly, my emotions numb from the constant fear and worry. We were still alive, but I felt as if it had cost me everything and upended my life in a way I'd never seen coming.

We ate in silence as Jack tried to assess the damage and get a feel for how bad it was outside.

The wind was still whistling around the building, but it grew quieter as we ate and looked around some more.

"I think it's worth taking a look outside," Jack said a moment later. "Before it gets too dark to see."

I paused, frozen. It hadn't occurred to me that it would be dark and there was no electricity anymore. Did we even have a way to communicate with anyone and ask for help?

Would help even be able to come? The boat had been heading to a port even nearer the storm. Would they have been emerging from shelters to similar scenes as this only a few hours earlier?

I had no idea, but the thoughts running through my head terrified me. I didn't know if I could cope, but I had nowhere to go. Being on a small island with Jack had been the worst decision of my entire life, and now I was stuck here, waiting to be rescued in a wrecked house with no heating or electricity and only so much food.

On top of that, I'd possibly just lost my most important possessions. The kind that money couldn't replace.

Jack moved to the nearest door and slowly unlocked it, pulling back the bolts and trying to ease it open. The water had warped the bottom, and it stuck at first, but eventually, he got it open.

Immediately, the water rushed out of the door, turning what had been a trickle into a torrent. I moved closer to watch it run down the hill toward the shore, the wind blowing it around before it reached the beach.

The pontoon was wrecked, a lot of the planks torn off. The smaller staff building and storage sheds had fared better from the outside, the lower profile and trees around them having possibly offered some protection, although I noticed shallow streams of water coming out of both of them as if they, too, had taken on water at some point but couldn't spit it out as fast as it had gushed in.

I walked out into the storm after Jack, although I kept close to the house. Here and there, trees were down, one having hit the patio at the side of the house but not broken anything.

The torn-off shutters were twisted hulks of metal farther up one of the pathways, having stuck on trees, mangling them and the living plants.

If I'd felt the storm had been destructive before, it was a thousand times worse now, surveying everything it had done to the island.

"I'm going to check out the generator and see if I can get some kind of power back on," Jack said a moment later. "Be careful where you step and what you do."

I nodded and headed to the most sheltered side of the house. After being in the water and now out in the wind, I was feeling cold. A few times, I tried to think of something I could use to get warm, but I hadn't brought a coat with me, and the blankets and towels were on the second floor of the house—unreachable, according to Jack's prior warning.

Deciding to keep moving for the warmth alone, I went after Jack in the end.

I found him in a small shed-like structure, the walls so solid they'd held, although a small corner of the roof had torn up. Inside was the generator, and as soon as I appeared in the doorway, Jack held out his hand to warn me from coming forward.

"It got wet in here. I don't want you to get hurt," he said.

"Yet you're in there," I replied, irritation coming to the surface as I lashed out at him with my words.

He ignored the snappy response, focusing on the machine in front of him and checking out panels and readings I didn't understand. Once again feeling adrift and unable to anchor myself to any task or function, I wandered off, checking out the destruction elsewhere.

It was clear that waves must have come right up and over the island. It was probably what had filled the buildings with water, but the water had receded back to previous levels, or at least close enough.

Even as I explored further, the storm grew quieter until it was no worse than a strong breeze.

If I'd seen the aftermath in pictures, I knew I wouldn't have felt impacted by it much. I'd have felt a small pang of sadness for the ruined beauty of the place, and I'd have been able to keep going and live my life normally, but there was something very different about seeing it close up.

My mind didn't want to think about anything but going home. Of running away from all of this. Yet, I had to wait until I was rescued.

By the time I made my way back to the house, I had started drying, no longer quite as cold, and the sun was setting. Jack wasn't by the generator, but it wasn't running either.

Anxiety crept into me again as the numbness faded at the thought of fresh difficulties through the night, and I went in search of Jack.

He was in the storage shed with a set of tools and instructions, trying to fix something, and it didn't look like he wanted to be interrupted. Knowing I needed a task, I looked through the contents of the shed, trying to figure out how we'd make food with no power, and stumbled upon the gas grill sitting in one corner.

It was wet at the bottom, a scummy water line and residue below that showing how high the water in the shed had come. Thankfully, it didn't seem to have reached the top of the gas tank or the cooking area.

Grabbing the handle, I lifted one end and wheeled the contraption into the open. Jack glanced my way a few times, but he didn't say anything until I'd gotten it set up. Then, he caught my eye.

"Cook whatever you want, and plenty of it. Unless I can get the generator working, it's all going to spoil. We might as well eat it."

I nodded, grateful to be doing something useful. I could feed us if nothing else. And the grill would be warm. At least until the gas ran out.

CHAPTER EIGHTY-ONE

As I handed Jack a plate of food I felt some satisfaction with what I'd achieved. The sun had set and we were sitting out beside a lamp, the house now as cold as outside.

The generator still wouldn't work. Jack had been forced to give up, focusing his attention on other forms of keeping us safe while I cooked. We had blankets wrapped around us now, Jack having ventured upstairs despite the risk and gathered some stuff.

A lot of the upstairs was wrecked, glass having torn through it, he'd said. Most of it was embedded in walls and furniture, but it had also reached the closets, torn apart clothing, and littered the carpets and floors.

Thankfully, the blankets were in a small closet out of the way, the door having been an awkward one that used to get stuck anyway. My clothes were ruined, as were many of Jack's.

It stung a little, having spent so much money on clothing only to wear two of the outfits once each so far. But the shelter had finally been pumped free of water, and Jack had retrieved the valuables we'd stowed down there.

The waterproof compartments had done their job for the

most part. My notebooks and laptop had survived. My phone and Jack's were both ruined, but Jack pointed out that both would have been useless anyway.

Not sure whether that comforted me, I tried to focus on the positive. I hadn't quite lost everything. I could still write, and all my ideas and thoughts were safe. I felt sorry for Jack at points as he discovered yet another thing was broken, soaked, or otherwise ruined.

If it bothered him, he took it well, sticking to problem-solving ideas instead. However, now that everything was calmer and we were sitting and eating, the emotions began to return.

After stealing over me in gradual degrees, the numbness gave way to tears and shaking until Jack noticed. He immediately came over to me and scooped me up, pulling me onto his lap as I started to sob.

For what felt like forever, I cried against him, not caring how I looked or if I ever stopped. All the while, Jack held me and rocked me back and forth gently, stroking my back.

I tried to calm down a few times, but then I'd think of some other element of what had gone wrong and how stranded we still were, and it would set more tears in motion until I was exhausted and spent, leaning against him, my head fuzzy and my eyes puffed up.

He felt warm, and I still didn't move, even once I was calm again. If Jack minded me seeking comfort from him like this, he still didn't say anything, merely holding me as darkness fell and brought out the stars here and there.

"We should light a fire or something. At some point, boats will start coming by to check on people. If we have a bonfire, we'll draw attention," Jack said. "It'll also keep us warm through the night."

I didn't question him, but it crossed my mind that he'd changed his comments from his boat coming back to get us to any boat coming by. Although his boat wasn't far away, it clearly wasn't coming back in a hurry.

Without any dry firewood, I wasn't sure how we would start a fire, though.

It didn't stop Jack. He gently set me on my feet, making sure I was all right before he got to his as well. Then he strode down to the beach.

Before my eyes, he dragged over a fallen tree, grabbed an ax, and started chopping it up. I found some smaller tools that looked as if they'd cut off branches and went down to help him. Keeping useful would help me both stay warm in the meantime and get the job done quicker.

I was impressed to notice that some of the smaller wood had already dried out a little, the tree dead in places. I pointed it out to Jack.

"Yeah, dead trees, or dying ones, are most likely to fall in a storm. Makes better firewood in this situation."

Grateful for that small mercy, we split the tree into three sizes of fuel—large logs, large branches, and the leafy canopy and twigs. Jack then started constructing a small bonfire and added everything, one pile at a time.

I expected that to be enough, but he then went to the shed and the pile of wood that had been stacked there. He found some matches and a large gas canister.

After helping him bring that to the bonfire, I helped him arrange even more wood on the pile, and then he drenched it in gas, pouring it so liberally that the entire beach soon stank of it.

"You'll want to stand back," he said, backing up with me.

After everything else, I definitely wasn't going to argue. I backed up with him until I was farther up the beach and waiting to see how he intended to light it from there.

He answered my unspoken questions in seconds, flicking a match against the edge of the slightly damp box and somehow managing to light it anyway. Pausing to give the match time to burn with a larger flame and spread down the stick, he focused on the pile of wood.

With a precision I hadn't expected, Jack flicked the match into the heart of the pile, and it went up with a *whoomph*. I stood back farther, the sudden heat startling me as Jack came to join me.

It crackled and spat, smoke rising in plumes that would have made us instantly spottable in daylight. I watched as the fire started to calm, the gas burning off as the wood caught alight.

After a few minutes, the smoke died down a little, and the wood burned itself. Jack spread one of the blankets on the sand a little closer to it on the side that would allow us to see out to the water and then encouraged me to sit down with him.

I did, not sure how I felt about being so close to him after deciding I was done with our relationship and I was going to leave. Was I really done?

My thoughts went back and forth. Sometimes, Jack could be perfect and everything I needed. But he was also so blind at other times to what was going on and how I felt. And his world was just too different from mine. I didn't belong with him, and I'd been a fool to think otherwise.

None of that changed the attraction I felt for him or that I was already head over heels in love with him. Nor did it change how much money I'd just wasted.

I felt like such a fool. I'd let my heart get carried away, and it had taken my head with it.

As I sat watching the fire and the stars come out above, I knew that a boat couldn't come soon enough to take me to the larger island and away from everything. Beside me, Jack didn't really speak, alternately gazing into the fire and out to sea. It was as if either he was heartbroken too, or he knew I wasn't his anymore.

We stayed like that, side by side in silence, for what felt like hours, time losing all meaning as the fire burned itself lower and we grew slowly colder.

CHAPTER EIGHTY-TWO

The fire was beginning to bank so low that Jack was considering dragging another fallen tree over and adding it to the pyre. I'd dozed in his arms several times over the course of the night, marveling at how awake he seemed to be and how he never once stopped taking care of me.

Part of me didn't want him to get up and walk away from me, but I knew we couldn't let the fire die, and it would need enough strength to dry out the next tree.

Instead, I got up to help him again. We would need to make the most of the situation, and this would put some distance between us for a while and keep me awake. I didn't want to fully fall asleep. Wasn't sure I even could. And I knew I had to keep some distance between Jack and me if I was going to walk away.

Before I could help Jack, I noticed a flash of light on the water. I stopped and turned to see if it was just a trick of my overtired eyes. As I looked out to the horizon, however, I was pretty sure there was a light out there.

"Jack, there's a boat," I called.

He immediately dropped his ax and came to my side so he could see through the gap in the trees better.

My heart hammered as I waited for him to confirm what I thought I'd seen. He looked at me and back out to sea and squinted a little.

"Yes," he said. "That's a boat."

He grabbed my hand and almost dragged me to the water's edge. I went with him, my heart pounding even faster. Was this rescue?

"Wave your hands and yell for them. They might not hear you at first, but they should see your outline moving in front of the firelight."

I did as I was bid as he made his way back to the house. I tried not to worry about him, but it wasn't easy. And despite my best efforts to attract the attention of the people on the boat, it didn't appear to change course or notice me, and I quickly grew hoarse.

Thankfully, Jack wasn't gone long, although he made me jump as he waved what looked like a gun in his hand. A moment later, he shot it into the sky, and a trail of bright orange smoke flew up into the air with a loud hiss. A few seconds after that, the boat let out a loud horn blast and visibly turned toward us.

"We need to get more wood on the fire. They need to be able to see as much as possible in case they don't have a floodlight," Jack said.

He practically ran back to the tree we were cutting down, and I sprinted after him. Although it felt like there was always yet another hurdle, I helped as quickly as I could, taking the piles of branches I lopped off and dragging them to the fire as Jack swung his ax again and again.

This time, he cut larger logs than before, making me wonder if they'd hold up, but I grabbed the end of one and dragged it toward the fire as he did the same with one in each hand.

We added the three large logs, and then I added the branches and leaves as quickly as I could. The fire grew again, although it smoked once more. I backed up, not wanting to inhale the smoke but not wanting to get too far away from the fire's warmth, either.

Jack moved out in front of it again and waved, shouting.

The boat came closer, someone calling back, although I couldn't make out the words.

"It's not our boat, but they're still likely to help us get somewhere," Jack said. "Pack up whatever you want to bring with you in as small a bag as you can manage."

I hurried to the house to do so, but it was hard to see so far from the firelight, and the flashlights had been wrecked in the shelter when it flooded. In the end, I only grabbed my laptop, notebooks, and purse. The latter was a little wet, but the contents were safe enough, and it meant I'd have credit cards.

After shoving my notebooks inside the bag, I carried it back to the beach and put it and the laptop on the blanket we'd been sitting on. I then took over briefly while Jack went to the house to fetch everything he wanted.

He had a much smaller pile, just some keys and a wallet, as well as the broken phone, and I worried for him for a moment. Admittedly, I hadn't fared much better.

Trying not to think about it, I focused on the boat again. It appeared to have stopped a little way out from us, but I couldn't be sure.

Not long later, they lowered a smaller rowboat, which came closer, three people aboard.

"Is it just the two of you?" a deep male voice called when they were a little closer.

"Yes, me and a woman. Our power is out, the house is uninhabitable, and we're low on food, too. How badly have the main islands been hit?"

"They've taken a beating, but it hit this run of islands harder. It's growing in strength as it heads on, so we'll take you back if you don't mind going a bit farther and checking the other smaller islands."

"No, that's fine. We should make sure no one else is stuck," Jack replied, getting closer to the water as the boat came up, his few possessions in one hand.

I grabbed my bag and laptop and followed, the idea of a rescue so welcome that I didn't care who these people were or if they planned to head anywhere else first. They'd offered to get us safe, and that was enough.

Within seconds, the boat reached the shore, the sound of the bottom hitting the sand and sliding into it an almost comforting noise.

Jack immediately grabbed the prow and held it still, waving me forward. I walked into the shallows, getting my feet wet yet again, and the man I could just see in the firelight held out a hand to help me step over the side.

The boat wobbled, but the strong hand in mine made sure I didn't fall, and I quickly sat down and scooted across the bench to the other side of the small boat to give Jack room to get in and sit.

He didn't right away, pushing the boat back off the sand before he waded in deeper and then accepted a sailor's hand to help him aboard. Immediately, he sat beside me and wrapped an arm around my back.

"You've got a familiar face," our rescuer said, the light not enough for anyone to make out much but the boat we were returning to.

It was only then I thought of the fire we'd left blazing.

"Shouldn't we put that out?" I asked.

Jack frowned for a moment, but the sailor was the first to respond.

"There's no point worrying about it. It's already getting smaller, and in the middle of the sand like that, it shouldn't spread to anything."

"What about other boats?" I asked. "What if someone else comes along and thinks we need rescuing?"

"There won't be other boats," the sailor replied. "At least, not before that dies down enough for them to know you're gone."

I blinked. No other boats? How bad had it been elsewhere?

Shuddering at the thought of more destruction, I felt Jack tighten the arm he'd put around me and pull me closer to him. Unable to speak and suddenly fearful that our rescue wasn't much of a rescue yet, I leaned closer and tried not to panic.

CHAPTER EIGHTY-THREE

<u>Jack</u>

The worst was over, and I felt myself relax a little as Juno and I were offered a cabin on the larger boat to rest in. Although they offered two, I'd declined the extra, and Juno hadn't objected. Despite her desire to be close to me, however, something was clearly wrong.

Not once had she tried to do more than lean into me as I held her, waiting for me to go to her or instigate contact. It could all be the shock of what happened, but it had been happening since we were in the shelter together and the power had gone out. It was as if she didn't feel safe with me any longer.

Part of me didn't have the energy to make her feel safer anymore. I wanted to. Wished she would feel it. I'd never hurt her, but if she was blind to that, there was nothing I could do, and I knew it.

I still planned to see her safely to shore and make sure she got back to England okay, but by the sounds of things, that would take time. Although I wanted to know what state the rest of the Bahamas was in and how hard it had been hit, I didn't dare ask the crew in front of Juno. Not while she was so scared. It would only worry her further.

On top of that, we both really needed some sleep. Juno didn't resist being led to the cabin or lying down on the bunk bed there. I encouraged her to make space for me. At first, I thought she was going to object, but she scooted over and let me wrap my arms around her.

"Sleep," I said. "We're safe for now."

She nodded and leaned into me. For a moment, everything felt right, her in my arms, but it felt like it might be the last time. For now, I'd appreciate it and hope I was wrong. I moved my head slightly so I could smell her scent, the smoke from the bonfire and her shampoo an interesting blend.

Closing my eyes as well, I tried to fight sleep to make the most of having her close one last time, but I was too tired, the ordeal having taken a toll on me, too. Within seconds, oblivion crept over me and stole me away.

When I came to, Juno was still asleep in my arms, her body peaceful and warm. I exhaled and didn't move. The boat was still moving, clipping along the water at a fast enough pace that I could hear it outside and feel the gentle sway as the waves rocked us.

It was peaceful, and I didn't want the moment to end. Sadly, the moment ended all too soon as Juno stirred and opened her eyes.

"We're still moving?" she asked.

I nodded, not sure what else to say. I didn't want her to move or pull away, but she did. My skin instantly felt cold everywhere she was no longer connected to me.

Despite the ache in my chest, I let her go and pulled back as well.

"I'll go find out how close to port we are," I said as I rolled away and got up.

Almost as if she didn't trust me to come back, Juno followed, leaving her stuff in a small pile in one corner of the cabin. I'd shoved my stuff in my pockets and almost told her to bring her things with her to make sure they were safe as well, but I pushed the fear away. These folks had rescued us and were highly unlikely to do anything else.

It took me a moment to remember which way we'd come below deck and lead us back up. The sunlight made me blink, and Juno leaned closer as the boat swayed and dipped. I looked around, seeing land on the horizon we were heading toward. It pretty much answered at least one of the questions I had.

Almost instantly, the sailor who had come to our rescue in the night approached, smiling at us.

"Looks like you two slept well," he said as he winked. "We're not far off porting now. Didn't find anyone else in need of rescue, though we did our best. Are either of you hungry?"

"Food would be really good," Juno said before I could reply.

The sailor gave us a nod and motioned for us to follow him back down below deck. Juno didn't hesitate, giving me little option but to go along as well. It was a good enough way to pass the time until we were on dry land again. As soon as we were led to a small table near a kitchen, my stomach rumbled.

I could smell bacon, and a guy dressed in a chef's white apron appeared as if he'd heard us coming.

"Another round of breakfast?" he asked, looking at Juno and me as if having extras on his ship to feed was nothing new.

"Please," Juno said before mentioning her allergies. Thankfully, the guy seemed to understand and promised he could accommodate the requirements before offering me a bunch of options.

I picked something substantial and then sat at the table beside Juno. She yawned as she appeared to relax, almost as if the sleep and the offer of food alone had revitalized her but encouraged her body to remind her it hadn't had as much of either as it truly needed.

"What do you think we'll find on the larger islands?" she asked as she looked out of the nearby porthole. I shifted so I could see through it, too, noticing land appearing on the horizon on that side as well.

"No idea. It will depend on how strong the storm was when it came over them. And how close. Considering our own boat never came back for us, though…" I trailed off, not sure I wanted to voice my worries and fears.

Most of me was sure they'd had time to get back without running into trouble, but the mind liked to doubt and play tricks that enough of me was considering the possibility they might not have. Because of it, I was slightly on edge. Would we find my friends alive?

The food came quickly, the chef skilled enough that neither of us had any complaints as we wolfed it down. Again, I relaxed a little more, but the feeling of being slightly on edge, of life not being quite right anymore, wouldn't go away.

My body was still expecting something to hurt or need me to act, and it wasn't fully letting up. And I knew it wouldn't until we had seen with our own eyes that the others were safe and we were both on dry land.

I tried not to think about the house and island I'd just left behind and abandoned for now. It wasn't going anywhere, but it was going to take a lot of money to fix it. The interior would need to be almost completely renovated.

However, there was nothing I could do now, and it was more important that we'd all survived.

As soon as we'd finished eating, Juno and I thanked the chef and made our way back up to the deck. She didn't look as if she felt entirely well, but I didn't say anything, just going with her and making sure she stayed safe.

I felt like a guardian angel, following her around and protecting her until she decided for sure on my part in her life. It was a strange feeling, my chest aching at the thought of being less to her, but my heart would be unsatisfied if that turned out to be all I ever was. I found myself willing to almost settle for it, however.

Juno glanced back at me as she stood at the side rail and watched the boat come toward the harbor. Relief washed through me, and I felt her relax a little as we came past the outer wall to reveal a mostly intact town, only the odd outhouse or shed looking damaged.

The harbor was another matter. Masts were broken all over the place, and some of the boats had come free of their moorings and been pushed up onto the streets or, in one case, into a cafe's dining area.

It had clearly been hit by the storm but weathered it better than my house had. Hope returned that my friends were okay.

CHAPTER EIGHTY-FOUR

<u>**Juno**</u>

Land had never been such a welcome sight before, but it took longer than I'd have liked to get docked somewhere. Because a bunch of the moorings had broken, there were boats floating free in the water, and people were trying to move everything around and fix the mess.

In the end, the captain of the boat that had rescued us ordered the smaller boat to be lowered again and to take us to a set of stairs on the harbor wall that ran up from the water.

We were being rowed there when I spotted Jack's boat in the harbor and pointed it out to him. He looked relieved for only a moment. The main mast was broken, and it was off its mooring as well and partially beached. It hadn't fared as badly as some of the other boats, but it was leaning at an angle, and I wouldn't have wanted to be the person trying to get it back in the water without breaking it.

"That explains why they didn't come get us," Jack said, his face unreadable.

"Sorry," I said, but he shrugged.

"It's a boat. As long as the crew and the band are okay, the boat can be fixed or replaced."

Although Jack's expression seemed to match his words, he regarded the stairs we were approaching with a sad look in his eyes. I bit my lip as I thought about what I wanted to do next.

I loved Jack. I knew that for sure, but I couldn't do this, and I knew I was about to hurt us both. There was no way I could go any deeper, and it was better to break both our hearts now before it got any worse.

Jack got onto the steps first and reached a hand back for me and my stuff.

With my laptop tucked as safely as I could get it under one arm and my bag on the same shoulder, I let him help me up one last time.

"Thank you," I called back to the sailors before we climbed the steps, and Jack led me along the wall to the town.

It was busier than I'd expected, but we didn't get much farther before a familiar male voice yelled Jack's name. Kai was standing on the street closest to Jack's boat and had spotted us approaching.

We immediately headed that way, Jack picking up speed. The two men hugged, and then Kai embraced me as well.

"Is everyone else okay?" I asked before Jack could.

"Yes. We're all fine. We took refuge in a well-built hotel a few blocks up the road, and they made sure we were all taken care of. The others are there now. We should let them know you're both alive and look well enough. What happened on the island?" Kai asked.

Jack's sigh and the slump of his shoulders said everything. Kai put a hand on his shoulder.

"We'll get it fixed. As long as you're both safe and unharmed."

"We are now," I replied for Jack.

This was enough to get us all moving again. Kai informed us

of the state of the much larger island, saying the airport was about to open again, but flights were fully booked. The private jet had taken a beating as well and was receiving a full inspection.

I listened, letting the two men talk about details I didn't entirely understand as we walked up the quiet streets toward the hotel.

Kai led us inside, and we found Alma and Eve waiting in the lobby. They both squealed when they saw us and came running up, although Eve made far more of a fuss about Jack being okay than me. Alma wouldn't stop hugging us both.

"We were so worried about you." Alma looked us over as if she was trying to figure out what had happened to us.

"And us you," Jack replied.

There were more hugs and exclamations as the rest of the group came down from the rooms they were staying in, and then we all found somewhere comfy to sit and catch up.

While Jack went off to get more information on the airport and how long we might be here for, I told the band and partners what had happened on the island.

I shook at a few points while I spoke, even tearing up when I thought of having to pull myself against the water flow to get out of the shelter, but Alma took my hand and gave me a sympathetic smile.

By the time I finished telling them our part of the story, Jack was back. He gave me a nod as if he appreciated what I'd said and wanted to talk to me. The others got the hint.

"Let's give these two some space to rest, and we'll all have lunch together in a bit," Kai said, encouraging the others to leave.

I got a look from Alma, but she let her husband pull her away until there was no one left but Jack and me. I wanted to follow them, sensing that we were getting to the moment I needed to tell Jack I was leaving.

"It looks like it's going to be a while until the flights start up again," he said. "I've booked us a room. We should probably get a little more sleep before we join the others."

I nodded, intending to go with him but not necessarily to sleep more. We needed to talk about everything in private, and then I needed to say goodbye.

Trying not to worry about it, I let Jack lead me to a room. Neither of us said anything at all, and it was clear that he had picked up on my change in attitude toward him. The tension between us grew until he managed to get the room door unlocked, and we both strolled in. I didn't put my stuff down, but Jack dropped the keys onto a small coffee table in front of a loveseat-style sofa.

The room wasn't anywhere near as fancy as the first one he'd ever taken me to, but it was still more plush than any I'd ever been in before that.

Still, neither of us spoke, standing in the room, looking toward each other but not meeting each other's gazes. I tried to think of a way to begin the conversation, but nothing I thought of sounded right, and Jack either didn't want to break the awkward silence or didn't know exactly how to either.

Eventually, he sat down. He leaned forward, one hand going through his hair, and exhaled. I finally looked at him, but he didn't even attempt to look my way.

An ache grew in my chest at the thought of walking out of the hotel door and never seeing him again, but I knew I had to. I couldn't seem to find a way to trust him, and I didn't belong in his world. I wasn't wealthy enough to take the rollercoaster ride.

But how did I tell him that? How did I tell him that without making him feel like I thought he was the monster the media portrayed? I didn't think he was the cruel, abusive man he'd been accused of being, but I was broken, and he deserved better.

I tried to move closer to get his attention. He finally glanced up, but he didn't speak. Instead, he sat back and surveyed me.

"You're trying to figure out how to tell me you're leaving for good, aren't you?" Jack asked, the pain it caused him making his voice crack slightly.

I felt tears sting my eyes as I nodded.

Yes. Yes, I was. And there was no stopping it now.

CHAPTER EIGHTY-FIVE

Jack

The look on Juno's face was too much to take. A mix of pity and hurt, but the decision had clearly been made. I'd seen it coming. Almost booked two rooms because I could feel her pulling away from me.

But now it hit home, and anger welled up in me. I got up and walked to the window, needing something else to take my focus so I didn't break something. Considering what she'd been through, I didn't want to make her feel like she was in danger. She wasn't. I'd never hurt her, no matter what she was doing to me.

"I'm sorry, Jack. I just don't feel safe enough with anything. And it's not fair to you," she said.

I growled in response, not sure I bought her reasons. Yeah, I could understand being scared of the storm, but I'd kept her safe. What else could she be scared of? The more I thought about it, the more anger built in me, my fists clenching and my body flushing with heat and tension until I knew I couldn't just let her walk out of here.

"I kept you as safe as I could during that storm, and I made sure you were comfortable, that you were happy and had people to talk to. Even though you offered to be my submissive and I wanted to be your dom, I kept things light and tried to help you grow to trust me, baby step by baby step. I even offered to choose a safe word with you. You turned me down on that one, remember?"

"I know," Juno replied, stepping closer. I moved aside to put more distance between us again. I didn't want her to be close anymore.

"I can't believe this. Eve was right. Kai, too. I should never have invited you to come and meet the band."

"Eve? Kai? What have they said?" She sounded innocent and made me almost want to explain everything.

"It doesn't matter now," I replied. "You're going anyway, aren't you?"

I looked at her again, and our eyes met. For a moment. she didn't reply, but she stared at me, her gaze searching, wide and almost pleading.

"I think I'd better. You're right. I never belonged in your world. Not only could I never afford it, but it seems no one likes or accepts me as much as I'd hoped. I'll find somewhere else to stay until I can get home."

Juno's words surprised me, and I almost told her exactly what I thought of her excuse of not being able to afford being in my world, especially now that she would receive such a high share of the royalties from our song. But the sadness in her last sentence and the way she turned away, almost defeated, stopped me from doing it.

The fight melted out of me as I watched her walk away and out of my life. How could I be angry at her when she seemed to be in need of protection all the time?

It also wasn't lost on me that the clothes she'd bought, including the dress I'd encouraged her to get, were all destroyed.

I had insurance. There was a good chance they would pay to replace everything. But her clothes…

I stopped the thought. She was getting money from the song, and it was clear she didn't love me as much as I did her. I didn't owe her anything.

Deflated, angry, and with a deep ache in my chest that I couldn't shift, I sat on the small loveseat and let the tears finally flow. I'd been so stupid! It was clear I'd fallen for yet another gold digger who had no desire to be with me beyond the money I could make her and the fame she could get.

When she got what she wanted, she'd run, taking everything with her.

It took me a while to calm down, my emotions passing through every state along the way. Anger at both her and me made my fists bunch, only to be followed by the hot gush of more tears and then embarrassment at how I never seemed to be able to have a long-term relationship anymore.

Eventually, I was calm again, my eyes dry and my mind made up. I needed to keep going, focus on fixing the house and island, and getting back to the band and what we were doing next as a group. Juno was in my past now, and that was where I needed to leave her.

With this thought and a deep breath, I made my way to Kai and Liam for lunch. I could worry about everything and everyone else later. It was enough to keep going and try and make the best of what had happened. And I needed a new phone, if nothing else.

The hotel's dining room was almost entirely empty aside from us, most of the rest of the hotel guests having gotten off the island by now.

"The others followed Juno and made sure she has somewhere safe for a day or so. She wanted to just go to the airport and wait for a flight there," Kai said, making it clear he knew enough of what happened to know it was over.

For a moment, I couldn't reply, not ready for someone to mention her despite calming myself down earlier. I wanted to scream and yell, and I felt anger rising inside me again. I'd done everything I could for her, yet I was the one holding a broken heart again.

Kai seemed to pick up on me not wanting to talk about it and needing a moment. He handed me a menu.

"They don't have any fresh fish, but they can still do the rest," he said.

I nodded, not surprised. No one was fishing today, and I doubted anyone had gotten a catch the previous day, either. It wasn't just us hurt by the storm. This thought helped me refocus.

We ordered and talked about all the things that were broken and would need fixing before moving on to more hopeful conversations about what the band was up to, Kai steering us in a happier direction.

When Alma and the others still hadn't appeared after we'd eaten some appetizers, Kai opted to go find them for us, leaving me with Liam.

"Let me get you a drink, man. You look like you need it," Liam said.

I shook my head. Although he was right, and I could really use a drink, I knew what I was like. It was too easy to be tempted into doing something I shouldn't, and I didn't need any more bad press. Not right now.

Liam opened his mouth as if he was going to say something else, and then closed it again. A moment later, he inhaled as if he was about to ask me a question. When he did it again, I looked at him and raised my eyebrow.

"Out with it," I said. "What are you trying to say but aren't?"

"It was something Eve said. Made me worried that you and Juno have fallen out over us. Eve implied she'd taken something the wrong way. I made sure she knew nothing had happened, but I just thought, what if she said something to you, too?"

"About you and Juno?" I replied, struggling to say her name.

"Yeah. She did say something, didn't she?" Liam asked.

"Yeah, but it wasn't…"

"It wasn't? Good. 'Cause Eve seemed to have some funny ideas about Juno flirting with me and me with her, and I don't know where she got them from. Juno's never even been alone with me, and she only ever talked about our band and you. She clearly wasn't interested in me. Didn't even seem that interested in letting me teach her like she was worried we'd be alone together."

I blinked as Liam spoke, the only outside reaction I had to his words. Eve had made up a pile of crap and accused Juno of flirting with him, and I told Liam as much.

"Stupid, jealous…" Liam trailed off as he shook his head.

"Sorry, brother. It seems we both picked wrong this time," I replied.

"No. Just me." Liam got up and looked me full in the face. "Juno worships the ground you walk on. I don't know what made you argue, but that girl…there aren't many who care the way she does."

With that, Liam walked away, leaving me sitting at the table waiting for a dinner no one else seemed to be eating anymore. Had I truly made a huge mistake? Maybe, but it hadn't been my decision. It had been hers, and although she might have been faithful, she'd still left me for her own reasons.

CHAPTER EIGHTY-SIX

<u>Juno</u>

I tried not to cry as Alma spotted me, her expression taking everything in, including the bag and laptop I still clutched and the sodden tissues grasped between my fingers.

"Tell me everything, now," she demanded.

I shook my head, unable to give her the information she wanted as tears threatened to fall again. I'd already had to hide in the alcove by the stairs, not daring to use the elevator, and calm myself down. It had taken several minutes, and I felt awful about what I was doing.

"It's over," I said when she didn't move and made it clear she would wait. "My fault."

"Oh, Juno. But Jack is so smitten with you."

"I know. But it's done now. Can't be undone. I need to get to the airport," I said as I fought back more tears and tried to focus on what came next instead.

Despite my desire to move on as quickly as possible and put distance between me and everything that was part of Jack's world, Alma refused to leave my side and put her arm around me.

"You can't go to the airport and wait there," she said. "You'll be treated like cattle in a stall. No. Stay here tonight, and try to book a flight for tomorrow. I'll pay for the—"

"No," I said, not wanting another penny from anyone.

I didn't want to owe anyone anything else, and I definitely didn't want to run the risk of bumping into Jack again. Getting to the airport was my only option.

Alma didn't let go of me, however.

"I can't," I said. "I just can't. I need to be somewhere else, and I need some distance. I also really need some sleep."

As I spoke the last words, I felt the weight of how true they were. I didn't doubt sleep would help, but I couldn't get it here. I needed to be locked in a hotel room somewhere else.

"There's another hotel right up the road. Let's try there. The buildings farther inland have fared even better, and I'm sure they'll have spare rooms just like here."

I nodded as Alma steered me, slipping her arm through mine. For a minute or two, I let her guide me and listened as she talked to Eve about how scared they'd been through the storm as well.

It gave me time to gain further control over my emotions and relax in their company.

Alma turned out to be right about another hotel nearby that had some space.

I quickly got checked in and requested information on the airport as soon as there were available flights out before ordering some lunch to my new room.

With the main essentials taken care of, I turned back to Alma and hugged her.

"Thank you for everything," I said as I pulled back.

"Now, don't say it like that. This isn't goodbye. You and Jack may have hit a bump, but I refuse to believe it's anything more than that. I've never seen him look at anyone the way he looks at you."

I looked down, not sure I could agree but feeling guilt wash over me. Despite the guilt, I knew I couldn't go back to him.

A moment later, Alma asked the receptionist for pen and paper and scrawled her number down.

"Here," she said, handing it to me. "When you're back in the UK and feeling a little better, call me, and we'll talk about everything."

I nodded, not sure I would but unwilling to argue.

"See you around, I guess," Eve said, giving me a quick hug, but she was clearly less concerned, and I couldn't blame her. We definitely hadn't bonded the way Alma and I had.

I watched the two women leave again before I returned to the hotel room and waited for my lunch.

As soon as I was alone, I sank onto the small sofa in the room and cried my eyes out. I was interrupted by a concerned-looking waiter, but I assured him I'd be fine and tried to eat some of the lunch he'd brought me, apologizing for having no cash to tip him with.

Not as hungry as I thought I'd be, I tried to figure out what to do next. I made the mistake of turning my laptop on and found a massive number of messages from friends trying to get hold of me and find out if I was okay.

Feeling guilty in a whole new way, I quickly let them know where I was and that I'd survived, and I would be flying home as soon as I could, but my phone was dead. I then did the same on a social media account that was public enough that it would be seen by pretty much everyone else I knew.

Before I'd managed to get away from the direct messages and people I needed to reassure, I had an email from my agent. It contained his number and the command to call him.

Although I wanted to sleep, I suddenly worried that Jack had dug his heels in about the song or something now that we'd broken up, and I wasn't going to get anything at all for it.

I was going to have to call and swallow the charges for using the hotel phone. As soon as I got to the airport, I would buy a cheap burner and make sure I could message and call again properly. Hopefully, my account would sync up, and I wouldn't have lost any numbers.

"Oh, thank God you're still alive," Harry said after picking up. "I was so worried I'd lost my most promising money-maker. I need something to retire on, you know."

I exhaled, smiling as I wondered how serious Harry was. I knew he liked me at least partially for the money I made him, but he always did right by me, too.

"Tell me you're not hurt, and that hunk of a man is still floating your boat through this little storm."

"I'm not hurt, but Jack and I aren't floating anything. Is that why you wanted me to call?" I asked, fear making me tense.

"Oh, no. What made you think I was calling about money? I might joke about it, and I might think more favorably because you make me wealthy, my dear, but you are also one of my favorite people on this planet. Well, you're one of the few I can stand..."

"So, nothing went wrong with the song deal?" I asked.

"No. It's all but signed. I'd have you signing it now, but I think it can wait till you're back in the UK."

"Thank you." I exhaled, feeling a little relief, at least. I wasn't sure I could have coped with a fight of that nature, too. Every inch of me would have wanted to give in, but Harry wouldn't hear of it.

"It's really over, then?" he asked, the sadness in his voice surprising me.

"Yeah. I think so," I replied, my voice breaking up as tears sprang up faster than I could stop them.

"Oh, Juno, darling, I'm so sorry. It sounds like you'd fallen pretty hard."

"Yeah. You could say that," I mumbled through the crying.

"Get some rest, get back home, and we'll find a project to distract you. Maybe see if we can add another hunk into the mix and really distract you."

I laughed, although it sounded slightly hysterical, and then Harry hung up again, and I was left to cry all by myself again.

Sighing, I removed my pants and got into the large bed. Maybe I could sleep some more, and it would hurt less when I woke up.

CHAPTER EIGHTY-SEVEN

I put the key in the lock of my apartment and turned it as relief swept through me. Pushing the pile of mail on the inside of the door out of the way, I walked in and flicked on a light.

The apartment was exactly the way I'd left it, with one exception. It smelled like yummy food, and someone was clattering in my kitchen.

A second later, Kit appeared, coming around the corner so she could see the door. She had a spoon in her hand.

"Good timing," she said. "I made us both some dinner. Put your stuff down and come to the table."

I could have cried again, the relief and gratitude I felt almost overwhelming. Instead, I did as she had suggested, noticing she'd made a large stew and there was something baking in the oven, too. Something chocolaty and divine-smelling.

"You are the world's best friend," I declared as I sat down, and she put a bowl in front of me.

"Yes, but you've been through hell by the sounds of it, and we all agreed you couldn't come home to an empty flat after everything else. I've also got tomorrow off. Happy to come shopping with you if you need to replace a bunch of stuff."

I nodded and took the first spoonful of food, burning my mouth. It tasted good, and for a few minutes, we focused on eating while I made a list of items I was going to need to buy the following day.

I'd already grabbed a new phone, but I needed to look at my contract and see if the phone insurance would cover a better one. I also needed a new toothbrush and a few other basics. And I was going to need more clothes.

As I thought about the credit card bill I currently had, I let out an exasperated sigh. I was going to have to spend more money again, and I would have very little to show for it.

"Want to talk about it?" Kit asked a moment later before going to the oven to check on the contents.

I got a peek at the chocolate muffins in there before she decided to give them a little longer. It gave me time to think about her question, and by the time she'd sat down again I knew I did. Over the last week or so the biggest problem had been that my usual friends, the people I already trusted completely, hadn't been there.

Alma and Kai had both been lovely to me, but it wasn't the same as sitting down with your best friend and talking over all your fears, worries, hopes, and the things you wished you'd said and done.

As we cleaned up, I began my tale, telling her everything and holding nothing back. It took the best part of an hour, the muffins finished and two of them eaten long before I was done. Kit was the perfect listener, sitting with me and only occasionally asking a question to understand what had happened.

"No wonder you feel so emotional," she said when I was done. "That's several adventures rolled into one. Are you sure you don't want to be with him anymore, though, Juno? It sounds like you really care about him."

Biting down on my lip, I tried to decide if I could tell Kit everything that had happened with Greg and why I truly didn't feel ready to trust Jack. I wasn't ready. At all.

"Too soon," was the only answer I could give. It was too soon.

Kit stayed with me only long enough for us to finish cleaning and put the leftover stew in pots. She took one home for her the following day, and then I made my way to my bedroom to sleep.

Before I could do so, a call came on my temporary phone. Recognizing my agent's number, I picked up again.

"Before you ask, I'm home. I'm safe, and my best friend's just made me dinner and chocolate muffins, so I'm also in a good mood," I said.

Harry laughed, not saying anything else.

"Well, I hopefully have more to put you in a good mood. The contract is all done and signed. Thank you for adding your signature somewhere over the Atlantic. And I've got some interview requests for you. The band asked if you'd help promote the single over the main release period."

I bit my lip, already feeling fear tighten my throat. Would Jack be there?

"There's only one where the band will actually be performing. Figured you wouldn't want to actually see the band much. The rest want to talk more in general about your writing. Now that you've been seen with Jack and you've got attention in the US, I think you should do them all."

"You'd think I should do them all anyway," I replied.

"Yes, I suppose that's true, my dear, but my point still stands. You should do them."

I chuckled at Harry's insistence that the interviews were good for me. Thinking back to the last TV interview I did, part of me wanted to say no anyway, but I couldn't bring myself to do it.

"Send the schedule to my email, and I'll take a look at it and make sure I can fit them in."

"Good. I'll say yes to them all provisionally," Harry replied, hanging up before I could request that he didn't.

I swore and went to fetch my laptop. If I was already going to be accepting these interviews, even if only a tentative acceptance via my agent, I needed to quickly make sure it was possible.

It took me a while to open my email system and find the attachment, but it wasn't as bad as I feared. They were all in a short window, four weeks from now.

A few mentioned the band, but one said it would just be Kai, and the other Harry had technically warned me about. I wasn't sure about approving it at first, but after a few minutes, I decided I'd be brave. I blocked off the time in my calendar and then put the laptop aside again.

It was in four weeks' time. That was enough time to heal my heart a little and move on. After all, I'd barely even known Jack more than two weeks. Anything could happen in another four.

But despite these assurances in my head, I had the sinking feeling it wasn't going to be that easy. It was a goal now—to spend four weeks doing anything but think of Jack. To focus on the rest of my life. And in about a month's time I'd know how successful I was.

CHAPTER EIGHTY-EIGHT

<u>Jack</u>

I felt my stomach tighten as I sailed back into the small harbor area of my island. The ashes of the large bonfire Juno and I had made still stuck out on the beach.

Part of me hadn't wanted to come back so soon. Not after everything that had happened here. The sweet woman I'd almost had as mine and all the time I'd hoped to spend with her at my mercy.

For a moment, it was all I could see. Everywhere Juno had been. The way she'd sat at the upper windows and written. Her legs dangling in the water off the now-mutilated pontoon. Even the way we'd sat and watched the bonfire together and she'd rested in my arms, trusting me even while she was terrified of what might come next.

And that was what made it hardest. She'd trusted me to keep her safe in so many ways. But somehow, it hadn't been enough.

On top of that, I still had no idea if she'd done all this for money or not. Kai had gone ahead and approved the contract for her to get credited with the song and the royalties, and I'd never brought it up with her again.

Standing and facing the wreckage of the house I'd loved, however, I couldn't help but wish she hadn't taken my share. The insurance company was already trying to claim they didn't have to pay for it all to be repaired. That I hadn't followed some of the procedures I was supposed to.

I'd have been a liar if I hadn't admitted that it had made me feel both angry and hopeless. Since all the rumors, I hadn't been making as much money as I used to. The band earned well, but my acting had paid for the island and everything on it.

With my housekeeper and some of the sailors, we made our way around the island and logged everything we could to try and prove to the insurance company that everything that could have been done to save the house had been done.

It felt like it took forever, and I had to resist the urge to straighten furniture and try to salvage things until everything was photographed properly.

However, nothing prepared me for walking into the bedroom and being confronted with the torn, glass-shredded remains of Juno's clothes and belongings. For a while, I could do nothing but stare at them. The only rational explanation was that she had stayed with me just long enough to ensure she had the money from the song.

I sighed and sat on the end of the shredded bed, careful not to perch on any glass shards. Looking around the room, I tried to think about what I'd do with the decor going forward, but all I could think about was having Juno there the last few days I'd been in it. It had felt as if I was in heaven. Having Juno with me in my world and seemingly happy.

I'd been an idiot, falling for the charms of yet another gold digger. And I'd paid for it. The only consolation I had was that the storm had wrecked all her expensive clothing. But as I thought about that as well, I knew it didn't make sense. If she had wanted my money, why hadn't she let me pay for the clothes?

Had it been part of some bigger plan? Had she been trying to lull me into trusting her so I'd give her the royalties?

I exhaled as the ache in my chest grew. I wanted to hurl things, or yell, or punch something until my fists hurt and I felt an emotion other than this lost, numb feeling I'd had since the storm.

The housekeeper came in a moment later and looked around the room.

"The upstairs really is a lot worse, isn't it?" she said, careful not to meet my gaze.

I could see the pity in her eyes when she did look my way. It only made me feel worse. Was I truly someone to be pitied? When had I become the poor sod who never got what they wanted?

Not wanting to be considered someone to pity, especially when I should have been the person who had everything, I tried to make myself busy again.

After making sure the room was completely photographed, I went to my wardrobe to see what I could salvage from the clothes I'd had in there. It wasn't as bad as I'd feared.

Either because I had more clothes than Juno or because they'd been in a more sheltered position, several sets of clothing near the back were completely unscathed.

I quickly pulled out everything that was salvageable and the housekeeper fetched me a bag to put it in. I was relieved to find some of my favorite clothes had survived. After all the emotional upheaval and the nightmares living through the storm had given me, it was only a small victory but it felt as if something was finally going more in my favor.

By the time everything had been checked over and the ruined possessions had been listed, it was getting dark and everyone was hungry. We made our way back to the boat still moored in the natural harbor. With the buildings on the island still uninhabitable, there was nowhere else to sleep for the night.

In the morning, we would need to board up all the windows and start drying the interior out before planning a path to fixing it all and getting workers in to make it happen. While my staff would handle a lot of that, I wanted to make sure they felt supported and heard as well. And I knew it was an opportunity to change a few things.

Everything about the house now reminded me of Juno. There was a chance I could change some elements and make that reminder less powerful, but I would have to think about it. I didn't want to act rashly either. Once the pain had faded, I might want some memories of her.

No sooner had I thought this than I walked into the cabin I'd shared with her on the boat. The same dull ache of heartbreak hit me hard in the chest again and I had to sit down on the end of the bed, winded and yearning for her to be with me.

What was it about Juno that had gotten her under my skin so badly, and why couldn't I seem to get her out of my head again? I had no idea, but I knew I wanted it to stop. I needed it to stop. Because in less than a month, I would be seeing her again, even if briefly, and I couldn't handle the thought of wanting her only to have her reject me again.

I tried to put her from my mind, but the pain was too great, and my mind seemed to want to think over all the looks she'd given me, every word and every interaction, to try and determine how true she had been.

It wasn't the first time, either. None of it made any sense, but I knew one thing for sure. I was going to wish I could wrap my arms around Juno and keep her safe for some time to come. And if she asked, I would have to remind myself that she'd done this for the money, even if I was still convincing myself of that.

CHAPTER EIGHTY-NINE

<u>Juno</u>

It almost seemed as if nothing had happened as I sat at our usual table in our favorite cafe to drink tea with my best friend again. Kit was staring at me with curiosity but she was waiting patiently for me to explain.

"You look like you've had a rough few days. Are you okay?" she asked, no doubt referring to getting stuck on the island and almost drowning.

"I will be, I think. I... I was in good hands," I replied, not sure how to talk about it, but knowing that I didn't want to say anything bad about Jack.

"Sounds like he really looked out for you. I've been following the news as much as it will tell me. You looked happy. Happier than I've seen you in a very long time." Kit put her drink down and leaned forward to study me. "But you're not now."

I looked away, not sure I wanted her to see so deeply into me. Since I'd gotten back from the island I hadn't known what to feel. It was still so raw.

"Do you want to talk about it? You know I won't push you. You definitely didn't seem ready the last time I saw you, but would it be so bad to open up a little?" she asked, her voice gentle. "I know you've kept a lot of what happened with you and Greg to yourself, but whatever this is or was, talking about it might help. And we both know that my love life is entirely non-existent right now. I might as well be here for yours instead."

I caught her smile and considered what to tell her. She was trying to be there for me and it had clearly not worked keeping everything about my relationship with Greg on the down low. And I appreciated that she hadn't demanded an answer the last time I'd seen her.

"He was amazing in lots of ways, but I never felt as if I belonged in his world." I shook my head, thinking back to how much I'd spent on clothes to try and fit in, not being sensible at all.

"Did he act like you had to fit in?"

"No," I replied. "If anything, he seemed to appreciate that I was different. Other than a few of his friends, no one seemed to like me, though. They all thought I wasn't…"

"When have you ever let the opinions of people with more money than sense stop you from doing what you thought was best for you?" She put her tea down again and stared at me. "It sounds to me like you let your fears get the better of you. And I understand why you might. The hurricane alone sounded terrifying."

"Oh, it was." I shuddered as I thought about it again and how scared I had been in the underground room with Jack. But then I thought about how little I had felt scared whenever he was with me and had his arms wrapped around me.

Every time I had been scared, it had been when he was absent or someone or some other event had made me scared. He had made me feel safe.

It had been so long since I felt safe because of another person that I had forgotten what it felt like. Everyone should have someone who respected you, cared for you, and wanted to make sure you were okay, but I had been with Greg for so long that I'd grown used to fear.

"Are you worried that you're not ready for another relationship?" Kit asked after a little while.

Although I wasn't completely sure, I nodded. It was a strange situation to be in and I knew that I was still more easily triggered by anger and aggression. I knew I was still getting panic attacks and struggling with certain aspects of life, but again, that was something I had kept to myself.

"Why don't you tell him some of this? Tell him you're scared and worried that you don't fit in. If he's as nice as he sounds, he'll be understanding and might even ask to take things slower with you as well."

Once again, Kit seemed to be spouting all the wisdom in the world, and it made some sense, but I remembered what I had said to him, and I was pretty sure that he was never going to forgive me. Somehow Kit made me feel as if the option might be open to me, however, if it was what I wanted.

"When did you get so wise about relationships?" I grinned now as well, and I saw the relief on her face as she sat back and picked up her tea again.

"I wouldn't say I'm that wise. All I really know for sure is that you appeared a lot happier and this life we get to live is too short to throw away not being happy. What can you lose by seeing him again and trying to make it work?"

Her words reminded me of my agent and how he had persuaded me to provisionally agree to do some publicity with the band. I still hadn't fully confirmed either way, and I filled Kit in on what my agent had planned and how oblivious he was to my pain.

"Agents have a habit of putting the money first, but your current one seems better than most. He'd understand if you told him you couldn't do it, and I think you know that. I don't want to tell you what you're feeling and that you don't know yourself best, but you should at least ask yourself why you let him persuade you to put yourself in the same place as Jack again."

It was yet another good point. Kit was right. I had let my agent convince me to do the shows, and I hadn't called to confirm or deny because I didn't dare admit to myself that I wanted to see Jack again. I wanted him to forgive me and make all the pain and hurt go away. Despite everything that happened, I wanted to feel safe again.

Even knowing all that, I knew I'd hurt Jack as well. He'd had a rough patch before me, too. It had been a leap from him to trust me, and I'd ruined that. As much as I was now willing to consider wanting him back, I had little hope he felt the same, and if anything, that made me hurt even more than before.

"I do want to do it," I said a few seconds later, looking up at Kit properly for the first time in several minutes. She smiled again, her expression full of warmth.

"If you need someone while you're out there, I'll be just a phone call away. Hopefully he will feel the same way you do. If not, he's an idiot for not appreciating you enough."

As Kit finished her tea and finished our conversation in the sweetest form of support I could have hoped for and just a little joking to help me relax, I let go of it all for now. I would do the promotional shows and see what happened.

And if I could do anything while I was out there to show Jack I'd never meant to hurt him and was sorry about everything, I wouldn't hesitate.

CHAPTER NINETY

<u>Juno, four weeks later</u>

I exhaled as the taxi pulled up outside the studio where I was doing another interview. This was the third of the seven I'd been asked to do over about ten days. Well, of the seven who had confirmed my attendance. It wasn't a perfect situation to be walking into, but I had agreed to it.

Today I was being interviewed on a daytime TV show along with Kai. Neither of us was going to need to say a lot. I got the impression we were only really on the show to add some variety and color.

Our questions were brief and we didn't need to answer them in much detail. But it meant seeing Kai again.

Although Alma and Kai had both been so kind to me, I hadn't been able to bring myself to message or call either of them. They were Jack's friends and his band, and I didn't want to make it awkward for them by talking to them about anything that mattered to Jack.

Feeling my hands shake a little, I walked into the building and tried to focus on the task at hand. I had to get to the right studio first.

"Juno!" I heard a familiar voice call.

I looked to my left to see Kai, a smile on his face and his arms open toward me. Not sure what else to do, I walked over to him and let him hug me. Immediately I felt the emotions I'd tried to bury come to the surface. I wanted to ask him how everyone was. Whether Jack missed me as much as I missed him. Instead, I pulled back and tried to smile.

"You look great," I said.

"As do you. Although I've seen you happier, my dear. But come, let us get this interview out of the way, and then we should go get some dinner somewhere." Kai motioned for me to go with him, already heading toward a door on the side of the building.

Grateful that he knew where to go and still trying to process his request to spend more time with me after the interview, I followed him. It wasn't long before we were met by an assistant and shown into makeup together.

We didn't talk much during that, focusing on the interview and getting ready for it instead. I tried not to let my nerves show but it wasn't easy. The shake in my hands had grown worse and my stomach was so tense I thought I might be sick.

In a lot of ways, I felt worse than I had for the first interview. Then, I'd only had my nerves at the interview itself to contend with. Now, I was also worried about dinner with Kai and what I might be asked about the song and the story it was based on, considering everything that had happened between me and Jack.

Would I find myself crying live on US television? I truly hoped not, but I was already a lot less calm than I had expected to be.

Kai smiled at me as we came out of makeup, the warmth in his expression helping. And unlike some of the other interviews I'd done, we didn't have long to wait after that, and spent all the time before being on set getting mic'd up and tested. It gave me no time to feel awkward or focus on anything but following instructions.

Before I knew it, I was in front of the live audience and sitting on a sofa beside Kai.

The interviewer, a middle-aged woman who had been hosting her own show longer than I'd been writing, focused far more on Kai to begin with, joking with him about past interviews, and then she finally looked at me.

"And I understand you helped write the song," the woman asked. "But you're normally a novelist, is that correct?"

"Yes," I replied, pausing to give myself time to think of a way of elaborating. "The lyrics were inspired by characters of mine, so I helped where I could, explaining them and offering suggestions, but the band did the hard work. For me, it was really an honor and a delight."

"And the characters were originally inspired by the band as well?"

"Yes, one of them was inspired by Jack." I struggled to say his name, but I wasn't sure anyone else had picked up on it. However, the interviewer seemed happy and didn't pry any further.

By the time I walked offstage again, I was so relieved I felt light as a feather.

It didn't take long to hand back all the tech I was wired up to either, and immediately Kai was back by my side.

"Well, I think that went well. Dinner as a reward. My treat."

I grinned at the enthusiasm in his voice as he offered me his arm in a gentlemanly fashion.

"Is Alma around?" I asked, not sure I could imagine the two of them not being in the same place together.

"Sadly not. Why? Are you worried the glam rags will insinuate you and I are up to something if Alma isn't with us and we dine together?"

I lifted an eyebrow and looked sideways at Kai as he laughed.

"I'm not sure anyone could imagine you doing anything but

going home to Alma," I replied, making Kai's grin grow even wider.

"Exactly, and she knows it, along with everyone else."

"I was worried she'd think I didn't want to be friends or something. I mean, I was worried about how all of you would feel about me." I couldn't look at Kai as I spoke, now out in the open again as he hailed a cab.

"Let's talk about it over dinner," he said as a car pulled up and he opened the door for us.

It felt ominous, but I wasn't entirely surprised he was reluctant to discuss it in the open. I'd broken Jack's heart, and I was well aware of it. I was the villain of this story.

In the end, I wouldn't have been surprised if they all hated me. Whatever happened, I knew I'd only ever feel one thing toward all of them—gratitude. They'd shown me their world and welcomed me in, and the royalties I'd already accrued from the song had surprised even me.

I'd already cleared the credit card with the first payment, and I had plenty more left over, making me feel cheeky for accepting Kai's invite to dinner at his expense. But I'd already decided I'd try to be sneaky and pay without him knowing if I got the chance.

Kai proved himself the perfect companion once more as we rode, asking me about my books and other topics to keep the conversation going until I felt more at ease with him again. It got us all the way to a stunning-looking Tex-Mex-style place, and once again I was on his arm as we went inside.

The waitstaff seemed to know he was coming. They immediately led us to a small table out of the way and handed us menus. Kai seemed to know what he wanted so I chose quickly and we ordered right away.

For a moment, we waited for the drinks to come, and Kai took a trip to the bathroom, but we were soon sitting with a clear window to not be interrupted and enough privacy to actually talk about important subjects.

Immediately, my palms felt sweaty, and I wanted to run away and hide. How could I have a conversation with him about the others?

"You know, he still feels for you, but he'd never hold a grudge. If you want to still spend time with us, Jack won't stop it. I wouldn't either. Alma and I both like you."

I exhaled at Kai's words, feeling some of the tension slip out of me. I had questions, but it made it easier for me to think of them and ask what was going on.

But what did I actually want to know? That was the big question.

CHAPTER NINETY-ONE

It took me a moment, but I finally looked Kai in the eyes and opened my mouth.

"How is everyone doing?" I asked, immediately mentally kicking myself. It was a copout question.

"They're all good. Liam and Eve broke up not long after the storm. She…wasn't a good fit for Liam, let's say. And it turned out she had her eye on Jack as well. Not that it got her anywhere."

I blinked as Kai talked, trying to keep my outward appearance steady, but I could feel Kai studying me.

"Alma is happy enough and wants me to tell you to call her, and to give you her number again in case you've lost it."

Chuckling, I shook my head. "I'll call her as soon as we're done."

"Good. Otherwise, she'll throttle me, and I like this life, so you'd better." Kai gave me a wink before growing serious again.

"And Jack, he's…"

For a moment, Kai didn't say anything, his gaze on me as if he was trying to figure out what I could handle hearing.

"I know it's my fault, and I've hurt him. Please tell me he's recovering, but don't lie," I said, my voice coming out quietly as guilt washed through me. I'd let fear get the best of me, and I knew it, but I had to hope he could move on quickly.

"He's doing better than I expected, but not by much. The island is keeping him busy. Getting it all repaired. And fighting with the insurance company over who's paying for it. Looks like Jack is going to be out of pocket for a lot of it. Plenty is done already, but…he's been hit hard financially."

"Have the new song royalties not been enough to cover it?" I asked, assuming Jack's share would have been far larger than mine since he'd come up with the majority of the lyrics and some of the instrumentation.

Kai didn't reply at first, sitting up a little straighter.

"He didn't tell you, did he?"

"Clearly not. What happened?" I asked, not sure what Kai was getting at, but finding my stomach tense. Anxiety crept into the back of my mind, my heart rate picking up as breathing became harder.

"He gave up his share to satisfy you. Or your agent, or whoever it was who insisted you get full credit." There was a bite to Kai's words, anger making his eyes flash.

I felt myself go cold as my mouth fell open.

"I had no idea. I'd never have agreed to that. He wrote most of the song. He should have had way more than me. I… I would have been happy with a tiny amount of money. Or none at all. I only asked my agent to have my name on it—nothing else, I swear."

Kai raised an eyebrow and opened his mouth before closing it and looking me over again.

"What?" I asked.

"You don't know how song royalties work with the unions and official music licensing board, do you?"

"Not a clue," I replied. "That's why I have an agent, but I

thought I'd made it clear I wasn't interested in the money. Is there—"

"It's okay, Juno," Kai said, reaching out and patting my hand. "It all makes sense now. Please don't fret, but for future projects and to make you aware, you can't be credited on the official hard copy of a song without getting a certain minimum percentage of the royalties. You can be credited unofficially, of course."

I felt even worse as I realized what Kai was telling me. My agent had inadvertently fought for a far larger amount than I'd wanted.

"Oh, my. I'm so sorry, Kai. I had no idea. Can we undo it? Can I give it back?"

"Jack would never let you now. And not easily. You'd have to sell us the rights back now that the contract is signed, and because of the unions and all the rules around it, we'd have to pay you a decent amount. It wouldn't be worth it."

"Can't I just give you the money? Or pay for something? Pay for the costs to refurbish the island if it's Jack's money I have?" The words rushed from my mouth so fast that I wasn't sure Kai would understand me, but he looked thoughtful for a moment.

"You'd really do something like that? Use the royalties for the song to help Jack?"

"Entirely. I swear I never wanted the money, only my name on the song credits somewhere. If I'd known how it all worked, I'd never have asked for anything officially."

"Your agent would have hated that, but okay. Leave it to me. I'll get Alma to help. We'll grab some of the bills and the details for them. You can then pay them if you really want to."

I nodded, determined to use every penny the songs had earned me to help Jack.

"You want me to tell him?" Kai asked.

I didn't know how to answer at first. Did I want him to know? I could almost imagine him trying to prevent it. Especially now that I knew he'd given up his royalties to appease me. I must have looked like a gold digger. In his life until I had the money I wanted.

"No. Not unless you'd have to lie to stop him from knowing, and preferably even then, not until I've paid what I can with the royalties."

Kai grinned and nodded. Not long after, the food arrived, and we changed the subject. Although he had been lovely to me at every moment, there seemed to be something more relaxed and happy about him after my offer to make things right. As if his opinion of me had changed, and I was no longer someone he merely liked but a true friend.

It helped me feel grateful for the opportunity to make things right and talk to one of the band, and I instantly regretted not doing it sooner. If only I'd called Alma, maybe I'd have known all this already.

Once more, I let Kai escort me away and fetch us another cab. It was only as I got into it that I realized I'd never remembered to try and pay for our meal. Then again, I hadn't seen Kai do it either. When I brought it up, he laughed.

"They know me there, and I own some shares in the chain. There's never a bill. One of the perks of being famous."

"Oh," I said as my mind caught up. I hadn't expected that either.

"You'll get used to all this fame stuff," Kai said. "One element at a time."

"I hope so," I replied. "Right now, I feel like I keep making blunder after blunder."

"You want to fix them when you do. That means more than you think."

Gratitude for Kai's understanding swept through me, taking away some of the tension I felt, but as we drove closer to the hotel he was staying in, all my worrying thoughts came back. I was seeing Jack in only a few days.

My emotions still in turmoil and my heart still so deeply

affected by Jack, I tried not to worry about the interview we had in three days' time. It would be the fifth of my little stint, but the whole band would be there, not just Jack. Could I trust seeing Jack again after all this and not want to ask if he'd take me back?

I had no idea what it would be like, but I had allies again. I just had to stay calm and be kind.

CHAPTER NINETY-TWO

<u>Jack</u>

I hurried through the apartment, trying to locate the bill for the largest portion of the renovations on the island. It didn't seem to be where I'd left it, and I knew it had to be paid.

"Come on, Jack. We've got to go," Kai's voice came from outside the apartment.

Sighing, I grabbed my jacket and followed him out of the building.

"Feels like so much keeps going wrong lately," I said as we rode the elevator down to the waiting cars.

· "We'll have a good patch again. Just give it time," he replied.

I wanted to believe him, but I had an interview to do with the band. We were singing the song I'd written about Juno's characters live for only the third time, and I wasn't sure I was ready for it, especially since Juno herself would be there.

It had been a month since I'd last seen her, and I knew she'd done an interview with Kai a few days earlier. He hadn't said much about her, and I hadn't asked. I didn't want to know how she was. I just wanted to survive the next few hours.

Part of me was still angry at her, and I was definitely angry at the insurance companies. It was all a big mess, and I'd been financially screwed over. I almost hadn't bothered to renovate the island house and make it nice again, but I knew I still needed the place to retreat to.

I'd just have to take another movie deal and hope it was good enough. Even they hadn't brought in as much as they once did.

The car journey was tense, and I found myself thinking of Juno despite not wanting to. How was she? Was she enjoying all the royalties she was getting from the song?

I had no idea, but it wouldn't make it any easier to see her either way. Yet part of me wanted to see her, wanted to know she was doing okay. Wanted to make sure her ex hadn't done anything else to her, and she'd healed.

And I wanted to know if she still cared, even just a fraction.

I wasn't over her. Not even a little.

For an entire month, I hadn't been able to sleep because of dreaming about her. Food didn't taste right, and there was an almost constant dull ache in my chest. The world was muted. And every performance of the song almost put me on the verge of tears.

It was horrible, and I was about to have to go through it all again.

The studio loomed large ahead of us as we got out of the car, Kai and Liam both having traveled with me. We were quickly ushered inside, and instantly, I felt myself looking around for Juno.

Thankfully, she either wasn't here yet or had already been whisked deeper into the building. For now, I could focus on getting ready. We had a sound check to do first and some other technical stuff, making sure we were ready to play.

I lost myself in getting ready, grateful until it came time to rehearse the song. Every inch of me wanted to walk back out of the building, but I carried on instead, singing the lyrics and trying not to think about anything but the words and what note I was playing.

It helped if I closed my eyes and focused on the music, singing words I could remember without trouble. By the time we'd played through the song a few times, the tech and sound team declared us done.

Turning, I saw Juno standing off to one side of the set, hurriedly wiping tears from her face and trying to back up.

"Juno. There you are, darling," Kai declared as he spotted her.

Immediately, she dropped her hands from her face, and I looked away so she wouldn't realize I'd spotted her emotions. By the time I dared look up again, she was giving Kai a hug before acknowledging Liam. I had no choice but to look like I hated her if I didn't walk over.

Seeming to understand it was awkward, she only gave me a smile and waited to see what I did. I couldn't move from the spot, but we were rescued by an assistant asking us all to go through makeup and get off the set so they could start bringing in the audience.

Relieved, I let myself be led away, but a rock had appeared in my stomach, and I couldn't get it to go away.

Makeup seemed to pass in a blur of voices as I lost mine. No words would come out, and I had to listen to Kai and Liam as they talked to Juno about the other interviews we'd all been doing and how well the song was going down with the fans.

It only made me feel worse, anger filling me that she was getting all the royalties I should have. And I'd let her. What had I been thinking?

Juno glanced my way a few times, but I refused to look at her directly. I'd appear friendly enough on air, but I just couldn't do anything else right now.

I was the first to finish in makeup, followed by Kai, and we were taken to a small waiting room with snacks and drinks before being called on stage.

Kai sat beside me and gave me a hard look as if he was trying to decide what to say to me and read me at the same time.

"What?" I asked, although I already suspected I knew what the problem was.

"I know you're hurting, Jack, but this isn't like you. You're giving her the silent treatment, and she still cares about you."

"She walked out on me, and she's the one who is getting everything out of our relationship afterward."

Kai lifted his hands defensively, my anger having come out in every word I'd uttered. I exhaled, trying to force myself to relax. It wasn't Kai's fault.

"There's no doubt that Juno isn't perfect, and I'm sure she deserves some of your anger, but she's not a gold digger."

"Isn't she?" I asked. Before Kai could reply, Liam and Juno entered the room, also done in makeup.

Immediately, our eyes met, and the same desire and warmth for her I'd had every day we'd been together rushed over me. I still wanted her, but I had to make sure I wasn't weak.

She smiled at me but sat down on the opposite end of the sofa, giving me space and putting the rest of the band between us.

It felt strange, knowing everything I did about her and seeing her emotional reaction. Anger warred with pity and desire inside me and made it hard to focus.

Taking a deep breath and looking away from her, I hoped Kai would come to the rescue and start some kind of conversation. Just a little longer, and this interview would be over, and we could all go our separate ways. With any luck, I would never have to see Juno again, and the band could move on to the next song.

Thankfully, Kai picked up on the awkwardness and made some quips about the snacks, which had everyone laughing, and the tension started to clear. Gratitude for my band swept through me. We could get through this.

CHAPTER NINETY-THREE

<u>Juno</u>

I tried to sit as calmly as possible, pretty sure I was doing a bad job, while we waited to be called onto the set. Seeing Jack again and hearing him sing the lyrics to the music he'd written had stripped away every bit of defense I'd had.

There was no doubt in my mind. I was as hopelessly in love with him as I'd ever been, and I knew I'd made the biggest mistake when I'd walked out on him. Over the past month I'd done nothing but wish I was his again.

Seeing Kai and being able to use the money I'd got so far from the song to help pay for Jack's repairs, even if I'd done it through Kai, had helped. And it made me realize I had grown stronger.

I felt less scared of Jack, but it was clear he was angry with me and had no desire to talk to me at all. I'd ruined everything.

Relief flooded through me as we were finally called onto the set, and the four of us trouped out, all waving and smiling. It was easier to pretend for an audience. They were at a distance, and they didn't know me so well. Couldn't necessarily read my fear in slight movements.

Following all three men out, I waited until they all sat on the sofa. To my surprise, I was forced to sit right next to Jack, Kai choosing to sit beside Liam instead of leaving that gap for me.

I only had a moment to wonder if it had been deliberate, Jack keeping his eyes fixed on our interviewer, a much-loved US television host.

Heat flushed through me, as the sofa was small and the three men solid enough that my body touched his, nowhere else for it to go.

Jack finally glanced my way, and I gulped, knowing I must look like a deer in headlights. Another quick flick of his eyes to our legs pressed side by side showed he noticed it too, but the interviewer started talking and drew our attention to him.

For a moment, he chatted about the band, the song, and how well it was doing, and then he started on the questions.

"Juno, what was it like watching one of your own personal fantasies come to life before your eyes?" the interviewer asked out of the blue, the first thing he'd said to me.

I blinked, too stunned by the question's phrasing to know how to respond.

"You admitted it was based on Jack and you, didn't you? And the two of you had a brief fling while the song was being written. That must have been a dream come true for a fan," he continued, smiling, his eyes lit up like a predator's.

"We didn't have a fling," Jack replied before I could say anything. "We're friends."

"Good friends," I said, trying to help sell the truth he wanted to give. Jack glanced my way, pity in his eyes and an almost pleading look. He hated this as much as I did.

It helped me find some courage.

"And it was inspired by Jack and I, not based on anything real. But you're right, it was a dream come true. Getting to work with such talented musicians and songwriters would be any creative's dream come true. I learned a lot, and I felt very welcome."

My words seemed to make the host back off a little, and he turned his attention to the others.

"What started the project? It appeared to come out of the blue, and it's a little different from the band's normal songs," he asked next, seeming to aim the comment at Kai.

"It was Jack who drove it. He came up with most of the song lyrics, and Juno helped us understand the characters and what drove them. The rest sort of fell into place, all of us doing what we do best. We've been doing this a long time, and even something with an unusual feel for us…we still know our process, you know?"

The interviewer nodded as if he understood every word, but I felt as if curiosity and more questions were coming anyway.

"We heard you say Jack himself was inspired by the characters, but it's come as a surprise to fans that Jack isn't credited for this song."

"He's not?" I asked without thinking, surprise making the words blurt out as I looked at the man beside me for an explanation.

He looked my way again and shook his head, seemingly unable to speak. The tension rose as the audience realized this wasn't normal and we'd been placed in an awkward position.

"Seems it's not just the fans who are surprised by that," the interviewer said, making it even more clear someone would have to explain.

"We had a misunderstanding," I said, the penny dropping on what must have happened.

Jack had to give up being credited for the lyrics so I could be credited instead, and then I'd ended up being paid instead of him. But how was I going to explain that to the audience?

"Sounds like it's quite a big misunderstanding. Care to clarify it?" the host asked.

I took a slow, steady breath as I tried to think of a way to answer this.

"Jack was really kind and basically let me have the accreditation," I said, feeling more confident as I spoke. "He's an amazing person, and I can't say I know his exact reasons, but I'm so grateful. He's a true gentleman and a thousand times better than any character in a book."

There were cheers and a few wolf whistles, and I felt my cheeks getting hotter as I spoke.

"It sounds like someone wants to be more than just friends," the host added, encouraging the audience with a glance their way. "What do you say to that, Jack? What made you give up not only the claim but the royalties to Juno?"

I exhaled, my heart missing a beat at the question that put him on the spot. How on Earth was he going to answer that, and how would he ever forgive me for setting the question up the way I had?

"It was a simple decision," Jack replied. "I never really do any of this for the money, just the love of doing it. It's rare that something inspires me so much, and it was a thrill to write."

The words were a non-answer, but they seemed to satisfy our host, or he realized that he wouldn't get a different answer out of either of us. Without further delay, he encouraged the band to get ready to perform the song, and they quickly moved to do so.

I exhaled, trying to calm myself down and feeling my heart race, pounding so much in my chest that I felt lightheaded and almost sick.

There was a brief moment as our host talked about what was coming up next on the show, and then the band was ready.

For a few minutes, I wasn't the focus again, and I could calm down, but all eyes were on Jack, and I was sure he was under the same level of pressure I'd felt only moments earlier.

As he sang, goosebumps rose on my arm, but I managed to keep the tears at bay this time. All too soon, it was over, and the band was coming back to the sofa. This time, Kai sat next to me, with Jack on his other side, but I tried to look normal.

It was almost over.

The host seemed to move on as well, talking about other news and asking questions related to future projects and other things the fans could look forward to. I was given an opportunity to mention my books and the TV series in production, and then the show came to an end.

My relief was immediate as we were all led back off set again, and I could stop being under the spotlight. It had been an awful interview.

I was more than ready to leave, and I headed to the door as soon as I thought I could get away with it.

CHAPTER NINETY-FOUR

Before I could make it to the door, Kai stepped out and wrapped his arms around me.

"Why don't you come for drinks?" he asked, quietly enough that only I would hear.

"No," I replied. "I don't think that would be a good idea. I'm pretty sure Jack never wants to see me again after I botched that interview so badly."

"That's not true. He still loves you, Juno. I swear he does."

"And I still feel for him, but I think it's too late now."

Kai exhaled and finally let me go. There was a sadness in his eyes but he didn't try to stop me as I walked away. I said goodbye to the others, meeting Jack's eyes only briefly, and hurried away. It was all I could do to keep walking and not throw up. It was too much.

I tried to get the elevator to take me back down, but it seemed busted, and I could feel the tears welling up. Hearing footsteps behind me and dreading that it might be Jack, I kept walking. The corridor turned back the way we'd come, ending in a closed door I didn't dare go through, but it gave me some privacy for a moment.

Drying my eyes, I tried to calm myself down again. The whole situation with Jack had been one huge screw-up after another, but he was so under my skin every time I was close to him that I wanted to offer myself up to him on a platter. My heart ached as I thought about what I'd thrown away. I wanted to go find him and hurl myself at his feet, but I didn't move.

"So, what else put you in a bad mood this evening?" Liam asked, his voice making me stiffen as several sets of feet strode closer. "You were pissed off before we even began the interview."

Fear at being found filled me, but they stopped just around the corner.

"It's nothing, really. Just can't seem to find the invoice that I need to pay. It's the really big one for the company that came in and did all the structural repairs, and I just want to get it paid and stop worrying about it before we head there on Wednesday."

There was silence as no one responded for a moment.

"What?" Jack suddenly said. "Kai. You've got that look on your face. Have you gone and fucking paid it for me? I asked you not to—"

"It wasn't me," Kai said, sounding more amused than annoyed that his friend was yelling at him. "But yeah, it's already paid."

"No. You didn't… I told you I didn't want anyone paying it for me. I might not be getting any royalties from the song because I trusted a gold digger, but that doesn't mean you guys—"

"Jack, I didn't pay for it," Kai interrupted him. "Someone else did, so just drop it, accept that someone wanted to do something kind, and let's go have some drinks and relax."

"If this elevator ever actually arrives," Liam added, his voice quieter. It was followed by the click-clack of someone pressing the button repeatedly.

"Then who did pay for it? You clearly know," Jack replied, not letting it go.

"They didn't want me to say."

"I want you to say."

Kai let out a loud sigh.

"It was Juno."

There was a stunned silence, and I froze, not even daring to breathe. Kai had told him.

"Juno?" Jack eventually asked, his voice quieter. "I don't—"

"When I had my interview with her a few days ago, we talked about the song and what all the terms meant, and she made it clear she'd never wanted the money, only to have the song credited to her name. She had absolutely no idea that one was tied to the other, thanks to the unions and the song going through her agent."

"So she paid for my repairs. Her idea or yours?"

"Hers, when I also told her you'd given up your share so none of the rest of us would lose out. She was mortified, Jack. Couldn't rest until she'd thought of a way to help put it right. I was more than happy to help her."

There was a *bing* as the elevator arrived, and the three men stopped speaking. I almost rushed out after them, half-finished sentences coming into my mind, but my feet didn't move. Before long, I heard the elevator doors shut, and the men were whisked away.

I couldn't think. All this time, Jack thought I only wanted his money. No wonder he was so angry at me, but did knowing I hadn't intended to take it all change anything?

There was no way to know, but my heart continued to race, and for the first time since I'd walked away from Jack and his island, I wondered if there might be a chance I could go back. Could I give myself to him completely?

Lost in a thousand thoughts and desperate to get back to my hotel room so I could think and figure out exactly how I felt, I finally exited the corridor I'd hidden in and rode the spare elevator back to the ground floor.

I kept replaying the conversation I'd overheard in my head as a taxi took me back to the hotel, and then I hurried inside and up to my room.

After ordering room service, I lay back on the bed and tried to calm myself. It was an almost impossible task, my pulse picking up every time I thought of Jack and how he'd sung the song earlier that day. The emotion he'd put into it and the way he'd made me feel.

Several times, I cried. Sad for everything I'd put him through, everything he'd thought was true, and for how much it hurt that it was all my fault.

Eventually, I managed to dry my eyes and begin thinking about what I actually wanted to do. I knew I had to do something. I had to try and get Jack to see that I loved him if there was even a small chance he'd take me back. And there was only one way I could think to do it. I had to give myself over to Jack completely.

If Jack still loved me, I had to make it clear I didn't just want to be his but that I trusted him and was willing to let him have control in every way possible. I had to show him that I wanted nothing from him but his love in return.

With shaking hands, I reached for my phone and finally pulled out the piece of paper Alma had written her number on. Would she help me? Would she know if Jack was likely to take me back?

It took me another half an hour to write a message I was happy with, but eventually, I sent it, hoping she understood what I was asking and didn't mind that my first message to her in a month was to ask for her help.

Admittedly, I started it by telling her I was a total idiot, and I hoped she could forgive me and help me apologize to Jack in a way that would let him know I was completely sincere.

As soon as it was sent, I got up and had to pace the room, nerves filling my body with adrenaline as I waited for a reply. I had no way of knowing if what I was trying to do was a good idea or not, but I had to try something, and I was going to need some help.

When my phone buzzed to let me know I had a reply, I couldn't get to it fast enough, my whole body a bundle of nerves and tension as I read it.

Of course I'll help you! He still loves you. I know it. And you know Kai told me what you did for him with the money. You've got a good heart.

I exhaled and sank onto the edge of the bed. Someone didn't think I was crazy, but I still had to make the rest work out, and I was going to need Alma's help getting everything in place and picking the right time.

CHAPTER NINETY-FIVE

Shivers ran through me as I thought about the plan Alma and I had made and how soon I was about to begin it. It wouldn't be easy to change my mind once I'd started down this path.

I was standing in front of a small carrying case. All I was taking with me. It had everything I was going to need and a few things I'd only need if Jack accepted me. Only an hour earlier, I'd finished the last of my interviews, and I was supposed to be heading to the airport to get on a plane back to the UK.

But I wasn't going home. Instead, I was flying somewhere very different.

Grabbing the case and slipping my phone into my pocket, I made my way to the waiting car and found Alma already inside, Kai with her.

"Hey, Juno. Alma tells me you're up to something but not to ask questions, so just let me say, if you can put a smile back on Jack's face, I'm willing to help you with whatever you need."

"I need to get onto Jack's island and into the house without him knowing," I replied without missing a beat.

Kai exhaled as Alma grinned and looked between us. I'd

already told her some of my plan, but not all of it. And I didn't plan to mention anything more to either of them.

"That's quite an ask. Jack's island is his safe space, and it's already been tarnished recently with the storm, and…" Kai trailed off.

"If Jack asks me to leave, I'll leave without a fuss, but if I'm going to show him how sorry I am and offer him what I should have done from the beginning, I can only think of one way to do it. I need to be in the house before Jack even realizes I'm on the island."

"All right," Kai replied. "I'll keep him busy at the right moments while Alma gets you where you need to go and sweet-talks everyone else into not noticing you, but you'll have to get to the Bahamas before us. We can't get you on the jet, even if we can get you on the boat."

"I've got another boat to do the drop-off onto the island," I replied. "Alma helped me organize that part already. I'll be on the island before you if you can delay the boat for half an hour."

"Half an hour?" Kai asked, lifting his eyebrows.

"Yeah. My boat is almost as fast, but I need time to get off it without being seen."

Once again, Alma grinned.

"All right. But I'm only doing this because I want Jack to be happy. You ever make him not happy, and I'm going to take it personally."

"Noted," I replied, a shudder of fear and anticipation running through my spine. I was about to do the craziest thing I'd ever done, and I didn't know if it was going to work.

Thankfully, Kai and Alma were their usual awesome selves and managed to help me focus on something else while we drove to the airport. However, there was nothing they could do while on the plane, both of them heading to join Jack and his party.

Now that everything on the island was fixed, Kai and Alma

had convinced Jack to let them all return for a couple of days to "help with the finishing touches," and I was taking the opportunity to surprise him while others could help smuggle me into the house.

The whole flight, I ran through the plan again and again, trying to imagine his reaction. In my mind, it was everything from flat-out rejection and hatred to full humiliation, but the moment I thought about the possibility he would accept me and take me back, every fear and negative outcome seemed worth it.

I hurried from the plane as soon as I could, grateful that I didn't have to wait by the luggage carousel. My carry-on bag was all I had with me. There was a slight holdup outside the airport, and I noticed the car for Jack and the others was already there and waiting for them.

Panic filled me at the idea that I might be seen before I could even get to my boat, but a taxi pulled up only a minute or so later. I quickly got inside and gave the driver instructions to take me to the harbor.

Feeling even more nervous as we approached, I tried to focus only on what I knew of the boat and its captain. Alma had given me the instructions on how to find it after setting it up for me, but it was up to me to find the right one. And I was against the clock.

The taxi ride only grew more tense when we hit some traffic, and I was at the mercy of the streets and the driver. I could only hope it held Jack and the others up just as much, if not more, as I finally got through it and was dropped off at the harbor.

I made my way to the jetty Alma's instructions indicated, and I was partway along it when someone stepped off a boat that was ready to leave, the engine running and someone ready to throw the last rope out to it.

"Are you Juno?" the man asked, his accent almost too thick for me to understand the question.

"Yes. Are you Ralph?" I replied.

"Aye. Come aboard. I understand you need to get to one of the islands nearby in a hurry."

"Yes. I've got to set something up before the owner arrives." I moved toward the boat, and thankfully, the captain pulled back and offered me a hand to get me on board.

It wasn't a large boat, and I wasn't entirely sure how they'd get me to shore on Jack's island, but I wouldn't object. They seemed to know what I was doing and where I was going, and I was quickly offered a spot at the table below or on deck.

After stowing my bag somewhere safe, I opted to sit out on deck, hoping that seeing the crew working and possibly having people to talk to would distract me from my nerves. The closer I got to Jack's island, the more I felt as if I was going to throw up or scream or do something even more embarrassing.

There was no turning back now. I had booked a one-way trip to Jack's island abode, and I was going to be on his island and at the man's mercy soon enough.

Although I was sure he wasn't a cruel man, I knew there was a good chance I would be rejected and slung back out again in front of everyone else on the island.

It wouldn't be easy to do what I needed to do, but I had a feeling sitting on a boat and waiting to reach the island was going to be the worst part.

Thankfully, the crew seemed to be talkative, and the boat moved faster than I had expected. I had to be careful about what I told the sailors when they asked who I was, but thankfully, none of them appeared to recognize me, and I simply implied I was there to help set up something for the party they were about to have and that I would return on Jack's yacht.

Some of it was sort of true. I did have to set up. But I wasn't there for anyone else.

Several times, I looked at my phone, wondering how far Alma

and the others were behind me, but I had no signal this far out from civilization, and I knew I wouldn't until we were actually on the island. Hopefully, Jack's small mast and satellite dish would be up and running again, and I could hook onto the internet and signal to find out.

CHAPTER NINETY-SIX

As the island came into sight and the boat moved off to one edge to drop me away from the jetty, I helped a couple of the crew get a small dinghy ready to take me the last of the way. It was something to focus on, but as soon as I was sitting inside it and the two burly sailors were picking up an oar each, I felt myself tense up.

This was the moment everything could begin to go wrong. If I wasn't dropped quickly enough and the boat was spotted, or if someone else on the island saw me, such as Jack's housekeeper, I would blow my chance. I needed to hide until Alma could get to the island. And then, we needed to scheme and plan.

We'd made a rough plan. I had a vague idea of where I could go, so I was out of the wind and sun and not visible easily, but it still had potential problems, and there was nothing to be done for the exact timing. Jack and all the other guests needed to be distracted, and Alma would need to let me know the coast was clear.

I could probably get into the house, but since I wasn't arriving at the island long before Jack and I wanted to minimize the chance that anyone discovered me, we'd agreed to keep me away until Jack had made it into the house and dumped his bag, and the housekeeper was off duty again.

As my little boat reached the shore, the two men expertly maneuvered it so I only had to wade through some shallows as I thanked them and carried my bag to the tree line.

I hurried away, making sure I was hidden behind the trees and unlikely to be seen before I dared to turn and look behind.

By then, the dinghy was already almost back to the main boat. I watched them for a few minutes, knowing my only means of leaving the island without Jack being aware was leaving with them.

As soon as the boat was out of sight, I started making my way deeper onto the island to find somewhere I could hide for a bit. Hopefully, I wouldn't have to wait long, but I had no way of being sure.

I hadn't been walking long when my phone buzzed.

Now leaving. Jack's not in a great mood. We got stuck in traffic.

At first, I almost swore, thinking I would have to wait a few hours for them to arrive, but then I noticed the time the message had been sent. It was over an hour earlier. I must have only just gotten enough signal for the message to come through.

It was an instant relief. I wouldn't have to wait too long before they arrived. I quickly tapped out a reply, letting her know I was on the island. Of course she wouldn't get it either until she was here, but it would ensure she was thinking of how to smuggle me into the house as soon as possible.

Wanting to make sure I could see their boat arrive, I made my way along the island's main path, going slowly enough to look out for the other staff. I felt increasingly nervous as I moved, terrified that Jack or someone else might find me before I could do as I intended.

Trying to ignore my fears and very aware I couldn't go back, I tucked myself behind one of the larger trees near the house, noticing that all the windows had new panes of glass and that everything else had been tidied or fixed.

I could just see the new pontoon and the patch of ash where we'd made a bonfire from where I was, and it made me instantly regret ever leaving him at that point. Now that I was calm and not scared of storms, I could look at it in a new light. Jack had protected me and kept me safe during the entire storm to the best of his ability.

After throwing it all away, I only hoped I could persuade him not to reject me a second time.

Seeing the house quiet and calm before me, I considered going to it now and sneaking into the room I needed, but I stayed where I was. If I went in now, there was a good chance I'd be found when all the luggage was taken up. And it was very important that only Jack found me.

Instead, I waited, my body shaking with fear and my stomach so tied in knots that I was sure I was going to throw up at any moment.

It wasn't long before I could hear the sound of the boat as it came up to the island and moored. I shrank back, making sure I was as hidden as possible and wasn't likely to be seen, and then I kept as still as I could.

As I'd expected, the staff went back and forth for some time, taking luggage up to the house and making me feel better about having stayed outside. With that many people bustling back and forth with luggage and food, I'd definitely have gotten caught.

A moment later, I spotted Jack and the others heading up to the house. My breath caught in my throat as I fixed my gaze on Jack. He looked as handsome as always, even though he clearly wasn't at his happiest.

The others around him were chatting merrily, and I soon spotted Kai and Alma, too. Liam had a woman I didn't recognize on his arm, and there were a few other folks I couldn't remember the names of but who had been at Alma and Kai's party. Thankfully, Logan wasn't among them.

They'd only been out of sight for a minute or two when my phone buzzed again. I quickly flicked open my messages.

Here now as well. Kai is persuading the others to go on a quick tour of the island. Going to go east first.

I swore. I was east, and that meant I needed to get around to the west before they came back out again, but I wasn't very close to a path, and I had no idea how long they'd be.

Moving as fast as I could on the difficult terrain, I scrambled back to the path, still clutching my carry-all and trying to be quiet. I made a lot of noise until I reached the path, and then I hurried down the other side, trying to move more quietly and loop around the north of the house while the staff were still going back and forth.

I had to move quietly again as I continued trying to work my way around to the house and then past it, the staff coming back out to get more luggage or food. A few times, I stopped entirely and hunkered down again, terrified of being seen before I could get out of the way.

Eventually, I managed it, keeping under the trees until I was on the northwest side and able to see the house but mostly out of the line of sight of anyone coming out.

I waited, the sun sinking lower in the sky as I tried not to panic. Having to move had increased my heart rate again, and now I was terrified this would go wrong. Although I was less exposed from the house direction, I could be more easily seen from the staff building farther away, and there were plenty of staff on the island with so many people here.

Time ticked by as I grew colder, exposed to a northern breeze and shaking with a combination of fear and cold. I could only hope it wasn't long before Jack appeared and took his friends on a tour.

CHAPTER NINETY-SEVEN

Ten minutes later, I was starting to worry they were going to delay leaving or do something else entirely, and I would be stuck outdoors for ages. If I could have given up in that moment, I would have.

It was terrifying, waiting for the hardest part of my mission. Sneaking into the house was going to be challenging, and I still had no way of knowing for sure that Jack wouldn't not only reject me, but make a fool of me if he didn't appreciate what I intended to do.

Eventually, the door on the back of the house opened, and Jack led his friends out. I noticed everyone but Alma and the other girl were there, and it made me feel a little better.

Keeping out of sight, I lowered myself farther down, shielded by the bushes nearby but equally unable to see Jack and everyone else for a moment.

I could hear them talking and chatting, but not what they were saying. For a while, it didn't seem to move, but eventually, the sound of their talking moved to the east of the island and away from the house.

With each second that passed, I felt more relaxed. If only

Alma and one other were in the house, I stood a much better chance of getting in without detection.

As the group traveled away, I came into their view again and had to move, trying to keep the closest bush between us. When I put my foot down and transferred my weight to it, the ground beneath it slid downward, and I almost fell over, sliding to that side and dropping my bag.

The rustle was followed by silence as I didn't dare move, unable to see the group but aware none of them were talking anymore. I held still, barely daring to breathe until they began talking again.

Jack got farther and farther away until I could move without fear of being detected. I was only starting to make my way closer to the house when my phone buzzed again.

Coast is clear, but you'll need to hurry. This new girl is pretty curious about everything, and I can only keep her distracted for so long.

It was all the encouragement I needed. Practically running for the house, I made my way out of the thick of the trees and around to the back door, closest to the stairs and farthest from any position Jack would notice.

I was still a few meters from the back door when I heard a sound in the open storage shed.

The housekeeper came out, and our gazes locked. Immediately, I stopped, rooted to the spot in fear.

"Juno, what are you doing here? How did you get on the island?" As the housekeeper spoke, I could see her mind catching up.

She knew I hadn't been on the boat with the others, and that meant I was in a world of trouble.

"I... I'm not supposed to be here. I won't lie. But. I wanted to surprise Jack. I was awful to him and I let fear get the best of me after the storm. I wanted to apologize in a way that would mean something. I promise I won't do anything to harm anyone or him. I—"

The housekeeper lifted her hand and shook her head.

"I want to let you through, Juno, but I can't. If Jack doesn't know you're here and hasn't given you permission, at the least, you need to come with me until I've talked to him."

"Please, I want to surprise him. I promise I won't cause a fuss. If he doesn't want me here, I'll leave immediately."

I could see the housekeeper wavering, but it wasn't enough. Again, she shook her head and stepped toward me to try and usher me away with her.

At the same time, Alma opened the back door, calling to me before she realized the housekeeper was even there. When Alma saw why I'd stopped, she did the same.

"Ah," she said, pulling a face. "Could we possibly persuade you not to say anything so Juno can try to put a smile back on Jack's face?"

The woman deciding my fate frowned.

"You knew about this?" she asked Alma.

"Yes. Kai does, too. We're both hoping it works, but if it helps, I'll bear all responsibility for the fallout. Although I don't think there will be any. He still loves her, and she's the one who paid for all the island fixes. If that doesn't show she cares…"

"You did?" the housekeeper asked, finally acknowledging me again.

I nodded and exhaled, desperate to be in the house or somewhere else. Anywhere but a place where Jack might notice me before I was ready for it.

"All right," she said, relenting. "Go inside. But if this goes badly, I will tell Jack I saw you, and you promised me you just wanted to apologize to him. Got that?"

"Thank you." I exhaled before Alma took my hand and pulled me inside.

"Clarice is in the bathroom. Get upstairs before she comes back out." Alma ushered me in that direction, giving me no other form of greeting.

I didn't hesitate, handing her the envelope I wanted her to pass to Jack and then hurrying toward the stairs and up them before anyone else could see me. My heart hammered in my chest, and for a moment, I had to pause on the landing, the decor changed so much it was unfamiliar and a little unsettling.

It made sense. The top floor had been ruined by the broken glass and water, as had much of the lower floor, but where the downstairs areas of the house had been kept in a similar style, the upper floors were a different color and feel.

Trying to move quietly along, I looked for Jack's room and hurried inside, shutting the door after myself. My legs gave way, and I sank toward the bed, relieved and still thrumming with adrenaline at the same time.

I'd ensured it would be Jack who discovered me now, but I still had his reaction to contend with. While Alma and Kai thought he would take me back in a heartbeat, I knew I would think twice after everything I'd done.

Taking several deep breaths, I stowed my bag in the closet and fetched one item—a pair of sturdy handcuffs. The key was in the envelope I'd handed Alma, and there was no way these things opened up again once they were closed, so I wasn't putting them on until I was sure I was ready for what might follow.

With shaking hands, I slowly took off all my clothing before slipping into the lingerie I'd brought with me and adjusting it. There wasn't much to it, but I had picked out the most enticing set I had, and I looked at my body in it now.

I wasn't the most attractive of women, my body never curving exactly the way the magazines said it should, but I wasn't unattractive, either. I didn't struggle too badly with my weight, and I had enough cleavage to not need to pad it out. It had been enough for Jack once before, however. I had to trust that it was enough again.

With my attire how I wanted it, I tried to decide where I wanted him to discover me. I wanted to appear vulnerable, but if someone else walked in, I didn't want them to see something intended only for Jack.

It was also a fraction too cold in the room to be comfortable wearing this little for a long time, and I had no idea how long Jack would be. I needed to find some way of staying warm and making sure I could ditch it with my hands cuffed behind my back.

Going to the bed, I lifted off the blanket and grabbed the sheet. It was lightweight enough to shrug off, but it would keep me a little warmer in the meantime.

After I'd made the bed again without it, I knelt on the floor and wrapped the sheet around me from the front so I could reach behind me and hold the ends in place.

The next minute or so was the hardest. I had to keep the sheet in place yet let go of it so my hands were free to do one last thing. It was time to put the handcuffs on and make it so I couldn't go anywhere or do anything without Jack's say-so. If this wasn't showing him I trusted him and intended to give myself over to him if he wanted me to, I didn't know what was.

Finally, it was done, the handcuffs attached to the bed with a cord and my body stuck on the floor at the foot of his bed, wearing nothing but panties and a sheet.

/ CHAPTER NINETY-EIGHT

Jack

The island looked different after the storm. I knew it would, but something about it didn't feel right anymore. The folks who had renovated everything and cleaned it up had done a good job. Even the new jetty to moor the boat was well done, especially considering how swiftly they'd done it.

Something didn't sit right, though. I couldn't stop thinking about the revelation Kai had given me that Juno had paid for it all. That she hadn't wanted me to lose out on her account. Considering I had a lot more money than her, it felt wrong that she'd paid for everything to be fixed. Especially now that she was gone from my life.

I wanted to message her, and almost had several times, to at least thank her, but the interview we'd had together kept coming back to mind as well. She'd been wary of me, as if she was deliberately keeping distance between us. I didn't want to push her for something she didn't want to give me.

And she'd also completely screwed the interview up. Put me on the spot. I hadn't been happy about it at the time, but I wasn't very good at interviews when I was first doing them, either. Not that I was great now.

I sighed as the friends I was with started talking about going back to the house. Part of me didn't want to, but I had no more of the island to show them.

The house was the worst part. I'd had it decorated differently. Partially for a change but partially to see if it helped me not see Juno everywhere. It didn't. I still thought of helping her up from the storm shelter. I still saw her naked on my bed, pinned beneath me and giving me whatever I wanted.

Just thinking about it made my crotch stir, and I had to hastily push the thought away and look for something else to focus on. Somehow, I found myself heading back to the house beside Kai, the familiar company helping despite the glances he kept giving me.

"Are you checking up on me?" I asked when he did it again.

"Sort of," he replied. "You've been brooding since we left the airport."

"I've been brooding since you told me Juno paid for those invoices."

Kai chuckled and nodded. "I wasn't going to say it."

"I don't understand it. And I'm tired of relationships not going well. I had just started daring to hope something deeper might happen with her. And now… I just want something to go right for a while. To get what I want without making it complicated."

Kai seemed to suppress a chuckle again, and I frowned. What was so funny?

"Give it time, Jack. Things will look up." Kai clapped me on the back as he spoke, and then Liam came closer, ending the conversation.

Part of me wanted to ask if Kai knew something I didn't, his responses a little off, but, given how I felt, I was pretty sure the problem was with me.

I let the others talk around me as we closed the distance to the house and went inside. Immediately, Kai suggested he stoke up the grill and called Liam and his new girlfriend out to help him.

The rest of the group agreed to bring chairs out as Alma approached me and asked me to show her where she could find a towel.

I lifted an eyebrow, pretty sure she knew where they were, but I made my way to the stairs anyway. Before we could climb them, she reached for my arm and held out an envelope.

I recognized the handwriting immediately. Juno had written my name on it.

"You're going to want to read this and then head up to your room," she said, fighting back a grin. "We'll save you some food."

My mouth fell open as I tried to find the words to ask her what was going on, but nothing came out. Before I knew it, I was alone. With nothing else to do, I opened the envelope, finding a small set of keys and a note.

Jack,

I know you have no reason to forgive me, but I wanted you to know I am so sorry for not trusting you when all you did was try to take care of me. I want you to know I'm completely yours if you ever want me, and if you'll give me the chance, I'd like to prove it.

I'm upstairs. At your mercy.

Juno

The last two sentences sent a thrill through my body, and for a moment, I could only read them again, not sure I believed it. Was Juno really upstairs? And what did she mean by at my mercy?

As I moved to fold the letter back up, I remembered the keys I was holding, and understanding dawned on me. Taking the steps two at a time, I made my way to my room.

I stopped at the doorway, not sure I could quite believe the note in my hands nor that Juno was here, and wondering if an elaborate prank was being played on me. After taking a deep breath, I pushed the door open and walked inside.

Juno knelt on the floor in front of the bed, her hair arranged around her shoulder and a white sheet draped around her body.

Entirely on autopilot and unable to speak, I shut the door. Almost immediately, Juno shifted, and the sheet fell to the floor, revealing her almost entirely naked body. Her breasts were out, her nipples quickly hardening in the cool air. And her arms were behind her.

She looked up at me with wide eyes, her chest rising and falling with each shallow, rapid breath she took. I could see the fear written all over her, but there she was, at my mercy, and she'd put herself there willingly. Her hands cuffed to the bed.

Her vulnerability made my cock hard in seconds, and I went to her, getting down on my knees until I had my arms around her, holding her against me.

Neither of us spoke, and I crushed my mouth upon hers, winding my hand through her hair to hold her head in place. She tasted so good, and for a moment, I lost myself in her, enjoying the way her body sculpted against mine, my leg between hers so close I could feel the wetness as she became more and more aroused.

It was all the consent I needed as I pushed her back against the bed and pulled her panties down, taking away the last scrap of modesty she had left.

"Are you mine?" I whispered in her ear as I did so.

"Completely," she replied, helpless to stop me.

I quickly pulled my own pants out of the way and pushed her legs apart. Within seconds I was deep inside her, the relief and pleasure immediate. She groaned and braced herself on the bed as I thrust hard into her for a second time.

Feeling as if I had everything I wanted and was truly having her and claiming her as mine for the first time, I screwed her rough and fast. Desperation drove me to push hard each time I was deep inside again, like the heaven I'd longed for.

She tilted her head back, growing tighter around me as my thrusts pleasured her as well. It took all my self-control not to blow my load inside her until I felt the pulsing of her pussy as she entered the throes of an orgasm.

Moaning deeply, she pulsated around me until I couldn't take it any longer and slammed myself into her one last time, filling her with my cum and groaning into her shoulder.

Slowly, we came down together, our mouths finding each other at some point along the way.

Juno was mine, and everything was finally right again.

CHAPTER NINETY-NINE

<u>Juno</u>

I couldn't get enough of Jack as I returned to Earth, still hand-cuffed to the end of his bed. It had felt perfect to finally be at his mercy and give myself to him entirely. All this time, I'd been holding back, and yet, when it actually came to it, I'd loved every second of it.

After kissing me some more, Jack slowly untangled us, pulling back and running his gaze over me. I felt almost drunk, my breathing erratic and my pulse racing. So many emotions ran through me, but I knew I wanted more. I didn't want Jack to be done with me at all.

For a moment I was vaguely aware of voices outside, but Jack never looked away from my body, his gaze roving over every inch of me. My thighs were slick with my own wetness and I was pretty sure my hair was a mess too, tousled by the hands he'd gripped it with while he fucked me. I also didn't doubt I was going to have marks on my wrists.

Slowly, Jack reached around behind me, following my arms with his hands until he reached the handcuffs. His gaze met mine as he wrapped a hand around each wrist, adding to the restraint.

"What made you change your mind?" he asked. "What made you want to let me control you completely?"

"A combination of things," I replied. "But mostly when I realized how safe you'd kept me here, and Kai telling me what you'd done with the song royalties. You'd been taking care of me in ways I hadn't noticed and didn't deserve."

"Will you let me take care of you?" he asked, his voice coming out deeper than normal, the emotion and desire in the question taking me by surprise.

"I'll let you do anything you want," I replied. "I should never have doubted you. I meant every word in that note Alma just gave you. I'm yours. Do what you want with me."

My words seemed to bring something out in Jack. His eyes lit up, and he seemed to come close to tears before he kissed me again.

Gently, he undid the handcuffs on one wrist and slipped the cord holding me in place out of the way. I slid my arms around to my front, rubbing them where they ached and trying to judge what Jack intended to do with me next.

I felt his arms reach around me again, and he lifted me up and onto the bed. I yielded to his control and suggestion, going where he placed me and letting him put me in the bed. He lifted my hands above my head and quickly handcuffed my free wrist again.

Trapped once more, I felt a small thrill of fear course through me, but it was far easier to ignore than ever before, my body already having been at Jack's mercy before. If he was going to hurt me, he could so easily have done it already.

All the worry I'd felt about him rejecting me was replaced by the high of knowing he wanted me. I was his now and it was perfect.

Slowly, he came closer, but I noticed something else in his hands. A familiar bandanna. Somehow, it must have survived the storm, and seeing it as he held it out near my head brought me a sort of comfort. He'd blindfolded me with it when I'd begun trying to trust him. It seemed fitting for him to use it now, after everything we'd already been through.

As if he sensed my permission, he laid it over my eyes, draping it in place and robbing me of sight before reaching behind my head and tying it in place.

"Do you remember our safe word?" he asked, his voice barely above a whisper.

"Yes," I replied, thinking of Hunter from my books. The character based on him. I hadn't done the real man justice, but in that moment, I was eternally grateful that I'd tried.

Jack gave me no other warning before his hands and mouth roamed, moving over my skin as he first gently stroked and then roughly kissed, nibbled and when he reached my nipples bit. He caused a heady mix of pleasure and pain, each sensation almost too much but never quite reaching the threshold that would have made me ask for mercy.

Moment by moment and inch by inch, he made my body heat up once more, desire making me wet and hungry for him. Unable to move far, his body mastering mine, I could only writhe and whimper, hungry to be screwed again.

He denied me for what felt like forever, holding his cock near my entrance and rubbing my nipples while he teased me.

"Do you want me?" he asked, his voice deep, almost mocking. He knew the answer already. I couldn't hide it even if I'd wanted to.

"I want you," I replied, each word an effort to say.

Jack chuckled and kissed me again. Still, I was left wanting, his hard manhood poised by my entrance, ready for him to thrust into my depths the moment he was ready.

"Please," I added. "Please, Jack. Take me."

Either Jack decided he'd made me wait long enough, or my words worked because he finally slid into me, as deep as he could get. Instantly, I moved my legs, lifting my knees and tilting my hips to try and get him deeper into me.

He moaned and seemed to shudder.

"Good god, you feel so perfect, Juno," he said as he held himself inside me for a moment.

I couldn't respond, enjoying being full of him too much to do anything but give in to the pleasure he was giving me.

Jack took me slowly, each deliberate stroke in and out in rhythm and timed to make me want him to go faster and, at the same time, appreciate how much longer I was going to have him inside me.

Time became meaningless. My only focus was his body near mine as I heated even further and felt each thrust taking me closer to heaven. Helpless and entirely his, I mewled as he pulled back and made me wait a fraction of a second before each thrust back into me.

Getting closer to his own pleasure, Jack finally picked up the pace, driving us both toward the peak until I cried out his name, my body shuddering with ripples of orgasm as it tore through me. It wasn't long after that Jack orgasmed as well, letting out a deep groan as his hips jerked with each blast of cum.

Slowly, we came down together, our bodies still close and entwined. I panted for what felt like hours, feeling sated and warm in Jack's arms and strangely not vulnerable despite still being bound and blindfolded.

Almost as if he sensed my calm and lack of fear, Jack reached up and took the blindfold off before using the keys I'd had Alma give him to undo the handcuffs.

He took my fingers in his and brought my arms back down the bed, almost cradling them as he gazed at me.

"Good girl," he said before he kissed my fingertips. He then kissed the marks on my wrists, almost as if he wanted to soothe them, but I felt strangely proud of them as if they showed the fear I had gotten over and how far Jack and I had come together.

Pride rippled through me, making me feel even warmer. I snuggled closer to Jack and let him wrap his arms around me. I didn't want to move or stop gazing at him. He was the dom I'd been looking for. Someone who wanted my submission, but only so they could both enjoy me and ensure that I enjoyed being claimed.

I was Jack's again. And for the first time in a long time, I felt like I was home.

CHAPTER ONE HUNDRED

<u>Jack</u>

Having Juno in my arms again felt so good I didn't want to move or do anything but hold her there. I felt as if I was still reeling, having thought she was gone from my life only a short while earlier.

I was convinced Kai and Alma had both known of Juno's plan, and I was both grateful and slightly irritated at them. Of course, I also had questions about how they'd got Juno onto the island without me knowing, but I still didn't want to do or say anything that would interrupt the moment I had with her right now.

Sadly, the rest of the world seemed to decide we'd had enough time together, and it pulled us back to reality. Laughter from outside reminded me that I had a house full of guests, and Alma had mentioned putting food aside.

It made me painfully aware of how long we'd been gone already and how it would be very obvious what we'd been doing to at least one, if not more, of the people having a barbecue without us.

"We should get dressed and go eat," I said when Juno's stomach rumbled.

"I didn't want to stop, but I am hungry. I haven't eaten since breakfast," she replied, looking almost guilty.

I wanted to ask her how she'd got onto the island and many other questions, but it was now my duty to take care of her, and I wanted her to have plenty of energy to give herself to my desire again later. That meant making sure she was well-fed now.

Taking her hand, I pulled her to her feet and helped her dress. She had brought some clothing with her, but I noticed it wasn't a lot and not of the quality that it had been when we went shopping together. Immediately, I felt a pang of sadness at the dress I'd persuaded her to buy. It had been ruined in the storm.

Once she was clothed again, I took extra time to help her fix her hair, feeling as if I wanted to make sure she felt adored after finally trusting me.

When her stomach rumbled for the third time, and even I felt like I could really do with some food, I took her hand and led her downstairs. She seemed to shy a little, hanging back and behind me as we went outside.

Alma spotted us first, taking in our entwined hands and smiling at both of us. She was already on her feet and grabbing two plates of food before anyone else noticed us.

Immediately, Kai also stood.

"Juno, darling, can I get you a drink?" he asked, flicking me a wink.

No one said anything to bring attention to the extra person, almost as if they all knew Juno was here and had been expecting it. It only made me even more curious about how she'd gotten here, but I didn't want to upset anything when we'd so recently come back together.

Sitting down beside her, I let her dig into the food and made sure she had everything she needed.

Alma and Kai continued talking with the group about our next tour dates and how we were going to fit everything in as if we hadn't interrupted their conversation. Everything felt right, but it made me realize that there was a lot I would have to discuss with Juno. I wanted her with me, but I also didn't want to force her to leave her world behind just to follow me on tour.

"Can we fly into the UK so I can grab some more of my stuff from my apartment and make sure I have all the forwarding set up properly?" Juno said a moment later, turning to me.

I nodded, unable to respond with words. She'd basically answered my question and allayed my fears at once.

"You want to come on the tour, then?" I asked.

"Of course," she replied. "Unless you'd rather I didn't. I've always wanted to travel, and I can work anywhere."

I reached for her hand, gratitude and desire flooding me again. Before I knew I was even moving, I was on my feet, and I'd pulled her to hers as well. My body continued to move automatically, getting down on one knee in front of her. One hand shot up to grab a Hula Hoop from a snack bowl nearby before I even knew I'd done it.

"Juno Fernsby, would you do me the honor of being my wife?" I asked, my heart barely beating as I surprised even myself.

Almost immediately, I wanted to kick myself. What was I doing, asking her so soon? There was no way she would say yes to me when we'd just gotten back together. However, I was stuck in position, waiting for her answer as everyone looked on.

"Yes," she replied, as tears welled up and started to flow down her face. "On one condition."

"Name it," I replied.

"I get to take your surname."

"You have to admit, Juno Starling has a good ring to it," Kai replied for me.

I chuckled and stood as I let Juno know I liked the idea of her taking my name. Juno Starling did have a nice ring to it. I wrapped my arms around my fiancée and kissed her passionately in front of everyone, much to the amusement of the whole group.

They congratulated us, and for the first time in a long time, I felt as if things were looking up, just as Kai had suggested they might.

Once we were all settled and calmer again, and someone had fetched champagne to celebrate with, I reached for Juno and pulled her into my arms.

"I have one more question," I said. "How did you smuggle yourself onto my island, and how on Earth did I not notice it?"

"That's technically two questions," she replied, grinning at me with a cheeky expression.

"Okay, so answer the first, and I'll decide how I didn't notice," I replied, putting a hand under her chin and lifting it up so I could get a good look at her.

Over the next few minutes, she explained her thought process, letting me know how Kai and Alma had helped her get to the island without me noticing. It explained several things. At the airport, I'd thought I'd seen someone waiting for a taxi that looked like her, and I informed her as much.

And then, when she'd made noise hiding among the trees, I'd almost gone to investigate. Every part of me was glad I hadn't. Finding her handcuffed and willing to be completely at my mercy had taken any sting out of finding her on my island unbidden. She'd faced her fear, and I knew it had meant a lot for her to offer herself up that way.

Just thinking about how brave she'd been and how much it must have scared her made my cock harden. And it had worked. I'd thought of nothing but how glorious it was to finally have her submit herself to me fully and make herself powerless so voluntarily. Having her want to be mine so completely was a heady feeling.

Hearing how she'd also put herself at risk and went to so much effort to make sure only I discovered her, that she was entirely at my mercy in so many ways, only made me feel the intensity of what she'd offered me more.

Juno was going to be my wife, and I was going to enjoy every minute of having her on my arm.

EPILOGUE

Juno

I exhaled as the last guest at our wedding reception walked away. We'd said goodnight to all of them, and that meant our wedding was finally over. It had been a whirlwind of a day, and I'd enjoyed it, all of it happening on Jack's island, but I was eager for what would follow once we were alone as well.

Jack took my hand, not saying a word as he finally led me away from the beach and patio, where a multitude of heat lamps, candles, and fairy lights lit the scene. At the bottom of the stairs, he paused, looking me over.

Heat ran through me at the look of hunger and appreciation in his eyes. Before I could do anything, he picked me up, pulling me into his embrace and holding me in place as if I weighed nothing while he climbed the stairs.

He took me all the way to the bedroom and then gently placed me on the bed. For a moment, I couldn't breathe, wanting him to claim me but terrified of asking for it. Despite having spent the last two months with Jack in a whirlwind of planning and prepa- ration for our wedding, I still felt nervous at the way he claimed me sometimes.

I wanted to be his completely, show him I would do anything he asked and that I trusted him enough that I knew we'd both enjoy whatever he wanted. But now and then, the fears crept back and reminded me I'd once trusted another.

But now I was Jack's wife as well. It felt even more serious, and at the same time, my heart felt light and happy at the thought of being his forever. We were beginning a whole new adventure together.

Not long after Jack laid me on the bed, he got on beside me, his arms reaching out for me as I reached for him. Our mouths found each other a moment later, our kisses already passionate. Hunger for him made me heat even more, wetness forming between my legs.

Wanting to give myself to him, I reached for the zipper of my dress. He stayed my hands almost immediately.

"No," he said as he pushed them up and over my head. "I'm doing this. I want you to submit to me completely."

"Always," I replied.

He growled as he pulled the zipper down as far as it went, his eyes drinking in the skin it revealed. It was a corseted wedding dress, and it instantly made it easier for me to breathe, my heart racing. As he peeled it away, freeing my breasts, he kissed my shoulders and neck.

I moaned as his mouth found my nipple, sucking on it until it was a hard nub, sensitive and at his mercy, just like the rest of me would no doubt be in only a few minutes more. When he repeated the motion with the other, I mewled, so wet he could have screwed me then and there.

Instead, he took his time, taking off the dress and kissing every inch of my skin along the way. Yielding to him and being patient became more of a struggle the closer his mouth grew to my pussy, until I was naked before him, his body still fully dressed.

For a moment, he simply gazed at me, making me feel both vulnerable and full of desire for him. Slowly, he resumed his kissing, teasing me by kissing closer to my most sensitive area.

I whimpered and mewled as he gently pressed his lips to my clit and then moved off again several times, but I kept myself still beneath him, making sure he knew he was in control. No matter what he did to me, I wanted him to know that. I'd vowed to be his forever, and I meant every word.

Slowly, he applied more pressure, lingering and leaving the gaps between kisses shorter and shorter. Pleasure grew in me, but I fought the feeling, not sure if I had permission to orgasm for him or not, and desperate to please him in any way I could.

As he flicked his tongue out for the first time, I gasped and grabbed the bed with both hands.

"Not yet, Juno," he said. "You're not allowed. Do you understand?"

"Yes, sir," I replied, desperate to disobey in so many ways but also determined to do as he commanded.

He resumed, being gentle but making the pleasure increase until I thought I would explode for trying to fight it off. Suddenly, he stopped, the lack of sensation almost as much torture as it had been having him stimulate me while trying to get me not to orgasm.

Slowly, I came back down, but before I could say I was safe, he resumed. The intensity grew even faster the second time until I was sure I would make Jack angry.

"Come for me, Juno," he said as he broke off again.

I whimpered, but the words and the relief were enough that he only had to blow a hot breath over me, and I tipped into oblivion. I shuddered and lost control of all my limbs while Jack looked on.

As I came back down again, Jack moved back up the bed and wrapped his arms around me. Feeling warm and grateful that he'd finally given me permission, I could only look at him with love and desire.

"Well done," he said. "But we've only just begun. You're going to have to do a lot more for me, kitten."

I exhaled, not sure how to respond but still wanting whatever he had for me.

Only a few seconds later, he pulled back and took my hands with him, so I was hauled to my feet as well. Standing naked before him, I felt exposed again, but he led me back to the end of the bed.

"On your knees," he commanded. "And hands behind your back. I want to see you the way you were when you snuck onto my island to offer yourself to me."

Feeling a thrill of delight at the memory he'd put in my head, I did as I was bid and knelt before him, my arms behind me. Almost immediately, he reached down and pulled something out from underneath the bed. I felt the cold of metal as he closed handcuffs around my wrists and fixed me in place.

As he stood, I tilted my head to look up at him. His hands moved to his pants, making the bulge of his hard cock very obvious. I had a feeling I was about to be given the command to pleasure him.

He slowly undid his belt and revealed himself, the tip of his cock already slick with precum.

"Open that pretty mouth of yours. I've got something for you to take."

Not hesitating, I did as I was bid, eagerly taking his hardness into my mouth. I ran my tongue over his head, tasting him and making him moan. He reached down and cradled the back of my head, taking control as he thrust in and out of my mouth.

I focused on his cock, wanting to pleasure him as much as possible. He pushed in and out at a slow pace to begin with, but as his breathing grew more ragged, he picked up the pace. I sucked and licked, feeling his throbbing cock and enjoying the effect I was having on him. I wanted to make him come as much as he'd just done me.

Each thrust gave him more pleasure, making him moan until he stopped, shuddering as he filled my mouth with salty cum. I swallowed, still sucking and running my tongue around his head, wanting him to enjoy every last sensation.

Slowly, he came back down and pulled out of me.

"That was perfect, Juno. You're perfect," he said, stroking my hair back down where his hands had ruffled it up in his desire and ecstasy.

I felt a thrill of delight run through me at pleasing him, and it helped still some of the fear inside me. Having him control me and do what he pleased with me made me feel amazing in so many ways. And now I was his forever.

Now I'd pleasured him, Jack reached down and freed one wrist from the handcuffs and unhooked me from the bottom of the bed. He then helped me to my feet before running his hands over me, stopping to cup my breasts and tug on my nipples.

"I'm going to have every inch of you tonight," he said. "I've started with your mouth. Your pussy's next. And I'm going to fuck your ass after that. Do you think you can cope with that, kitten?"

"I'd like to try," I replied, knowing it was true without thinking about it.

"Good girl," he said before turning me around. "Now, bend over and open your legs."

I did as I was told, Jack moving so he could stretch my arms out in front of me and handcuff them again. He then used another rope to attach them to the top of the bed. It made me nervous for a moment, but Jack returned to the end of the bed and gently ran his hands down my sides and around my legs before slipping a hand between them.

Immediately he rubbed at my clit, stirring my pleasure again and making me heat up for a second time. Without another word, he reached down and slipped something around each ankle, holding them in place, open and now unable to close.

If I'd felt vulnerable before, I felt it even more now. He had access to my most intimate areas, and I couldn't move or stand up again.

Once I was in place and he was comfortable with my position, he reached between my legs again. His fingers found me wet, my body growing more and more aroused despite the vulnerability I felt.

Slowly, he ran circles around my clit, making me even wetter and more aroused, until I was shivering with desire, wanting him to embed himself in my pussy but not sure I could ask for it before he was ready.

Before I could come close to orgasming, he stopped and removed his hand again. Frustration tore through me at the denial as he stepped away again.

A moment later, I saw him go to the closet and pull out a now-familiar bandanna. Within seconds, he had it folded and over my eyes, tying it in place behind my head. A shudder ran through me when he touched my skin again, the sensation feeling even more intense for being robbed of others.

His fingers trailed down my side as he moved back to the end of the bed, and then I could feel him, his hard cock suddenly pressing against my entrance. With no more warning and no words, he pushed hard into me. I gasped but immediately relaxed into him, enjoying how deep he could get and how full I felt from this angle.

Pulling out, he slammed back inside, fucking me far harder than I'd expected him to. He continued to take me, pushing deep and filling me only briefly before he retreated to impale me again.

Despite the roughness, the pleasure rolled over me, taking me to heaven and making me moan and tighten around Jack as he continued. As I moaned, he slowed only briefly before continuing, holding onto my hips and driving himself even harder and deeper while I pulsed around him.

As I came back down, he continued, using me to sate his own needs and keeping me wet and hot around him. His rhythm increased until he also exploded, yelling as he filled me full of cum for a second time and then held himself deep inside me.

Satisfaction made me grin as he leaned over and kissed my back and neck.

"I'm going to take your ass soon. Do you need to move, or can you stay here while I get you ready for me?"

"I'm all yours," I replied, feeling a little apprehensive but otherwise relaxed. Both orgasms he'd given me had made my head feel buzzed, and I liked how full I felt when I had him inside me, no matter where he was.

I felt his fingers as he parted my ass cheeks and exposed the final part of me he wanted to claim. He slipped his thumb into me, the feeling cold as he lubricated my depths and helped ready me for the hard cock I was going to have to take.

I did my best to relax as he added more and probed into me. And as he slipped fingers into my pussy as well, I moaned at the fullness.

Before I could decide what I liked more, he pushed even more fingers into my pussy and used the other hand to start working my clit, rubbing his thumb over it as he filled me.

Already partially horny from the fucking he'd given me after the last orgasm, it didn't take me long to near a third turn in oblivion. Right before I could orgasm again, he pulled one hand away, leaving my ass and pussy empty but continuing to put pressure on my clit.

I mewled at the sudden lack of penetration, but my frustration was short-lived, his cock pushing against my asshole within seconds. With only a moment of warning and his hand still working my clit and distracting me with an impending orgasm, he impaled me slowly but confidently.

Giving way before him, I gasped and moaned, the pain mingling with the pleasure until I cried out, his name coming with waves of pleasure. Once again, Jack didn't stop, his cock thrusting into me again and again while I enjoyed my reward and slowly came back down.

Surprised by how good it felt having him in my ass, I moaned as he picked up the pace and drove deep inside me. His hands reached for my hips again, holding onto me to help himself get deeper and deeper. All the while, the movement rubbed my body against the bed beneath, his weight and down thrusts forcing me into a slightly different position.

Slowly, I felt myself heating up and my pussy getting wet and tight for a fourth time. At the same time, Jack grew even faster, enjoying me and taking himself to his own peak.

We cried out together, my body trembling with each wave of orgasm as he filled my ass full of cum and finished claiming every inch of my body as his. I moaned and collapsed onto the bed, unable to bear my own weight anymore. Slowly, Jack eased out of me, making it clear I was going to know I'd been fucked in every way possible the following day as well.

High on the pleasure Jack had given me and the satisfaction of pleasing him, I didn't move as Jack undid all the ropes and hand-cuffs that held me in place. As soon as I was free, he slipped the blindfold off my head.

I blinked at first, my eyes adjusting before I looked at him. He smiled and kissed me a few times as he helped me into the bed and climbed in beside me.

We cuddled, his arms wrapped around me and holding me close.

Although I'd loved every minute of what we'd done together, I felt more tired than I'd expected, and the warmth and gentleness he was showing me helped to calm me and make me feel relaxed and cozy.

"I've claimed you completely," he whispered. "You're mine now, Juno."

"And always will be," I replied, leaning my head against his chest and closing my eyes.

For the first time in my life, I was right where I wanted to be.

THE STORY CONTINUES

The story continues with book two, *Billionaire Blaze*, coming soon to Amazon and Kindle Unlimited.

ACKNOWLEDGMENTS

Thank you to everyone at Florid Romance for taking a chance on this series of mine. I am grateful to every single one of you for being there for me.

Thank you to my muse. You're not a rockstar in the literal sense, but you do make my world go round.

And a big thank you to my readers, for giving my characters the chance to talk to you and make you feel the same emotions they did me.

Finally, to my mum, for not reading these books.

CONNECT WITH THE AUTHOR

Email Address: elizalockhartauthor@gmail.com
Mailing list sign up

facebook.com/elizalockhartauthor

ABOUT THE AUTHOR

Eliza Lockhart is a made-up name for someone who likes to not have her friends and family read her steamy books. She lives somewhere pretty but not as pretty as she wishes it to be in a place on Earth that lets her write whatever she wants.

When she was younger, she used to read her mother's books off the adult shelves, and no genre was off limits. Now she writes the books she wanted to read ever since then but didn't find. And whatever else takes her fancy along the way.

When she's not writing, she likes to travel, enjoy good food, and discover new experiences and adventures with those she cares about.

BOOKS BY ELIZA LOCKHART

Fame and Flames Series:

Hard Rock Heat

The Twisted Mafia Fairytales Series:

Taken by the Beast

Taught by the Beast

Protected by the Beast

Rescued by the Beast

Forever with the Beast

Claimed by the Thief

Taken by the Thief

Forever with the Thief

Almost Immortal Courtesan:

Resurrected

Surrendered

Taken shorts:

Taken by the Vampire

Holidays with the Pack:

Lycans and Lawyers at Christmas

Coming soon:

Fame and Flames series:

Billionaire Blaze

Twisted Mafia Fairytales Series:

Tamed by the Prince

www.ingramcontent.com/pod-product-compliance
Lightning Source LLC
Chambersburg PA
CBHW031233310726
48971CB00004B/991